RUSSIA

ISTANBUL

BLACK SEA

ARMARA SEA

LÖSUNG 1914

BEHEMOTH

BEHEMOTH

Written by

MR. SCOTT WESTERFELD

Illustrated by Mr. Keith Thompson

SIMON PULSE

New York · London · Toronto · Sydney

SIMON PULSE

An imprint of Simon & Schuster Children's Publishing Division
1230 Avenue of the Americas, New York, NY 10020
First Simon Pulse hardcover edition October 2010
Copyright © 2010 by Scott Westerfeld
For information about special discounts for bulk purchases, please contact
Simon & Schuster Special Sales at 1-866-506-1949
or business@simonandschuster.com.
The Simon & Schuster Speakers Bureau can bring authors to your live event.
For more information or to book an event, contact the Simon & Schuster Speakers
Bureau at 1-866-248-3049 or visit our website at www.simonspeakers.com.
Designed by Mike Rosamilia
The text of this book was set in Hoefler Text.
Manufactured in the United States of America
2 4 6 8 10 9 7 5 3 1
Library of Congress Cataloging-in-Publication Data
Westerfeld, Scott.
Behemoth / written by Scott Westerfeld ; illustrated by Keith Thompson.
— 1st Simon Pulse hardcover ed.
p. cm.
Sequel to: Leviathan.
Summary: Continues the story of Austrian Prince Alek who, in an alternate 1914
Europe, eludes the Germans by traveling in the Leviathan to Constantinople,
where he faces a whole new kind of genetically engineered warships.
ISBN 978-1-4169-7175-7 (hardcover)
[1. Science fiction. 2. Imaginary creatures—Fiction. 3. Princes—Fiction.
4. War—Fiction. 5. Genetic engineering—Fiction.]
I. Thompson, Keith, 1982– ill. II. Title.
PZ7.W5197Beh 2010
[Fic]—dc22
2010009755
ISBN 978-1-4424-0957-6 (eBook)

To Justine:

nine years, seventeen novels, and counting

⊙ ONE ⊙

Alek raised his sword. "On guard, sir!"

Deryn hefted her own weapon, studying Alek's pose. His feet were splayed at right angles, his left arm sticking out behind like the handle of a teacup. His fencing armor made him look like a walking quilt. Even with his sword pointed straight at her, he looked barking silly.

"Do I have to stand like *that*?" she asked.

"If you want to be a proper fencer, yes."

"A proper idiot, more like," Deryn muttered, wishing again that her first lesson were someplace less public. A dozen crewmen were watching, along with a pair of curious hydrogen sniffers. But Mr. Rigby, the bosun, had forbidden swordplay inside the airship.

She sighed, raised her saber, and tried to imitate Alek's pose.

It was a fine day on the *Leviathan*'s topside, at least.

The airship had left the Italian peninsula behind last night, and the flat sea stretched in all directions, the afternoon sun scattering diamonds across its surface. Seagulls wheeled overhead, carried by the cool ocean breeze.

Best of all, there were no officers up here to remind Deryn that she was on duty. Two German ironclad warships were rumored to be skulking nearby, and Deryn was meant to be watching for signals from Midshipman Newkirk, who was dangling from a Huxley ascender two thousand feet above them.

But she wasn't really dawdling. Only two days before, Captain Hobbes had ordered her to keep an eye on Alek, to learn what she could. Surely a secret mission from the captain himself outweighed her normal duties.

Maybe it was daft that the officers still thought of Alek and his men as enemies, but at least it gave Deryn an excuse to spend time with him.

"Do I look like a ninny?" she asked Alek.

"You do indeed, Mr. Sharp."

"Well, you do too, then! Whatever they call ninnies in Clanker-talk."

"The word is '*Dummkopf*,'" he said. "But *I* don't look like one, because my stance isn't dreadful."

He lowered his saber and came closer, adjusting Deryn's limbs as if she were a dummy in a shop window.

"MARTIAL LESSONS ON THE SPINE."

"More weight on your back foot," he said, nudging her boots farther apart. "So you can push off when you attack."

Alek was right behind her now, his body pressing close as he adjusted her sword arm. She hadn't realized this fencing business would be so touchy.

He grasped her waist, sending a crackle across her skin.

If Alek moved his hands any higher, he might notice what was hidden beneath her careful tailoring.

"Always keep sideways to your opponent," he said, gently turning her. "That way, your chest presents the smallest possible target."

"Aye, the smallest possible target," Deryn sighed. Her secret was safe, it seemed.

Alek stepped away and resumed his own pose, so that the tips of their swords almost touched. Deryn took a deep breath, ready to fight at last.

But Alek didn't move. Long seconds passed, the airship's new engines thrumming beneath their feet, the clouds slipping slowly past overhead.

"Are we going to fight?" Deryn finally asked. "Or just *stare* each other to death?"

"Before a fencer crosses swords, he has to learn this basic stance. But don't worry"—Alek smiled cruelly—"we won't be here more than an hour. It's only your first lesson, after all."

"What? A whole barking hour . . . without moving?" Deryn's muscles were already complaining, and she could see the crewmen stifling their laughter. One of the hydrogen sniffers crept forward to snuffle her boot.

"This is nothing," Alek said. "When I first started training with Count Volger, he wouldn't even let me hold a sword!"

"Well, that sounds like a daft way to teach someone sword fighting."

"Your body has to learn the proper stance. Otherwise you'll fall into bad habits."

Deryn snorted. "You'd think that in a fight *not moving* might be a bad habit! And if we're just standing here, why are you wearing armor?"

Alek didn't answer, just narrowed his eyes, his saber motionless in the air. Deryn could see her own point wavering. She set her teeth.

Of course, barking *Prince* Alek would have been taught how to fight in the proper way. From what she could tell, his whole life had been a procession of tutors. Count Volger, his fencing master, and Otto Klopp, his master of mechaniks, might be the only teachers with him now that he was on the run. But back when he'd lived in the Hapsburg family castle, there must have been a dozen more, all of them cramming Alek's attic with yackum: ancient languages, parlor manners, and Clanker superstitions. No wonder he thought that standing about like a pair of coatracks was educational.

But Deryn wasn't about to let some stuck-up prince outlast her.

So she stood there glaring at him, perfectly still. As the minutes stretched out, her body stiffened, her muscles beginning to throb. And it was worse inside her brain, boredom twisting into anger and frustration, the rumble of the airship's Clanker engines turning her head into a beehive.

The trickiest part was holding Alek's stare. His dark green eyes stayed locked on hers, as unwavering as his sword point. Now that she knew Alek's secrets—the murder of his parents, the pain of leaving home behind, the cold weight of his family squabbles starting this awful war—Deryn could see the sadness behind that gaze.

At odd moments she could see tears brightening Alek's eyes, only a fierce, relentless pride holding them back. And sometimes when they competed over stupid things, like who could climb the ratlines fastest, Deryn almost wanted to let him win.

But she could never say these things aloud, not as a boy, and Alek would never meet her eyes like this again, if he ever learned she was a girl.

"Alek . . . ," she began.

"Need a rest?" His smirk wiped her charitable thoughts away.

"Get stuffed," she said. "I was just wondering, what'll

you Clankers do when we get to Constantinople?"

The point of Alek's sword wavered for a moment. "Count Volger will think of something. We'll leave the city as soon as possible, I expect. The Germans will never look for me in the wilds of the Ottoman Empire."

Deryn glanced at the empty horizon ahead. The *Leviathan* might reach Constantinople by dawn tomorrow, and she'd met Alek only six days ago. Would he really be gone so quickly?

"Not that it's so bad here," Alek said. "The war feels farther away than it ever did in Switzerland. But I can't stay up in the air forever."

"No, I reckon you can't," Deryn said, focusing her gaze on their sword points. The captain might not know who Alek's father had been, but it was obvious the boy was Austrian. It was only a matter of time before Austria-Hungary was officially at war with Britain, and then the captain would never let the Clankers leave.

It hardly seemed fair, thinking of Alek as an enemy after he'd saved the airship—two times now. Once from an icy death, by giving them food, and the second time from the Germans, by handing over the engines that had allowed them all to escape.

The Germans were still hunting Alek, trying to finish the job they'd started on his parents. *Someone* had to be on his side. . . .

And, as Deryn had gradually admitted to herself these last few days, she didn't mind if that someone wound up being her.

A fluttering in the sky caught her attention, and Deryn let her aching sword arm drop.

"Hah!" Alek said. "Had enough?"

"It's Newkirk," she said, trying to work out the boy's frantic signals.

The semaphore flags whipped through the letters once more, and slowly the message formed in her brain.

"Two sets of smokestacks, forty miles away," she said, reaching for her command whistle. "It's the German ironclads!"

She found herself smiling a little as she blew— Constantinople might have to wait a squick.

The alarm howl spread swiftly, passing from one hydrogen sniffer to the next. Soon the whole airship rang with the beasties' cries.

Crewmen crowded the spine, setting up air guns and taking feed bags to the fléchette bats. Sniffers scampered across the ratlines, checking for leaks in the *Leviathan*'s skin.

Deryn and Alek cranked the Huxley's winch, drawing Newkirk down closer to the ship.

"We'll leave him at a thousand feet," Deryn said,

watching the altitude markings on the rope. "The lucky sod. You can see the whole battle from up there!"

"But it won't be much of a battle, will it?" Alek asked. "What can an airship do to a pair of ironclads?"

"My guess is, we'll stay absolutely still for an hour. Just so we don't fall into any bad habits."

Alek rolled his eyes. "I'm serious, Dylan. The *Leviathan* has no heavy guns. How do we fight them?"

"A big hydrogen breather can do plenty. We've got a few aerial bombs left, and fléchette bats . . ." Deryn's words faded. "Did you just say 'we'?"

"Pardon me?"

"You just said, 'How do *we* fight them?' Like you were one of us!"

"I suppose I might have." Alek looked down at his boots. "My men and I *are* serving on this ship, after all, even if you are a bunch of godless Darwinists."

Deryn smiled again as she secured the Huxley's cable. "I'll make sure to mention that to the captain, next time he asks if you're a Clanker spy."

"How kind of you," Alek said, then raised his eyes to meet hers. "But that's a good point—will the officers trust us in battle?"

"Why wouldn't they? You saved the ship—gave us engines from your Stormwalker!"

"Yes, but if I hadn't been so generous, we'd still be

stuck on that glacier with you. Or in a German prison, more likely. It wasn't exactly out of friendship."

Deryn frowned. Maybe things *were* a squick more complicated now, what with a battle coming up. Alek's men and the *Leviathan*'s crew had become allies almost by accident, and only a few days ago.

"You only promised to help us get to the Ottoman Empire, I suppose," she said softly. "Not to fight other Clankers."

Alek nodded. "That's what your officers will be thinking."

"Aye, but what are *you* thinking?"

"We'll follow orders." He pointed toward the bow. "See that? Klopp and Hoffman are already at work."

It was true. The engine pods on either side of the great beastie's head were roaring louder, sending two thick columns of exhaust into the air. But to see the Clanker engines on a Darwinist airship was just another reminder of the strange alliance the *Leviathan* had entered into. Compared to the tiny British-made engines the ship was designed to carry, they sounded and smoked like freight trains.

"Maybe this is a chance to prove yourself," Deryn said. "You should go lend your men a hand. We'll need good speed to catch those ironclads by nightfall." She clapped him on the shoulder. "But don't get yourself killed."

"I'll try not to." Alek smiled and gave her a salute. "Good luck, Mr. Sharp."

He turned and ran forward along the spine.

Watching him go, Deryn wondered what officers down on the bridge were thinking. Here was the *Leviathan*, entering battle with new and barely tested engines, run by men who should by all rights be fighting on the other side.

But the captain didn't have much choice, did he? He could either trust the Clankers or drift helplessly in the breeze. And Alek and his men had to join the fight or they'd lose their only allies. Nobody seemed to have much choice, come to think of it.

Deryn sighed, wondering how this war had got so muddled.

◦ TWO ◦

As he ran toward the engines, Alek wondered if he'd told Dylan the whole truth.

It felt wrong, hurrying to join this attack. Alek and his men had fought Germans—even fellow Austrians—a dozen times while fleeing to Switzerland. But this was different—these ironclads weren't hunting him.

According to wireless broadcasts that Count Volger had overheard, the two ships had been trapped in the Mediterranean at the start of the war. With the British in control of Gibraltar and the Suez Canal, there'd been no way for them to get back to Germany. They'd been running for the past week.

Alek knew what it felt like to be hounded, trapped in a fight that someone else had started. But here he was, ready to help the Darwinists send two ships full of living, breathing men to the bottom of the sea.

The vast beast rolled under his feet, the tendrils that covered its flanks undulating like windblown grass, pulling it into a slow turn. Fabricated birds swirled around Alek, some already harnessed and carrying instruments of war.

That was another difference. This time he was fighting side by side with these creatures. Alek had been raised to believe they were godless abominations, but after four days aboard the airship, their squawks and cries had begun to sound natural. Except for the awful fléchette bats, fabricated beasts could even seem beautiful.

Was he turning into a Darwinist?

When he reached the spine above the engine pods, Alek headed down the port side ratlines. The airship was tilting into a climb, the sea falling away below him. The ropes were slick with salty air, and as he strained to keep from falling, questions of loyalty fled his mind.

By the time he reached the engine pod, Alek was soaked in sweat and wishing he hadn't worn fencing armor.

Otto Klopp was at the controls, his Hapsburg Guard uniform looking tattered after six weeks away from home. Beside him stood Mr. Hirst, the *Leviathan*'s chief engineer, who was studying the roaring machine with a measure of distaste. Alek had to admit, churning pistons and spitting glow plugs looked bizarre beside the undulating flank of the airbeast, like gears attached to a butterfly's wings.

"Master Klopp," Alek shouted over the roar. "How's she running?"

The old man looked up from the controls. "Smoothly enough, for this speed. Do you know what's going on?"

Of course, Otto Klopp spoke hardly any English. Even if a message lizard had brought the news up to the pod, he wouldn't know why the airship was changing course. All he'd seen were color codes flashed from the bridge to the signal patch, orders to be obeyed.

"We've spotted two German ironclads." Alek paused—had he said "we" again? "The ship is giving chase."

Klopp frowned, chewing on the news for a moment, then shrugged. "Well, the Germans haven't done us any favors lately. But it's also true, young master, that we could blow a piston at any time."

Alek looked away into the spinning gears. The newly rebuilt engines were still cantankerous, with unexpected problems always cropping up. The crew would never know if a temporary breakdown were intentional.

But this was no time to betray their new allies.

For all the talk of Alek saving the *Leviathan*, the airship had really saved him. His father's plan had been for Alek to hide in the Swiss Alps for the entire war, emerging only to reveal his secret—that he was heir to the throne of Austria-Hungary. The airship's crash landing had rescued him from long years of skulking in the snow.

He owed the Darwinists for saving him, and for trusting his men to run these engines.

"Let's hope that doesn't happen, Otto."

"As you say, sir."

"Anything wrong?" Mr. Hirst asked.

Alek switched to English. "Not at all. Master Klopp says she's running smoothly. I believe Count Volger is assigned to the starboard engine crew. Shall I stay here and translate for you two?"

The chief engineer handed Alek a pair of goggles to protect his eyes from sparks and wind. "Please do. We wouldn't want any . . . misunderstandings in the heat of battle."

"Of course not." Alek pulled on the goggles, wondering if Mr. Hirst had noticed Klopp's hesitation. As the airship's chief engineer, Hirst was a rare Darwinist with an understanding of machines. He always watched Klopp's work on the Clanker engines with admiration, even though the two didn't share a language. There was no point in arousing his suspicions now.

Hopefully this battle would be over quickly, and they could head on to Constantinople without delay.

As night fell, two dark slivers came into view on the horizon.

"The little one's not much to look at," Klopp said, lowering his field glasses.

Alek took the glasses and peered through them. The smaller ironclad was already damaged. One of its gun turrets had been blackened by a fire, and an oil slick spread in the ship's wake, a shimmering black rainbow in the setting sun.

"They've been in a fight already?" he asked Mr. Hirst.

"Aye, the navy's been hunting them all over the Mediterranean. They've been shelled a few times from a distance, but they keep slipping away." The man smiled. "But they won't escape this time."

"They certainly can't outrun us," Alek said. The *Leviathan* had closed a gap of sixty kilometers in a few hours.

"And they can't fight back either," Mr. Hirst said. "We're too high for them to hit. All we have to do is slow them down. The navy's already on its way."

A *boom* rang out on the spine above, and a swarm of black wings lifted from the front of the airship.

"They're sending in fléchette bats first," Alek said to Klopp.

"What sort of godless creature is that?"

"They eat spikes," was all Alek could say. A shudder passed through him.

The swarm began to muster, forming a black cloud in the air. Searchlights sprang to life on the gondola, and as the sunlight faded, the bats gathered in the beams like moths.

The *Leviathan* had lost countless beasts in her recent battles, but the airship was slowly repairing itself. More bats were already breeding, like a forest recovering after a long hunting season. The Darwinists called the ship an "ecosystem."

From a distance there was something mesmerizing about the way the dark swarm swirled in the searchlights. It coiled toward the smaller ironclad, ready to unleash its rain of metal spikes. Most of the crew would be safe beneath armor plating, but the men at the smaller deck guns would be torn to pieces.

"Why start with bats?" Alek asked Hirst. "Fléchettes won't sink an ironclad."

"No, but they'll shred her signal flags and wireless aerials. If we can keep the two ships from communicating, they're less likely to split up and make a run for it."

Alek translated for Klopp, who pointed a finger into the distance. "The big one's coming about."

Alek raised the field glasses again, taking a moment to find the larger ship's silhouette against the darkening horizon. He could just read the name on her side—the *Goeben* looked far more formidable than her companion. She had three big gun turrets and a pair of gyrothopter catapults, and the shape of her wake revealed a set of kraken-fighting arms beneath the surface.

On her aft deck stood something strange—a tall tower that bristled with metal rigging, like a dozen wireless transmitters crammed together.

"What's that on her back side?" Alek asked.

Klopp took the glasses and stared. He'd worked with German forces for years, and usually had a lively opinion on military matters. But now he frowned, his voice hesitant.

"I'm not sure. Reminds me of a toy I once saw . . ." Klopp squeezed the glasses tighter. "She's launching a gyrothopter!"

A small shape hurtled into the air from one of the catapults. It banked hard and came whirring toward the bats.

"What's he up to?" Klopp asked softly.

Alek watched with a frown on his face. Gyrothopters were fragile machines, barely strong enough to lift a pilot. They were designed for scouting, not attack. But the little aircraft was headed straight at the cloud of bats, its twin rotors spinning wildly.

As it neared the fluttering swarm, the gyrothopter suddenly kindled in the darkness. Bolts of flame shot from its front end, a spray of brilliant crimson fireworks that stretched across the sky.

Alek remembered something that Dylan had said about the bats—they were deathly afraid of red light; it scared the spikes right out of them.

The stream of fire tore through the swarm, scattering bats in all directions. Seconds later the cloud had disappeared, like a black dandelion in a puff of wind.

The gyrothopter tried to veer away, but was caught

beneath a wave of fleeing bats. Alek could see fléchettes falling, glittering in the searchlights, and the gyrothopter began to shudder in midair. The blades of its rotors tore and crumpled, their remaining energy twisting the delicate frame into wreckage.

Alek watched as the flying machine tumbled from the sky, disappearing in a small white splash on the ocean's dark surface. He wondered if its unlucky pilot had survived the fléchettes long enough to feel the water's cold.

The *Leviathan*'s searchlights still swept across the sky, but the swarm was too scattered to resume the attack. Small fluttering shapes were already streaming back toward the airship.

Klopp lowered his glasses. "The Germans have some new tricks, it seems."

"They always do," Alek managed, staring at the ripples

spreading out from where the gyrothopter had crashed.

"Orders coming in," Mr. Hirst said, pointing at the signal patch. It had turned blue, the sign to slow the engine. Klopp adjusted the controls, giving Alek a questioning look.

"Are we giving up the attack?" Alek asked in English.

"Of course not," Mr. Hirst said. "Just changing course. I reckon we'll ignore the *Breslau* for now and go after the big one. Just to make sure that other gyrothopter doesn't trouble us with those sparklers."

Alek listened to the thrum of the ship for a moment. The starboard engine was still running high, pushing the *Leviathan* into a slow turn toward the *Goeben*. The battle wasn't over yet. More men would die tonight.

He looked back at the whirling gears of the engine. Klopp could halt them in a dozen subtle ways. One word from Alek would be enough to stop this battle.

But he'd promised Dylan to fight loyally. And after throwing away his hiding place, his Stormwalker, and his father's gold to make these Darwinists allies, it seemed absurd to betray them now.

He knew Count Volger would agree. As heir to the throne of Austria-Hungary, Alek had a duty to survive. And survival in an enemy camp didn't start with mutiny.

"What happens next?" he asked Hirst.

The chief engineer took the field glasses from Klopp.

"We won't waste any more time tearing up their signal flags, that's for certain. We'll probably go straight in with aerial bombs. A gyrothopter can't stop those."

"We're going to bomb them," Alek translated for Klopp. "They're defenseless."

The man just nodded, adjusting the controls. The signal patch was turning red again. The *Leviathan* had found her course.

• THREE •

It took long minutes to close the final distance to the *Goeben*.

The ship's big guns boomed once, spilling fire and smoke into the night sky. But Mr. Hirst was right—the shells flew well beneath the *Leviathan*, erupting into white columns of water kilometers away.

As the *Leviathan* drew closer, Alek watched the German ship through the field glasses. Men scrambled across the ironclad's decks, hiding her small guns under what looked like heavy black tarps. The coverings shone dully in the last flickers of sunset, like plastic or leather. Alek wondered if they were made of some new material strong enough to stop fléchettes.

But no plastic could stop high explosives.

The men on the ironclad hardly seemed worried, though. No lifeboats were readied, and the second gyrothopter stayed on its catapult, the rotors strapped down against the wind. Soon it too was veiled with a glossy black covering.

"Young master," Klopp said, "what's happening on her aft deck?"

Alek swung the field glasses, and saw lights flickering atop the ironclad's strange metal tower.

He squinted harder. There were men working at the tower's base, dressed in uniforms made from the same shiny black that covered the deck guns. They moved slowly, as if encased in a fresh layer of tar.

Alek frowned. "Take a look, Master Klopp. Quickly, please."

As the old man took the field glasses, the flickering lights grew brighter—Alek could see them with his naked eyes now. Shimmers slid along the struts of the tower, like nervous snakes made of lightning. . . .

"Rubber," Alek said softly. "They're protecting everything with rubber. That whole tower must be charged with electriks."

Klopp swore. "I should have realized. But they only showed us toys and demonstration models, never one that huge!"

"Models of *what*?"

The old man lowered the glasses. "It's a Tesla cannon. A real one."

Alek shook his head. "As in Mr. Tesla, the man who invented wireless? You mean that's a transmitting tower?"

"The same Mr. Tesla, young master, but it's not a transmitter." Klopp's face was pale. "It's a weapon, a lightning generator."

Alek stared in horror at the shimmering tower. As Dylan often said, lightning was an airship's natural enemy. If raw electriks flowed across the airship's skin, even the tiniest hydrogen leak could burst into flame.

"Are we in range yet?"

"The ones I've seen could hardly shoot across a room," Klopp said. "They only tickled your fingers or made your hair stand on end. But that one's *huge*, and it's got the boilers of a dreadnought to power it!"

Alek turned to Mr. Hirst, who was watching their conversation with an air of disinterest, and said in English, "We have to come about! That tower on the aft deck is some kind of . . . lightning cannon."

Mr. Hirst raised an eyebrow. "A lightning cannon?"

"Yes! Klopp has worked with the German land forces. He's seen these things before." Alek sighed. "Well, toy ones, anyway."

The chief engineer peered down at the *Goeben*. The electriks were sparkling brighter now, unfolding into spidery forms that danced along the tower's struts.

"Can't you see?" Alek cried.

"It is rather odd." Mr. Hirst smiled. "But lightning? I doubt your Clanker friends have mastered the forces of nature just yet."

"You have to tell the bridge!"

"I'm sure the bridge can see it well enough." Hirst pulled a command whistle from his pocket and blew a short tune. "But I shall inform them of your theory."

"My *theory*?" Alek shouted. "We don't have time for a debate! We have to turn around!"

"What we'll do is wait for orders," Mr. Hirst said, dropping the whistle into his pocket.

Alek swallowed a groan of frustration, then turned back to Klopp.

"How long do we have?" he said in German.

"Everyone's cleared the deck, except for those men in protective suits. So it could be any moment." Klopp lowered the glasses. "Full reverse on this engine will turn us around fastest."

"Full reverse from full ahead?" Alek shook his head. "You'll never make that look like an accident."

"No, but I can make it look like my own idea," Klopp said, then grabbed Alek by the collar and shoved him hard to the floor. As Alek's head cracked against the metal deck of the engine pod, the world went starry for a moment.

"Klopp! What in blazes are you—"

The shriek of gears drowned out Alek's words, the whole pod shuddering in its frame around him. The air suddenly stilled as the propeller sputtered to a halt.

"What's the meaning of this!" cried Hirst.

Alek's vision cleared, and he saw Klopp brandishing a wrench at the chief engineer. With his free hand the old man deftly shifted the engine into reverse, then pushed the foot pedal down.

The propeller sputtered back to life, drawing air backward across the pod.

"Klopp, wait!" Alek began. He tried to stand, but his head spun, and he fell back to one knee.

Blazes! The man had actually *hurt* him!

Hirst was blowing on his whistle again—a high-pitched squeak—and Alek heard a hydrogen sniffer howling in response. Soon a pack of the ugly creatures would be thundering down upon them.

Alek pulled himself up, reaching out for the wrench. "Klopp, what are you *doing?*"

The man swung at him, yelling, "Got to make this convincing!"

The wrench whistled over Alek's head. He ducked and fell back onto one knee again, cursing. Had Klopp gone *mad*?

Mr. Hirst reached into a pocket and pulled out a compressed air pistol.

"No!" Alek cried, leaping for the gun. As his fingers wrapped around Hirst's wrist, the pistol exploded with a deafening *crack*. The shot missed Klopp, but the bullet rang like an alarm bell as it ricocheted around the engine pod.

Something kicked Alek in the ribs, hard, and searing pain blossomed in his side.

He fell backward, his fingers slipping from Hirst's wrist, but the man didn't raise the gun again. Hirst and Klopp both gaped, dumbstruck, at the *Leviathan*'s flank.

Alek blinked away pain and followed their stares. The cilia were in furious motion, rippling like leaves in a storm. The airbeast's vast length was bending, twisting harder than he'd ever seen. The great harness groaned around them as it stretched, joined by the *pop* of ropes snapping in the ratlines.

"The beast knows it's in danger," Klopp said.

Alek watched in wonder as the airship seemed to curl around them in the air. The stars spun overhead, and soon the huge animal had turned itself entirely around.

"Back to full . . . ," Alek began, but it hurt too much to speak. Every word was another kick in the ribs. He looked down at his hand pressed against his left side, and saw blood between the fingers.

Klopp was already working, reversing the engine once more. Mr. Hirst clutched his pistol tight, still staring in wonder at the airbeast's flank.

"Get out of the pod, young master," Klopp yelled as the propeller's gears caught again. "It's metal. The lightning will jump to it."

"I don't think I can."

Klopp turned. "What . . . ?"

"I'm shot."

The old man dropped the controls and bent beside him, eyes wide. "I'll lift you."

"Mind your engine, man!" Alek managed.

"Young master—," Klopp began, but his words were drowned out by a crackling in the air.

With a painful heave Alek pulled himself up to look backward. The *Goeben* was falling behind them, but the Tesla cannon was blindingly bright. It flickered like a welding lamp, sending jittering shadows across the dark sea.

Beside him the airship's cilia still seethed and billowed, pushing at the air like a million tiny oars.

Faster, Alek prayed to the giant airbeast.

A great fireball formed at the tower's base, then swiftly rose, dancing and shimmering as it climbed. When it reached the top, a thunderous *boom* rang out.

Fingers of lightning, jagged and colossal, shot up from the Tesla cannon. They stretched across the whole sky at first, a tree of white fire, then leapt toward the *Leviathan* as if drawn by scent. The lightning spread a fiery web across

the airbeast's skin, a dazzling wave that surged down its length. In an instant the electricity flowed three hundred meters from tail to head, leaping eagerly across the metal struts that supported the engine pod.

The whole pod began to crackle, the gears and pistons flinging out radiant spokes of fire. Alek was seized by an invisible force; every muscle in his body tightened. For a long moment the lightning squeezed the breath from him. Finally its power wilted, and he slipped back to the metal deck.

The engine sputtered to a halt again.

Alek smelled smoke, and felt an awful pounding in his chest. His ribs ached with every heartbeat.

"Young master? Can you hear me?"

Alek forced his eyes open. "I'm all right, Klopp."

"No, you aren't," the man said. "I'll get you to the gondola."

Klopp wrapped one big arm around Alek and pulled him up, sending a wave of fresh agony through him.

"God's wounds, man! That *hurts!*"

Alek wavered on his feet, dumbstruck by the pain. Mr. Hirst didn't lend a hand, his nervous eyes scanning the length of the *Leviathan* beside them.

Somehow, the airship was not aflame.

"The engine?" Alek asked Klopp.

The man sniffed the air and shook his head. "All the

electrikals are cooked, and the starboard side is silent as well."

Alek turned to Hirst and said, "We've lost the engines. Perhaps you could put that gun away."

The chief engineer stared at the air pistol in his hand, then slipped it into his pocket and pulled out a whistle. "I'll call a surgeon for you. Tell your mutinous friend to set you down."

"My 'mutinous friend' just saved your—," Alek started, but a fresh wave of dizziness passed over him. "Let me sit," he muttered to Klopp. "He says he can get a doctor up here."

"But he's the one who shot you!"

"Yes, but he was aiming at you. Now please put me down."

With an unkindly look at Hirst, Klopp leaned Alek gently against the controls. As Alek caught his breath, he glanced up at the airship's flank. The cilia were still rippling like windblown grass. Even without the engines to motivate it, the great beast was still headed away from the ironclads.

Alek looked sternward through the motionless propeller. The ironclads were steaming away.

"That's odd," he said. "They don't seem to want to finish us off."

Klopp nodded. "They've gone back to their north-northeast heading. They must be expected somewhere."

"North-northeast," Alek repeated. He knew that was significant somehow. He also knew that he should be worried that the *Leviathan* was now drifting southward, away from Constantinople.

But breathing was worry enough.

FOUR

Deryn stood up slowly, blinking away spots from her eyes.

A barking lightning bolt! That was what had fizzled up from the Clanker warship and leapt across the sky, dancing on every squick of metal on the *Leviathan*'s topside. The Huxley winch had thrown out a blinding flock of white sparks, knocking her half silly in the process.

Deryn looked in all directions, terrified that she would see fires bursting willy-nilly from the membrane. But it was all dark except for the jaggy shimmers burned into her vision. The sniffers must have done their jobs brilliantly before the battle. Not a squick of hydrogen had been leaking from the skin.

Then she remembered—the *Leviathan* had spun around just in time, the whole airship twisting like a dog chasing its own tail.

Hydrogen . . .

She looked up into the dark sky, and her jaw dropped.

There was Newkirk, his arms waving madly, the Huxley blazing over his head like a giant Christmas pudding soaked with brandy.

Deryn felt sick, the way she had in a hundred nightmares replaying Da's accident, so close to the awful sight above her. The Huxley tugged at its cable, carried higher by the heat of the flames, spinning the winch's crank.

But a moment later, its hydrogen expended, the airbeast began to drop.

Newkirk was twisting in the pilot's rig, still alive somehow. Then Deryn saw a misting in the starlight around the Huxley. Newkirk had spilled the water ballast to keep himself from burning. Clever boy.

The dead husk of the airbeast billowed out like a ragged parachute, but it was still falling fast.

The Huxley was a thousand feet up, and if it missed crashing against the *Leviathan*'s topsides, it would drop another thousand feet before the cable snapped it to a halt. Best to make that trip as short as possible. Deryn reached for the winch—but her hand froze.

Did electricity linger?

"*Dummkopf!*" she cursed herself, forcing herself to grasp the metal.

No sparks shot from it, and she began to turn as fast

as she could. But the Huxley was coming down faster than she could reel it in. The cable began to coil across the airship's spine, tangling in the feet of crewmen and sniffers running past.

Still spinning the crank wildly, Deryn looked up. Newkirk was hanging limply beneath the burned husk, which was drifting away from the *Leviathan*.

The engines had stopped, and the searchlights had gone dead too. The crewmen were using electric torches to call the bats and strafing hawks back from the black sky—the Clanker lightning contraption had knocked everything out.

But if the airship was powerless, why was the wind pushing Newkirk away? Shouldn't they all have been drifting together?

Deryn looked down at the flank, her eyes widening.

The cilia were still moving, still carrying the airship away from danger.

"Now, that's barking odd," she muttered.

Usually a hydrogen breather without engines was content to drift. Of course, the airbeast *had* been acting strangely since the crash in the Alps. All the old crewmen said that the crash in the Alps—or the Clanker engines—had rattled its attic.

But this was no time to ponder. Newkirk was gliding past only a hundred feet away, close enough that Deryn could see his blackened face and soaking uniform. But he didn't seem to be moving.

"Newkirk!" she yelled, her hand raw on the winch's handle. But he fell past without answering.

The coils of slack cable began to rustle, like a nest of snakes strewn across the topside. The Huxley was dragging its cable behind as it dropped below the airship.

"Clear those lines!" Deryn shouted, waving off a crewman standing among the slithering coils. The man danced away, the cable snapping at his ankles, trying to drag him down as well.

She went at the crank again, till the line snapped tight with a sickening jerk. Deryn hit the brake and checked the cable markings—just over five hundred feet.

The *Leviathan* was two hundred feet from top to bottom, so Newkirk would be dangling less than three hundred feet below. Strapped into the pilot's rig, he was probably all right. Unless the fire had got him, or he'd been jolted to a neck-breaking stop . . .

Deryn took a deep breath, trying to stop her hands from shaking.

She couldn't crank him back up. The winch was designed for a hydrogen-filled Huxley, not to haul dead weight.

Deryn followed the taut cable, climbing down the ratlines on the airbeast's flank. From the ship's waist she could just see the Huxley's dark shape fluttering against the whitecaps of the waves.

"Barking spiders," she murmured. The water was much closer than she'd expected.

The *Leviathan* was losing altitude.

Of course—the great airbeast was trying to find the strongest wind to pull itself away from the German ironclads. It wouldn't care about smacking poor burnt Newkirk against the ocean's choppy surface.

But the officers could drop ballast, and drag the ship up against its will. Deryn pulled out her command whistle and blew for a message lizard, then stared again at the Huxley below.

There was no human movement that she could see. Newkirk had to be stunned, at least. And he wouldn't have the right equipment to climb the cable. No one expected to climb *up* from an ascender.

Where was that barking message lizard? She saw one scrambling across the membrane, and whistled for it. But the lizard just stared at her and jabbered something about an electrical malfunction.

"Brilliant," she murmured. The bolt of Clanker lightning had scrambled the wee beasties' brains! Down below, the dark water looked closer every second.

She was going to have to rescue Newkirk herself.

Deryn searched the pockets of her flight suit. In

airmanship class Mr. Rigby had taught them about how riggers "belayed," which was Service-speak for sliding down a rope without breaking your neck. She found a few carabiners and enough line to make a pair of friction hitches.

After attaching her safety clip to the Huxley's cable, Deryn twisted the carabiner tight. She couldn't wind the rope around her hips because the weight of the dead Huxley would snip her in half. But after a moment's fiddling, she attached the extra carabiners to her harness and strung the cable through them.

Mr. Rigby wouldn't approve of this method, Deryn thought as she kicked herself away from the membrane.

She slid down in short jerks, the carabiners' friction keeping her from falling too fast. But the rope was hot beneath her gloves, its fibers fraying wherever she snapped to a halt. Deryn doubted this cable was designed to hold the weight of a dead Huxley and two middies.

The ocean thundered below Deryn, the wind growing colder now that the sun had fully set. The peak of a tall wave smacked against the Huxley's drooping membrane, cracking like a gunshot.

"Newkirk!" Deryn shouted, and the boy stirred in his pilot's rig.

A shudder of relief went through her—he was alive. Not like Da.

She let herself fall the last twenty yards, the rope hissing like mad and spilling a burnt smell into the salt air. But her boots landed softly on the squishy membrane of the dead airbeast, which smelled of smoke and salt, like jellyfish cooked on a hearth fire.

"Where in blazes am I?" Newkirk mumbled, barely audible over the rumble of the waves. His hair was scorched, his face and hands blackened with smoke.

"Almost in the barking ocean, that's where! Can you move?"

The boy stared at his blackened hands, wriggling his fingers, then unstrapped himself from the harness. He stood up shakily on the frame of the pilot's rig.

"Aye. I'm just singed." He ran his fingers through his hair, or what was left of it.

"Can you climb?" Deryn asked.

Newkirk stared up at the *Leviathan*'s dark belly. "Aye, but that's *miles* away! Couldn't you have cranked faster?"

"You could have *fallen slower!*" Deryn shouted back. She unclipped two carabiners and shoved them into his hands, along with a short length of line. "Tie yourself a friction hitch. Or don't you remember Mr. Rigby's classes?"

Newkirk stared at the carabiners, then up at the distant airship.

"Aye, I remember. But I never thought we'd be ascending that far."

"Ascending," of course, was Service-Speak for climbing *up* a rope without breaking your neck. Deryn's fingers worked fast with her own line. A friction hitch slid freely up a rope, but held fast when weight was hanging from it. That way, she and Newkirk could stop and rest without relying on their muscles to keep them from sliding back.

"You go first," she ordered. If Newkirk slid down, she could stop him.

He pulled himself up a few feet, then tested his hitch, swinging freely from the rope. "It works!"

"Aye. You'll be conquering Mount Everest next!" As she spoke, another wave slapped at the Huxley, splashing across them both. Deryn lost her footing, but her friction hitch held.

She spat out salt water and yelled, "Get going, you *Dummkopf*! The ship's losing altitude!"

Newkirk started climbing, scrambling with feet and hands. He had soon cleared enough distance that Deryn could haul herself off the dead Huxley.

Another wave hit the airbeast, snapping the line tight, and Newkirk skidded down till he was almost on top of her. If the *Leviathan* dropped any lower, the beastie's carcass would be dragging in the water. If the membrane filled up, it would pull on the rope like a barrel full of stones.

Enough to break any cable . . . She had to cut the Huxley loose.

"Higher!" she yelled, and started climbing madly.

About twenty feet above the Huxley, Deryn halted, hanging just above a badly frayed spot. She pulled out her rigging knife, reached down, and started hacking at the line. Huxley cable was barking thick, but when the next tall wave struck the airbeast, the fibers unraveled in a blur and snapped.

Without the beastie's dead weight anchoring them, suddenly they were swinging across the black sea, cast about by the wind. Newkirk cried out with surprise overhead.

"Sorry!" Deryn yelled up. "Should have warned you."

But with the Huxley's weight gone, the rope wouldn't snap . . . probably.

She started climbing again, wishing for the hundredth time that she had the arm strength of a boy. But soon the waves no longer threatened her dangling boots.

Halfway up, Deryn took a long breather, searching the dark horizon for the two German ironclads. They were nowhere to be seen.

Maybe the Royal Navy was close by, and had kept the ships running. But Deryn couldn't see any sign of surface ships. The only shape on the water was the Huxley's carcass, a lonely black smear on the waves.

"Poor beastie," she said, shivering. The whole airship and its crew might have wound up like that—burnt black, as lonely as driftwood on the dark sea. If the hydrogen sniffers had missed a single leak, or if the airbeast hadn't spun itself around just in time, they'd all have been done for.

"Barking Clankers," Deryn murmured. "Making their own *lightning* now."

She closed her eyes to shut her dark memories away, the roar of skin-prickling heat and the smell of burnt flesh. This time she'd won. The fire hadn't taken anyone she loved.

Deryn shuddered once more, then started to climb again.

● FIVE ●

"This is entirely unacceptable!" Dr. Barlow cried.

"I'm s-sorry, ma'am," the guard sputtered. "But the captain said the Clanker boy wasn't to have visitors."

Deryn shook her head—the man's resistance was already faltering. He was backed up against Alek's stateroom door, sweat breaking out on his forehead.

"I am not a visitor, you imbecile," Dr. Barlow said. "I'm a doctor here to see an injured patient!"

Tazza's ears perked up at the lady boffin's sharp tone, and he let out a low growl. Deryn held his leash a squick tighter. "Shush now, Tazza. No biting."

"But the surgeon was already here," the guard squeaked, staring wide eyed at the thylacine. "Said the boy only bruised a rib."

"On top of suffering from shock, no doubt," Dr. Barlow said. "Or did you fail to notice our recent encounter with a prodigious amount of electricity?"

"Of course not, ma'am." The guard swallowed, still eyeing Tazza nervously. "But the captain was quite specific—"

"Did he *specifically* forbid doctors from seeing the patient?"

"Er, no."

Just give up, thought Deryn. It didn't matter that Dr. Barlow was a boffin—a fabricator of beasties—and not a pulse-taking stick-out-your-tongue doctor. She'd be seeing this particular patient one way or another.

Deryn hoped that Alek really was all right. The Clanker lightning had danced across the whole ship, but it must have been worst in the engine pods, with all that metal about . . . Well, second to worst, anyway. Newkirk's hair was half burnt off, and he had a knot on his head the size of a cricket ball.

But how had Alek bruised a rib? That didn't sound like something an electric shock would do.

Finally the guard surrendered his post, slinking off to check with the watch officer and trusting Dr. Barlow to wait till he got back. She didn't, of course, just pushed the door straight open.

Alek lay in bed, his ribs wrapped in bandages. His skin was ashen, his dark green eyes glistening in the dawn light streaming through the portholes.

"Barking spiders!" Deryn said. "You're as pale as a mealyworm."

A wan smile spread across the boy's face. "It's good to see you, too, Dylan. And you, Dr. Barlow."

"Good morning, Alek," the lady boffin said. "You *are* pale, aren't you? As if you've lost some blood. An odd symptom for electrocution."

Alek grimaced as he struggled to sit up higher. "I'm afraid you're right, ma'am. Mr. Hirst shot me."

"Shot you?" Deryn cried.

Alek nodded. "Luckily it was one of your feeble compressed air guns. Dr. Busk said the bullet hit a rib and bounced off, but nothing's broken, thanks partly to my fencing armor. I should be walking about soon enough."

Deryn stared at the bandages. "But what in blazes did he shoot you *for*?"

"He was aiming for Klopp. They had a . . . disagreement. Klopp realized what was about to happen—what the Tesla cannon was—and decided to turn us around."

"A Tesla cannon?" Dr. Barlow repeated. "As in that awful Mr. Tesla?"

"That's what Klopp says," Alek said.

"But you Clankers didn't turn us around," Deryn said. "Everyone says that the beastie itself turned, because it got scared."

Alek shook his head. "Klopp reversed the port engine

first, then the airbeast followed suit. It seems the *Leviathan* has more sense than its own officers."

"You said they had a disagreement?" Dr. Barlow asked. "You mean you changed course without orders?"

"There wasn't time to wait for orders," he said.

Deryn let out a low groan. No wonder Alek was under guard.

"That's barking mutiny," she said softly.

"But we saved the ship."

"Aye, but you can't disobey orders just because the officers are being daft. Especially not in battle—that's a hanging offense!"

Alek's eyes widened, and the room was silent for a moment.

Dr. Barlow cleared her throat. "Please don't say alarming things to my patient, Mr. Sharp. He's no more a member of this crew than I am, and is therefore not subject to your brutish military authority."

Deryn bit down a reply. She doubted Captain Hobbes would see it that way. This had probably been his worry since the Clankers had come aboard, that they'd ignore the bridge and pilot the ship whichever way they wanted.

Changing course wasn't like skylarking or learning to fence on duty. It was mutiny, pure and simple.

The lady boffin sat primly on the stateroom's only chair, snapping her fingers for Tazza to come to her.

"Now, Alek," she said, stroking the thylacine's striped flank. "You say that Klopp was operating the engine. So this 'mutiny' wasn't your idea?"

The boy thought for a moment. "I suppose not."

"Then, pray tell, why are *you* under guard?"

"When Mr. Hirst pulled the pistol, I tried to take it from him."

Deryn shut her eyes. Striking an officer—*another* hanging offense.

"Very sensible of you," Dr. Barlow said. "This ship won't get very far without its master of mechaniks, will it?"

"Where is Klopp now?" Alek asked.

"I reckon he's in the brig," Deryn said.

"And *not* at work on the engines, thus further delaying my mission." Dr. Barlow stood up, straightening her skirts. "Don't you worry about Master Klopp, Alek. Now that I

have all the facts, I'm sure the captain will see reason."

She handed the leash to Deryn.

"Please walk Tazza and then check on the eggs, Mr. Sharp. I don't trust that Mr. Newkirk, especially with his head swelling up like a melon." She turned. "In fact, I'd much rather that you were watching them, Alek. Please do get better soon."

"Thank you, ma'am. I'll try," the boy said. "But if you don't mind, could Dylan stay a moment?"

The lady boffin's eyes measured them both, and then she smiled. "Of course. Perhaps you could amuse Mr. Sharp with whatever you know about this . . . Tesla cannon? I have some familiarity with the inventor, and it seemed a most intriguing device."

"I'm afraid I don't know much—," Alek began, but Dr. Barlow was already out the door and gone.

Deryn stood silently a moment, wondering where to start. With the Clankers' lightning contraption? Or how Newkirk had almost burnt to a crisp? Or the possibility that Alek would be court-martialed and hanged?

Then her eyes fell on his bandages, and an awful feeling went through her. If the gun had been pointed a few inches higher, Alek might be dead.

"Does getting shot hurt much?" she asked.

"Like a mule kicked me."

"Hmm. I've never been daft enough to let that happen."

"Nor have I." Alek smiled weakly. "But it feels about right."

The two were silent again, Deryn wondering how things had gone pear-shaped so fast. Before Newkirk had spotted the ironclads, she'd been hoping that Alek would wind up staying on the *Leviathan* somehow. But she hadn't meant lying wounded in bed, or clapped in irons for mutiny, or *both*.

"This is the second time someone's shot at me," Alek said. "Remember those gunners on the zeppelin?"

Deryn nodded slowly. Back in the Alps, the daft prince had stepped out into the middle of a battle, right in front of a machine gun. Only a hydrogen leak had saved him, the German gunners setting their own airship aflame.

"Perhaps I wasn't meant to die that day," he said. "Or last night, either."

"Aye, or perhaps you were just barking *lucky*."

"I suppose," Alek said. "Do you really think they'll hang us?"

Deryn thought a moment, then shrugged. "There aren't any rules for something like this, I reckon. We've never had Clankers aboard before. But they'll listen to the lady boffin, because of her grandfather's name."

Alek grimaced again. Deryn wondered if it was his wound, or being reminded that Dr. Barlow was related to old Charles Darwin himself. Even after serving on a living airship, the Clankers were still superstitious about life threads and fabrication.

"I wish we *had* mutinied," Alek said. "And ended that pointless battle before it started. Klopp and I thought about stopping the engines and making it look like a malfunction."

"Well, thinking isn't the same as doing," Deryn said, slumping onto the chair. She'd entertained madder ideas than mutiny. Like telling Alek that she was a girl, or giving Dr. Barlow a smack—the latter more than once. The trick was never to let what you were thinking slip out into the world.

"And anyway," she continued, "I haven't heard about this mutiny business, so the officers must be keeping dead quiet. Maybe the captain wants to let you off without looking soft. Everyone thinks it was the airbeast who turned us around, for fear of that Clanker cannon."

"The beast *did* turn us around. It must have smelled the lightning—it knew we'd all burn."

Deryn shuddered again, as she did every time she thought of how close they'd come. She could still see the Huxley, blazing in midair just like Da's balloon.

"But Newkirk isn't dead," she told herself softly.

"Pardon me?"

Deryn cleared her throat. She didn't want to wind up with her voice squeaking like a girl's. "I said, the engines are dead. And the airbeast has gone bonkers, and thinks it's still running away from that Tesla thingie. We're half-way to Africa!"

Alek swore. "I suppose those ironclads are already there."

"What, in Africa?"

"No, *Dummkopf*—Constantinople." He pointed at the desk in the room. "There's a map in that drawer. Kindly fetch it for me."

"Aye, your princeliness," Deryn said, hauling herself up to get the map. It was just like Alek, to be thinking of maps and schemes while lying wounded, guilty of a hanging offense.

She sat on the bed beside him, smoothing out the roll of paper. It was labeled in Clanker writing, but she could see it was the Mediterranean.

"The ironclads were headed north into the Aegean," Alek said. "See?"

Deryn traced the *Leviathan*'s course from southern Italy with one finger, until she found the spot where they'd fought the *Goeben* and *Breslau*—almost due south of Constantinople.

"Aye, they were headed that way." She pointed at the Dardanelles, the narrow stretch of water that led to the ancient city. "But if they head north, they'll be trapped in the strait, like a fly in a bottle."

"What if they plan to stay there?"

Deryn shook her head. "The Ottoman Empire is still neutral, and ships at war can't hang about in a neutral port. Dr. Barlow says we're only allowed to stay in Constantinople for twenty-four hours. It must be the same for the Germans."

"But didn't she also say that the Ottomans were angry with the British? For stealing their warship?"

"Well, aye," Deryn said, then muttered, "but that's just borrowing, really."

To be truthful, though, it *had* been a bit like stealing. Britain had just completed a new dreadnought for the Ottoman navy, along with a huge companion creature, some new sort of kraken. Both the warship and the creature had already been paid for, but when the war had begun, the First Lord of the Admiralty had decided to keep the ship and its beastie, at least until the conflict ended.

Borrowing or stealing, it had caused the diplomatic ruckus that Dr. Barlow and the *Leviathan* had been sent to sort out. Somehow the mysterious eggs in the engine room were meant to help.

"So the Ottomans might decide to let the ironclads stay," Alek said. "Just to get back at your Lord Churchill."

"Well, that would make everything trickier, wouldn't it?"

Alek nodded. "It would mean even more Germans in Constantinople. It might even bring the Ottomans over to the Clanker side! The *Goeben*'s Tesla cannon is pretty convincing."

"Aye, it convinced me," Deryn said. She wouldn't fancy sharing the same city with that contraption.

"And what happens if the Ottomans close the Dardanelles to British shipping?"

Deryn swallowed. The fighting bears of the Russian army needed lots of food, most of which was brought in by ship. If they were cut off from their Darwinist allies, the Russians would have a long, hungry winter.

"But are you sure that's where the ironclads were headed?"

"No. Not yet." He raised his dark gaze from the map. "Dylan, can you do me a favor? A *secret* favor?"

She swallowed. "That depends on what it is."

"I need you to deliver a message."

◦ SIX ◦

"Barking bloody princes," she muttered, pulling Tazza along the airship's corridors.

She'd hardly slept a wink last night, what with looking after Newkirk, and the thylacine needed to go for a walk soon. On top of which, Deryn still had to check on Dr. Barlow's precious eggs. But instead of attending to her duties, here she was delivering secret messages for the Clankers.

Aiding the enemy in wartime. How was that for mutiny?

As she drew closer to the cabin, Deryn began to formulate excuses and explanations—"*I was just asking our count friend if he needed anything.*" "*I was on a secret mission from the captain.*" "*Someone had to keep an eye on those mutinous Clankers, and this was the best way!*"—all of them barking pathetic.

She knew the real reason she'd said yes to Alek. He'd

looked so helpless lying there, pale and bandaged, not knowing if they were going to hang him tomorrow at dawn. It had only made the way she felt harder to ignore.

Deryn took a deep breath, and rapped on the stateroom door.

After a long moment it opened to reveal a tall man in a formal uniform. He stared down his sharp nose at her and Tazza, not saying a word. Deryn wondered if she should bow, because he was a count and all. But Alek was a prince, which sounded more important, and no one ever bowed to him.

"What is it?" the man finally asked.

"Pleased to meet you, Mr. . . . , um, Count Volger. I'm Midshipman Dylan Sharp."

"I know who you are."

"Right. Because Alek and I, we've been fencing and that. We're friends."

"You're that idiot boy who put a knife to Alek's throat."

Deryn swallowed, willing her tongue to untangle. She'd only been pretending when she'd taken Alek hostage back in the Alps, to force the Clankers to negotiate instead of blowing up the airship.

But under the man's imperious gaze, the explanation wouldn't come.

"Aye, that was me," she managed. "But it was only to get your attention."

"You succeeded."

"And I used the dull edge of that knife, just to be safe!" She looked both ways down the corridor. "Do you suppose I could come in?"

"Why?"

"I've got a message from Alek. A secret one."

With those words Count Volger's stony countenance shifted a squick. His left eyebrow arched, then finally he stepped back. A moment later she and Tazza were inside the room, the thylacine sniffing at the man's boots.

"What is this creature?" he asked, taking another step backward.

"Oh, that's just Tazza. He's harmless," Deryn said, then remembered the damage he'd done to the lady boffin's cabin. "Well, unless you're a set of curtains, which, um, you're clearly not."

She cleared her throat, feeling like a ninny. The man's cold, haughty manner had started her babbling.

"Will it repeat our words?"

"What, Tazza, *talk?*" Deryn stifled a laugh. "He's no message lizard. He's a natural beastie, a thylacine from Tasmania. Dr. Barlow has him as a traveling companion, though, as you can see, he's mostly *my* responsibility. Anyway, I've got a message from—"

Volger silenced her with an upheld hand, then glanced up at the message tubes in the cabin. A lizard was poking its head from one, and the count clapped his hands once to scare it off.

"Those godless things are everywhere," he muttered. "Always listening."

Deryn rolled her eyes. The other Clankers were even more twitchy about beasties than Alek. They seemed to think that everything living aboard the airship was out to get them.

"Aye, sir. But lizards only carry messages. They don't eavesdrop."

"And how can you be sure of that?"

Now, that was a daft question. Message lizards might repeat snatches of conversation by accident now and then, especially when they'd been recently dazzled by a Tesla cannon. But that wasn't the same as eavesdropping, was it?

Then she remembered how Count Volger had pretended not to speak English when he'd come aboard, in hopes of overhearing secrets. And how Dr. Barlow had pulled the same trick on the Clankers, pretending not to know any German. No wonder those two were always suspicious of everyone—they were both sneaky-beaks themselves.

"Those lizards have got brains no bigger than walnuts," she said. "I don't reckon they'd make very good spies."

"Perhaps not." The count sat down at his desk, which was covered with maps and scrawled notes, a sheathed sword serving as a paperweight. "And what about *your* brains, Mr. Sharp? You're clever enough to be a spy, aren't you?"

"What, me? I told you, Alek sent me here!"

"And how do I *know* that? Last night I was informed that Alek was hurt in the battle, but I haven't been allowed to see him or Master Klopp. And now I receive this 'secret' message from Alek, courtesy of a boy who held him hostage?"

"But he . . . ," Deryn began, then groaned with frustration. This was what she got for doing favors for Clankers. "He's my friend. *He* trusts me, even if you don't."

"Prove it."

"Well, of course he does! He told me his little secret, didn't he?"

Count Volger's eyes narrowed at her a moment, then he stared down at the sword on the table. "His secret?"

"Aye, he told me who he . . . ," Deryn began, but a slow realization was creeping over her. What if Alek had never mentioned to Volger that he'd spilled the beans to her? Finding out now might give the man a wee startle. "You know, his *big* secret?"

The air hissed as Volger whirled around, sunlight flashing on steel, the chair spinning across the floor and sending Tazza leaping to his feet. The sword suddenly stretched from Volger's hand, its cold, naked tip at Deryn's throat.

"Tell me what secret," the wildcount demanded. "*Now.*"

"A-about his parents!" she sputtered. "His father and mother were assassinated, which is what started this barking war! And he's a prince or something!"

"Who else knows this?"

"Just me!" she squeaked, but the metal prodded her. "Um, and Dr. Barlow. But no one else, I swear!"

He glared at her for an endless moment, his eyes prying their way into hers. Tazza let out a low growl.

Finally the wildcount pulled the saber a few inches back. "Why haven't you informed your captain?"

"Because Alek made us promise." Deryn stared at the sword point. "I thought you knew he'd told us!"

Count Volger lowered the sword. "Obviously I did not."

"Well, that's not *my* fault!" Deryn cried. "Maybe it's *you* he doesn't trust!"

The man looked at the floor. "Perhaps."

"And you didn't have to cut my barking head off!"

Volger gave her a thin smile as he righted the overturned chair. "It was only to get your attention. And I used a dull edge. Surely you know a fencing saber when you see one?"

Deryn reached out and grabbed the weapon's blade. She swore—it was the very saber she'd practiced with yesterday, no sharper than a butter knife.

Count Volger sat heavily, shaking his head as he cleaned the sword with a pocket handkerchief and then

"AN ALTERCATION."

sheathed it again. "That boy will be the death of me."

"At least Alek trusts someone!" Deryn said. "The rest of you *Dummkopfs*, you're all as mad as a box of frogs! Lying and sneaking and . . . scared of *message lizards*. With all your scheming it's no wonder the world's in a barking great war!"

Tazza growled again, then made his strange little yelp, hopping on his hind legs. Deryn knelt to calm him down, and to hide her burning eyes from Count Volger.

"Is Alek really hurt?" the man asked.

"Aye. But it's only a bruised rib."

"Why won't they let me see him or Klopp?"

"Because of what Master Klopp did during the battle," Deryn said, stroking Tazza's flank. "He turned the ship around just before the Tesla cannon fired. Without orders."

Volger snorted. "So *this* is why your captain has summoned me? To discuss the chain of command?"

She glared up at him. "He might reckon it was mutiny— a hanging offense!"

"An absurd notion, unless he wants his ship to drift forever."

Deryn took a slow, deep breath and petted Tazza again. It was true—the *Leviathan* still needed the Clankers and their engines. More so than ever, with the airbeast acting up.

"I suppose the captain just wants to make a point," she said. "But that's not what I'm here about."

"Ah, yes. Your secret message."

Deryn gave the man a hard look. "Well, maybe you don't care one way or the other. But Alek thinks those two ironclads are headed for Constantinople, just like us!"

Volger raised an eyebrow at that, then pointed to the fallen chair.

"Sit down, boy, and tell me everything."

SEVEN

"Hear that?" Corporal Bauer asked.

Alek wiped his hands on an oily rag, listening. The air trembled with the distant clamor of an engine coming to life, sputtering at first, then settling into a low and steady roar.

He stared at the tangle of gears before him and said to his men, "Three against one, and Klopp has his engine working first!"

"Hate to say so, sir." Bauer spread his grease-blackened hands. "But you and I aren't much help."

Master Hoffman clapped the gunner on his back and laughed. "I'll make an engineer of you one day, Bauer. It's that one who's hopeless." He glanced at Mr. Hirst, who was watching them glumly from the engine pod strut, his hands perfectly clean.

"What's this about?" the man asked.

Alek switched to English. "Nothing, Mr. Hirst. Just that it sounds as though Klopp has beaten us."

"So it would seem," the man said, and fell back into silence.

It was late afternoon, less than forty-eight hours after the unlucky encounter with the *Breslau* and the *Goeben*. Alek, his men Hoffman and Bauer, and Hirst had been assigned to the starboard pod, while Master Klopp was over on the port side, under armed guard, with Count Volger translating for him.

Since the incident with the air pistol, it had been decided that Klopp and Mr. Hirst would no longer share the same engine pod. Alek was not under guard, but he suspected that was only because of the bandages wrapped around his injured rib. Every time he lifted a wrench, he winced in pain.

But no one was locked in the brig, at least. True to her word, Dr. Barlow had convinced the captain to accept reality—without Klopp's help, the airship would drift on the winds. Or worse, the great airbeast might take them on a journey of its own choosing.

The captain's goodwill had come with certain conditions, however. The five Austrians were to stay aboard the *Leviathan* until the Darwinists understood their new engines fully, however long that took.

Alek suspected they wouldn't be getting off in Constantinople.

⊙　　⊙　　⊙

Half an hour later, the starboard engine finally sparked to life. As smoke poured from the exhaust pipes, Master Hoffman engaged the gears, and the propeller began to spin.

Alek closed his eyes, reveling in the steady thrum of pistons. Freedom might not be any closer, but at least the airship was whole again.

"Feeling all right, sir?" Bauer asked.

Alek took a deep breath of sea air. "Just happy to be under way."

"Feels good to have an engine rumbling underfoot again, doesn't it?" Hoffman nodded at Mr. Hirst. "And maybe our sulky friend here has finally picked up a few tricks."

"Let's hope so," Alek said, smiling. Since the battle, Bauer and Hoffman had taken a dislike to the *Leviathan*'s chief engineer. After all, the two had been at Alek's side since the awful night his parents had died, and had given up their careers to protect him. They hadn't taken kindly to Mr. Hirst shooting at him and Master Klopp, mutiny or not.

Soon both engines were working in tandem, and the *Leviathan* set a northward course again. The water's surface slid by beneath them faster and faster, until the airship had left behind its escort of hungry seagulls and curious dolphins.

Moving air tasted better, Alek decided. The airbeast

had let itself drift most of the day, matching the speed and direction of the wind, wrapping everything in a dead calm. But now that they were under power, the salt air was sharp and alive against his face, driving away the feeling of being imprisoned.

"One of those talking things," Bauer said, frowning.

Alek turned to see a message lizard making its way across the airship's skin, and sighed. It was probably Dr. Barlow putting him on egg duty again.

But when the lizard opened its mouth, it spoke with the master coxswain's voice. "The captain wishes the pleasure of your company on the bridge, at your earliest convenience."

Bauer and Hoffman looked at Alek, recognizing the English word "captain."

"Wants to see me at my earliest convenience," he translated, and Bauer gave a snort. There wasn't much convenient about climbing down to the gondola with a bruised rib.

But Alek found himself smiling as he wiped engine grease from his hands. This was the first time any of them had been invited to the bridge. Since coming aboard, he'd wondered how the officers controlled the airship's interwoven complements of men, fabricated animals, and machines. Was it like a German land dreadnought, with the bridge crew directly controlling the engines and cannon? Or an oceangoing ship, with orders dispatched to the boiler rooms and weapon stations?

Alek turned to Mr. Hirst. "I leave you to it, sir."

The man nodded a bit stiffly. He'd never apologized for shooting Alek, and none of the officers had ever admitted that Klopp had saved the ship. But as they'd started work that morning, Hirst had quietly turned out his pockets, showing that he wasn't carrying a pistol anymore.

That was something, at least.

Alek found Volger waiting for him on the gondola's main staircase.

It was strange to see the wildcount's riding clothes spotted with oil, his hair tangled by propeller wash. In fact, Alek hadn't seen Volger since the battle. They'd both been working on the engines every waking moment since Alek's release.

"Ah, Your Highness," the wildcount said, offering a half-hearted bow. "I was wondering if you'd been summoned too."

"I go where the lizards tell me."

Volger didn't smile, just turned and started down the stairs. "Beastly creatures. The captain must have important news, to let us see the bridge at last."

"Perhaps he wants to thank us."

"I suspect it's something less agreeable," Volger said.

"Something he didn't want us to know until *after* we got his engines working again."

Alek frowned. As usual the wildcount was making sense, if only in a suspicious way. Living among the godless creatures of the *Leviathan* hadn't improved his disposition.

"You don't trust the Darwinists much, do you?" Alek said.

"Nor should you." Volger came to a halt, looking up and down the corridors. He waited until a pair of crewmen had passed, then pulled Alek farther down the stairway. A moment later they were on the lowest deck of the gondola, in a dark corridor lit only by the ship's glowworms.

"The ship's storerooms are almost empty," Volger said quietly. "They don't even guard them anymore."

Alek smiled. "You've been sneaking about, haven't you?"

"When I'm not adjusting gears like a common mechanik. But we must speak quickly. They've caught me here once already."

"So, what did you think of my message?" Alek asked. "Those ironclads are headed for Constantinople, aren't they?"

"You told them who you were," Count Volger said.

Alek froze for a moment as the words sank in. Then he blinked and turned away, his eyes stinging with shame and frustration. It felt like being a boy again, when Volger had landed hits with his saber at will.

He cleared his throat, reminding himself that the wild-count was no longer his tutor. "Dr. Barlow told you, didn't she? To show that she has something over us."

"Not a bad guess. But it was simpler than that—Dylan let it slip."

"Dylan?" Alek shook his head.

"He didn't realize you kept secrets from me."

"I don't keep any . . . ," Alek began, but it was pointless arguing.

"Have you gone mad?" Volger whispered. "You're the heir to the throne of Austria-Hungary. Why would you *tell our enemies that?*"

"Dylan and Dr. Barlow aren't enemies," Alek said firmly, looking Count Volger full in the eye. "And they don't know I'm the legal heir to the throne. Nobody knows about the pope's letter but you and me."

"Well, thank heaven for that."

"And I *didn't* tell them, not really. Dr. Barlow guessed who my parents were, quite on her own." Alek looked away again. "But I'm sorry. I should have told you they knew."

"No. You should have never admitted anything, whatever they'd guessed! That boy Dylan is completely guileless—incapable of keeping a secret. You may think he's your friend, but he's just a peasant. And you've put your future in his hands!"

Alek shook his head. Dylan might be a commoner, but he *was* a friend. He'd already risked his life to keep Alek's identity a secret.

"Think for a moment, Volger. Dylan let it slip to *you*, not to one of the ship's officers. We can trust him."

The man stepped closer in the darkness, his voice hardly above a whisper. "I hope you're right, Alek. Otherwise the captain is about to tell us that his new engines will be taking us back to Britain, where they'll have a cage waiting for you. Do you think being the Darwinists' pet monarch will be agreeable?"

Alek didn't answer for a moment, replaying all of Dylan's earnest promises in his mind. Then he turned away and started up the stairs.

"He hasn't betrayed us. You'll see."

The bridge was much larger than Alek had imagined.

It took up the entire width of the gondola, curving with the gentle half circle of the airship's prow. The afternoon sun streamed through windows that stretched almost to the ceiling. Alek stepped closer to one—the glass leaned gently outward, allowing him to peer straight down at the dazzling water slipping past.

Reflected in the window, a dozen message lizard tubes coiled along the ceiling; others sprouted from the floor like shiny brass mushrooms. Levers and control panels

lined the walls, and carrier birds fluttered in the cages hanging in one corner. Alek closed his eyes for a moment, listening to the buzz and chatter of men and animals.

Volger gently pulled his arm. "We're here to parley, not to gawk."

Setting a serious expression on his face, Alek followed

Volger. But still he watched and listened to everything around him. No matter what the captain's news turned out to be, he wanted to soak in every detail of this place.

At the front of the bridge was the master wheel, like an old sailing ship's, carved in the Darwinists' sinuous style. Captain Hobbes turned from it to greet them, a smile on his face.

"Ah, gentlemen. Thank you for coming."

Alek followed Volger's lead and offered the captain a shallow bow, one suited for a minor nobleman of uncertain importance.

"To what do we owe the pleasure?" Volger asked.

"We're under way again," Captain Hobbes said. "I wanted to thank you personally for that."

"We're glad to help," Alek said, hoping that for once Count Volger's suspicions had proven overblown.

"But I also have bad news," the captain continued. "I've just received word that Britain and Austria-Hungary are officially at war." He cleared his throat. "Most regrettable."

Alek drew in a slow breath, wondering how long the captain had known. Had he waited until the engines were fixed to tell them? Then Alek realized that he and Volger were smeared with grease, dressed like tradesmen, while Captain Hobbes preened in his crisp blue uniform. Suddenly he hated the man.

"This changes nothing," Volger said. "We're not soldiers, after all."

"Really?" The captain frowned. "But judging by their uniforms, your men are members of the Hapsburg Guard, are they not?"

"Not since we left Austria," Alek said. "As I told you, we had to flee for political reasons."

The captain shrugged. "Deserters are still soldiers."

Alek bridled. "My men are hardly——"

"Are you saying we're prisoners of war?" Volger interrupted. "If so, we shall collect our men from the engine pods and retire to the brig."

"Don't be hasty, gentlemen." Captain Hobbes raised his hands. "I merely wanted to give you the bad news, and to beg your indulgence. This puts me in an awkward situation, you must understand."

"We find it . . . *awkward* too."

"Of course," the captain said, ignoring Alek's tone. "I would prefer to reach some arrangement. But try to understand my position. You've never told me exactly who you are. Now that our countries are at war, that makes your status rather complicated."

The man waited expectantly, and Alek looked at Volger.

"I suppose it does," the wildcount said. "But we still prefer not to identify ourselves."

Captain Hobbes sighed. "Then I shall have to turn to the Admiralty for orders."

"Do let us know what they say," Count Volger said simply.

"Of course." The captain touched his hat and turned back to the wheel. "Good day, gentlemen."

While Volger bowed again, Alek turned stiffly about and walked away, still angry at the man's impertinence. But as he headed back toward the hatchway, he found himself slowing a little, just to listen for a few more seconds to the thrum of the airship at its heart.

There were worse prisons in the world than this.

"You know what his orders from the Admiralty will be," Volger muttered out in the corridor.

"To lock us up," Alek said. "As soon as he can do without our help."

"Exactly. It's time to start planning our escape."

EIGHT

That night in the machine room, Alek stared at the eggs, his mind drifting.

They were such insignificant-looking objects, but this giant, marvelous airship had fought its way across Europe to bring them here. What was inside them? What sort of godless creature could keep the Ottomans from joining the war?

The heaters packed around the eggs glimmered softly, and in the ship's quiet, Alek felt sleep creeping up on him. He stood and shook himself awake.

It was just after three a.m., time to get started.

As he pulled off his boots, a twinge crept down his side. But the pain in his rib cage was only a dull ache. Nothing that would trouble him tonight.

It had taken an hour of arguing to make Count Volger see the logic of this plan. Klopp was still under guard, Bauer and Hoffman were busy with the engines, and Volger had already been caught skulking below. It was up to Alek to find their avenue of escape.

He pressed an ear against the machine room door, holding his breath.

Nothing.

He turned the latch and pushed it slowly open. The electrikal lamps were dark. Only the glimmer of glow-worms lit the corridors, a green radiance as faint as starlight. Alek stepped into the hall, dead silent in his stocking feet, and eased the door shut behind him.

He waited for a moment to let his eyes adjust, then started for the stairs. There had to be an escape hatch somewhere, a way for the crew to abandon ship by rope or parachute. The lowest deck of the gondola was the logical place to look for it.

Though, where they would find five parachutes—or a few hundred meters of rope—was beyond Alek. They would have to escape when the ship was grounded in Constantinople, then buy their way to safety with the last bar of his father's gold.

The stairs made no complaints beneath his weight. The Darwinists' wood came from fabricated trees, and was lighter than natural wood and stronger than steel. The airship didn't groan and creak like a sailing ship, but felt as still as a stone castle. The distant, rumbling engines were reduced to the barest trembling under his feet.

Alek slipped past the central deck of the gondola quickly. At night a guard stood at the door to the bridge, two more were stationed at the armory, and the ship's cooks were always in the galley before dawn. But after the ship's five days on the glacier, the lower cargo holds and storerooms lay empty and unguarded.

Halfway down the last flight of stairs, a sound froze Alek in his tracks.

Was it a crewman walking past on the upper deck? Or someone behind him?

He turned and looked back up the stairs—nothing.

Alek wondered if airships had rats. Even metal land dreadnoughts could be infested. Or did the six-legged sniffer dogs hunt for pests as well as leaks?

He shuddered and kept moving.

At the bottom of the stairs, the deck was chill beneath Alek's feet. The night air was coursing past just below, thin and close to freezing at this altitude.

The corridors were wider down here, with two rails set in the floor for cargo trolleys. On either side lay open storerooms. They were shrouded in darkness, the glow-worms reduced to a few green squiggles on the walls.

The sound came again—the scrape of boots on wood. There *was* someone behind him!

His heart racing, Alek walked faster toward the bow. A few half-empty feed sacks sat in the shadows, but there was no good place to hide.

The corridor ended at a closed doorway. Alek turned and saw a silhouette moving behind him. For a split second he considered giving himself up and pretending he'd gotten lost. But Volger had already been caught down here . . .

Alek pushed his way through the door and shut it behind himself.

The room was pitch-black, and a heavy smell hung in the air, like old straw. He stood there in the darkness, breathing hard. It felt small and crowded in here, but the click of the closing door seemed to echo for a moment.

Alek thought he heard mutterings. Was this a bunk room full of sleeping airmen?

He waited for his eyes to adjust to the blackness, willing his heart to stop pounding in his ears. . . .

Someone, or some*thing*, was breathing in here.

For an awful moment Alek wondered if there were creatures aboard the *Leviathan* that Dylan hadn't told him about. Monsters, perhaps. He remembered his military toys, and the Darwinist fighting creatures fabricated from the life threads of extinct and giant reptiles.

"Um, hello?" he whispered.

"Hello?" someone answered.

Alek swallowed. "Oh, I seem to have gotten lost. I'm sorry."

"Gotten lost?" came the reply. The words sounded hesitant, and there was something eerily familiar about the voice.

"Yes. I'll just be going." Alek turned back to the doorway and felt blindly for the knob. The metal squeaked a little as he turned it, and he froze.

Suddenly the room was full of tiny screeches and complaints.

"I'm sorry," a voice said. Then another whispered, "Hello?"

The murmurs increased, building in intensity. The room felt no bigger than a closet, but it sounded as though a dozen men were waking up around him. They muttered half-formed words, in a nervous and agitated babble.

Was this the airship's *madhouse*?

Yanking open the door, Alek banged it into his bare foot. He yelped with pain, and a symphony of angry voices answered. More cries filled the darkness, as though a brawl were breaking out!

Through the half-open door a green face stared back at him.

"Barking spiders! What are you *doing*?" the intruder said.

"Spiders! Barking spiders!" came a dozen cries from every direction.

"SURREPTITIOUS IN A ROOM OF MESSENGERS."

Alek opened his mouth to scream, but then a low whistling sound floated through the room. The cacophony instantly went silent.

A glowworm lantern lifted in front of Alek's face. In its green light he made out Dylan squinting back at him, a command whistle in one hand.

"I reckoned it was you," the boy whispered.

"But . . . but who are these—"

"Shush, you ninny. Don't get the beasties started again." Dylan pushed him backward and slipped into the room, closing the door behind them. "We'll be lucky if the navigators haven't heard this ruckus already."

Alek blinked, and in the light of the wormlamp finally saw the stacks of cages climbing the walls. They were full of message lizards, crowded together like puppies in a pet store.

"What is this place?" he breathed.

"It's the barking lizard room, isn't it?" Dylan whispered. "It's where Dr. Erasmus takes care of the beasties."

Alek swallowed, his eyes falling on a table where a dissected lizard lay pinned. Then he saw that the ceiling was covered with the gaping mouths of message tubes, tangled like railroad tracks at a station. "And it's a sort of junction, too, isn't it?"

"Aye. Dr. Erasmus is in charge of all that palaver— origin and destination tags, emergency alerts, clearing up traffic jams."

Alek stared at the dozens of tiny eyes peering at him, all glowing with wormlight. "I had no idea it was so . . . complicated."

"How did you think the beasties always found you? By magic?" Dylan snorted. "It's a tricky job, even for a boffin, especially with half the lizards still dizzy from that Clanker lightning. Look at the poor things, and here's you riling them up!"

A few of the lizards started to murmur, repeating Dylan's words. But when he blew another soft, low note on his command whistle, they settled again.

Alek looked at Dylan. "You didn't just happen along, did you?"

"No. I couldn't sleep. And you know how Dr. Barlow doesn't want us bothering each other on egg duty? Well, I thought if I dropped by now, she wouldn't be about."

"But I wasn't there," Alek said.

Dylan nodded. "And *that* was a wee bit odd. So I thought I'd sniff around and see what you were up to."

"Didn't take you long to find me, did it?"

"The beasties' ruckus helped, but I reckoned you'd be down here in the storerooms." Dylan leaned closer. "You're looking for a way to escape, aren't you?"

Alek felt his jaw clench. "Am I that obvious?"

"No. I'm just dead clever," the boy said. "Have you not noticed?"

Alek took a moment to think about this, then smiled. "I have."

"Good." Dylan took a step past him and knelt at a small hatch on the opposite side of the room. "Come through here, then, before we start the beasties yammering again."

◦ NINE ◦

Dylan went first through the hatchway, climbing down a few rungs mounted on the slanted wall.

Alek passed the wormlamp down, spilling light into the small spherical chamber. He'd seen this place from outside the airship: a round bulge in the gondola's underbelly. The space was crowded by what looked like a mismatched pair of telescopes pointed down at the sea.

"Is that a weapon?" he asked.

"No. The fat one is a reconnaissance camera," Dylan said. "And the wee one's a sight for aerial bombs and navigation. But they're useless at night, so it'll be private enough."

"If not luxurious," Alek said. He climbed down and wedged himself onto a corner, half squatting on a giant gear attached to the camera's side. "But aren't we right below the bridge?"

Dylan glanced up. "That's the navigation room over us, and the bridge is above that. But it's safer here than in the lizard room. You're lucky you didn't send out an alert to the whole barking ship!"

"That might have been awkward," Alek said, imagining an army of lizards scampering through the airship's message tubes, shouting in his voice to the sleeping crew. "I'm a pretty useless spy, I suppose."

"At least you were clever enough to be caught by me," Dylan said. "And not someone who might have objected to you skulking about."

"Not so much skulking as bumbling," Alek said. "But thank you for not reporting me."

The boy shrugged. "I reckon it's a prisoner's duty to escape. After all, you Clankers keep saving the ship—that's *three* times now—and the captain's treating you like enemies! And just because Britain declared war on your granduncle. I think it's dead rotten."

Alek found himself smiling. On the subject of Dylan's loyalty, at least, Volger's suspicions were completely wrong.

"So that's why you were looking for me," Alek said. "To talk about how we can escape."

"Well, I'm not keen to *help* you. That might be a squick too treasonous, even for me. It was only . . ." Dylan's voice faded.

"What?"

"We'll be in Constantinople by noon tomorrow, so I reckoned you might be slipping away soon, and this might be our last chance to talk." The boy wrapped his arms around himself. "And I've hardly slept anyway."

Alek squinted through the darkness. Dylan's fine features looked drawn, even in the soft light of the glow-worms. His usual smile was missing.

"What's wrong?"

"It was what happened to Newkirk. It's left me dead shattered."

"Shattered?" Alek frowned. Dylan's strange way with the English language was playing tricks again. "Newkirk is the midshipman whose Huxley burned, right?"

"Aye, it was so much like . . . what happened when my da died. It's given me nightmares."

Alek nodded. The boy had never said much about his father's death. Only that he'd been lost in an accident, and that Dylan hadn't spoken for a whole month afterward.

"You've never told anyone about it, have you?"

The boy shook his head, then fell still.

Alek waited, remembering how hard it had been to tell Dylan about his own parents. In the silence he could hear the wind sweeping around the prow of the airship, testing its joints and seams. A draft swirled up from where the camera thrust out into the night sky, snatches of cold air coiling around their feet.

"I mean, since you're leaving the ship anyway," Dylan said, "I reckoned it wouldn't burden you too much to hear it."

"Of course you can tell me, Dylan. You know plenty of my secrets, after all."

The boy nodded, but fell silent again, his arms still wrapped tight around himself. Alek took a slow breath. He'd never seen Dylan afraid to speak his mind. The boy had never seemed afraid of anything before, much less a memory.

Perhaps he didn't want anyone to see him this way, looking weak and . . . shattered.

Alek slipped off his jacket and laid it over the worm-lamp. Darkness wrapped around them both.

"Tell me," he said gently.

A moment later Dylan began to speak.

"Da flew hot-air balloons, you see, even after the hydrogen breathers got so big. I always went up with him, so I was there when it happened. We were still on the ground, the burners firing to warm up the air in the envelope. Then suddenly there was this great blast of heat, like opening a boiler door. One of the kerosene tanks . . ."

Dylan's voice had gradually gone softer, almost like a girl's, and now it faded away altogether. Alek slid closer, putting his arm around the boy until he spoke again.

"It was just like with Newkirk. The fire shot straight up

until the whole balloon was burning overhead, the heat pulling us skyward. The tethers held, even though they must have been on fire too. And my da pushed me out of the basket."

"So he saved you."

"Aye, but *that's what killed him.* With my weight gone, the ropes broke, all at once, like knuckles cracking. And Da's balloon went roaring away."

Alek's breath caught. He remembered again the German zeppelin in the Alps, falling right in front of him, its hydrogen ignited by machine-gun fire. He could still hear the snow beneath the wreck hissing as it turned to steam, and the thin screams from inside the gondola.

"Everyone saw how he'd saved me," Dylan said, reaching into his pocket. "They gave him a medal for it."

He pulled out a small decoration, a rounded silver cross that dangled from a sky blue ribbon. In the darkness Alek could just make out the face of Charles Darwin engraved upon its center.

"It's called the Air Gallantry Cross, the highest honor they can give a civilian for deeds in the air."

"You must be proud," Alek said.

"Back in that first year, when I couldn't sleep, I used to stare at it at night. But I thought the nightmares were over and done with, until what happened to Newkirk." Dylan looked at him. "Maybe you understand a wee bit, how it comes back? Because of your ma and da?"

Alek nodded, staring at the medal and wondering what to say. He still had dreams, of course, but his own parents' death had happened in far-off Sarajevo, not in front of his eyes. Even his nightmares couldn't compare with what Dylan had described.

But then he remembered the moment when the Tesla cannon had fired, his horror that the *Leviathan* would be engulfed in flame.

"I think you're very brave, serving on this ship."

"Aye, or mad." The boy's eyes glistened in the glimmers of wormlight from beneath Alek's jacket. "Don't you think it's daft? Like I'm trying to burn to death, same as he did?"

"Don't be absurd," Alek said. "You're honoring your father. Of course you'd want to be on this ship. If I weren't . . ." He paused. "I mean, if things were different, I'd want to stay here too."

"You would?"

"Well, maybe it's silly. But the last few days, it's like something's changing inside me. Everything I ever knew is upside down. Sometimes it's almost as if I'm . . . in love . . ."

Dylan's body tightened beside Alek.

"I know it sounds silly," Alek said quickly. "It's quite obviously ridiculous."

"But are you saying that . . . ? I mean, what if things *were* different than you thought? If I were . . . or have you guessed already?" Dylan let out a groan. "Just what are you *saying*?"

Alek shook his head. "Perhaps I'm putting this stupidly. But it's almost as though . . . I'm in love with your ship."

"You're in love," Dylan said slowly, "with the *Leviathan*?"

"It feels *right* here." Alek shrugged. "As if this is where I'm meant to be."

Dylan let out a strange, choked laugh as he put the medal back into his pocket.

"You Clankers," he muttered. "You're all cracked in the head."

Alek pulled his arm from the boy's shoulders, frowning. Dylan was always explaining how the airship's interwoven species sustained one another, how every beast was part of the whole. Surely he could understand.

"Dylan, you know I've always been alone. I never had schoolmates, just tutors."

"Aye, because you're a barking prince."

"But I'm hardly even that, because of my mother's blood. I never mixed with commoners, and the rest of my family has always wanted me to disappear. But here on this ship . . ." Alek laced his fingers together, searching for the right words.

"This is one place where you fit," Dylan said flatly. "Where you feel real."

Alek smiled. "Yes. I knew you'd understand."

"Aye, of course." Dylan shrugged. "I just thought you might be saying something else, that's all. I feel the same way as you . . . about the ship."

"But you're not an enemy here, or hiding what you are," Alek said, sighing. "It's much simpler for you."

The boy gave a sad laugh. "Not quite as simple as you'd think."

"I didn't say *you* were simple, Dylan. It's just that you've got no secrets hanging over you. No one's trying to throw you off this ship and put you in chains!"

Dylan shook his head. "Tell that to my ma."

"Oh, right." Alek recalled that Dylan's mother hadn't wanted him to join the military. "Women can be quite mad sometimes."

"In my family they're a squick madder than most." Dylan pulled Alek's jacket from the wormlamp. "Full of stupid ideas. Mad like you wouldn't believe."

In the sudden wash of green light, Dylan's face was no longer sad. His eyes had their usual spark, but there was an angry gleam in them. He tossed the jacket to Alek.

"We both know you can't stay aboard this ship," Dylan said quietly.

Alek held his gaze a moment, then nodded. He would never be allowed to serve on the *Leviathan*, not once the Darwinists understood their new engines. They would take him and the others back to Britain for safekeeping, whether or not they learned exactly who he was.

He had to escape.

"I should get back to my skulking, I suppose."

"Aye, you should," Dylan said. "I'll go up and watch the eggs for you. Come back before dawn, though, or the lady boffin will have both our heads."

"Thank you," Alek said.

"We can only stay in Constantinople twenty-four hours. You'll have to find whatever you're looking for tonight."

Alek nodded, his heart beating a little faster. He reached

out a hand. "In case we don't talk again, I hope we'll stay friends, whatever happens. Wars don't last forever."

Dylan stared at the offered hand, then nodded.

"Aye, friends." He stood up. "Keep that lamp. I can find my way in the dark."

He turned and climbed up into the blackness without another word.

Alek looked down at his hand, wondering for a moment what had happened, why Dylan had turned suddenly cold. Perhaps the boy had let more of his feelings show than he'd meant to. Or maybe Alek had said the wrong thing somehow.

He sighed. There wasn't time to think about it—he had skulking to do. Once the *Leviathan* started back for Britain, there wouldn't be another chance to escape. He had to be off this ship in less than two days.

Alek picked up the wormlamp and started for the hatch.

◦ TEN ◦

Deryn had never seen a Clanker city before.

Constantinople rolled past below, the hills filled to bursting with humanity. Pale stone palaces and domed mosques squashed against modern buildings, some rising up six stories tall. Two narrow arms of sparkling water carved the city into three parts, and a placid sea stretched away to the south, peppered with countless merchant ships under steam and sail, flying a dozen different flags.

A pall of smoke hung over everything, coughed up from countless engines and factories, veiling the walkers striding the narrow streets. The muddled air was empty of messenger birds; only a few biplanes and gyrothopters skimmed the rooftops, skirting stone spires and bristling wireless aerials.

It was odd to imagine Alek being from a place just like this, full of machines and metal, hardly alive except

for human beings and their bedbugs. Of course, it was strange to think of Alek at all right now. She'd made such a *Dummkopf* of herself last night, blethering on about Da's accident, then mistaking Alek's confidences for something more than they were.

How completely daft, imagining for a moment that a barking prince would think of her *that* way. Alek didn't even know her real first name. And if he learned somehow that she was a girl in boy's clothes? He'd run a mile.

Thankfully, Alek was planning to run in any case. Sometime tonight he and his Clanker friends would slip away into that smoky mass of city, and be gone for good. Then she'd be done with acting like some village girl, her fists twisting in her skirts whenever a certain boy walked by.

Not that pathetic unsoldierly fate for Deryn Sharp.

The *Leviathan* swept in low over the water, and Newkirk leaned closer to the big window of the middies' mess, staring down, wide eyed. No doubt he was searching the forest of masts and smokestacks below for the deadly spindle of the *Goeben*'s Tesla cannon.

"See any German ships?" he asked nervously.

Deryn shook her head. "Just a few merchants and a coaler. I told you those ironclads would be long gone."

But Newkirk, his dress uniform cap pulled down tight over his singed hair, didn't look entirely reassured. The sea below them stretched all the way back to the Dardanelles, with plenty of nooks and crannies to hide a dreadnought in. The *Leviathan* had come to Constantinople over land, after all, not wanting to risk the ironclads' Clanker lightning again.

"Midshipmen Sharp and Newkirk!" came a voice from the doorway. "I must say you're both looking handsome."

Deryn turned and bowed a squick to the lady boffin, feeling awkward in her full-dress uniform. She'd worn it only once before, at her swearing-in ceremony. The tailor who'd made it for her in Paris had probably wondered why some daft girl was going to so much fuss for a costume ball.

Now, a month later, the fancy jacket stretched tight over the new muscles in her shoulders, and the shirt felt as stiff as a vicar's collar.

"Frankly, ma'am, I feel a bit like a penguin," Newkirk said, adjusting his silk bow tie.

"That may be," Dr. Barlow said, "but we must look respectable for Ambassador Mallet."

Deryn turned back to the window with a sigh. The storerooms were empty, and they had only twenty-four hours to resupply the whole ship. It seemed daft to bring diplomats along to the Grand Bazaar, especially if it meant dressing up. Dr. Barlow was all in riding clothes, like a duchess on a fox hunt.

"Do you reckon we'll find corned beef in Constantinople?" Newkirk asked hopefully.

"Is-tan-bul," Dr. Barlow said, tapping her riding crop against her boot once for each syllable. "That's what we must remember to call this city. Otherwise we shall annoy the locals."

"Istanbul?" Newkirk frowned. "But it's 'Constantinople' on all the maps."

"On *our* maps it is," the lady boffin said. "We use that name to honor Constantine, the Christian emperor who founded the city. But the residents have called it Istanbul since 1453."

"They changed the name four hundred-odd *years* ago?"

Deryn turned back to the window. "Maybe it's time to fix our barking maps."

"Wise words, Mr. Sharp," Dr. Barlow said, then added quietly, "I wonder if the Germans have already fixed theirs."

The *Leviathan* came down on a dusty, mile-wide airfield on the western edge of the city.

A mooring mast stood at the center of the field, like a lighthouse in a sea of grass. It looked no different from the mast back at Wormwood Scrubs. Deryn supposed that whether Darwinist or Clanker, an airship had to be secured from the fancies of the wind in pretty much the same way. The dozens of ground men certainly looked sharp as they corralled the landing ropes, their fezzes bright red against the grass.

"Mr. Rigby says they get plenty of practice on German airships," Newkirk said. "Says we should study their technique."

"We could, if we were closer," Deryn said. She itched to be down there helping, or at least working with the riggers topside. But Dr. Barlow had warned the two middies not to muss their dress uniforms.

The engines were pulsing overhead, turning the ship into the wind. Even Alek and his Clanker friends had honest work to do.

Ten minutes later the *Leviathan* was secured by a dozen

ropes, each held by ten men, and the airbeast's nose was pressed against the mooring mast, its great eyes covered with blinders.

Deryn frowned. "They've lashed us a bit high. We're still fifty feet off the ground!"

"All according to plan, Mr. Sharp," said Dr. Barlow, pointing her riding crop into the distance.

Deryn looked up and saw what was coming out of the trees—her jaw dropped open.

"I didn't know Clanker countries had elephantines!" Newkirk cried.

"That's no beastie," Deryn said. "It's a barking *walker*."

The machine lumbered forward on huge legs, its tusks swaying back and forth as it moved. Four pilots in blue uniforms sat on saddles that stuck out from its haunches, one pilot working the controls for each leg. A mechanical trunk, divided into a dozen metal segments, swept slowly back and forth, like a sleeping cat's tail.

"It must be fifty feet tall," Newkirk said. "Even bigger than a real elephantine!"

Sunlight struck the walker as it left the trees, and its polished steel skin glittered like mirrors. The platform on its back was covered by a parasol shaped like a strafing hawk's cowl. A handful of men in dress uniform stood on the platform, while a fifth pilot perched in the front, working the trunk. The elephant's large metal ears flapped slowly, stirring the brilliant tapestries that hung down its sides.

"As you can see," Dr. Barlow said, "the ambassador travels in style."

"I know we can't use beasties here in Clanker-land," Deryn said, "but why make a walker look like an animal?"

"Diplomacy is all about symbols," Dr. Barlow said. "Elephants signify royalty and power; according to legend an elephant divined the prophet Mohammed's birth. The sultan's own war machines are made in this same shape."

"Do all the walkers here look like beasties?" Newkirk asked.

"Most of them, yes," the lady boffin said. "Our Ottoman friends may be Clankers, but they haven't forgotten the web of life around us. That is why I have hope for them."

Deryn frowned, thinking for a moment of the mysterious eggs in the machine room. What did the creatures inside them signify?

But there wasn't much time to wonder. Soon the metal elephant was beside the airship's gondola, with a gangway level between them.

"Look smart, gentlemen," Dr. Barlow said. "We have an elephant to catch."

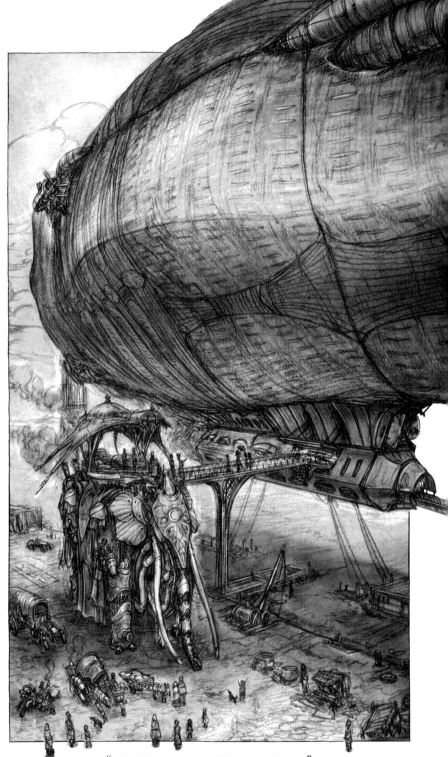

"DOCKING WITH THE DAUNTLESS."

◦ ELEVEN ◦

The howdah, as the ambassador had called the *Dauntless*'s platform, felt a bit like a small boat at sea. It rocked from side to side with the elephant's gait, but the motion was steady and predictable. Not enough to make Deryn seasick.

Newkirk, of course, was another matter.

"I can't see why we should have to ride in this contraption," he said, his face growing paler with every step. "We joined the *Air* Service, not the barking Elephant Service!"

"And not the diplomatic corps either," Deryn muttered.

Since being introduced the ambassador and his assistants had ignored the two middies. They were prattling away to Dr. Barlow in French, which was daft, as they were all English, but that was diplomacy for you. And, as far as Deryn could tell, no one was saying anything about transporting supplies.

She wondered how the *Dauntless* would carry all the provisions the airship needed. There wasn't much room in the howdah, which was all silk and tassels in any case, too fancy for stacks of crates. The machine could pull a sledge or wagon like a real elephantine, she supposed, but there was none in sight. Maybe when they got to the Grand Bazaar . . .

"Mind if I ask you boys some questions?"

Deryn turned. The man who'd interrupted her thoughts wasn't dressed like the diplomats. In fact, his slops were a dog's breakfast. His jacket was patched at the elbows, his hat a shapeless mass on his head. An unwieldy camera hung around his neck, and some sort of frog perched on his shoulder.

The ambassador had introduced him as a reporter for a newspaper in New York, so Deryn supposed that his strange accent must be American.

"You'd best ask the lady boffin, sir," Newkirk said. "Midshipmen aren't allowed to have opinions."

The man laughed, then

leaned forward and said quietly, "Off the record, then. Any particular reason why your airship is here in Istanbul?"

"Just a friendly visit." Deryn nodded at the ambassador. "Diplomacy and all that."

"Oh," the man said, and shrugged. "And here I was thinking it might be because of all the Germans pouring in."

Deryn raised an eyebrow, then glanced at the bullfrog. It had the big-brained look of a memory frog, the sort of beast that recorded court proceedings and sessions of parliament. She decided to watch her words carefully.

"Engineers, mostly," the reporter continued. "They're building all sorts of things. Just finished a new palace for the sultan."

"Aye, the lady boffin's headed there tomorrow," Newkirk said.

Deryn silenced him with an elbow between the ribs, then turned to the reporter. "What's your name again, sir?"

"Eddie Malone, of the *New York World*. And please don't call me 'sir.'" He offered his hand, smiling again. "I won't ask your name, of course, since this is all off the record."

Deryn shook the man's hand, wondering if he was full of yackum. When the ambassador had introduced them, she'd seen the reporter scribbling all their names into his battered notebook. He'd taken pictures, too, the battered old camera blazing with light from a fabricated firefly living in its flash apparatus.

Americans were an odd bunch—neither Clanker nor Darwinist. They dabbled with both ways, mixing technologies as they saw fit. Everyone reckoned they would stay out of the war, unless somebody was daft enough to drag them in.

"There are German officers here too." Malone pointed at the guards standing at attention beside the approaching airfield gates. Instead of red fezzes they wore pointy helmets that looked a bit like Alek's piloting hat.

"Those are Germans?" Newkirk said with alarm.

"No, Ottoman soldiers," the reporter said. "But just look at them. They used to have more colorful uniforms, until the field marshal dressed them up in gray, like proper Clankers."

"Who's that?" Deryn asked.

"Field Marshal Liman von Sanders. German fellow—a good friend of the kaiser's. The Ottomans made him head of the army here in Istanbul. Your diplomat friends kicked up a fuss, of course, and he bowed out." Malone strutted across the howdah with a comically high step. "But not before he got them marching like Germans!"

Deryn glanced at Newkirk. The man was clearly cracked. "The Ottomans put a German in charge of their own barking army?"

Malone shrugged. "Maybe they're getting tired of being pushed around. The French and the British used to run things here, but not anymore. I suppose you've heard about the *Osman?*"

Deryn nodded slowly. "Aye, the ship that Lord Churchill borrowed."

"'Borrowed'?" Malone chuckled, scribbling in his notebook. "Now, *that* I can use."

Deryn muttered under her breath, cursing herself for a *Dummkopf.* "So that must be news here."

"News? It's the biggest story in Istanbul! The sultan is half broke, you see, so that dreadnought was bought with money raised by the people. Grannies sold their jewelry and handed over the money. Kids coughed up pennies, and bought shadow puppets of its companion creature. Everyone in the empire owns a piece of that ship! Or at least they did, till your Lord Churchill went and pinched it." The man's smile was maniacal, the bullfrog on his shoulder poised to memorize whatever she said.

Deryn cleared her throat. "I suppose they're a wee bit angry now?"

Malone nodded at the airfield gates parting before them, then licked the tip of his pen. "You'll see soon enough."

Through the gates a broad avenue stretched toward the city. As the walker plodded ahead, the streets grew busier, the buildings rising up as tall as the howdah. People and pushcarts bustled past windows full of carpets and dishes, everything decorated with mad checkerboard patterns that dazzled Deryn's eyes. The footpaths were crowded with stalls selling stacks of nuts and dried fruit, or meat roasting on rotating skewers. Powdered spices lay in rust red and dusty yellow piles, or spilled bright green from sacks as large as feed bags. Rich and unfamiliar scents cut through the smell of engines, so heavy she could taste them in her mouth, like the air inside a fabrication greenhouse.

Deryn saw now what the walker's trunk was for. As the machine lumbered through the crowd, its trunk swept gracefully from side to side, nudging pedestrians out of the way. The howdah pilot's fingers moved nimbly on the controls; he pushed carts aside, and even rescued a child's fallen toy from being crushed by the walker's giant feet.

Other walkers pulled wagons through the streets. Most looked like camels or donkeys, and one took the form of a horned creature that Eddie Malone explained was a water buffalo. A metal scarab beetle as big as an omnibus carried passengers through the crowds.

Down a narrow side street Deryn saw a pair of walkers constructed almost in the shape of men. They stood almost as tall as the *Dauntless*, with squat legs, long arms, and featureless faces. They were decorated with striped cloths and strange symbols, and carried no weapons in their giant clawed hands.

"Army walkers of some kind?" Deryn asked the reporter.

"No, they're iron golems. They guard the Jewish neighbor-hoods." Malone waved his hand across the crowd. "Most of the Ottomans are Turks, but Istanbul is a melting pot. Not only Jews, but Greeks, Armenians, Venetians, Arabs, Kurds, and Vlachs all live here."

"Blisters," Newkirk said. "I never heard of half of those."

The man smiled and scribbled in his notebook. "And all of them have their own combat walkers, just to keep the peace."

"Sounds like a flimsy sort of peace," Deryn muttered, watching the streets below. The people were dressed in a dozen different ways—in tasseled fezzes, desert robes, women under veils, and men wearing jackets like any in London. Everyone seemed to be getting along, though, at least under the impassive stares of the iron golems.

"What's that?" Newkirk asked, and pointed ahead.

A quarter mile in front of the elephant, the street seemed to be churning, a mass of crimson trickling through the crowd—moving closer.

Eddie Malone licked his pen. "That would be your wel-coming committee."

Deryn stepped to the front of the howdah and shielded her eyes against the sun. She made out a group of men wear-ing red fezzes, their fists waving in the air. Behind her the diplomat's French prattle faded suddenly away.

"Oh, dear," Ambassador Mallet said. "Those chaps again."

Deryn turned to the howdah pilot. "Who are they?"

"A bunch called the Young Turks, sir, I think," the man said. "This town is full of secret societies and revolutionaries. Can hardly keep track of them all, myself."

There was a burst of light as Eddie Malone took a photograph.

The ambassador began to clean his eyeglasses. "The Young Turks tried to depose the sultan six years ago, but the Germans put them down. Now they hate all foreigners. I suppose this was to be expected. From what my sources tell me, the newspapers have been riling them up about the *Osman*."

"Your *sources* tell you?" Dr. Barlow asked.

"Well, I don't speak Turkish, of course, and none of my staff does either. But I have excellent sources, I assure you."

The lady boffin raised an eyebrow. "Are you telling me, Ambassador, that none of you can read the local newspapers?"

The ambassador cleared his throat, and his assistants stared off into space.

"Not much point," Eddie Malone said, feeding the firefly in his camera's flashbulb a sugar cube. "From what

I've heard, the Germans own half of them anyway."

Dr. Barlow stared at the ambassador with fresh alarm.

"The Germans only own *one* of the newspapers," he protested, still cleaning his glasses. "Though it seems quite influential. Very clever of them, spreading their lies here in Constantinople."

"It's called *Istanbul*," Dr. Barlow said quietly, her fingers clenched around her riding crop.

Deryn shook her head and turned back toward the crowd.

The men were surging closer, chanting, their fists pumping in unison. They rushed through the bustle of people and carts, their fezzes like crimson water flowing past pebbles in a stream. They soon surrounded the walker, yelling up at the pilots on their saddles, waving newspapers. Deryn squinted—every front page showed a picture of a ship under a huge headline.

The crowd was chanting *"Osman! Osman!"* But there was another word in all the hubbub—"behemoth"—that Deryn didn't recognize at all.

"Well," Dr. Barlow said, "this *is* a discouraging start."

The ambassador drew himself up, patting the railing at the howdah's edge. "There is no reason to worry, madam. We've ridden out far worse on the *Dauntless*."

Deryn had to admit that they were safe enough up here, fifty feet above the mob. No one was throwing anything, or trying to climb the elephant's huge legs. The howdah pilot was deftly nudging the protesters aside with the trunk, so the walker's progress was hardly slowed.

But Dr. Barlow wore an icy expression. "It's not a question of 'riding it out,' Ambassador. My objective is to keep this country friendly."

"Well, talk to Lord Churchill, then!" the man cried. "It's hardly the Foreign Office's fault when he goes and snatches a . . ."

His words faded as a metal groan filled the air, the world tilting beneath them. Deryn's dress boots skidded sideways on the silk carpet, and everyone went stumbling toward the howdah's starboard side. The railing caught Deryn at stomach level, and her body pitched halfway over before she righted herself.

She stared down—the foreleg pilot below had toppled from his perch, and lay sprawled in a circle of protesters. They looked as surprised as the pilot did, and were bending down to offer help.

Why had the man fallen from his saddle?

As the machine stumbled to a halt, something flickered in the corner of Deryn's vision. A lasso flew up from the crowd and landed around the shoulders of the rear-leg pilot, then he, too, was yanked from his seat. A man in a blue uniform was scrambling up the front leg.

"We're being boarded!" Deryn cried, running to the

port side of the howdah. The *Dauntless* was under attack there too. The man driving the rear leg had already been yanked from his perch, and the foreleg pilot was pulling against a rope around his waist.

Deryn watched as another man in blue uniform—a *British* uniform—took the place of the rear-leg pilot and grasped the controls.

Suddenly the machine lurched back into motion, taking a massive stride into the crowd. Someone screamed as a huge foot bore down to shatter cobblestones into dust, and the protesters in red fezzes began to scatter.

◉ TWELVE ◉

"*Do* something, Mr. Sharp," cried Dr. Barlow above the din. "We appear to have been captured!"

"Aye, ma'am, I noticed!" Deryn reached for her rigging knife, but of course her full-dress uniform had no pockets to speak of. She'd have to use bare fists.

"How do I get down to the saddles?" she asked the howdah pilot.

"You can't from here, sir," he said, his knuckles white on the trunk's controls. He was pushing people to safety as the machine stumbled through the panicking crowd. "The leg pilots climb on from the ground, while the elephant's kneeling."

"Blisters! Do you have any rope aboard?"

"Afraid not, sir," the man said. "This isn't a sailing ship."

Deryn groaned in frustration—how could any ship not have *rope*? The machine stumbled again, and she grabbed the railing to keep her footing.

Making her way around the edge of the howdah, Deryn saw that three of the pilots had been replaced by impostors in blue uniforms. Only the foreleg pilot on the port side remained in his seat. But the rope was still around him, stretching down into the crowd. He'd be pulled off soon enough.

In the meantime three of the walker's legs were scraping and stamping, trying to get the contraption moving again. As she watched, the huge right forefoot stamped down on a vendor's cart, scattering peeled chestnuts like hailstones across the street.

"Barking stupid machines!" Deryn muttered. A real beastie would know who its proper masters were.

Suddenly the trunk swung to the port side. It reached among the protesters and found the man trying to drag the foreleg pilot off his seat. The man shrieked, letting go of the rope as he was flicked aside.

"Good work!" Deryn said to the howdah pilot. "Can you yank the impostors off?"

The man shook his head. "Can't reach the rear saddles at all. But maybe . . ."

He twisted at the controls, and the trunk whipped about to the starboard side. It curled back, reaching for the pilot on the foreleg, but stopped a yard short, metal segments grinding.

"It's no use, sir," the man said. "She's not as flexible as a real beastie."

However inflexible, the machine was barking powerful. It was lurching down the street now, scattering people and vehicles in all directions. One of its huge feet stamped down on a wagon and smashed it into splinters. The remaining British pilot struggled to bring the machine to a halt, but there was only so much that one leg could do against three.

"Can you grab something to use as a weapon?" Deryn asked the howdah pilot. "You only need another few feet of length!"

"This is a Clanker contraption, sir! It's hardly as nimble as that."

"Blisters," Deryn swore. "Then I suppose it'll have to be me!"

The man took his eyes from the controls for a second. "Pardon me, sir?"

"Bend that trunk up this way. And make it fast, man!" she ordered, pulling off her fancy jacket. She turned to toss it back at Newkirk, then climbed out of the howdah and onto the elephant's head.

"What in blazes are you doing?" Newkirk cried.

"Something barking daft!" she called as the tip of the

metal-jointed trunk reared up before her. She readied herself on the rocking surface of the elephant's head.

And jumped . . .

Her arms wrapped around the shining steel. The segments rasped and clanked as the trunk flexed, carrying her high above the crowd. Her feet swung out from the centrifugal force, as if she were riding the end of a huge whip whistling through the air.

The blur of passing shapes resolved around her—she was swinging toward the starboard foreleg. The impostor pilot stared, wide eyed, as she aimed both feet at him.

But he ducked at the last second, her dress boots whistling over his head. As she swung past, Deryn's palms skidded on the shiny metal trunk, her grip sliding.

The man scowled at her and drew a knife.

There was something about his face—he was paler than most of the protesters in the street.

"*Dummkopf!*" she shouted at him.

"*Sie gleichen die!*" he yelled back. Clanker-talk!

Deryn narrowed her eyes—this was no Turk, or Vlach, or Kurd, or whatever else they had here in Istanbul. The man was a German, as certain as anything.

The trouble was, how to get *rid* of him? She didn't fancy her dress boots in a fight against that knife.

She glanced up at the howdah. Dr. Barlow was shouting something at the howdah pilot, and Deryn hoped

"A DARING MIDSHIPMAN HANDLES THE SITUATION."

whatever the boffin was cooking up would work quickly. With every lurching step the elephant took, her grip on the polished steel loosened a squick.

The trunk began to flex again, swinging Deryn low over the street, a blur of paving stones passing below. She wondered what sort of boffin-inspired strategy she was expected to figure out while hurtling through the air.

Then the trunk came to a shuddering halt, the pilot keeping her steady as the machine lurched along. Deryn glanced down. She was hanging just above a table piled with spices.

"What in blazes?" she muttered. Did Dr. Barlow expect her to tempt the German off his perch with a home-cooked meal?

But after a moment of hanging there, a tickle started in the back of Deryn's throat, and her eyes began to burn. Even an arm's length away, the spices were fiery enough to notice.

"Not bad, Dr. Barlow," she muttered, then sneezed.

Deryn reached down, snatching up the reddest and meanest-looking bag of spices.

The trunk swung back into action, whipping her back toward the German driving the starboard foreleg. She could see the cold look on the man's face as she zoomed toward him, the knife flashing in his hand.

"Try this for dinner, bum-rag!" she shouted, and flung the entire bag straight at him.

The momentum of the speeding trunk redoubled the force of her throw, and the sack hit the German like a cannonball. It exploded against his chest, enveloping him in a dark red cloud. Spice billowed in all directions, swirling back at Deryn.

Red-hot fingers clamped shut her eyes. She gasped for breath, and liquid fire spilled down her lungs. Her chest felt stuffed full of embers of coal, and her grip was slipping. . . .

But she landed softly—the howdah pilot had set her down. She lay there coughing and sputtering, her body trying to expel the spices from her lungs.

Finally Deryn forced open her burning eyes.

The metal elephant stood motionless. Both its front legs were bent, as if the huge machine were bowing down to her. The back legs alone had not been enough to keep it moving.

Deryn saw flashes of blue slipping through the crowd, the two other impostors running away. But the German she'd blasted with spice lay in a pile of red dust, still coughing and sputtering.

As she rose to her feet, Deryn looked down at herself.

"Barking spiders!" she cried, then sneezed. Her uniform was ruined.

But the loss of one middy's dress slops was nothing compared to the trail of destruction that stretched down the street—overturned carts and wagons, a donkey-shaped walker squashed as flat as a metal bug. The gathering crowd was quiet, still in shock at what the rampaging elephant had done.

A gangway descended from the walker's belly. Two of the ambassador's assistants grabbed the spice-addled German, while Newkirk and Eddie Malone ran through the crowd to her.

"Are you all right, Mr. Sharp?" Newkirk cried.

"I think so," Deryn said as Malone's camera flashed with a *pop*, blinding her again.

"Then, we'd better get back aboard," Newkirk said. "These chaps could get unruly again."

"But someone might be hurt." Deryn blinked away spots, looking down the street. Were there bodies anywhere among the splintered wood and broken windows?

"Aye, that's why we're in a hurry. We need to find our pilots and get moving again, before things get ugly!"

"Things already look ugly to me," Eddie Malone said, feeding a handful of sugar cubes to his firefly. He aimed his camera down the devastated street.

Still blinking away red spice, Deryn followed Newkirk back toward the *Dauntless*. She wondered how many people had seen the impostor pilots coming aboard a hundred yards back. Would anyone realize that the elephant's British crew hadn't caused this disaster?

Even if the crowd had seen what had happened, the newspapers wouldn't report it that way. Not the ones the Germans owned.

"You saw, right?" she said to Eddie Malone. "It was impostors driving! Not our men."

"Don't you worry. I saw them," the reporter said. "And we only print the truth in the *New York World.*"

"Aye, in New York," Deryn sighed as she climbed the gangway. The crowd was already stirring around them as the shock of the rampage faded away.

The question was, would anyone believe them here in Istanbul?

THIRTEEN

Alek waited in the machine room, wondering when the signal would come.

He loosened another button on his jacket. Dr. Barlow had made the room as hot as an oven tonight. She always seemed to add more heaters when Alek watched the eggs, just to annoy him.

At least he wouldn't have to suffer much longer. He could already hear the distant rumble of glow plugs firing in the starboard pod. Klopp, Hoffman, and Bauer were up there, pretending to work on the engine. And being noisy about it, so no one would be surprised to see Alek heading up to help.

After the disastrous start of Dr. Barlow's mission today, the escape plan had changed. Alek had watched the elephant-shaped walker's hasty return, carrying no supplies, its side spattered with some sort of red dust. Rumors had spread through the ship that the walker had been attacked, an incident in which dozens of civilians had been injured.

Within an hour angry crowds had arrived at the airfield's gate, threatening to attack the *Leviathan*. Guards were posted at all of the airship's hatches now, and a ring of Ottoman soldiers surrounded the gondola. There would be no sneaking out through the cargo deck tonight.

From his station up in the engine pod, however, Klopp had reported that no one was guarding the mooring tower. It was connected to the airbeast's head by a single cable that hung eighty meters in the air. If the five of them could climb across and down, perhaps they could escape across the darkened airfield.

Alek listened to the engine misfiring, waiting for the signal. Now that the captain considered him a prisoner of war, he was happy to leave the airship behind. He'd been a fool to let himself grow so attached. Volger was right— pretending that this flying abomination was his home had lead only to misery. Dylan might have been a good friend in some other world, but not this one.

There it was—five sharp coughs from the glow plugs. The signal meant that Bauer and Hoffman had subdued the Darwinist crewmen in the pod. Volger would be headed up from his stateroom.

They were really leaving. Tonight.

Alek adjusted the eggs one last time. He picked up a

fresh heater and shook it to life, then tucked it into the hay. As hot as the machine room was, Dr. Barlow's mysterious cargo would most likely be fine until dawn. In any case, it wasn't his concern anymore.

Alek noticed an old smear of grease on the egg box and rubbed a finger across it. Then he drew a stripe across his cheeks, as if he'd been working up in the engine pod. If anyone saw him, they would assume that Dylan was down here with the eggs and that Alek was fetching parts for the engineers.

He stood and hefted his toolbox. It was stuffed with spare clothes and the wireless set from the Stormwalker. The set was heavy, but once he and his men were hidden in the wilds, radio might be their only means of contact with the outside world.

Alek sighed. Here aboard the *Leviathan* he'd almost forgotten how lonely it was to run and hide.

The door opened with a soft squeak, and he stared out into the hall, listening to the murmurs of the ship.

A small tapping noise reached his ears. Was someone headed this way?

He swore softly. It was probably Dylan, coming to talk one last time. Seeing the boy again would only make this harder, and Alek needed to start toward the engine pod.

But the noise was coming from *behind* him. . . .

He turned around—one of the eggs was moving.

In the rosy light of the heaters, he could see a tiny hole forming at the top of the egg. Little chips were breaking free and sliding down the smooth white surface. Fleck by fleck the hole grew larger.

Alek stood there, his hand on the doorknob. He should be heading up, leaving these godless creatures behind. But he'd spent seven long nights watching the eggs and wondering what would emerge from them. In another few moments he would finally see.

Alek pulled the door softly closed.

The odd thing was, it was the middle egg hatching—the one Dr. Barlow had said was sick.

Something was poking its way out of the hole now. It looked like a claw—or was it a *paw?* There was pale fur on it, not feathers.

A small black nose poked its way out, sniffing the air.

Alek wondered if the creature was dangerous. Of course, it was only a baby, and he had a rigging knife sheathed on his belt. But Alek stayed close to the door, just in case.

The beast emerged slowly, reaching out to grip the edge of the box with tiny four-fingered hands. Its fur was damp, and its huge eyes blinked in the glow of the heaters. It looked about attentively, twitching as it pulled itself farther from the broken egg.

God's wounds, but the thing was *homely.* Its skin seemed too large for its body, drooping like an old man's.

It reminded Alek of his aunt's hairless cat, bred for its bizarre looks.

The beast stared at him and made a soft, plaintive noise.

"You must be hungry," Alek said softly. But he hadn't the first idea what it ate.

At least it was clear enough that the creature *didn't* eat humans. It was far too small for that, and too . . . appealing, even with its strange excess of skin. Somehow the large eyes seemed wise and sad. Alek found himself wanting to pick the animal up and comfort it.

The creature extended a tiny hand.

Alek put down the tool kit and took a step closer. When he reached out a hand, the animal touched his fingertips, squeezing them one by one. Then it leaned forward, letting itself slide from the edge of the egg box.

Alek caught it just in time. Even in the sweltering machine room, the creature's body felt warm, its short fur as soft as the chinchilla coat his mother had always worn in winter. When Alek held it closer, the beast made a cooing noise.

The huge eyes blinked slowly, staring straight into his. Thin arms wrapped around Alek's wrist.

It was strange, how the creature didn't give him the same uneasy feeling as other Darwinist creations. It was too small and sleepy-looking, and gave off an air of preternatural calm.

The engine sputtered again, and Alek realized that he was behind schedule.

"I'm sorry," he whispered, "but I have to go."

He placed the creature back in the box amid the warm glow of the heaters. But as his hands pulled away, the animal made a high-pitched mewling noise.

"Shush," Alek breathed softly. "Someone will be along soon."

He wondered if that were true. Dylan would be here at dawn, but that was hours away.

He took a step backward, kneeling to pick up the tool

kit. The creature's eyes grew wider, and it let out another cry that ended in a high, sweeping note, as pure as a flute.

Alek frowned—that last sound was oddly like the whistles the crew used to command their beasts. And it was loud enough to wake someone up.

He reached out again, shushing the creature. The instant his hand touched it, the animal went silent.

Alek knelt there for a moment, stroking the soft fur. Finally the large eyes closed and Alek dared to pull away.

The beast instantly sprang awake and began to mewl again. Alek swore. This was absurd, being held hostage by this newborn. He turned away and crossed the room.

But as the door opened, the screams shifted into a burst of whistling noises. The glowworms in the machine room reacted, green light spilling from the walls. Alek imagined the whole airship waking up, message lizards scampering from all directions in response to the creature's cries.

"Quiet!" he whispered, but the beast didn't stop until he went back and picked it up again.

As Alek stood there stroking its pale fur, he came to a horrible realization.

To have any hope of escaping, he had to take the newborn animal with him. He could hardly leave it sitting here, bawling its tiny misshapen head off for the whole ship to hear.

He had no idea what to feed the creature or how to

take care of it, or even what it *was*. And what would Count Volger say when he showed up with this abomination in his arms?

But Alek didn't have much choice.

When he lifted the animal up from the hay, it scampered up his arm and clung to his shoulder like a cat, the tiny claws stuck fast in the wool of his mechanik's suit.

It looked at him expectantly.

"We're going for a walk now," he said softly, hefting the tool kit again. "You're going to stay quiet, right?"

The creature blinked at him, a look of smug satisfaction on its face.

Alek sighed, and went to the door. He opened it again, looking up and down the corridor. No one was coming to investigate the strange noises—not yet, anyway.

He loosened his jacket, ready to shove the creature inside if he encountered anyone. But for the moment the animal seemed happy on his shoulder—and quiet. It felt as light as a bird there, as if designed to travel this way.

Designed, Alek thought. This animal was fabricated, not born of nature. It had some purpose in the Darwinists' plans, a role in Dr. Barlow's schemes to keep the Ottomans out of the war.

And he had no idea what that purpose was.

Alek shuddered once, then strode into the darkened hall.

· FOURTEEN ·

"There you are!" Count Volger called softly from the support strut of the engine pod. "We'd almost given up on you."

Alek made his way along the ratlines, feeling the creature move inside his jacket. It was flexing its claws again, like tiny needles piercing his flesh.

"I had a small . . . problem."

"Did someone see you?"

Alek shrugged. "A few crewmen on the way. But they didn't ask where I was headed. You play a very convincing broken engine, Maestro Klopp."

From down in the pod the master of mechaniks saluted, a broad smile on his face. Beside him was a very angry-looking Mr. Hirst, gagged and bound fast to the control panel.

"Then it's time to get moving," Volger said. "I trust you're all ready for a fight, if it comes to that."

Bauer and Hoffman brandished tools in their hands, and Volger was wearing his saber. But Alek could hardly wield a knife with the creature hiding under his coat. The time to tell them was now, not in the middle of the escape.

"There's still my small problem."

Volger frowned. "What are you talking about? What happened?"

"Just as I was leaving, one of Dr. Barlow's eggs hatched. Some sort of beast came out. Quite a loud one. When I tried to leave, it began to howl, like a newborn baby crying, I suppose. I thought it would wake the whole ship up!"

Volger nodded. "So you had to strangle it. Most unpleasant, I'm sure. But they won't find its body till morning, and by then we'll be long gone."

Alek blinked.

"You did get rid of it, didn't you, Alek?"

"In fact, that strategy didn't cross my mind." Inside his jacket the creature moved, and Alek winced.

Volger put a hand on his sword hilt and hissed, "What in blazes is under your coat?"

"I assure you, I have no idea." Alek cleared his throat. "But it's perfectly well behaved, as long as one doesn't try to abandon it."

"You brought it with you?" Volger leaned closer. "In case it has escaped your notice, Your Highness, we are currently trying to escape the Darwinists. If you have one of their abominations with you, kindly *fling it over the side!*"

Alek tightened his grip on the ratlines. "I certainly will not, Count. For one thing, the beast would make considerable noise on the way down."

Volger groaned softly, his fists unclenching. "Very well, then. I suppose if it comes to a fight, we could use it as a hostage."

Alek nodded, unbuttoning his jacket. The creature poked its head out.

Volger turned away with a shudder. "Just keep it quiet, or I shall silence it myself. After you, Your Highness."

Alek began to make his way toward the bow, the others following in silence. They climbed along the ratlines just above the airship's waist, the ropes sagging under the weight of the five men and their heavy bags. It was slow going, and poor old Klopp wore a look of terror on his face, but at least no one on the spine could see them.

When the newborn beast began to squirm, Alek opened his jacket the rest of the way. It crawled out and climbed onto his shoulder, its huge eyes narrowing in the breeze.

"Just be careful," he whispered. "And stay quiet."

The creature turned to him with a bored expression, as if Alek were saying something terribly obvious.

Soon the awful fléchette bats were everywhere.

The bow of the airship was covered with them, a seething mass of small black shapes all softly clucking. Dylan had once explained to Alek that the clicks made echoes, which the creatures used to "see" in the dark. They had eyes as well—a thousand beady pairs were following Alek expectantly. No matter how carefully he moved, the bats fluttered about him. It was like trying to sneak through a flock of pigeons on a footpath.

"Why are they watching us so keenly?" Klopp whispered.

"They think we're here to feed them," Alek said. "Dylan always feeds the bats at night."

"You mean they're *hungry*?" Klopp asked, his face shiny with sweat in the moonlight.

"Not to worry. They eat figs," Alek said, leaving out the part about metal spikes.

"I'm glad to hear—," Klopp began, but suddenly a bat fluttered up in front of him. As it shot past his face, his boots slipped from the ratlines.

Klopp jerked to a halt a moment later, his hands white-knuckled on the ropes, but his large body swung into the side of the airship's membrane, sending it billowing out in all directions. Around them bats launched into the air, their clicking noises changing into shrieks and calls.

Alek grabbed for Klopp's wrist as the man struggled to get his feet back on the ropes. A moment later he was safe, but the disturbance was spreading, bats fluttering outward like ripples in a dark pond.

We're done for now, Alek thought.

The creature on his shoulder perked up, its claws sinking painfully into Alek's shoulder. A soft clucking noise came from its mouth—the sound the bats had been making a moment before.

"Keep that beast—," Volger hissed, but Alek waved him silent.

All around them the bats were growing quieter. The screeches faded out, the carpet of black shapes settling back onto the airship's skin.

The creature went silent and turned its big-eyed gaze upon Alek again.

He stared back at it. Had the thing, whatever it was, just silenced the fléchette bats?

Perhaps . . . by accident. It was some kind of mimic, like the message lizards. And yet the creature had required no training, no mothering at all. Perhaps that was the way with all newborn Darwinist beasts.

"Keep moving," Volger whispered, and Alek did.

The mooring tower stretched into the air before them, but Alek found himself staring downward. In the foggy darkness the ground seemed to be a thousand kilometers below.

"Does that rope look strong enough?" he asked Hoffman.

The man knelt to feel the slender cable that stretched across to the tower, perhaps thirty meters away. It seemed too thin to hold a man's weight, though the Darwinist's fabricated materials were always stronger than they looked.

"From what I've seen, sir, the heavy cables are all attached to the gondola below. But this must be here for some reason. Pretty useless, if it can't hold a man's weight."

"I suppose," Alek said. He could think of other creatures that could use the cable. It might be for message lizards to dart across, or for strafing hawks to roost on.

Hoffman shrugged a loop of rope from his shoulder. "This line will hold any two of us, along with our gear. We should send someone over carrying one end of it."

"I'll go," Alek said.

"Not with your injury, young master," Klopp said.

"I'm the lightest of us." Alek held out his hand. "Give me the rope."

Klopp looked at Volger, who nodded and said, "Tie that around his waist, so he doesn't kill himself."

Alek raised an eyebrow, a little surprised that Volger was letting him go first.

The wildcount read his expression and smiled. "If that cable breaks, we'll *all* be stuck here, so it hardly matters who goes first. And you are the lightest, after all."

"So my foolhardiness has produced the correct strategy, Count?"

"Even a stopped clock is right twice a day."

Alek didn't answer, but the creature bristled on his shoulder, as if sensing his annoyance.

Klopp let out a chuckle as he knelt and tied the heavier rope around Alek's waist. Soon it was secure, the other end gripped by Bauer, Hoffman, and Klopp in a tug-of-war line.

"Quickly now," Volger said.

Alek nodded and turned away, walking down the slope of the airbeast's head. The others let the rope out slowly, a gentle pull at his waist. It reminded Alek of when he was ten and his father would let him lean out from castle parapets, keeping a firm hand on his belt. Of course, back then he'd felt much safer.

The slender cable stretched out ahead, disappearing among the dark struts of the mooring tower. Alek grasped the cable in both hands.

"I hope you're not afraid of heights, beastie."

The newborn creature just looked at him and blinked.

"Right, then," Alek said, and stepped off into the void. He dangled for a moment from his hands, then swung his legs up to wrap them around the cable. Though its claws sank deep into his shoulder, the beastie didn't make a sound.

There was one good thing about hanging faceup like

"CROSSING A GULF INTO THE DARKNESS."

this—Alek couldn't see the dark ground below, only his own hands clenching the rope and the stars above. He pulled himself away from the airship hand over hand, the cable cutting into the backs of his knees as he inched along.

Halfway across, Alek was breathing hard. His injured rib had begun to throb, and his hands were losing feeling. The night air turned the sweat on his forehead cold. As he inched away from the airship, the rope hanging from his waist grew longer and heavier.

He imagined the cable snapping, or his fingers slipping. He would fall for an awful moment, but the rope around his waist would swing him back toward the airship, smashing him into its nose—maybe hard enough for the whale itself to awaken and protest. . . .

The mooring tower grew closer, but the cable in his aching hands sloped gently upward now, and was harder than ever to climb. The creature began to moan softly, mimicking the wind in the struts of the tower.

Alek gritted his teeth and pulled himself the last few meters, ignoring his burning muscles. For once he was thankful for the years of Volger's cruel fencing lessons.

Finally a metal strut came within reach, and Alek wrapped an arm around it. He hung there for a moment, panting, then hauled himself up onto the cold steel of the tower.

With shaking fingers he untied the thick rope from around his waist and knotted it to the strut. Now that it stretched all the way back to the airship's head, the rope seemed to weigh a ton. How had he carried it so far?

Alek lay on his back and watched as the others prepared to cross, dividing up the satchels of tools and weapons. It was odd to see the *Leviathan* from this head-on perspective. It made Alek feel insignificant, like some minuscule creature about to be swallowed by a whale.

But the darkness beyond the airship was vaster still. It was dotted with the fires of the protesters at the airfield gate, and past those, the lights of the city.

"Constantinople," he said softly.

"Mmm, Constantinople," the creature said.

⦿ FIFTEEN ⦿

Climbing down the tower was simple. A set of metal stairs spiraled through its center, and the five of them descended quickly.

Or was it *six* of them now? Suddenly Alek could feel the weight of the fabricated beast riding on his shoulder. The single word it had spoken made the animal heavier somehow, as if its uncanniness were something solid.

Alek hadn't told the others, of course. Volger was terrified enough of message lizards. Why provide him with another excuse to get rid of the newborn creature?

At least it seemed to know when to stay quiet. Since speaking that one word, it hadn't uttered another sound.

As they neared the bottom of the stairs, Alek found himself level with the airship's bridge. Light from worm-lamps shone through the windows, silhouetting two officers on duty inside. But the faint green glow didn't reach the shadows within the tower.

The *Leviathan*'s guards stood at attention in the airship's hatches. Ground men in red fezzes faced them, the two groups watching each other warily. The rest of the Ottomans were at the airfield gates, keeping an eye on the protesters.

No one was guarding the base of the mooring tower.

The moon was climbing, a fat crescent in the sky, and the tower cast a long shadow pointing west, away from the city and the crowds. Volger lead the others along that slender finger of darkness, heading for an empty stretch of fence at the airfield's edge.

Alek wondered what would happen if they were spotted now. The *Leviathan*'s crew had no authority here on Ottoman soil. But he doubted that the Darwinists would let their only engineers slip away without a fight. For that matter, the Ottomans mightn't take kindly to foreigners trespassing on their airfield.

All in all, it seemed better to remain unseen.

Suddenly the newborn creature stood up on its hind legs, its ears twisting back toward the ship. Alek came to a halt and listened. The distant shriek of a command whistle reached his ears.

"Volger, I think they've—"

A hydrogen sniffer's howl pierced the night. The sound

came from near the engine pod—someone had found the bound and gagged Mr. Hirst.

"Keep moving," Volger whispered. "We're half a kilometer from the fence. They'll search the ship before they think to look out here."

Alek broke into a run, shuddering to think what beasts the Darwinists would send after them. The six-legged sniffer dogs? The awful fléchette bats? Or were there even worse creatures aboard the ship?

The alarm spread along the long, dark silhouette behind them, the gondola lights flickering from soft green to brilliant white. On Alek's shoulder the creature softly imitated the sounds of the alert, the barks and cries of the hounds, the shouts and whistles of command.

"I'm not sure that's helpful," he muttered to it.

"Helpful," the creature repeated softly.

A minute later a blinding searchlight lanced out from the ship's spine. At first it pointed at the airfield gate, but slowly it began to turn, like a lighthouse on a dark ocean.

So much for the Darwinists letting them slip away.

"You four go ahead," Klopp said, his face bright red. "I can't keep running like this!"

Alek slowed his pace, taking the man's heavy tool kit from him. "Nonsense, Klopp. Spreading out just makes it easier for them to spot us."

"He's right," Volger said. "Stick close together."

Alek glanced over his shoulder. The light was swinging toward them, rippling across the grass like a luminous wave.

"Get down!" he whispered, and the five of them dropped flat to the ground.

The blinding light flashed past, but didn't stop on them—it had been aimed too high. The spotlight crew were searching the airfield from the outside in, checking the boundaries first. But Alek doubted Klopp could make it to the fence before the light swung round again.

The newborn creature's claws tightened on his shoulder, and it made a new noise in his ear . . . a sound like fluttering wings.

Alek glanced back at the ship, his eyes widening. A dark cloud was boiling up from beneath the gondola, thousands of black forms spilling into the air. The tempest of wings climbed through the searchlight's beam, glittering with the flash of steel talons.

"Strafing hawks," Alek breathed. Back on the glacier, he'd seen the hawks in action against German soldiers. And just yesterday he'd seen a crewman sharpening the steel talons they wore, like a razor on a leather strap.

The birds spread out from the ship, and soon the air above was full of fluttering shapes.

Alek looked ahead—the fence was only a hundred meters away.

But a moment later the hawks had begun to circle, a whirlwind of wings and glinting steel forming overhead. Alek stooped his shoulders, waiting for an attack.

"Just keep running!" Volger cried. "We're no good to them dead."

Alek ran, hoping the man was right.

As the spinning mass grew larger and larger, the spotlight altered course, heading toward the towering whirlwind of birds. It arrived in seconds, pinning Alek like the stare of a great, blinding eye.

The howl of hydrogen sniffers reached Alek's ears again, closer than before. The beast on his shoulder imitated the sound.

"They're coming on foot," Alek said.

"Go on, Bauer," Volger shouted. "You've got the cutters!"

Alek followed as the man spurted ahead. The airfield's edge wasn't far now; the spotlight streaming past them glinted on the coils of barbed wire.

When Bauer and Alek reached the fence, Bauer pulled out the bolt cutters and set to work. He snipped at the mesh of wire, slowly opening a way through. But the cries of the beasts behind them were growing louder every second.

Bauer was halfway done when the others caught up.

"The forest is heavy this way," Volger said, pointing at the blackness past the fence. "Run due west until you drop, then find a place to hide."

"What about you?" Alek asked.

"Hoffman and I will hold the breach for as long as we can."

"Hold the breach?" Alek said. "With wrenches and a fencing saber? You can't fight off those beasts!"

"No, but we can slow them down. And once the Darwinists realize they have an engineer and a translator in hand, they may decide it's not worth chasing the rest of you. Especially across Ottoman territory."

"We've thought this out, young master," Klopp said, panting. "It's all in the plan!"

"*What* plan?" Alek cried, but no one answered. "Why didn't you tell me?"

"My apologies, Your Highness." Volger drew his sword. "But you've been a bit loose with our secrets lately."

"God's wounds, Volger! Are you playing the martyr?"

"If they weren't right behind us, I'd be going with you. But someone has to hold them here. And between the two of us, Hoffman and I offer them a chance to keep their ship flying, as long as they don't treat us too roughly."

"But I can't . . ." Alek swallowed.

"It's done, sir," Bauer said.

"Go, then," Volger said, handing his bag to Klopp, who scrambled through the breach. The shadows of hydrogen sniffers and men loomed, made huge by the searchlight.

"A STAND."

"But, Volger." Alek clenched his fists. "I can't do this without you! Not any of it!"

"I'm afraid you must." Volger saluted with his saber. "Good-bye, Alek. Make your father proud."

But my father is dead . . . and you're not.

"Come, sir." Bauer grabbed his arm. Alek tried to pull away, but the man was bigger and stronger. Alek found himself dragged through the opening in the fence, his jacket nipped at by the wire's barbs, the creature on his shoulder ducking low and howling like a hydrogen sniffer on the hunt.

A moment later they were among dark trees, Klopp's panting ahead of them. Corporal Bauer still pulled him along, apologizing under his breath. The forest soon smothered the battle's sounds, the searchlight barely glimmering through the leaves. The sniffers' howls were muted, the strafing hawks forced higher by heavy branches.

The three of them thrashed deeper into the trees, until everything was swallowed up by blackness. All Alek could see were spots burned into his vision by the searchlight. Behind them the sounds faded abruptly.

Volger would be negotiating now, offering Hoffman and himself in exchange for the others' freedom. The Darwinists would have little choice. If they fought their way through the fence, they'd risk killing their last engineer and translator.

Alek found himself slowing. Count Volger's plan had worked to perfection.

Bauer tightened his grip. "Please, sir. We can't go back."

"Of course not." Alek shook himself free and came to a halt. "But there's no need to rush, unless we want to give poor old Klopp a heart attack."

Klopp didn't argue. He stood, stooped and panting, his hands on his knees. Alek looked back the way they'd come, listening for sounds of pursuit—nothing. Not even a bird in the sky.

He was finally free, but he'd never felt more alone.

Prince Aleksandar knew what his father would have said. It was time for him to take command.

"Did we drop anything?"

Bauer quickly counted the bags. "The wireless set, the tools, the gold bar—we've got it all, sir."

"The gold . . . ," Alek said, wondering how much the last of his father's fortune had slowed them down. He would've traded all of it for the extra minutes that Volger's sacrifice had bought them.

But this was no time for self-pity, or for wishing that things were different.

"And there's this," Klopp added, pulling a leather scroll case from his jacket. It was marked with the crossed keys of the papal seal. "He said you should carry it from now on."

Alek stared at the object. It was a letter from the pope stating that Alek was heir to his father's titles and estates, despite the wishes of his granduncle, the emperor. One could argue that it made Alek the heir to the throne of Austria-Hungary as well. It was why the Germans were hunting him—he might one day have the power to end this war.

As Alek's fingers closed around the case, he realized that he'd always relied on Volger to keep the letter safe. But now he had to carry his own destiny.

He slid the case into a pocket and buttoned it shut. "Very good, Klopp. Shall I take Volger's bag for you?"

"No, young master," the man panted. "I'll be fine."

Alek held out his hand. "I'm afraid I must insist. You're slowing us down."

Klopp paused. This was the moment when he would normally have glanced at the wildcount for approval, but no longer. He handed the bag over, and Alek grunted as the weight hit him.

Volger, of course, had been carrying the gold.

The creature mimicked the grunt, and Alek sighed. Less than an hour old, and already it was becoming tiresome.

"I hope you learn some new tricks soon," he muttered, to which the creature blinked its eyes.

Bauer hoisted the other two bags. "Which way, sir?"

"You mean Count Volger didn't provide you with any more secret plans?"

Bauer looked at Klopp, who shrugged.

Alek took a slow breath. It was all up to him now.

To the west lay Europe, descending into madness and war. To the east was the Ottoman Empire, stretching, vast and alien, into the heart of Asia. And spanning the two continents was the ancient city of Constantinople.

"We stay in the capital, for now. We'll need to buy clothes . . . and perhaps horses." Alek paused, realizing that with the gold bar they could buy their own walker if they wanted. The possibilities were endless. "At least in the city some of the storekeepers will understand German."

"Very sensible," Klopp said. "But where *tonight*, young master?"

Bauer nodded, staring back the way they'd come. The woods were silent, but the searchlight still glimmered on the horizon.

"We head west for an hour," Alek said. "Then circle back toward the city. Perhaps we'll find a friendly inn."

"An inn, sir? But won't the Ottomans be looking for us?" Bauer asked.

Alek thought for a moment, then shook his head. "They won't know who to look for, unless the Darwinists tell them. And I don't think they will."

Klopp frowned. "Why not?"

"Don't you see, the Darwinists don't *want* us to be caught." As Alek spoke the words, his own thoughts became clearer. "We know too much about the *Leviathan*—how its engines work, the nature of its mission. It won't help them to have us in Ottoman hands."

Klopp nodded slowly. "They could say it was only Volger and Hoffman who tried to escape, and they've caught them. So there's no one else to look for!"

"Exactly," Alek said. "And as a warship, the *Leviathan* has to leave neutral territory by tomorrow. Once they're gone, no one will know we're here."

"What about the Germans, sir?" Bauer said quietly. "They saw the Stormwalker in the Alps, with its Hapsburg crest, and saw the *Leviathan* mounted with our engines. They must know we were aboard, and they'll guess who was trying to escape tonight, even if the Ottomans don't."

Alek swore. German agents were everywhere in Constantinople, and tonight's ruckus hadn't been subtle.

"You're right, Bauer. But I doubt there are any Germans in these woods. I still say we sleep in an inn tonight—a quiet, comfortable one that will take gold shavings in payment. Tomorrow we'll disguise ourselves properly."

He walked into the darkness, setting his course by the last glimmer of searchlights behind them. The other two hoisted their bags and followed. No arguments, no debate.

As simple as that, Alek was in command.

· SIXTEEN ·

Deryn carried the tray carefully, barely trusting herself to walk straight.

The Clankers' escape had kept her awake all night—scrambling to the rookery to release the strafing hawks, being dragged about by a pack of excited sniffers, then two hours with the officers as they explained it all to the Ottoman authorities, who thought it a squick rude for the *Leviathan*'s crew to be gallivanting across their airfield without permission.

When Deryn had finally found a moment to check the machine room, Dr. Barlow was already there. One of the eggs had hatched in the night, and the newborn beastie was missing!

The odd thing was, the lady boffin had hardly seemed upset. She'd ordered Deryn to take a good look around the ship, but had only smiled when Deryn had come back empty-handed.

That was boffins for you.

By the time Deryn had stumbled to her own cabin, it had been dawn—time to go back on duty. To add insult to injury, her first orders had been to deliver breakfast to the man who'd caused the whole palaver.

A guard stood in front of Count Volger's stateroom. He looked as tired as Deryn felt, and stared hungrily at her tray full of toast, boiled eggs, and tea.

"Shall I knock for you, sir?" he asked.

"Aye, feel free to wake his countship up," Deryn said. "Seeing as how he kept *us* up all night."

The man nodded and gave the door a good piece of his boot.

Volger opened it a moment later, looking as though he hadn't been to bed yet either. His hair stuck out at all angles, and his riding breeches were still spattered with mud from the airfield.

He gave the tray a hungry look and stepped aside. Deryn pushed past him and set it down on the desk. She noted that Volger's saber was gone, along with most of his papers. The officers must have ransacked the room after the escape.

"Breakfast for a condemned man?" Volger asked, closing the door.

"I doubt they'll hang you, sir. Not today, anyhow."

The man smiled, pouring himself tea. "You Darwinists are so forgiving."

Deryn rolled her eyes at that. Volger knew he was indispensable. The lady boffin might speak Clanker, but she didn't know the fiddly words for mechanical parts. And she certainly wasn't going to spend her days up in an engine pod. Volger would be treated well as long as Hoffman was needed to keep the engines running.

"I'd hardly say you're forgiven," Deryn said. "There'll be a guard on your door day and night."

"Well, then, Mr. Sharp, I am your prisoner." Volger pulled out the desk chair and sat down, then gestured at an empty cup on the windowsill. "Tea?"

Deryn raised an eyebrow. His countship was offering *her*, a lowly middy, a cup of tea? The floral smell rising from the pot had already set her mouth watering. Between the ruckus last night and resupplying the ship before they left today, it might be hours before she sat down to her own breakfast.

Better a quick cup of tea and milk than nothing.

"Thank you, sir. I believe I will." Deryn picked up the cup. It was fine porcelain, as light as a hummingbird, with Alek's mechanical eagle crest inlaid in gold. "Did you bring this fancy china all the way from Austria?"

"One advantage to traveling in a Stormwalker, there's plenty of room for luggage." Volger sighed. "Though I'm afraid you hold our last surviving piece. It is two centuries old. Pray, don't drop it."

Deryn's eyes widened as the wildcount poured. "I'll try not to."

"Milk?"

She nodded dumbly and sat down, wondering at the transformation that had come over Count Volger. He'd always been a dark presence on the ship, skulking through the corridors and glaring at the beasties. But this morning the man seemed almost . . . *pleasant*.

Deryn took a sip of tea, letting its warmth spread through her.

"You seem in good spirits," she said. "Considering."

"Considering that my escape was foiled?" Volger stared out the window. "Odd, isn't it? I feel somewhat light-hearted this morning, as if all my cares had lifted."

Deryn frowned. "You mean because Alek's got away, and you haven't?"

The man stirred his tea. "Yes, I suppose that's it."

"Well, that's a bit hard, isn't it?" Deryn said. "Poor Alek's out there on the run, while you're sipping tea out of a fancy cup, safe and sound."

Volger raised his cup, which had the *Leviathan*'s silhouette and nautilus spirals stamped on its side in black. "That would be you, boy. Mine is quite plain."

"To blazes with your barking teacup!" Deryn cried, annoyance rising in her. "You're *happy* that Alek's gone, aren't you?"

"Happy that he's off this ship?" The wildcount salted his boiled eggs and took a bite of one. "That he's no longer destined to spend the war in chains?"

"Aye, but the poor boy's all on his own. And here you are having breakfast, smug as a box of cats! I think it's dead rotten of you!"

Volger paused, a forkful of potatoes now halfway to his mouth. He looked her up and down.

Deryn swallowed her next words, realizing she'd let exhaustion get the better of her. Her voice had gone all high and squeaky, and she was gripping the antique teacup so hard it was a wonder it hadn't shattered.

During the alert there'd been so much commotion, it had been easy to forget that Alek was out there running for his life. But sitting here watching Volger salt his eggs with a self-satisfied expression, the enormity of it all had finally struck home.

Alek was gone, and he wasn't coming back.

Deryn set the teacup carefully on the desk. Careful to use her boy's voice, she said, "You seem dead pleased with yourself, is all. And I reckon it's because Alek isn't your problem anymore."

"My problem?" Volger asked. "Is *that* what you think he was?"

"Aye. You're glad to see the backside of him, just because he had a mind of his own sometimes."

Volger's face fell back into its usual stony expression, as if Deryn were a bug crawling across his breakfast. "Listen, boy. You have no idea what I've given up for Alek—my title, my future, my family's name. I'll never see my home again, no matter who wins this war. I'm a traitor in the eyes of my people, and all of it to keep Alek safe."

Deryn held his stare. "Aye, but you're not the only one who's had to go against his own country. I kept Alek's secrets and looked the other way when you lot were planning to escape. So don't go getting all high and mighty on *me*."

Volger glared at her another moment, then let out a tired laugh. He finally took his bite of potatoes, and chewed them thoughtfully.

"You're as worried about him as I am, aren't you?"

"Of course I am," Deryn said.

"It's quite touching, really." Volger poured more tea for them both. "I'm glad Alek had you as a friend, Dylan, even if you are a commoner."

Deryn rolled her eyes. Aristocrats were so barking stuck up.

"But Alek has trained for this moment his whole life," Volger went on. "His father and I always knew that one day he would be alone, with the whole world against him. And Alek has made it amply clear that he was ready to go on without me."

Deryn shook her head. "But you've got it all wrong, Count. Alek didn't want to go it alone; he wanted *more* allies, not less. He even said he wanted to . . ."

She remembered the last time they'd spoken, two nights before. Alek had wished that there were a way for him to stay aboard the *Leviathan*, because the airship felt like the only place he'd ever belonged. And she'd been a bum-rag about the whole thing, just because he hadn't been declaring his undying love for *her*.

Suddenly her throat was too tight to speak.

Volger leaned forward and regarded her. "You're a very sensitive boy, Dylan."

Deryn glared back at him. It didn't mean she was barking "sensitive," just because she knew when things *mattered*.

"I just hope he's all right," she said after a good swallow of tea.

"As do I. Perhaps we can still help Alek, you and I together."

"How do you mean?"

"He has a bigger part to play in this war than you understand, Dylan," the count said. "His granduncle the emperor is a very old man."

"Aye, but the throne doesn't mean anything to Alek, because his mum isn't royal enough. Right?"

"Ah, I see he told you everything," Volger said, giving her an odd smile. "But in politics there are always exceptions.

When the right time comes, Alek could tip the balance of this war."

Deryn frowned. What the count was saying didn't quite square up with Alek's story, about how his family had always looked down on him and his mother. But back in the Alps, of course, the Germans had sent a massive fleet of airships to capture him. They, at least, seemed to think he was important.

"But what can we do to help him?"

"At the moment, not much. But one never knows what opportunities might present themselves. The problem is that I no longer have a wireless set."

Deryn frowned. "You had a wireless? Did the officers know about that?"

"They didn't ask." Count Volger waved a hand at his breakfast. "And I see you haven't thought to bring me the morning newspapers. So if you could keep me apprised of events, I would appreciate it."

"What? Spy for you?" Deryn cried. "Not barking likely!"

"I could make it worth your while."

"With what? Cups of *tea*?"

The wildcount smiled. "Perhaps I can do better than that. For example, you must be wondering about a certain missing creature."

"The beastie that hatched last night? You know where it is?" The man didn't answer, but Deryn's mind was already spinning. "Then it must have hatched *before* Alek left the machine room! He's got it with him, hasn't he?"

"Perhaps. Or perhaps we strangled it to keep it quiet." Volger took his last bite of toast and dabbed his mouth with a napkin. "Do you think your Dr. Barlow would be interested in the details?"

Deryn narrowed her eyes. The way the lady boffin was acting, she already had a good idea where the newborn creature had gone. Suddenly it all made sense. Deryn would've seen it herself if she hadn't been so exhausted.

Now that she thought about it, quite a few peculiarities surrounding the eggs were beginning to make sense.

"Aye," Deryn said. "She might be interested."

"Then, I'll tell you exactly how your creature fared last night, as long as you keep me informed over the next few days." The count looked out the window. "The Ottomans will soon make their decision about entering this war. Alek's next step will depend greatly on that choice."

Deryn followed his gaze out the window. The spires of Istanbul were just visible in the distance, the haze of engine smoke already rising over the city. "Well, I could tell you what the newspapers say. *That's* not spying, I suppose."

"Excellent." Count Volger stood, offering his hand. "I think you and I may be allies after all."

Deryn stared at his hand a moment, then sighed and

shook it. "Thank you for the tea, sir. And by the way, next time you try to escape, I'd be much obliged if you did it more quietly. Or at least in the middle of the day."

"Of course." Volger bowed gracefully, then said, "And if you ever want to learn to fence *properly*, Mr. Sharp, do let me know."

SEVENTEEN

Halfway back to the bosun's cabin, a message lizard stopped on the ceiling overhead and fixed her with its beady eyes.

"Mr. Sharp," it squawked in the lady boffin's voice, "I shall need you in full dress today. We'll be visiting the sultan."

Deryn stared up at the beastie, wondering if she'd heard right. *The* sultan? The man who ruled over the whole barking Ottoman Empire?

"I have told Mr. Rigby to relieve you of other duties," the lizard continued. "Meet me out on the airfield at noon, and make sure you look sharp."

Deryn swallowed. "Aye, ma'am. I'll be there. End message."

As the beastie scuttled away, she closed her eyes and softly swore. She didn't even have a dress uniform to wear, not since yesterday. Deryn had taken off her jacket before she'd jumped onto the *Dauntless*'s trunk, but her only fancy shirt was still bright red from the spice bomb. Even after two washings, one whiff of the shirt was strong enough to make a dead horse sneeze. She'd have to borrow one of Newkirk's, and that meant making adjustments with her sewing kit. . . .

She groaned, then headed toward her cabin at a run.

As Deryn descended the gangway hours later, the rumble of Clanker engines sprang to life around her. In the airship's shadow Newkirk, the bosun, and a dozen riggers were loading themselves onto a squadron of walkers in the shapes of donkeys and water buffaloes. They were headed to the markets for supplies, and looked to be in a hurry. If the *Leviathan* didn't leave the city by late afternoon today, the Ottomans would have every right to impound it.

The officers hadn't let on where the ship was going next. But wherever they were bound, Deryn doubted she would be seeing Istanbul or Alek again, not until the war was over.

She watched Newkirk for a moment, envious of his disguise. The whole party was dressed in Arab robes to keep the Young Turks from spotting them and starting up another protest. If only she could be doing proper ship's work instead of diplomacy . . . or whatever Dr. Barlow was up to.

The lady boffin waited a hundred yards from the *Leviathan*, on a stretch of empty airfield past the mooring tower. She was dressed in her finest traveling coat, twirling a parasol and standing beside a small hay-filled box. One of the last two eggs sat inside it, shining like a huge pearl in the sun. So Dr. Barlow's secret cargo would at last be delivered to the sultan.

But why take a spare middy along?

As Deryn drew near, Dr. Barlow turned and said, "You're a bit late, Mr. Sharp, and looking positively unkempt."

"Sorry, ma'am," Deryn said, adjusting her collar. Her shirt fitted all wrong despite a mad hour of sewing. Worse, it still smelled of Newkirk—the bum-rag hadn't bothered to wash it since yesterday. "I had to borrow this shirt. Mine was still a bit spicy."

"You possess only one dress uniform?" Dr. Barlow clicked her tongue. "We shall have to remedy that, if you're going to continue assisting me."

Deryn frowned. "Assisting you, ma'am? Frankly, I never fancied myself much of a diplomat."

"Perhaps not. But this is what comes of making yourself useful, Mr. Sharp. You were invaluable during the battle of the *Dauntless*, while the ambassador and his lackeys were quite hopeless." Dr. Barlow sighed. "Soon I shall be afraid to leave the airship without your protection."

Deryn rolled her eyes. Even when dispensing compliments, the lady boffin always managed a mocking tone. "I hope you're not expecting to be attacked again today, ma'am."

"One never knows. We are not as welcome here as I might have liked."

"That's right enough," Deryn said, still hearing the anger in the protesters' voices. "But I've been meaning to ask you, ma'am. What's a behemoth?"

Dr. Barlow looked at her with narrowed eyes. "Wherever did you hear that word, Mr. Sharp?"

"It was just something they were shouting yesterday. The Young Turks, I mean."

"Hmm, of course. That is the name of the *Osman*'s companion creature, and thus part of Lord Churchill's unfortunate appropriation."

Deryn frowned. "But krakens don't have names. No beastie does, unless it's a whole ship."

"'Behemoth' is not a proper name, young man, but a species. You see, this creature is not a kraken at all but something altogether new. And a military secret, so perhaps we should drop the subject." Dr. Barlow tipped back her parasol to look into the sky. "I believe this is our airship."

Deryn shielded her eyes against the high sun, and saw a peculiar craft coming into view. "It's quite . . . conspicuous, isn't it, ma'am?"

"Of course. Guests of the sultan are expected to arrive in style."

The Clanker airship was less than a quarter of the *Leviathan*'s length, but was as fancy as a wedding cake. A

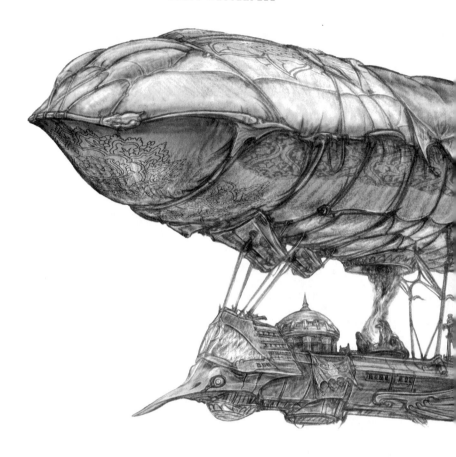

fringe of tassels fluttered from its airbag, and canopies of
billowing silk covered the gondola, as if some Ottoman
prince had decided to go soaring on his four-poster bed.

The craft was held aloft by a long cylindrical balloon
with several funnels leading up into its belly, each fed with
hot air by a blazing smokestack in the shape of a monstrous
head. Propellers thrust out on long and jointed arms, some
pointing up, some down, the two largest pushing the craft

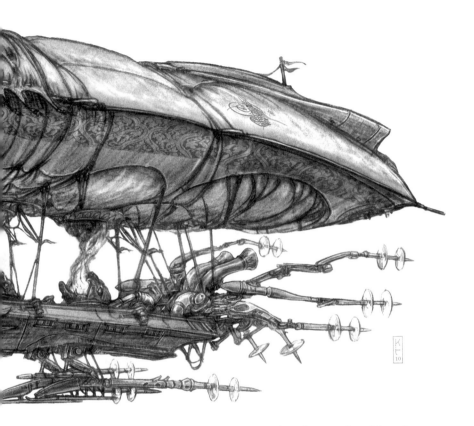

forward. The prow was carved in the shape of a falcon's hooked beak, and wings unfolding like straight razors were carved into the gondola's sides.

The craft's propellers turned and twisted, until it had settled gently on the scrub grass of the airfield.

As a short gangway unfolded from its gondola, Dr. Barlow closed her parasol and pointed it at the egg box. "If you please, Mr. Sharp."

"Invaluable, that's me," Deryn said, lifting the box with a grunt.

She followed the lady boffin up the gangway to an open platform surrounded by a low railing, like the top deck of a sailing ship. The propeller wash swirled about them, ruffling the veil tucked into Dr. Barlow's bowler.

The crew were all dark-skinned men, but they weren't wearing desert robes, like the Africans that Deryn had seen from the elephant's howdah the day before. Instead they wore silk uniforms and tall turbans of brilliant red and orange. Two of them took the egg box from Deryn, lashing it fast to metal cleats on the deck.

One of the men wore a tall conical hat, his eyes protected by piloting goggles. Some sort of mechanical beastie perched on his shoulder, like an owl with big eyes and a wide-open mouth. A tiny cylinder sat on the machine's chest, a metal stylus scratching against its spinning surface.

The man stepped forward and bowed to Dr. Barlow.

"Peace be upon you, madam. I am the Kizlar Agha. Welcome aboard."

The lady boffin replied in a language Deryn didn't recognize, one made of softer sounds than German. The man smiled, repeating the same phrase as he bowed to Deryn.

"Midshipman Dylan Sharp," she said, bowing in return. "Pleased to meet you, Mr. Agha."

Dr. Barlow laughed. "Kizlar Agha is a title, Mr. Sharp, not a name. He is the head of the palace guard and of the treasury. The most important man in the empire, after the sultan and grand vizier. A carrier of important messages."

"And important visitors as well," the man said, raising a hand. The smokestacks belched fire, sending ripples of heat through the air.

Deryn's nose caught the sweet smell of burning propane. She shuddered and clenched her jaw, turning to grip the rail as the airship lifted into the sky.

"Are you unwell, Mr. Sharp?" the Kizlar Agha said, leaning closer to her. "Airsickness seems a strange malady for an airman."

"I'm quite all right, sir," Deryn said stiffly. "It's just that hot-air balloons make me a wee bit nervous."

The man crossed his arms. "I assure you, the Imperial Airyacht *Stamboul* is as safe as any airbeast."

"I'm sure it is, sir," Deryn said, but her hands still gripped the railing. The smokestacks belched fire again, roaring like an angry tigeresque.

"We had something of a battle yesterday," Dr. Barlow said, putting a cool hand against Deryn's cheek. "And alarms and excursions again last night. Mr. Sharp has been quite busy, I'm afraid."

"Ah, yes. I heard of the Young Turks pestering you," the Kizlar Agha said. "Revolutionaries are everywhere now. But they will not trouble us at the palace, nor in the sky."

The craft had cleared the airfield fence now, and the protesters at the gate looked as small as ants below.

While Dr. Barlow and the Kizlar Agha talked, Deryn stared down at the city, trying to ignore the air wrinkling with heat around her. The tangled streets of Istanbul were soon beneath the *Stamboul*, the metal flash of walkers glinting through the veil of smoke. Gyrothopters flittered past, looking as delicate as butterflies.

Alek was down there somewhere, she supposed. Unless he'd already headed into the wilds of the empire, where the Air Service maps showed only mountains and dusty plains on the way to the Far East.

When the Kizlar Agha returned to his duties, Dr. Barlow joined Deryn at the railing. "Are you quite sure you weren't bumped on the head last night, Mr. Sharp? You look unwell."

"No, I'm feeling brilliant," Deryn said, gripping the handrail tighter. She wasn't going to spout off about her father's accident again. Best to change the subject. "It's just that I had an odd chat with Count Volger over breakfast . . . about our missing beastie."

"Really? How enterprising of you."

"He said he saw it last night. The beastie must've hatched before Alek left, and the daft boy took it with him." Deryn turned to Dr. Barlow and narrowed her eyes. "But you already knew that, didn't you, ma'am?"

"The possibility had crossed my mind." The lady boffin shrugged. "It seemed the only logical explanation for the creature's disappearance."

"Aye, but it wasn't just logic, was it? You knew Alek would try to escape before we left Istanbul, so you put him on egg duty last night."

A smile appeared behind Dr. Barlow's veil. "Why, Mr. Sharp, are you accusing me of *scheming*?"

"Call it what you like, ma'am, but Alek was always complaining that you rearranged the heaters when he was watching the eggs. Made it hotter for him than for me." As Deryn spoke her suspicions aloud, more pieces fell into place. "And you never wanted me to visit while he was on egg duty. So that when the beastie hatched, it would be just him in the machine room, all alone!"

Dr. Barlow looked away and said sternly. "Are you

certain you weren't bumped on the head last night, Mr. Sharp? I'm not sure what you're talking about."

"I'm talking about the beasties inside those eggs," Deryn said, staring at the cargo box. "What *are* they, anyway?"

"They are a military secret, young man."

"Aye, and now we're taking one to this sultan fellow. A Clanker aristocrat, just like Alek!"

Deryn stared straight at Dr. Barlow, waiting for a reply. It was the rudest she'd ever dared be with the lady boffin, but between the sleepless night and this morning's realizations, anger had taken control of her tongue.

It was all starting to make sense. Why Dr. Barlow had been willing to keep Alek's secret from the officers, and why she'd put him on egg duty almost from the start. She'd *wanted* one of the eggs to hatch while Alek was alone in that room.

But what on earth was the beastie's purpose? And why hadn't Alek simply left the barking thing behind?

After a moment of cold stares between them, Dr. Barlow broke the silence. "Did Count Volger say anything *specific* about the creature?"

"Not really." Deryn shrugged. "He may have mentioned something about strangling it to keep it quiet."

Dr. Barlow's eyebrows shot up, and Deryn smiled. Two could play at this game of keeping secrets.

"But I think he was just trying to be clever."

"Indeed," Dr. Barlow said coldly. "There appears to be a lot of that going about."

Deryn held the woman's gaze. "I'm not trying to be clever, ma'am. I just want to know . . . Is Alek in danger from that beastie?"

"Don't be absurd, Mr. Sharp." Dr. Barlow leaned closer, lowering her voice. "The perspicacious loris, as it is known, is quite harmless. I would never put Alek in danger."

"Then you *did* try to make an egg hatch while he was in there with them!"

Dr. Barlow looked away. "Yes, the loris was designed with a high degree of nascent fixation. Like a baby duck, it bonds with the first person it sees."

"And you made it bond with Alek!"

"A necessary improvisation. After we crashed in the Alps, it seemed that we wouldn't reach Istanbul in time. I didn't want to see all my years of work wasted." She shrugged. "Besides, I'm quite fond of Alek, and wish him every advantage in his travels. To those who listen carefully, the perspicacious loris can be quite helpful."

"Helpful?" Deryn asked. "How, exactly?"

"By being perspicacious, of course."

Deryn furrowed her eyebrows, puzzling over what "perspicacious" might mean. She wondered if she could trust the lady boffin's words at all. Dr. Barlow always seemed to have a larger plan than whatever she let on.

"But it wasn't just to help him," Deryn said. "Alek's an important Clanker, just like the sultan, and that's why you wanted him to have this loris beastie."

"It is as I said yesterday." Dr. Barlow gestured at the beaklike prow before them, at monstrous heads belching fire. "Unlike the other Clanker powers, the Ottomans have not forgotten the web of life. And I think that in his short time with us, Alek may have become amenable to reason as well."

"Reason?" Deryn swallowed. "But what does some newborn beastie have to do with *reason?*"

"Nothing, of course, as per my grandfather's law: 'No fabricated creature shall show human reason.'" The lady boffin waved her hand. "Take it as a figure of speech, Mr. Sharp. But one thing is certain—this war will make a mess of Europe's royal houses. So it's possible that young Alek may one day be as important as any sultan, proper royalty or not."

"Aye, that's what Count Volger was saying too."

"Was he?" Dr. Barlow drummed her fingers on the railing. "How interesting."

Just ahead, the strait was shining in the noon sun. Almost directly below were two huge buildings of marble and stone—mosques, of course, their domed roofs like giant shields arrayed against the sky, their minarets thrusting up like spears around them. The plaza between the buildings was crowded with people, their faces turning upward as the *Stamboul*'s shadow slid across them.

The Kizlar Agha shouted orders, and the propellers shifted on their long, spindly arms. The aircraft began to descend toward what looked like a park surrounded by high walls. Inside it were dozens of low buildings, all stitched together with paths and covered walkways, and one great cluster of still more domes and minarets, almost another city within the palace walls.

"Perhaps we should keep an eye on Count Volger, then," Dr. Barlow said.

Deryn nodded, remembering the wildcount's offer to tell her more about the beastie if she brought him news from outside. He was certainly open to an exchange of information.

"Well, ma'am, he did say he'd give me fencing lessons."

The lady boffin smiled. "Then, dear boy, you shall have to learn to fence."

◦ EIGHTEEN ◦

The *Stamboul* descended just inside the palace walls, in an overgrown garden the size of a cricket field.

The Kizlar Agha stood at the airship's prow, shouting directions to the propeller men, making adjustments all the way down. Deryn soon saw why—there was barely room to land an airship. But the craft settled precisely at a spot where five paths crossed, as soft as a kiss, like a gaudy pavilion completing the garden's design. The fronds of palm trees around them shivered in the wash from the airship's propellers.

The gangway dropped, and the Kizlar Agha led Deryn, Dr. Barlow, and the two crewmen with the egg box down into the sultan's garden.

A hundred windows looked down upon them, but all were covered with metal lattices that shimmered gold in the sunlight. Deryn wondered if there were people watching them through the narrow slats, courtiers and advisers, or the sultan's famous harem of countless wives.

This was nothing like Buckingham Palace, where Deryn had watched the changing of the Royal Lionesque Guard her first day in London. That was four stories tall and as square as a cake. But here the buildings were low and surrounded by colonnades, their arches decorated with checkerboards of black and white marble, as shiny as piano keys. Steam pipes wound across the mosaicked walls like message lizard tubes, sweating and huffing with the energies inside them. Guards stood at every door, Africans in bright silk uniforms armed with halberds and scimitars.

Deryn wondered what it would be like to live among all this spectacle and pomp, all of it designed to dazzle the eye. Had poor Alek grown up in a place this fancy? It would be enough to drive you mad, having a million servants watching your every move.

The guards all made elaborate bows to the Kizlar Agha, murmuring the same greeting that Dr. Barlow had used.

"Is that Turkish for 'hello'?" Deryn whispered, wondering if she should learn the phrase.

"Arabic. Many languages are spoken here in the palace." Dr. Barlow glanced up at the steam pipes. "Let us hope that German is not one."

Soon they were led to a large marble building that

stood apart from the rest of the palace. Three blazing smokestacks thrust skyward from its roof, and the sound of grinding gears rumbled within.

The Kizlar Agha stopped before an archway sealed by two stone doors. "We enter the throne room of Sultan Mehmed V, Lord of the Horizons."

He clapped his hands three times, and the doors opened with a hiss of steam. A smell rolled out—burning coal and engine grease covered over with incense.

The throne room was dark after the brilliant sunlight outside, and Deryn could hardly see at first. But before her rose what seemed to be a giant sitting cross-legged, as large as the iron golems in the street the day before. It was a metal statue dressed in countless yards of black silk, a sash of silver cloth spread across its medaled chest, and a crimson fez the size of a bathtub on its strange horned head.

As her eyes adjusted, Deryn noticed a man beneath the statue. He was dressed in exactly the same clothes, and sat on his silk divan in the same position, cross-legged, his hands resting on his knees.

"Welcome, Dr. Barlow," he said, his right hand turning over to show an empty palm.

Behind him the statue stirred, mimicking his movements. It was an automaton—the whole throne room one huge mechanism! But the rumble of engines and gears was

"HEAD OF THE OTTOMAN EMPIRE: SULTAN AND CALIPH."

muffled to a whisper by thick tapestries and stone walls, so the huge statue seemed almost alive.

In the corner of Deryn's vision the lady boffin was curtsying smoothly, as if she met giant statues every day. Deryn recovered from her surprise and bowed from the waist, the way Alek always had when addressing the *Leviathan*'s officers. She realized she had no idea how to behave around a barking emperor, and wished the lady boffin had spared a moment to tell her.

"My Lord Sultan," Dr. Barlow said. "I bring you greetings from His Majesty, King George."

"Peace be upon him," the sultan said, bowing his head a little. Behind him the giant automaton followed in kind.

"I bring you a gift as well." Dr. Barlow gestured at the egg box.

The sultan's eyebrows rose. Deryn found herself relieved that the automaton didn't make facial expressions. The giant machine was uncanny enough as it was.

"An odd shape for a dreadnought," the sultan said. "And a bit small for a behemoth."

After a moment of uncomfortable silence, the lady boffin cleared her throat. "Our little gift is not, of course, a replacement for the *Osman* or its companion creature. Though His Majesty regrets that unfortunate affair."

"Does he?"

"Profusely," Dr. Barlow said. "We have only borrowed

the *Osman* because our need is greater. Britain is at war, and your empire is—and hopefully shall stay—at peace."

"Peace has its burdens too." The sultan crossed his arms, and the statue followed suit.

Watching more closely now, Deryn noticed that the machine's movements were a bit stiff, like a sailor caught with too much rum under his belt and trying to act sober. Perhaps to aid the illusion, the sultan moved slowly and carefully, like an actor in a pantomime show. Deryn wondered if he controlled the automaton himself, or whether there were engineers watching from some hidden cubbyhole, their hands scurrying across levers and dials.

Somehow, wondering about its inner workings made the huge contraption less unsettling.

"I am sure your cares are great, My Lord Sultan." Dr. Barlow looked toward the egg box. "And we hope that this fabricated creature, humble though it is, will prove a welcome distraction from them."

"The Germans give us railroads, airships, and wireless towers," the sultan replied. "All the glories of the *mekanzimat*. They train our armies and service our machines. They rebuilt this palace and helped us crush the revolution six years ago. And all your king can offer is a *distraction*?"

The sultan gestured at the egg box, and the automaton's hand stretched out across the room, stirring the air as it passed over Deryn's head. She hunched her shoulders, wondering how powerful those giant fingers were.

Dr. Barlow didn't seem ruffled at all. "Perhaps it is only a start," she said, bowing her head a little more. "But we offer this gift with hope for a happier future."

"A gift? After so many humiliations?" The sultan looked at the egg again. "Perhaps we have been distracted long enough by your gifts."

Suddenly the giant fingers wrapped around the box, closing into a fist. The crackle of splintering wood echoed from the stone walls, and pieces skittered like matchsticks across the floor. The egg burst with a sickening crack, and translucent strands oozed between the metal fingers. As they pooled together on the stone floor, the reek of sulfur joined coal smoke and incense.

A gasp of horror escaped the lady boffin's mouth, and Deryn stared, wide eyed, at the closed fist, then at the sultan. Oddly, the man seemed surprised himself, as if he hadn't realized what he was doing. Of course, *he* hadn't done anything—the automaton had.

Deryn looked at the sultan's outstretched hand. His fingers were still open, simply gesturing at the egg box, not curled into a fist. . . .

Her eyes darted around the room. The Kizlar Agha and the crewmen who had carried the egg box wore astonished expressions, and there was no one else in the room.

"A CRUSHED GIFT."

But then she spotted an upper gallery behind the statue's head. It was covered over with latticed windows, and for a moment Deryn thought she saw eyes peering down between the slats.

She glanced at Dr. Barlow, trying to get her to notice the sultan's open hand. But the lady boffin's face was pale and frozen, her poise shattered along with the egg.

"I see, Lord Sultan, that I have come too late." Despite her devastated expression, there was steel in her voice.

The sultan must have heard it too. He cleared his throat softly before speaking.

"Perhaps not, Dr. Barlow." He brought his palms together, but the automaton stayed motionless, its giant hand frozen around the shattered, leaking egg. "In a way the scales have already been balanced."

"How do you mean?"

"Just today we have been able to replace the dreadnought you 'borrowed' from us, with two ships instead of one." The sultan smiled. "May I present to you the new commander of the Ottoman navy, Admiral Wilhelm Souchon."

A man strode from the shadows, and Deryn's jaw dropped. He wore a crisp blue German naval uniform, except for the crimson fez on his head. He clicked his heels and bowed to the sultan, then turned to salute Dr. Barlow.

"Madam, I welcome you to Istanbul."

Deryn swallowed. So that was how the two German ironclads had disappeared—the Ottomans had hidden them, for the price of owning them! And they hadn't just taken the ships, they'd put the master of the *Goeben* in charge of their whole barking navy.

The lady boffin simply stared, dumbstruck for the first time Deryn had ever seen. The silence stretched out awkwardly, the only sound the last innards of the egg dripping onto the stone floor.

Finally Deryn cleared her throat and returned the German's salute.

"As ranking officer present, I extend the thanks of the British Air Service. For all your, um, hospitality."

Admiral Souchon looked coolly at her. "I don't believe we are acquainted, sir."

"Midshipman Dylan Sharp, at your service."

"A midshipman. I see." He turned back to Dr. Barlow and offered his hand. "Forgive me, madam, for the military formalities. I almost forgot you were a civilian. It is a pleasure to meet you. And how lucky that, thanks to my recent appointment, we do not meet as enemies."

The lady boffin extended her hand and let the admiral kiss it.

"Charmed, I'm sure." She slowly gathered herself, turning back to the sultan. "Two ironclads is indeed a most impressive gift. In fact, I am so moved by this German generosity that I must offer another gift on behalf of the British government."

"Really?" The sultan leaned forward. "And what would that be?"

"The *Leviathan*, Lord Sultan."

The room went silent again, and Deryn blinked. Had the lady boffin gone *completely barking mad*?

"It is the most famous of the great hydrogen breathers," Dr. Barlow continued. "As valuable as the *Osman* and its companion put together, and a creation that your German friends could never match."

The sultan looked quite pleased, and Deryn noticed that Admiral Souchon's smile had frozen on his face. She herself was dizzy, unable to believe what the lady boffin was saying.

"Dr. Barlow," she spoke up. "It is, of course, customary to check with the captain before, um . . . giving away his ship."

"Ah, of course." Dr. Barlow waved her hand. "Thank you for reminding me, Mr. Sharp. We shall require a few days to communicate with the Admiralty, Lord Sultan, before effecting this transfer."

"That is unfortunate, Dr. Barlow," Admiral Souchon said, putting a hand on the hilt of his sword. "The limit for harboring a combatant ship in wartime is twenty-four hours. International law is very strict on this matter."

"May I remind you, Admiral," the sultan said mildly, "that your own grace period was extended while negotiations took place?"

The German opened his mouth, then closed it and bowed, low. "Of course, My Lord Sultan. I am at your command."

Leaning back on his divan, the sultan smiled and folded his hands. Without the automaton mimicking him, Deryn noticed that he moved more fluidly. Or perhaps he was simply enjoying pitting two great powers against each other.

"Then we are all agreed," he said. "Dr. Barlow, you have four days to get me the *Leviathan*."

Thirty minutes later the *Stamboul* rose into the air again. As it passed over the shimmering strait in a slow turn back toward the airfield, the Kizlar Agha joined Deryn and Dr. Barlow at the railing, his face pale.

"I do not know what to say, madam. My Lord Sultan was not himself today."

"He seemed firm enough in his convictions," Dr. Barlow said, her voice still quavering from shock.

"Indeed. But he has not been the same since moving back into the palace. The Germans have changed so much there. Not all of us approve."

Deryn frowned, wanting to mention what she'd noticed

about the automaton. But she couldn't in front of the sultan's closest adviser.

The mechanical owl still perched on the Kizlar Agha's shoulder, but she noticed that the cylinder on its chest was no longer spinning. Perhaps it was some sort of recording machine, and the man had switched it off to keep his words a secret.

"Are you saying that he may change his mind about the kaiser's gifts?" Dr. Barlow asked carefully.

The Kizlar Agha spread his hands. "That, I do not know, madam. But our empire has fought two wars in the last ten years, and a bloody revolution as well. Not all of us want to join this madness in Europe."

Dr. Barlow nodded. "Pray, then, make yourselves heard."

"We shall try. Peace be upon you, and upon us all," he said, then bowed and returned to the prow of the airship.

"How interesting," the lady boffin said as he walked away. "Perhaps there is still hope for this country."

"What did he mean exactly?" Deryn asked.

"Perhaps he plans to give his emperor good advice." She shrugged. "Or perhaps something more. Sultans have been replaced before."

Deryn turned back to the railing, and suddenly there they were below—the *Goeben* and the *Breslau* harbored in the Golden Horn.

"The admiral wasn't lying," she said, seeing crimson

Ottoman flags fluttering from the ironclads' mainmasts. "They must have been hiding up in the Black Sea yesterday."

"I should have known," Dr. Barlow said. "Those ships were trapped, worthless to the Germans. So why not offer them as bribes?"

"Aye, and speaking of bribes . . ." Deryn swallowed, almost afraid to ask. "What was that about giving the *Leviathan* away? You haven't gone barking mad, have you?"

Dr. Barlow gave her a sidelong glance. "Don't be tiresome, Mr. Sharp. That was merely a ploy to extend our time here. Which of course you knew, as you played your part to perfection. Another four days may prove quite useful."

Deryn frowned. Played her part? She'd only said the first thing that had come into her head. "But if we're not going to give the Ottomans the ship, what's the point of staying?"

"Really, Mr. Sharp," the lady boffin said, the steel returning to her voice. "Do you suppose I would journey across Europe without an alternate plan?"

"And *this* is your plan, ma'am? Making false promises to the sultan to make him even angrier?"

"Hardly." The lady boffin sighed. "I doubt the sultan's anger will make much difference, one way or the other. The Ottoman Empire is already in the Germans' hands."

"Aye, that's true enough," Deryn said. "And speaking of hands, I'm not sure that the sultan really meant to crush that egg."

Dr. Barlow turned a cold gaze on Deryn. "Are you saying that my life's work was destroyed *by accident?*"

"Not by accident, ma'am. But the sultan didn't make a fist. He was just pointing at the egg, and then the automaton went and squashed your poor beastie, all on its own!"

Dr. Barlow was silent for a moment, then slowly nodded. "Of course. I'm an idiot! That throne room was built by German engineers, so *they* were in control, not the sultan. They forced his hand, so to speak."

"Aye." Deryn stared back at the water. The *Stamboul* had completed its turn, and the *Goeben* was receding into the distance. But she could still see the forbidding shape of the Tesla cannon, its struts covered with fluttering seabirds. "Makes you wonder how they'll force the sultan's hand next, doesn't it?"

"Indeed, Mr. Sharp."

Deryn looked at the water stretching into the distance. The Royal Navy's Mediterranean fleet was stationed just south of the strait, still waiting for the *Goeben* and *Breslau* to emerge. And in the opposite direction, the Russian navy sat in its Black Sea ports, not yet aware that their old enemy the sultan had two new ironclads.

All it would take was a quick sortie by Admiral Souchon in either direction, and the Ottomans would be dragged into war.

NINETEEN

"It's probably foolish, leaving the hotel with so many Germans about."

There was no reply as Alek buttoned the jacket of his new suit.

"But the Germans don't know what I look like," he continued. "And the Ottomans don't even know we're here."

Alek put on the fez and stared at himself in the mirror, waiting. But again no reply came.

"Anyone would think I was a proper Turk in these clothes." Alek flicked at the fez's tassel. Was it meant to hang on the left or the right? "And if I have to speak German, at least I've been practicing my common accent, so I don't sound like such a prince anymore."

"Such a prince," the creature finally said.

"Well, that's your opinion," Alek said, then sighed.

How had he gotten into this habit of talking to the beast? The animal was probably memorizing all his secrets.

It was better than sharing his doubts with the men, he supposed. And there was something about the creature's wise, contented expression that made Alek feel as if it really were listening, not just repeating words at random.

Alek checked himself in the mirror one last time, then turned toward the door.

"Be a good little beastie, and Master Klopp will come and feed you. No whining. I'll be back soon."

The creature gave him a long, hard look, then seemed to nod.

"Be back soon," it said.

Corporal Bauer was dressed in his new civilian clothes and was waiting in the room he shared with Klopp. The master of mechaniks himself couldn't leave the hotel. He was too well known among the Clanker technical class, and Constantinople was full of German engineers.

On their way into the city the night before, Alek had counted a dozen construction projects flying a black eagle on a yellow pennant, the kaiser's flag of friendship. The ancient walls of the city bristled with shiny new smoke-stacks, steam pipes, and wireless antennae. Alek remembered his father talking about Germany sponsoring this policy of *mekanzimat*, the reformation of Ottoman society around the machine.

"I still say this is a bad idea, young master," Klopp said, turning away from the wireless and a pad full of dots and dashes.

"No one will recognize me," Alek said. "My father was very careful to not let me sit for portraits or photographs. Hardly anyone outside my family knows what I look like."

"But remember what happened in Lienz!"

Alek drew a slow breath, remembering the first time he'd been in disguise among commoners. "Yes, Klopp, I acted exactly like a little prince. But I think my common touch has improved since then, don't you?"

Klopp only shrugged.

"And if we're going to hide in the Ottoman Empire," Alek continued, "we need to know what the great powers are up to here. I'm the only one of us who can speak anything besides German."

The old man held his gaze for a moment, then looked away. "I can't argue with your logic, young master. I just wish it weren't *you* going."

"I wish Volger were here too," Alek said softly. "But I'll be taken good care of. Right, Bauer?"

"At your service, sir," Bauer said.

"Indeed," Alek said. "But that reminds me, no *sirs* while we're outside this room."

"Yes, sir. That is, um . . . What should I call you, sir?"

Alek smiled. "Well, no one who hears us talking will think we're Turkish, so let's pick a good German name. How about Hans?"

"But that's *my* name, sir."

"Ah, yes, of course." Alek cleared his throat, wondering if he'd ever known Corporal Bauer's first name. Perhaps he should have asked before now. "I'll be Fritz, then."

"Yes, sir. I mean—yes, Fritz," Bauer said, and Alek saw that Klopp was slowly shaking his head.

So much for the common touch.

The hotel was near the Grand Bazaar, the largest market in Constantinople, and the streets were full tonight. Alek and Bauer followed the crowds, looking for a place where German workers might congregate and gossip.

Soon they were inside the bazaar, a gaslit labyrinth of shops under high arched ceilings. The owners cried their wares—lamps, linens, carpets, silks, jewelry, tooled leather, and machine parts—in half a dozen languages. Mechanikal donkeys pushed their way through the crowds, chestnuts and skewers of meat roasting on their steaming engine blocks. Veiled women rode on sedan chairs with silent clockwork legs, wary servants walking on either side.

Alek remembered his first time disguised as a commoner, in the market at Lienz, when the press of bodies and smells had sickened him. But the Grand Bazaar was almost otherworldly, the scents of cumin, paprika, and rose water mixing with the bitter pall of tobacco coiling up from burbling water pipes. Jugglers jostled for space with fortune-tellers and musicians, while tiny clockwork walkers danced on a blanket spread out before a cross-legged man, the crowd clapping with appreciation.

The man at the hotel desk had said this was a holy month, and that the Muslims of the city would be fasting while the sun was up. They seemed to be making up for it now that night had fallen.

"Not many Germans about," Bauer said. "Do you suppose they have a beer hall in this city?"

"I don't know if the Ottomans have a love for beer." Alek gestured to a boy carrying a small tray with empty glass cups. "But coffee is another matter."

He stopped the boy and pointed at the tray. The boy nodded and waved for them to follow, skipping deftly through the crowds, waiting impatiently for Bauer and Alek to catch up.

The boy soon brought them to a large public room on the edge of the market. The smell of chocolate-tinged coffee and black tea spilled out of its doors, and tobacco smoke hung in a pall across the ceiling.

As Alek tipped the boy for his trouble, Bauer said, "Looks like we've found the right place, sir."

Alek looked up. A row of the kaiser's friendship flags fluttered along the awning, and a German drinking song was rumbling along inside.

"That boy spotted us as Clankers right off." Alek sighed. "Watch your step, and no more *sirs*. Remember, Hans?"

"Sorry . . . Fritz."

Alek hesitated at the door, the sound of so many German accents sending a shiver through him. Of course, the kaiser's airships had found him even hidden on a mountain peak in the Alps. Perhaps it was safer to keep one's enemies in sight.

He squared his shoulders and strode in.

Most of the men inside appeared to be German engineers. Some still wore their mechaniks' coveralls, shiny with grease from the day's work. Alek felt out of place in his new Turkish clothes.

He and Bauer found an empty table, then ordered coffee from a young turbaned boy who spoke excellent German.

As the boy darted away, Alek shook his head. "Whether the Ottomans join the war or not, the Germans are already running this country."

"And you can see why." Bauer pointed to the wall behind them.

Alek turned to see a large poster tacked to the wall, the

sort of crude propaganda his father had always hated. At the bottom was a cartoon city labeled Istanbul, festooned with steam pipes and train tracks. The city sat astride The Straits, with the Russian bear looming over the Black Sea and the British navy threatening from the Mediterranean.

Dominating the poster was a giant chimera striding over the horizon, a Darwinist beast fabricated from half a dozen creatures. It wore a misshapen bowler hat, and carried a dreadnought in one clawed hand and a sack of money in the other. A tiny fat man labeled Winston Churchill rode on its shoulder, watching as the obscene beast menaced the tiny spires and domes below.

"Who will protect us from these monsters?" read the legend across the top.

"That must be the *Osman*," Bauer said, gesturing at the dreadnought.

Alek nodded. "It's odd to think, but if it weren't for Lord Churchill stealing that ship, the *Leviathan* would never have headed across Europe. We'd still be in that castle in the Alps."

"We might be a bit safer there," said Bauer. Then he smiled. "But a lot colder, too, and no one would be bringing us good Turkish coffee."

"So you think I made the right choice, Hans? Leaving safety behind?"

"You didn't have much of a choice, sir—I mean, Fritz."

Bauer shrugged. "You had to face what was in front of you, whatever your father's plans. Every man arrives at that point, sooner or later."

Alek swallowed, grateful for the words. He'd never asked Bauer's opinion before, but now that he was in command, it was good to know that the man didn't think he was a complete idiot.

"What about your father, Hans? He must think you're a deserter."

"My parents sent me off a long time ago." The man shook his head. "Too many mouths to feed at home. It was the same with Hoffman, I think. Your father only chose men without families to help you."

"That was kind of him, I suppose," Alek said, struck by the thought that he and his men were, in a way, all orphans together. "But once this war is over, Hans, I swear you'll never go hungry again."

"No need, Fritz. This is duty. And besides, one could hardly go hungry in this city."

The coffee arrived, smelling of chocolate and as thick as black honey. It certainly tasted better than anything that could have been cooked up over a fire in the freezing Alps.

Alek took a long drink, letting the rich flavors sweep away his dark thoughts. He eavesdropped on the surrounding tables, hearing complaints of delayed shipments of parts, and censored letters from home. The conquest of

"COFFEE IN A DEN OF SNAKES."

Belgium was almost complete, and the engineers were celebrating. France would fall soon after. Then would come a quick campaign against Darwinist Russia and the island fortress of Britain. Or it might be a long war, some argued, but Germany would prevail eventually—fabricated beasts were no match for Clanker bravery and steel.

It didn't sound as though anyone cared if the Ottomans joined the war or not. The Germans were confident in themselves and their Austrian allies.

Of course, the high command might have a different view.

Suddenly Alek's ears caught the sound of English. He turned and saw a man moving slowly among the tables, asking questions that drew only shrugs and uncomprehending stares. The man was scruffily dressed in a traveling coat and a shapeless hat, with a folding camera strapped around his neck. Some sort of fabricated beast rode on his shoulder—a frog, perhaps, its beady eyes peering out from beneath the man's jacket collar.

A Darwinist, here, in what was practically German territory?

"Pardon me, gentlemen," he said when he reached Alek's table. "But do either of you speak any English?"

Alek hesitated. The man's accent was unfamiliar, and he didn't look British. His camera seemed to be a Clanker design.

"I do, a little," Alek said.

The man's face broke into a broad smile as he thrust out his hand. "Excellent! I'm Eddie Malone, reporter for the *New York World*. Do you mind if I ask some questions?"

· TWENTY ·

The man sat down without waiting for an answer, snapping for a waiter and ordering coffee.

"Did he say *reporter*?" Bauer muttered in German. "Is this wise, Fritz?"

Alek nodded—this was the perfect opportunity. The job of a foreign reporter, after all, was to understand the politics around him, the maneuverings of the great powers here in the Ottoman Empire. And talking to Malone was much safer than trying to extract gossip from a German, who might notice Alek's aristocratic accent.

A few men at the other tables had glanced at the reporter as he'd sat down, but no one was staring now. The streets of Constantinople were full of stranger sights than a fabricated frog.

"I don't know how much we can help you," Alek said. "We haven't been here very long."

"Don't worry. My questions won't be too tricky." The reporter pulled out a battered notebook. "I'm just curious about what they call the *mekanzimat*—all the new buildings the Germans are putting up in Istanbul. Are you here to work on something?"

Alek cleared his throat. The man had assumed they were Germans, of course. He probably couldn't tell an Austrian accent from the croak of his own bullfrog. But there was no point in correcting him. "We aren't in construction, Mr. Malone. At the moment we're just traveling. Seeing the sights."

Malone's eyes scanned Alek up and down, coming to a halt on the fez on the chair beside him. "I can see you've been shopping already. Funny thing, though. Men of military age, on a vacation in wartime!"

Alek swore silently. He'd always been hopeless at any sort of lying, but pretending to be a tourist was absurd when every man in Europe was reporting for duty. Malone probably thought they were deserters, or spies.

Of course, a certain amount of mystery might be useful.

"Let's just say you needn't know our names." Alek gestured at the camera. "And no photographs, if you please."

"No problem. Istanbul is full of anonymous people." The man reached up to scratch his bullfrog's chin. "I suppose you came in on the Express?"

Alek nodded. The Orient-Express ran straight from Munich to Constantinople, and he could hardly admit they'd arrived by airship.

"Must've been crowded, with all the new workers coming in."

"The train might have been crowded, but we had our own cabin." As the words came out, Alek cursed himself again. Why did he always find ways to make it obvious that he was wealthy?

"So you didn't talk to any of the folks working on that wireless tower, did you?"

"Wireless tower?" Alek asked.

"Yep. The one you Germans are building on the cliffs out to the west. A special project for the sultan, they say. It's huge—has its own power station!"

Alek glanced at Bauer, wondering how much the man was following with the English he'd picked up aboard the *Leviathan*. A large wireless tower might need its own power station, but so would a Tesla cannon.

"I'm afraid we don't know anything about that," Alek said. "We've only been in Constantinople for two days."

Malone looked at him closely for a moment, a gleam in his eye, as if Alek had just told a subtle but clever joke. "Not long enough to start calling it Istanbul, I see."

Alek remembered Dr. Barlow saying that the locals used another name for their city, but the staff at his hotel hadn't seemed to mind. "Whatever the city's called, we haven't seen much of it."

"So you haven't been down to the docks yet to see the sultan's new warships?"

"New warships?"

"Two ironclads, just handed to the Ottomans by the Germans." Malone's eyes narrowed. "You haven't seen them? They're pretty hard to miss."

Alek managed to shake his head. "No, we haven't been to the harbor at all."

"Haven't been to the *harbor*? This is a peninsula, you know. And doesn't the Orient-Express come in right along the water?"

"I suppose," Alek said stiffly. "But we were quite tired when we arrived, and it was a dark night."

The man looked amused again—this was hopeless. Next, Malone would tell him that the moon was full, or that the Orient-Express never arrived at night.

But what did it matter? He didn't believe a word Alek was saying anyway. Perhaps it was time to change the subject.

"It's odd, seeing that creature here," Alek said, pointing at the bullfrog. "I didn't know the Ottomans allowed Darwinist abominations in their country."

"Oh, you just have to know who to bribe." The man laughed. "And I wouldn't go anywhere without Rusty. He's got a much better memory than me."

Alek's eyes widened. "He . . . remembers things?"

"Sure. Ever seen one of those message lizards?"

"I've heard of them."

"Well, Rusty is a close relation. Except he's all brain and no hop." The man patted the bullfrog on its head, and the beady eyes blinked. "He can listen to an hour's worth of conversation and repeat it back to you, word for word."

Alek frowned, wondering if the newborn creature back at the hotel was some sort of recording beast. "Is this animal memorizing what we're saying right now?"

The reporter shrugged. "In as much as you're saying anything at all."

"As I said, we've just arrived."

"Well, at least your English is easy on the ears." The man laughed again. "It's like you've been practicing up, just for me."

"You're too kind," Alek said. For the past two weeks, of course, he'd spoken more English than German. "And you have a sharp ear. Do you mind if I ask *you* some questions?"

"Sure. Why not?" The reporter licked his pen.

"Do you think the Ottomans will join the Clankers in this war?"

Malone shrugged again. "I doubt the Germans care, one way or the other. They're here for the long term. Defeat the Darwinists in Europe, then expand across the whole world. They're already extending the Express to Baghdad."

Alek had heard his father say the same, that the Orient-Express had been built to spread Clanker influence into the Middle East, and then deeper into the heart of Asia.

Malone gestured up at the propaganda poster behind Alek. "All they want now is for the Ottomans to close the Dardanelles, so the Russians can't ship food in from the south."

"It's easier to starve a man than to fight him," Alek said. "But can the Ottomans hold the strait against the British navy?"

"Surface ships can't make it past the mines and the cannon, and they have nets to keep the krakens out. That's everything but airships, and the Ottomans may get one of those soon."

"Pardon me?"

Malone's face brightened. "That's a sight you'll definitely want to see. The *Leviathan*, one of the great hydrogen breathers, is here in Istanbul."

"It's still . . . I mean, there's a British airship here? Isn't that a bit odd, with a war going on?"

"I'll say it is. And what's odder still, the British are thinking of *giving* it to the sultan!" Malone shook his head. "Seems the Germans donated a pair of ironclads to the Ottomans, and the British want to up the ante. The sultan himself will be taking a joyride tomorrow, along with some of us reporters."

Alek was almost too stunned to speak. That the *Leviathan* might be handed over to a Clanker power was absurd. But if the airship hadn't left yet, then Count Volger was still in Istanbul.

"Are you going on this . . . joyride?"

Malone beamed. "Wouldn't miss it for the world. We've got hydrogen breathers in the U.S., but nothing half that big. Just watch the skies tomorrow, and you'll see what I mean!"

Alek stared hard at the man. If he was right about the *Leviathan*, then Volger might have another chance to escape. Of course, Volger thought that Alek and the others had already disappeared into the wilds.

It was madness to trust this strange American, but Alek had to take the chance. "Perhaps you could do something for me," he said quietly. "There's a message I want delivered to that ship."

Malone's eyebrows rose. "Sounds interesting."

"But you can't put any of this in your newspaper."

"I can't promise that. But remember, my paper's way off in New York City, and I use messenger terns to file my stories. Anything I write will take four days to get back to New York, and it'll take another day or so for the news to find its way back here. See what I mean?"

Alek nodded. If Volger really could escape, five days would be plenty of time for them to disappear.

"All right, then." Alek took a slow breath. "There's a man aboard the *Leviathan*, a prisoner."

Malone's scribbling pen came to a halt. "A German fellow, I presume?"

"No. Austrian. His name is . . ."

Alek's voice faded—the gaslights were suddenly sputtering around them, the room plunging into darkness.

"What's happening?" Bauer hissed.

Malone held up a hand. "Don't worry. It's just a shadow play."

The coffeehouse went silent, and soon the back wall was flickering to life. Alek realized that it wasn't a wall at all but a thin screen of paper with powerful gaslights burning behind it.

Dark forms came into focus on the paper screen, shadows in the shapes of monsters and men.

Alek's eyes widened. One of his aunts in Prague had collected shadow puppets from Indonesia, leather creations with moving arms and legs, like marionettes with sticks instead of strings. But the shadows here danced in perfect clockwork patterns. They were Clanker puppets, moved not by hand but by machines concealed behind the wall.

The hidden actors spoke in what sounded like Turkish, but the story was easy enough to understand. Across the bottom of the screen, waves rose and fell, and a sea creature bounded among them, a Darwinist monster with flailing tentacles and huge teeth. It approached a ship where two men stood on deck talking, unaware of the kraken coming for them. Alek caught the name Churchill among the unfamiliar words.

Then suddenly the creature leapt from the waves, snatching one of the men and dragging him into the water. Oddly, the other man only laughed. . . .

Alek jumped as someone squeezed his arm. It was Bauer, who nodded at a pair of German soldiers making their way through the coffeehouse. The two were going from table to table, checking faces against a photograph in their hands.

"We should go, Fritz," Bauer whispered.

"They're here for someone else," Alek said firmly. No photograph of him had ever been taken.

Malone had noticed their nervous glances, and turned to look at the German soldiers. He leaned forward to whisper, "If you two are busy, perhaps we should meet tomorrow. Noon, at the gateway to the Blue Mosque?"

Alek began to explain that there was no need to leave, but then one of the soldiers stiffened. He glanced down at the photograph in his hands, then up at Alek.

"Impossible," Alek breathed. Then he realized that the soldier wasn't looking at him after all.

He was looking at Bauer.

· TWENTY-ONE ·

"I'm a fool," Alek whispered to himself.

The Germans had, of course, investigated the other men who'd disappeared the night he'd run away. Bauer, Hoffman, and Klopp were all Hapsburg House Guards, with photographs in their military files. But somehow Alek had forgotten that commoners could be hunted too.

He looked frantically around the room. Two more German soldiers stood at the door, and the coffeehouse had no other exits. The soldiers who'd noticed Bauer were talking to each other intently, one glancing at their table.

Malone leaned back in his chair and casually said, "There's a door to the alley in the back."

Alek looked—the back wall was entirely covered by the glowing screen, but it was made of paper.

"Hans, do you have a knife?" Alek asked softly.

Bauer nodded, reaching into his jacket. "Don't worry, sir. I'll keep them busy while you run."

"No, Hans. We're escaping together. Give the knife to me, then follow."

Bauer frowned, but handed over the weapon. The two German soldiers were signaling to their compatriots at the door. It was time to move.

"Noon tomorrow at the Blue Mosque," Alek said, reaching for his fez . . .

He leapt to his feet and ran through the tables toward the glowing screen.

The bright expanse of paper parted with a swift stroke of the knife, revealing whirling gears and gaslights behind. Half blinded, Alek crashed through silhouettes of ocean waves, stumbling against a large, humming contraption. His hand banged against one of the hissing gaslights, which burned like a branding iron against his hand. The light crashed to the ground, spilling naked flames and shards of glass across the floor.

Shouts exploded from behind them, the crowd panicking at the smell of burning gas and paper. Alek heard one of the soldiers yelling at the customers to let him through.

"The door, sir!" Bauer cried. Alek could see nothing but the spots burned into his vision, but Bauer dragged him along, their boots skidding on machinery and broken glass.

"A SLASHING AND ESCAPE."

The door crashed open onto darkness, the night air blessedly cool on Alek's burned palm. He followed Bauer, trying to blink away spots as he ran.

The alley was like a miniature version of the Grand Bazaar, lined with market stalls the size of closets, and crowded with small tables piled with pistachios, walnuts, and fruit. Surprised faces looked up at Alek and Bauer as they ran past.

Alek heard the slam of the door bursting open behind them. Then a gunshot boomed through the alley, and dust sprayed from the ancient stones beside his head.

"This way, sir!" Bauer cried, dragging him around a corner. People were scattering now, the alley turning into a tumult of men and overturned tables. Shutters flew open overhead, and cries in a dozen languages echoed from the walls.

Another shot shook the air around them, and Alek followed Bauer into a side passageway between two buildings. It was narrow and empty, and their boots slapped through a runnel of drainage that ran down its middle. They had to duck beneath low stone arches as they ran.

The alley didn't lead back to the Grand Bazaar, or to an open street—it seemed to wind around itself, following the hissing spirals of steam pipes and wiring conduits. Only the barest hint of moonlight made its way down to the paving stones, and soon Alek had lost all sense of direction.

The walls here were chalked with a tangle of words and symbols—Alek saw the Arabic, Greek, and Hebrew alphabets mixed together, along with signs he didn't recognize. It felt as though he and Bauer had stumbled into an older city hidden inside the first, Istanbul before the Germans had widened its boulevards and filled them with polished steel machines.

As they turned a corner, Bauer pulled Alek to a halt.

Above them loomed a walker, six stories high. Its body was long and sinuous, like a snake rearing up, a pair of arms jutting out from its sides. The front of the pilot's cabin looked like a woman's face, which seemed to be staring down at them, absolutely still.

"Volger told us about these," Alek whispered. "Iron golems. They keep the peace among the different ghettos."

"It looks empty," Bauer said nervously. "And the engines aren't running."

"Perhaps it's only for show. It doesn't even have guns."

There was something magnificent about the walker, though, as if they were staring up at a statue of some ancient pagan goddess. The expression of the giant face seemed to hint at a smile.

Shouts came from the distance, and Alek tore his eyes from the machine.

"We could break in somewhere and hide," Bauer said, pointing at a low doorway in the alley wall, an iron-grilled window at its center.

Alek hesitated. Crashing into a strange house would only stir up more trouble, especially if the owners of the motionless walker were about.

The shriek of whistles echoed around them, as if pursuers were closing in from every direction. . . .

Almost every direction.

Alek looked up at the steam pipes climbing the stone walls. They sweated and trembled with heat, but he dashed down the alley, testing them until he found an old tangle of pipes that was cold to the touch.

He thrust the knife into his belt. "Let's try for the rooftops."

Bauer gave the pipes a shake, and brick dust floated down from the rusty bolts. "I'll go first, sir, in case it breaks off."

"If that happens, Hans, I suspect we'll both be in trouble, but be my guest."

Bauer took a firm grip and pulled himself up.

Alek followed. His boots found steady purchase on the rough stone wall, and the rusty pipes were good handholds. But halfway up his burned palm began to complain, throbbing as though a splinter of flame were trapped beneath the skin. He let go with that hand and shook it, trying to put out the fire coursing through his nerves.

"Not much farther, sir," Bauer said. "There's a rain gutter just above me."

"I hope there's some rain in it," Alek muttered, still waving his hand. "I'd kill for a bucket of cold water."

His right boot skidded a few centimeters, and Alek grabbed the pipes with both hands again. Better a little agony than a long fall onto paving stones.

Soon Bauer had hauled himself over the edge and out of sight. But as Alek reached up for the gutter, shouts came from below.

He pulled himself closer to the wall, and froze.

A group of soldiers was running down the alley, wearing German gray. One called out, and they came to a ragged halt directly beneath Alek. The man who'd shouted knelt, lifting something from the ground.

Alek softly swore. Bauer's knife had fallen from his belt.

It was Hapsburg Guard issue, the hilt marked with Alek's family crest. If the Germans had been wondering whether he was here in Istanbul or not, this would remove all doubt.

The men stood there talking, but none of them paid any notice to the steam pipes climbing the wall beside them. The officer was pointing in all directions, splitting up his men.

Go away! Alek pleaded silently. Hanging there motionless was a hundred times harder than climbing. His burned hand was cramping, and the week-old injury in his ribs was pulsing with his heartbeat.

Finally the last man had passed out of sight, and Alek reached out and grabbed the rain gutter. But as he hauled himself up, metal groaned, and the gutter pulled itself from the stone with a series of *pops*.

Alek felt a sickening lurch downward, the rusted bolts spitting out into his face. The gutter held for another moment, but he could feel it twisting in his hands.

"Sir!" Bauer reached out from the rooftop, trying to grab Alek's wrists, but the gutter had pulled too far away from the wall.

Alek kicked out, trying to swing himself closer, but the movement only tore more bolts from the wall.

"The walker!" Bauer cried.

Alek realized that a huge shadow was moving beneath him, steam huffing from its joints into the cool night air. One of the great claws was reaching out. . . .

He fell, dropping into the giant metal hand. The impact knocked the breath from him, sending pain shooting through his sore ribs. He skidded for a moment, the buttons of his tunic snapping against steel, but the claw closed into a huge bowl around him.

He looked up—the arm was still moving, carrying him closer to the walker. Its face was splitting open, like a viewport cranking wider and wider. A moment later the pilot's cabin was exposed.

There were three men inside. Two stood leaning over

the edge, peering down at the alley, pistols gripped tightly in their hands. The third sat at the walker's controls, a curious look on his face.

Clouds of steam swirled around them, puffing from the joints of the machine. Alek realized that its engines were still silent; it had used stored pneumatic pressure to spring to life.

"You speak German," the man at the controls said. "And yet the Germans are chasing you. How interesting."

"We're not Germans," Alek answered. "We're Austrian."

The man frowned. "But still Clankers. Are you deserters?"

Alek shook his head. His allegiances might have been tangled lately, but he was no deserter. "May I ask who *you* are, sir?"

The man smiled and worked at the controls. "I'm the fellow who just saved you from falling to your death."

"Sir, should I . . . ," came Bauer's voice from the rooftop, but Alek waved him silent.

The giant hand drew closer to the walker's head, and opened flat. As Alek rose to his feet, one of the other two men said something in a language he didn't recognize. It sounded more like Italian than the Turkish he'd heard on the streets today. It also sounded unfriendly.

The first man laughed. "My friend wants to throw you back, because he thinks you're Germans. Perhaps we should pick another language."

Alek raised an eyebrow. "By all means. Do you speak English?"

"Exceedingly well." The man switched effortlessly. "I studied at Oxford, you know."

"Well, then. My name is Aleksandar." Alek bowed a little, then pointed up at the rooftop, where Bauer was staring down, wide eyed. "And this is Hans, but I'm afraid he has no English."

"I am Zaven." The man waved a hand dismissively at the others. "These two barbarians speak nothing by Romanian and Turkish. Ignore them. But I can see you are an educated gentleman."

"Thank you for saving me, sir. And for not . . . throwing me back."

"Well, you can't be all bad, if the Germans are chasing you." Zaven's eyes twinkled. "Did you do something to annoy them?"

"I suppose so." Alek took a slow breath, choosing his words carefully. "They've been hunting me since before the war started. They had issues with my father."

"Aha! A second-generation rebel, as am I!"

Alek looked at the others. "So that's what you three are? Revolutionaries?"

"We are more than three, sir. There are thousands of us!" Zaven snapped upright in his piloting chair and saluted. "We are the Committee for Union and Progress."

Alek nodded. He remembered the name from six years before, when the rebellion had demanded a return to elected government. But the Germans had stepped in to crush them, keeping the sultan in charge.

"So you were part of the Young Turks' rebellion?"

"Young Turks? Fah!" Zaven spat into the alley below. "We split off from those cretins years ago. They think that only Turks are true Ottomans. But as you can see, the Committee takes in all kinds." He gestured at the other two men. "My friends are Vlachs, I am Armenian, and we have Kurds, Arabs, and Jews among us. And plenty of Turks, of course!" He laughed.

Alek nodded slowly, remembering the chalk scratchings in the passageways below, some sort of code assembled from the empire's jumble of tongues.

And all of them fighting the Germans—together.

For a moment Alek felt unsteady on the giant metal hand. Perhaps it was just an echo of his near fall, but his heart was racing again.

These men were allies. At last, here was a chance to do more than simply run and hide, a way to strike back at the powers that had murdered his parents.

"Mr. Zaven," Alek said, "I think you and I are going to be friends."

TWENTY-TWO

"Get out, you barking horrible spice!" Deryn yelled, then sneezed for the hundredth time that day. The sultan and his entourage would be aboard in an hour, and the whole crew was due in full-dress uniform in half that time. But no matter how hard she scrubbed, the red stain in her shirt wouldn't budge.

She was well and truly stuffed.

A yip came from the door of her cabin, and Deryn turned to see Tazza bouncing happily on his hind legs, a fresh bone in his mouth. That was one benefit of Dr. Barlow's mad scheme of pretending to give the *Leviathan* away—the beasties were eating better. Over the last two days the crew had made more trips to the markets and smithies of Istanbul, trading the airship's ambergris for food and parts. Except for Deryn's uniform, the ship was fit to receive a foreign emperor, which it shortly would.

The lady boffin appeared, right behind her thylacine. She'd managed to dig another dazzling dress out of her luggage, and a hat with abundant ostrich feathers that matched her long white gloves. Even Tazza was wearing a fancy collar, a band of diamonds glittering around his neck.

"Mr. Sharp," she said, and tutted. "Once more I find you in a state of disrepair."

Deryn held up her dress shirt. "Sorry, ma'am. But this is ruined, and I haven't got another!"

"Well, it's lucky you won't be serving the sultan this evening. Mr. Newkirk will be stepping in for you."

"But the whole crew is meant to be in full dress!"

"Not those with more important matters to contend with." Dr. Barlow handed over the thylacine's leash. "After you walk Tazza, please join me and the captain in the navigation room. I think you'll find our conversation interesting."

Tazza tried to pull her out the door, but Deryn stood firm. "Pardon me, ma'am. The barking *captain* wants to see me? Is this about your alternate plan for the Ottomans?"

The lady boffin smiled coolly. "Partly. But it also concerns your recent behavior. If I were you, I wouldn't dawdle on your way there."

The navigation room was at the bow of the ship, just below the bridge. It was a small, quiet cabin where the captain sometimes retreated to think, or to have an awkward conversation with a wayward crewman.

Deryn felt her stomach tighten as she drew near. What if the officers had noticed her fencing lessons with Count Volger? Whenever Deryn brought him a meal, she stayed for twenty minutes or so, practicing swordplay with mop handles.

But the captain himself wouldn't issue a reprimand for mere dawdling, would he? Unless he also knew that she'd been supplying Volger with newspapers, and had even told him about Admiral Souchon and the *Goeben*. Or how she'd looked the other way while the Clankers had been planning to escape!

But when the lady boffin had announced this meeting, she'd been *smiling*. . . .

The late afternoon sun was slanting in through the windows that curved around the navigation room. Dr. Barlow and the captain were already there, along with the bosun and Dr. Busk, the officers all in resplendent dress uniforms for the sultan's visit.

Deryn frowned. If she was about to receive a reprimand, why in blazes was the ship's head boffin here?

When she clicked her heels, the four of them clammed up quickly, like children caught telling secrets.

"Ah, Mr. Sharp, glad you could join us," Captain Hobbes said. "We need to discuss your recent exploits."

"Um . . . my exploits, sir?"

The captain raised a dispatch. "I have communicated with the Admiralty about the matter, and they concur with my recommendations."

"The Admiralty, sir?" Deryn managed. If the Admiralty was involved, this had to be a hanging offense! She looked at Dr. Barlow, racking her brain for what had given her treason away.

"Don't look so surprised, Mr. Sharp," the bosun said. "Even in all the recent ruckus, your rescue of Mr. Newkirk has not been forgotten."

The rest of them broke into broad smiles, but Deryn's brain ground to a halt.

"Pardon me, sir?"

"I wish we had time to do this properly," Captain Hobbes said, "but other duties await."

He lifted a velvet jewelry case from the map table, opened it, and produced a rounded silver cross that dangled from a sky blue ribbon. The face of Charles Darwin was engraved upon its center, the Air Service wings at its top.

Deryn stared at it, wondering what the captain was doing with her father's medal, and how it had got so shiny and new. . . .

"Midshipman Dylan Sharp," the captain began, "I hereby award you the Air Gallantry Cross for your brave and selfless actions of August 10, wherein you saved the life of a fellow

[230]

crewman at great risk to your own. Congratulations."

As he pinned the medal to Deryn's chest, Dr. Barlow applauded softly with gloved hands. The captain stepped back, and the officers saluted as one.

A realization meandered its slow way through Deryn's brain—this wasn't her father's medal . . .

It was hers.

"Thank you, sir," she said at last, barely remembering to return the officers' salutes. Instead of charging her with treason, they'd gone and *decorated* her?

"Now, then," Captain Hobbes said, turning back to the map table. "We have other matters to discuss."

"Well done, Mr. Sharp," the lady boffin whispered, patting Deryn on the shoulder. "If only you were properly dressed!"

Deryn nodded dumbly, trying to gather her thoughts. She was a decorated officer now, pinned with the same medal her father had won. And unlike him, she was still alive. She could still hear her own heart beating, sure enough, like a drummer marching her off to war.

Part of her wanted to weep, to let all the nightmares of the last week spill out of her. And another part wanted to shout aloud that this was madness. She was a traitor, a spy—a *girl*, for heaven's sake. But somehow she managed to hold the jumble of feelings inside by staring down at the table as hard as she could.

On it was a map of the Dardanelles, with mines and fortifications drawn by hand in red. As Deryn took slow breaths, her brain gradually focused on the matter at hand.

The Dardanelles strait was the heart of the Ottoman defenses. It squeezed all ships headed for Istanbul into a channel less than a mile wide, which was stuffed with sea mines and lined with forts and cannon on high cliffs.

Whatever the lady boffin's alternate plan was, Deryn had a feeling it didn't involve more diplomacy.

"We're forbidden to fly down the strait," Captain Hobbes was saying. "The Ottomans don't want us spying on their fortifications during the sultan's joyride. But they've given us permission to travel down the ocean side—so the sultan can watch the sunset, we've told them."

The bosun chuckled as the captain's finger traveled down the western edge of Gallipoli, the rocky peninsula that separated the strait from the Aegean Sea.

"Just here is a ridge known as the Sphinx, a natural landmark. We can find our way back to it easily, day or night. So can your landing party, Mr. Sharp."

"Landing party, sir?"

"That's what I said. You'll have to keelhaul drop from cruising altitude."

Deryn raised her eyebrows. A keelhaul drop meant sliding down a cable to the ground. But according to the *Manual of Aeronautics*, drops were only for abandoning ship.

The bosun saw her expression, and smiled. "A bit lively, eh, Mr. Sharp? Especially for your first command."

"I'll be *in command*, sir?"

The captain nodded. "Can't have a full officer in charge, in case you're captured. Better a middy, so it's less of an incident."

"Oh." Deryn cleared her throat, realizing why they'd been in such a rush to give her the barking medal. In case she didn't make it back. "I mean, yes, sir."

The captain's finger slid across Gallipoli. "From the Sphinx your landing party will cross the peninsula to Kilye Niman—a bit more than two miles away." He pointed at a narrow passage at a bend in the strait, which was marked with a dotted red line. "That's where the Ottomans have their heavy kraken nets, according to our best dolphin-esques."

"Pardon me, sir," Deryn said, "but if the dolphins have already scouted them, what am I going for? To take photographs?"

"Photographs?" The captain chuckled. "This isn't a sightseeing trip, Mr. Sharp. Your job is to bring those nets down."

Deryn frowned. Heavy kraken nets were strong enough to stop even the largest beasties from getting through. How was her landing party meant to cut them up? With a pair of clippers?

"Allow me to explain," Dr. Barlow said, gesturing to two jars on the map table. They were crowded with tiny beasties, a honeycomb of white shells clinging to the interior of the glass. She twisted off the top of one, and the smell of salt water filled the room. "Did you know, Mr. Sharp, that my grandfather was an expert in the field of barnacles?"

"Barnacles, ma'am?"

"Amazing creatures. They spend their humble lives clinging to ships, to whales, to rocks and driftwood, and yet they are implacable. Enough of them can foul even the largest dreadnought's engines." She pulled on heavy gloves and lifted a pair of tongs from the table, then fished out a single beastie from the jar. "Of course, these are no ordinary barnacles. They're a species of my own devising, prepared in case the Ottomans proved troublesome. You shall have to be careful with them."

"Don't worry, ma'am. I won't hurt your beasties."

"Hurt *them*, Mr. Sharp?" the lady boffin asked, and Dr. Busk laughed.

Suddenly Deryn smelled something besides seawater. It was a dark scent, like smoke from a smithy. Then she realized that the tongs were slowly drooping in Dr. Barlow's hand.

The metal itself was . . . *melting*.

Dr. Barlow maneuvered the tongs carefully, so that they dropped the barnacle back into the jar of brine before disintegrating altogether. "I call them vitriolic barnacles."

"Of course, Midshipman Sharp, you must keep this mission secret from the rest of the crew," the captain said. "Even the men in your landing party won't know the entire plan. Is that clear?"

Deryn swallowed. "Perfectly clear, sir."

Dr. Barlow carefully screwed the top back onto the jar. "Once the vitriolic barnacles are on the kraken nets, they'll begin to multiply, interbreeding with the natural barnacles already there. In a few weeks the colony will be overcrowded, like these in the jar. Then they shall begin to struggle, trying to dislodge each other's relentless grip. Their vitriolic ooze will tear away at the nets, turning the cables into a stringy paste of metal at the bottom of the sea."

"We'll return a month from now," the captain said. "In the dark of the new moon, the *Leviathan* will guide a creature down the strait by searchlight. The Ottoman coastal artillery won't be able to hit us in the air, and the beastie will swim deep underwater, unharmed by magnetic sea mines."

"But won't the Ottoman navy have plenty of warning, sir?" Deryn asked—the strait was almost a hundred miles from Istanbul.

"Indeed," Dr. Busk said. "But Admiral Souchon won't guess what sort of creature the *Leviathan* is bringing. It's a new species, more formidable than any of our navy krakens."

Deryn nodded, remembering what Dr. Barlow had told her on the sultan's airship.

"It's called a behemoth," the head boffin said.

By the time she left the navigation room, Deryn felt unsteady on her feet.

First a decoration for gallantry, when she'd half expected to be hanged for treason. Then her first command, a secret attack against an empire that Britain was at peace with. That didn't seem right at all. It was more like being a spy than a soldier!

And the final shock was the drawing of the behemoth that Dr. Busk had shown them. It was a huge creature, with tentacles like a kraken and a maw big enough to swallow one of the kaiser's submarines. The body was nearly as big as the *Leviathan*, but made of muscle and sinew instead of hydrogen and fragile membranes.

No wonder Lord Churchill hadn't wanted to hand it over!

As Deryn neared the central stairs, she frowned—a civilian was lurking about in the corridor ahead of her. She recognized the shapeless hat and the bullfrog on his shoulder. It was Eddie Malone, the reporter she'd met aboard the *Dauntless*, no doubt here to cover the sultan's joyride.

But what was he doing so close to the bow?

"Excuse me, Mr. Malone," she said. "Are you lost?"

The man spun around on one heel, a guilty expression on his face. Then he frowned and took a closer look. "Oh, it's you, Mr. Sharp. How lucky!"

"Indeed you are, sir. You're wandering about in a restricted area." She pointed back toward the stairs. "I'm afraid you'll have to rejoin the other reporters in the mess hall."

"Well, of course," Malone said, but he made no move to turn around, just stood there watching a message lizard scuttling past overhead. "I just wanted a better look at your magnificent ship."

Deryn sighed. She had only a few hours to learn how to use a diving apparatus, how to keelhaul drop onto solid stone, and how to handle acid-spitting barnacles! She wasn't in the mood for pleasantries.

"You're very kind, sir." She pointed down the corridor again. "But if you *please*."

Malone leaned closer and spoke quietly. "Here's the thing, Mr. Sharp. I'm checking out a story. One that might make your ship look bad, if reported in a certain way. Perhaps you could clear things up for me."

"Clear what up, Mr. Malone?"

"I have it on good authority that you're holding a prisoner here. He should be a prisoner of war, but you're not treating him properly."

Deryn took a long moment to speak. "I'm not sure who you're talking about."

"I think you are! A man named Volger is aboard this ship. You're making him work on those Clanker engines of yours, even though he's a real-life count!"

Deryn's hand went to her command whistle, ready to call for the guards. But then she realized how Malone must have learned about Volger . . . *from Alek.*

With a quick look in both directions, she pulled Malone out of the main corridor and into the officers' baths.

"Where did you hear this?" she whispered.

"I met an odd fellow," he said softly, scratching the chin of his bullfrog. "I thought he was a bit suspicious, and suddenly the Germans were chasing him. That didn't seem right, as he was Austrian, a fellow Clanker!"

"Germans?" Deryn's eyes widened. "Is he all right?"

"He gave them the slip, and I saw him again today at lunch." The man smiled. "He knew a lot about your ship, which was also odd. Do you think I could meet this Volger fellow? I have a message to deliver."

Deryn groaned, her stomach winding into the same tight coils it always did when she was contemplating treason. But Alek was still here in Istanbul, and the Germans were after him! Maybe Count Volger could help.

She held out her hand. "All right. I'll take the message to him."

"It won't work that way, I'm afraid." Malone pointed at his bullfrog. "Rusty here has the message in his head, and you don't know how to make him speak."

Deryn stared at the frog, wondering if it was memorizing everything she was saying right now. Could she really trust this reporter?

Her thoughts were shattered by a whistle echoing through the ship—the all-hands signal. The sultan was almost here. In a few minutes all the ship's marines would be arrayed along the gangway, waiting for his arrival.

Which meant that there wouldn't be a guard at Volger's stateroom door . . .

Deryn reached for her ring of keys.

"Come with me," she said.

TWENTY-THREE

As expected, no one was guarding the count's stateroom.

Deryn opened the door to the sight of Volger leaning halfway out his window, trying to get a better view of the sultan's magnificent walker. Before she'd left the navigation room, Deryn had seen the elephant-shaped machine approaching across the airfield. It was even larger than the *Dauntless*, its howdah as ornate as a lady's hat on Derby Day.

"Excuse me, sir," she said to Volger's backside, "but you have a visitor."

As the wildcount extracted himself from the window, Deryn checked the empty corridor and closed the door behind them.

"A visitor?" Volger said. "How interesting."

The reporter stepped forward and thrust out his hand. "Eddie Malone, reporter for the *New York World*."

Count Volger said nothing, eyeing Malone up and down.

"He has a message from Alek," Deryn said.

Volger's face froze for a moment. "Alek? Where is he?"

"Right here in Istanbul." Malone pulled out his battered notebook. "He told me about you being a prisoner aboard this ship. Are you being well treated, sir?"

Volger didn't answer, his expression still one of shock.

"Blisters, Malone!" Deryn swore. "We haven't got time for you to do a barking interview. Can your wee beastie please just deliver the message!"

"Alek said it was private, just for the count."

Deryn groaned with frustration. "Alek won't mind me hearing whatever he has to say. Right, your countship?"

Volger regarded the bullfrog with an expression of infinite distaste, but he gave the reporter a nod.

Malone took the beastie from his shoulder and set it on the desk. He scratched beneath its chin, tapping a sort of code with his fingertip. "Okay, Rusty. Repeat."

The frog began to speak in Alek's voice. "I can't be sure if this is really you, Count, but I have to trust this man. We're still here in Istanbul, you see, which I'm sure upsets you greatly. But we've met some friends—allies, I suppose you'd call them. I'll say more about that when we meet face-to-face."

Deryn frowned. Allies? What was Alek blethering about?

"Mr. Malone tells me that the *Leviathan* is still here

as well," the beastie continued. "If you and Hoffman can escape, you can join us! We're at a hotel in the old city, with a name like my mother's. We'll stay here as long as we can."

At this, Count Volger softly groaned, his fists clenching at his sides.

"Oh, and I apologize for making you listen to this abomination. But I need your help, Count, more than ever. Please try to join us. Um, end message, I suppose."

The bullfrog went silent.

"Do you mind if I ask you some questions, sir?" Malone said, his pen at the ready.

Count Volger didn't answer, but sank into his desk chair, staring hatefully at the frog. "I suppose that's really him?"

"It sounds like Alek, right enough," Deryn said. "And the beasties can only repeat what they've heard."

"Then why was he speaking in English?" Volger asked.

"My name's not Rosencrantz," Eddie Malone said. "I wasn't going to carry a message I didn't understand."

"That little fool," the count said quietly, shaking his head. "What's he playing at now?"

Eddie Malone picked up the bullfrog and placed it on his shoulder, a frown on his face. "You don't sound glad to hear from this fellow. He seemed to think highly of you."

"Do you know what he was talking about?" Volger asked Malone. "Who these new 'allies' of his are?"

The man shrugged. "He was being cagey about it.

Istanbul is full of secret societies and conspiracies. There was a revolution just six years ago."

"So he's fallen in with anarchists? Splendid."

"Anarchists?" Deryn frowned. "Alek's not completely daft, you know!"

Volger waved his hand at the bullfrog. "I believe this proves that he is. All he had to do was leave Istanbul, then find somewhere to hide."

"Aye, but *why* would he do that?" Deryn said. "You and his da kept him cooped up his whole life, like a budgie in a fancy cage, and now he's finally free. Did you really think he'd find some hole to hide in?"

"The situation would seem to call for it."

"But Alek can't keep running forever," she cried. "He needs allies, like he had on this ship before the barking war got in the way. He needs somewhere to belong. But I will say this—I'm glad he ran away from the likes of *you*, even if he's joined the barking Monkey Luddite Brigade! At least he can find his own way now!"

Count Volger stared at her for a long moment, and Deryn realized that she'd let her voice go all squeaky. That was what came of thinking too hard about Alek—it turned her pure dead girly sometimes.

"This Alek fellow just gets more and more interesting," Malone said, pen scratching against his pad. "Can you give me a bit more background on him?"

"No!" Deryn and Volger said together.

The cast off alert sounded, and Deryn heard footsteps scrambling in the corridor outside. She swore—the captain had ordered a fast ascent. They had to make it down the peninsula before sunset, or her landing party would be keelhaul dropping in the dark.

"We have to go now," she said, dragging Malone toward the door. "They'll be coming for his countship soon, to help with the engines."

"What about my interview?"

"If they catch us in here, you'll be interviewing a barking hangman!" Deryn eased open the door, peeking out and waiting for the corridor to clear.

"Mr. Sharp," Count Volger said from behind her. "I hope you understand that this complicates things."

She looked over her shoulder. "What are you blethering about?"

"I need to rejoin Alek and talk him out of this madness. And that means escaping from this ship. Hoffman and I shall need your help with that."

"Have you gone barking mad as well?" she cried. "I'm not a traitor . . . not *that* much of one, anyway."

"Perhaps, but if you don't help us, I shall be forced to reveal your little secret."

Deryn froze.

"I had begun to suspect during our fencing lessons,"

the count said coolly. "There's something about the way you stand. And your outbursts on Alek's behalf have also been revealing. But really it was the look on your face just now that removed all doubt."

"I don't know . . . what you're talking about," she said. The words came out ridiculously low, like a wee boy trying to sound like a man.

"Neither do I," Eddie Malone said, his pen flying across the page. "But this is sure getting interesting."

"So if you want to continue serving on this ship, *Mr. Sharp*, I think you will be helping us to escape." A cruel smile spread across Count Volger's face. "Or shall I give our reporter friend here the news?"

Deryn's head was spinning like mad. She'd lived this moment in a hundred nightmares, but now the moment had arrived like a bolt of lightning from a clear sky. And from barking *Count Volger*, of all people.

Suddenly Deryn hated all sneaky, clever people.

She bit her lip, forcing her thoughts into focus. She was Midshipman Dylan Sharp, a decorated officer in His Majesty's Air Service, not some ninny about to lose her head. Whatever she said now, she could scheme her way out of this later.

"All right, then," she spat. "I'll help you escape."

Volger drummed his fingers. "It'll have to be tomorrow night, before the *Leviathan* leaves Istanbul for good."

"Don't you worry. I'll be glad to see the back side of you!"

With that, she dragged Eddie Malone out the door.

Three hours later Deryn found herself staring out the *Leviathan*'s open cargo door, a heavy pack on her back and a rocky expanse rolling past below.

She sighed. *Might as well jump now, without a barking rope.*

No matter how she thought the matter through, everything was hopeless and ruined. The count had guessed her secret, and he'd done so right smack in front of a reporter. Her first command was about to begin, but her career was practically over.

"Don't worry, lad," the bosun said from beside her. "It's never as far as it looks."

She nodded, wishing that it was something piffling like a keelhaul drop that had her jittery. Gravity was something you could beat; all it took was hydrogen, hot air, or even a bit of rope. But being a girl was a miserable, never-ending struggle.

"I'm fine, Mr. Rigby. Just can't wait to get started." She turned toward her men. "How about you lot?"

The three men in her landing party put on brave faces, but their eyes stayed glued to the passing landscape. As the Sphinx drew closer, the airship slowed, turning into the stiff breeze coming off the ocean. But the officers couldn't come to a full halt without giving the sultan and his men too clear a view of the ground beneath them.

A bit cheeky, committing espionage right in front of a nation's sovereign.

The bosun consulted his watch. "Twenty seconds, I'd say."

"Clip your lines!" Deryn ordered. Her heart was starting to race now, driving out her gloomy thoughts. Volger and his threats could get stuffed. She could always toss him out his stateroom window.

The terrain was rising beneath the ship now, turning from trees to scrub grass and rock, then finally sand. To her right was the Sphinx, a natural formation thrusting up like an ancient statue of some pagan god.

"Get ready, lads." She shouted, "Three, two, one . . ."

. . . and jumped.

The rope hissed through her safety clip, angry and piping hot in the sea breeze. She heard her comrades descending around her, a chorus of whirring cables slicing through the air.

The ground came up fast, and Deryn snapped on a second clip. The friction doubled, jerking her into a slower fall. But solid rock and scrub grass still blurred beneath her, too fast for comfort.

Then she felt it, a sway in her line. The airship was

"KEELHAUL DROP."

slowing just a squick. Her rope swung forward with her momentum, then began a slow swing backward, so that her position was almost static with the ground below.

"Now!" Deryn cried, and pulled her second clip from the line.

She dropped fast, hitting hard sand and loose, flat rocks that crunched and powdered under her boots. The impact shook her spine, but she stumbled along, managing to keep her feet. The rest of the cable whipped through her safety clip, smacked her hand spitefully, then skipped across the beach toward the sunset.

As the *Leviathan* slid away into the distance, its engine noise faded into the crash of the waves. Deryn felt her gloom descend again, along with a lonely feeling of being left behind.

She turned around, counting three other figures on the ridge. At least none of her command had been dragged into the sea.

"Everyone all right?" she called.

"Aye, sir!" two calls from the growing darkness, followed by a soft groan.

It was Matthews, ten yards away and still not on his feet. Deryn scrambled across the loose rocks, and found him curled into a tight ball.

"It's my ankle, sir," he said, teeth clenched. "I've turned it."

"All right. Let's see if you can stand." Deryn waved for the other men, then shrugged out of her heavy pack. She knelt and checked the glass case that held the vitriolic barnacles; it hadn't broken.

When Airmen Spencer and Robins had made their way over, she had them lift Matthews to his feet. But the moment his weight settled on the twisted right ankle, he cried out in pain.

"Set him down," she ordered, then let out a slow breath.

The man's ankle was stuffed. There was no way he could walk two miles across the rocky peninsula and back.

"You'll have to wait here, Matthews."

"Aye, sir. But when are they picking us up?"

Deryn hesitated. Of the four of them, only she knew exactly when the *Leviathan* would return to the Sphinx. That way, if the men were captured, the Ottomans couldn't set a trap for the airship.

As for Deryn herself, well, she was a decorated hero, wasn't she? The Ottomans would never drag the truth from her.

"I can't tell you, Matthews. Just wait here, and don't let anyone see you." The man winced in pain again, and she added, "Trust me, the captain won't leave us behind."

They knelt and divided the four packs among the three of them, giving Matthews most of the water and a little bully beef. Then Deryn, Robins, and Spencer headed down the ridge toward the strait, leaving him all alone.

A few minutes into her first command, and she was already one man down.

TWENTY-FOUR

Two miles hadn't looked very far on the map, but the real Gallipoli was a different matter.

The peninsula was crisscrossed by high steep-sided ridges, as if mountains of limestone had been raked to pieces by giant claws. The valleys between were choked with dry, brittle undergrowth. And whenever Deryn and her party rested, ants made their way out of the sandy ground to torment their ankles.

To make things worse, the Royal Navy's maps of Gallipoli were useless, showing only a fraction of the ridgelines and overgrown ravines. Deryn kept an eye on her compass and on the stars overhead, but the tangled geography still forced her into tortured zigzags.

By the time they reached the other side of the peninsula, it was after midnight.

"I reckon this has to be Kilye Niman, sir," Spencer

said, dropping his heavy pack to the ground.

Deryn nodded, peering down at the beach through her field glasses. Two lines of buoys stretched across the narrow strait, bobbing gently on the waves. The giant metal barrels were covered with cruel-looking barbs and phosphorous bombs. Hanging unseen beneath them would be the kraken nets, a thick lattice of metal cables threaded with more spikes and explosives.

Rising from the water at either end of the nets were tall towers, their searchlights sweeping slowly across the water. Deryn made a quick sketch of the fortifications she could see—at least a score of twelve-inch guns aiming down from the cliffs, all sheltered in bunkers cut deep into the limestone.

Impossible for ships to get past, but the behemoth could slip by beneath the water's surface.

"I reckon the navy will owe us a few favors after this, sir," said Robins.

"Aye, but it's the Russians who'll really thank us," Deryn said, spotting a cargo ship waiting for daylight to arrive so it could sail past the nets. "This is their lifeline."

When she'd told Volger about the *Goeben* and the *Breslau*, he'd agreed that the Germans' ultimate plan was to close The Straits. Starving the Russian army's fighting bears was worth giving the sultan a pair of ironclads.

She pulled the diving gear from their packs, and knelt

in the brush to put the suit together. It was a Spottiswoode Rebreather, the first underwater apparatus created from fabricated creatures. The suit had been woven from salamander skin and tortoise shell. The rebreather itself was practically a living creature, a set of fabricated gills that had to be kept wet even in storage.

In short, the suit was a Monkey Luddite's nightmare. Deryn felt a squick of jitters herself as she crawled inside, the wrinkled skin of reptiles slithering over her own. At least it made Spencer and Robins nervous too; they were happy to turn away as she put it on. Even as dark as it was, it would have been tricky stripping down to her skivvies in front of two airmen.

When Deryn was ready, she and Spencer crept down to the beach, leaving Robins to guard the packs. At the water's edge the tides had carved a yard-high bank of sand to hide behind.

They waited there for the searchlights to sweep past, then slapped across the luminous wet sand of the beach, wading into the cool salt water of the strait.

"Here you go, sir," Spencer said, handing her the rebreather. "I'll stay right here by the water."

"Just stay hidden." Deryn dipped her goggles and strapped them on. "If I'm away longer than three hours, go back and see to Matthews before it's light. I can get back on my own."

"Aye, sir." Spencer saluted and crept back to the shadows. When he was out of sight, Deryn finally unwrapped the glass cases of vitriolic barnacles. As per the captain's orders, she hadn't let the men catch even a glimpse of them.

The searchlight was sweeping around again, and she sank down to her neck, pressing the rebreather to her mouth.

Just as in Dr. Busk's office a few hours before, the feeling was uncanny and a bit horrid. The tendrils of the beastie crept into her mouth, seeking a source of carbon dioxide. A fishy taste covered her tongue, and the air she breathed turned warm and salty, like in the *Leviathan*'s galley when the cooks were frying up anchovies.

Deryn bent her knees, dropping beneath the surface.

The searchlight flickered past overhead, and then it was very dark. She squatted on the sand for a moment, forcing herself to take slow and even breaths.

When she'd stopped shivering from the cold, Deryn pushed out toward the first line of nets, staying just beneath the surface. She'd swum in the ocean plenty of times, but never at night. The blackness around her seemed full of huge shapes, and the strange taste of the rebreather was a constant reminder that she didn't belong in this cold and inky realm. She remembered her first sea training exercise aboard the *Leviathan*, watching a kraken crush a wooden schooner into matchsticks.

But there would be no krakens in this strait, not yet. This was Clanker territory, where the worst beasties were sharks and jellyfish, neither of which could harm her through the Spottiswoode armor.

After a long swim she reached one of the buoys, which bobbed in the water like a spiky metal hedgehog. Deryn took hold of one of the spurs gingerly. They were sharp enough to puncture kraken skin, and tipped with phosphorous bombs that would automatically ignite when the beastie tried to struggle free.

She clung there, resting before heading down. The vitriolic barnacles had to be placed deep beneath the waterline, so the colony wouldn't gobble up the buoys and give away their presence too soon.

When Deryn had caught her breath, she let herself sink, descending until the last glimmer of the waning moon disappeared above. The net was easy to find even in the blackness, its cables as thick as her arm and studded with spurs the size of boat hooks. But it was tricky opening the glass cases while blind and wearing thick gloves of salamander skin, and it took Deryn long minutes to deposit six of the wee beasties a few feet apart. They had to be close enough to create a colony, Dr. Barlow had explained, but not so close that the fighting would start right away.

Deryn kicked her way back to the surface, partly to orient herself and partly to recover from the cold of the deeper water. She stared tiredly down the line of buoys stretching across the half mile to the other shore. The job would take a dozen more dives, at least.

It was going to be a long, cold night.

Her fingers were dead numb by the time the last barnacle was in place. The cold had seeped through the salamander skin and deep into her bones, and Deryn realized that this was her second lost night of sleep in three days.

On top of the cold and her exhaustion, the rebreather seemed to be slowly sucking the life from her. It felt as though she hadn't had a proper gulp of air since its tendrils had crept into her mouth. So when she came up for the last time, Deryn decided to risk the searchlights and swim back on the surface.

The rebreather came out a bit stickily, like pulling toffee stuck between her teeth. But it was worth a moment of irksomeness to taste the pure night air again. She headed back, ducking low in the water whenever the searchlights swung round.

Halfway back to shore, the sharp slap of a gunshot rolled across the strait.

Deryn's exhaustion vanished in a flash, and she sank down until her eyes were just above the surface. A large black shape was lumbering across the sand, perhaps twenty yards from where she'd left Spencer waiting.

It was a walker, a machine in the form of a scorpion, with six legs and two grasping claws in front. The long tail curled up into the air, the beam of a spotlight flaring from its tip.

Deryn swam closer, hearing shouts and another gunshot. The spotlight was trained on a lone figure in a British flight suit, while a dozen or so men scrambled across the sand in pursuit. The searchlight from the nearest tower left its slow path and swung toward the beach, forcing Deryn underwater again.

She stuffed the rebreather back into her mouth, then swam closer beneath the surface, her heart pounding in her ears. One of her men had obviously been caught, but perhaps the other was still hidden. If she could find him, they could swim away, sharing the rebreather between them.

A few yards from the beach, Deryn lifted her head above the water, letting herself rise and fall with the swell of the waves. Her eyes swept the shadows behind the shelf of sand, but she saw no one hidden there. She crawled closer, as slow as some primordial beastie taking its first steps on land.

The scorpion's spotlight shifted closer to the tree line, revealing another figure in a flight suit lying on the ground. Two Ottoman soldiers stood nearby, watching the downed man with their rifles pointed at him.

Deryn swore silently—both her men had been captured. She clung to the darkness behind the shelf of sand, wondering what to do. The walker was moving now, making the sand tremble beneath her knees. How was she meant to take on a giant scorpion and a score of soldiers with nothing but a rigger's knife?

She poked her head up. The two Ottomans were lifting the downed man now, helping him up from the sand. He was limping on his right foot. . . .

Deryn frowned. That was *Matthews*, the man she'd left at the Sphinx. The Ottomans must have captured him. Had he led them here? Or had the Ottomans simply guessed that the kraken nets were their objective?

And where was her third man?

Then the spotlight shifted again, and machine-gun fire erupted from the tip of the scorpion's tail, raking the trees along the beach. The branches thrashed madly in the hail of bullets, and sand sprayed into the air.

Finally the machine gun went silent, and a group of Ottoman soldiers charged into the brush. A moment later they dragged something out. It was a body, motionless and as white as a sheet except for the red stains on the flight suit.

Deryn swallowed. Her first command had been killed and captured down to the last man.

With a noisy grinding of gears, the scorpion moved closer to the dead body. One of its massive front claws dug into the sand, then came up, lifting the lifeless form into the air. The Ottomans were taking her men somewhere, probably to interrogate the survivors and take a closer look at their uniforms and equipment.

They would soon guess that the landing party had come from the *Leviathan*, even if they hadn't forced it out of Matthews already. But her men knew nothing about the vitriolic barnacles, and even if the Ottomans inspected the nets, they wouldn't notice a few more beasties among the millions already living along the miles of cable.

Hopefully they would think this had been a simple reconnaissance mission, and an utter failure. The Ottomans would probably lodge a protest with the *Leviathan*'s captain, but as far as they knew, this mission had not been an act of war. Deryn was the only one who could explain otherwise.

"AN OTTOMAN ARTHROPOD AND ITS PREY."

She had to get away from here, or risk everything. There could be no heroic attempt to rescue her men, and no heading back to the Sphinx now either. The Ottomans would be patrolling the whole peninsula for weeks to come.

There was only one place to go.

Deryn stared back out across the black water, to where the cargo ship she'd seen earlier waited to transit the strait. Once the sun rose, it would head for Istanbul.

"Alek," she said softly, and slipped back into the sea.

· TWENTY-FIVE ·

The minarets of the Blue Mosque rose up behind the trees, six tall spires like thin freshly sharpened pencils standing on end. The graceful arc of the mosque's dome stood out dark gray against the hazy sky, and sunlight shimmered from the spinning blades of gyrothopters and aeroplanes overhead.

Alek sat outside the small coffeehouse where Eddie Malone had taken him the day before. It was on a quiet side street, and Alek was sipping black tea and studying his collection of Ottoman coins. He had begun to learn their names in Turkish, and which ones to hide from shopkeepers if he wanted a fair price.

With the Germans handing out photographs of Bauer and Klopp, it was up to Alek to buy supplies. He'd learned a lot, though, wandering the streets of Istanbul on his own. How to bargain with merchants, how to slip through the

German parts of town unnoticed, even how to tell time by the prayers drifting down from the city's minarets.

Most important of all, he'd realized something about this city—he was meant to be here. This was where the war would turn, either for or against the Clanker side. A slender strip of water glittered in the distance, the fog sirens of cargo ships wailing softly as they crept along it. This passage from the Mediterranean to the Black Sea was the Russian army's lifeline, the thread that held the Darwinist powers together. That was why providence had brought him halfway across Europe.

Alek was here to stop the war.

In the meantime he'd also taught himself a little Turkish.

"*Nasılsınız?*" he practiced.

"*İyiyim,*" came an answer from the covered birdcage on his table.

"Shush!" Alek looked about. Fabricated beasts might not be strictly illegal here, but there was no point in drawing attention to himself. Besides, it was insufferable that the creature's accent was better than his own.

He adjusted the cage's cover, closing the gap the creature had been peeking through. But it was already sulking in a corner. It was uncannily good at reading Alek's mood, which at the moment was one of annoyance.

Where was Eddie Malone, anyway? He'd promised to

be here half an hour ago, and Alek had another appointment soon.

He was just about to leave when Malone's voice called from behind him.

Alek turned and nodded curtly. "Ah, here you are at last."

"At last?" Malone raised an eyebrow. "You in a hurry to get somewhere?"

Alek didn't answer that. "Did you see Count Volger?"

"I did indeed." Malone waved for a waiter and ordered lunch, consulting the menu and taking his time about it. "A fascinating ship, the *Leviathan*. The sultan's joyride turned out to be more interesting than I expected."

"I'm pleased to hear it. But I'm more interested in what Count Volger said."

"He said a lot of things . . . most of which I didn't understand." Malone pulled out his notebook and readied his pen. "I'm curious if you know the fellow who helped me get in to see Volger. Name of Dylan Sharp?"

"Dylan?" Alek asked, frowning. "Of course I know him. He's a midshipman aboard the *Leviathan*."

"Did you ever notice anything odd about him?"

Alek shook his head. "What do you mean by odd?"

"Well, when Count Volger heard your message, he decided that joining you might be a good idea, and said so. I thought it was downright rash of him to talk about

escaping right in front of a crewman." Malone leaned
closer. "But then he *ordered* Mr. Sharp to help him."

"He ordered him?"

Malone nodded. "Almost as if he were threatening
the boy. Looked like a case of blackmail to me. Does that
make any sense?"

"I . . . I'm not sure," Alek said. Certainly Dylan had
done a few things he wouldn't want the ship's officers to
hear about—like keeping Alek's secrets. But Volger could
hardly blackmail Dylan on that subject without revealing
to the Darwinists who Alek really was. "It doesn't sound
right, Mr. Malone. Perhaps you misheard."

"Well, maybe you'd like to hear for yourself." The man
took the frog from his shoulder, set it on the table, and
scratched it under the chin. "Okay, Rusty. Repeat."

A moment later Count Volger's voice emerged from
the bullfrog's mouth.

"Mr. Sharp, I hope you understand that this complicates things," it said, then switched to Dylan's voice. "What
are you blethering about?"

Alek looked around, but the handful of other patrons
didn't seem to notice. They looked off into the distance,
as if talking frogs came to dine at this establishment every
day. No wonder Malone had insisted on meeting here.

The frog started up a whooping noise, like the *Leviathan*'s Klaxon sounding an alert. Then it continued in a

tangle of voices, with the wail of the Klaxon breaking in at odd times, most of the words flying by too fast for the frog to render clearly.

But then Count Volger's voice came out of the muddle. "Perhaps, but if you don't help us, I shall be forced to reveal your little secret."

Alek frowned, wondering what was going on. Volger was talking cryptically about fencing lessons. At first Dylan sputtered that he didn't understand, but his voice was shaky, almost as if he were about to cry. Finally he agreed to help the count and Hoffman escape, and with one last shriek of the Klaxon, the bullfrog went silent.

Eddie Malone lifted it from the table and placed it gently back on his shoulder. "Care to shed any light on the matter?"

"I don't know," Alek said slowly, which was the truth. He'd never heard such panic in Dylan's voice before. The boy had risked being hanged for Alek. What threat of Volger's could frighten him so much?

But it was no good thinking aloud in front of this reporter. The man knew too much already.

"Let me ask *you* a question, Mr. Malone." Alek pointed at the frog. "Did they know this abomination was memorizing their words?"

The man shrugged. "I never told them otherwise."

"How honest of you."

"I never lied," Malone said. "And I can promise you that Rusty isn't memorizing now. He won't unless I ask him to."

"Well, whether he's listening or not, there's nothing I can add." Alek stared at the frog, still hearing Dylan's voice. He'd almost sounded like a different person.

With Dylan's help, of course, Volger and Hoffman stood a better chance of escaping.

"Did Volger say when they would try?"

"It has to be tonight," Malone said. "The four days is almost up. Unless the British really do plan on giving the *Leviathan* to the sultan, it has to leave Istanbul tomorrow."

"Excellent," Alek said, standing up and offering his hand. "Thank you for carrying our messages, Mr. Malone. I'm sorry that I must beg your leave."

"An appointment with your new friends, perhaps?"

"I leave that to your imagination," Alek said. "And by the way, I hope you won't write about any of this too soon. Volger and I might decide to stay in Istanbul a bit longer."

Malone leaned back in his chair and smiled. "Oh, don't worry about me making a mess of your plans. As far as I can see, this story is just getting interesting."

Alek left the man scribbling in his notebook, no doubt writing down everything they'd said. Or perhaps he'd been lying and the bullfrog had memorized it all. It was mad to trust a reporter with his secrets, Alek supposed, but being reunited with Volger was worth the risk.

He wished the wildcount could be here for his next appointment. Zaven was introducing him to more members of the Committee for Union and Progress. Zaven himself was a friendly sort, and an educated gentleman, but his fellow revolutionaries might not be so welcoming. It wouldn't be easy for a Clanker aristocrat to earn their trust.

"You were very good at staying quiet," Alek whispered to the birdcage as he walked away. "If you keep behaving, I shall buy you strawberries."

"*Mr.* Sharp," the creature answered, then made a giggling sound.

Alek frowned. The words were a snatch of the conversation the bullfrog had repeated. The creature didn't imitate voices, but Count Volger's sarcastic tone was quite recognizable.

Alek wondered why the beast had chosen those two words from everything it had heard.

"*Mr.* Sharp," it said again, sounding abundantly pleased with itself.

Alek shushed it and pulled a hand-drawn map from his pocket. The route, labeled in Zaven's flowery handwriting, took him north and west from the Blue Mosque, toward the neighborhood he'd stumbled into two nights before.

The buildings grew taller as he walked, and the Clanker

influences stronger. Tram tracks braided through the paving stones, and the walls were stained by exhaust, almost as black as the steel spires of Berlin and Prague. German-made machines huffed down the streets, their spare, functional designs strange to Alek after days of seeing walkers shaped like animals. The signs of rebellion also grew—the mix of alphabets and religious symbols filled the walls again, marks of the host of smaller nations that made up the Ottoman Empire.

Zaven's map led Alek deep into a tangle of warehouses, where mechanikal arms stood beside loading docks. The stone walls loomed high above the narrow streets, so tall they almost seemed to touch each other overhead. Sunlight filtered grayly through the fumes.

There were few pedestrians here, and Alek began to feel wary. Before yesterday he'd never walked alone in a city, and he didn't know which sorts of neighborhoods were safe and which were not.

He came to a halt, setting down the birdcage to check Zaven's map once more. As he squinted at the flamboyant handwriting, Alek noticed a figure out of the corner of his eye.

The woman was dressed in long black robes, her face covered by a veil. She was hunched with age, and a few silver coins were sewn into her headdress. He'd seen plenty of desert tribesmen like her on the streets of Istanbul, but never a woman walking alone before. She stood, motionless, beside a warehouse wall, staring down at the cobblestones.

When Alek had passed that building a moment ago, she hadn't been there.

He quickly folded the map, then picked up the cage and started walking again. A moment later he glanced backward.

The old woman was following him.

Alek frowned. How long had she been there?

He chewed his lip as he walked. He was close to the address Zaven had given him, but he could hardly lead this stranger straight to his new allies. Istanbul was full of spies and revolutionaries, and of secret police as well.

But surely he could outrun an old woman. Hoisting the heavy birdcage higher, Alek quickened his pace. He let himself take longer and longer steps, ignoring the complaints from beneath the birdcage cover.

And yet when he looked back, his pursuer was still there, gliding gracefully across the paving stones, her robes rippling like waves of black water.

This was no old woman, perhaps no woman at all.

Alek's hand went to his belt, and he softly swore. He was armed only with a long knife he'd bought at the Grand Bazaar that morning. Its curved steel blade had looked exotically lethal laid out on red velvet. But its edge hadn't been sharpened yet, and Alek had never trained to use a weapon of its kind.

He rounded the last corner, almost at the address on Zaven's map. With his pursuer out of sight for a moment, he dashed ahead, ducking into the entrance of an alley.

"Shush," he breathed through the birdcage's cover. The creature made an unhappy noise at being bounced about again, but fell silent.

Alek placed the cage carefully on the ground and peeked out.

The dark figure appeared, moving slowly now, and came to a halt in front of a loading dock on the other side of the street. Alek saw the symbol painted on the dock, and frowned.

It was the same symbol Zaven had drawn extravagantly on his map.

Was this a coincidence? Or had this pursuer already known where Alek was headed?

The black-robed figure jumped up onto the loading dock in a single bound, confirming that this was no woman. The man backed into the shadows, but his robes were just visible, billowing softly in the breeze.

Alek stood there in the alley, his back pressed hard against cold stone. Thanks to Eddie Malone, he was already half an hour late. If he waited for his pursuer to give up and go away, it might take ages more. What would his new allies think if he arrived at their secret meeting hours behind schedule?

Of course, if he brought them this spy as his prisoner, they might be somewhat more impressed. . . .

A six-legged German walker was headed up the street, dragging a heavy cargo train behind it—the perfect cover. Alek knelt and spoke softly to the birdcage. "I'll be right back. Just stay quiet."

"Quiet," the creature muttered in reply.

Alek waited until the cargo train was lumbering past, between him and the other man. He stole out of the alley and scampered along behind the train, then slipped between two cars and across the street.

His back to the stone warehouse wall, Alek inched his way toward the loading dock. The long, curved knife felt unfamiliar in his hand, and he wondered for a moment if the man had spotted him.

But it was too late for doubts. Alek crept closer. . . .

Suddenly a maniacal peel of laughter came from across the street, echoing from the alley where he'd left the beast!

Alek froze. Was it in trouble?

A moment later the black-robed figure jumped down onto the street. It crept toward the maniacal laughter, crossing the street to peer into the alleyway.

Alek saw his chance, stealing up behind to press his knife against the man's throat. "Surrender, sir! I have the advantage."

The man was smaller than he'd thought—and quicker.

"THE STRANGER WITH THE CURVED KNIFE."

He whipped around within Alek's grip, and suddenly they faced each other.

Alek found himself staring into deep brown eyes framed with ringlets of black hair. This wasn't a man at all!

"Not quite an advantage, boy," the girl said in perfect German. "Unless you want to join me in death."

Alek felt a nudge, and looked down.

The tip of her knife was pressed against his stomach.

Alek swallowed, wondering what to do. But then the door to the loading dock began to rise, rattling with the clatter of chains and pulleys.

Both of them looked up, still locked in their lethal embrace.

Zaven stood there in the doorway, beaming down at them.

"Ah, Alek! You're finally here. And I see you've met my daughter!"

TWENTY-SIX

"You should have let me kill him," Zaven's daughter said as they climbed the broad staircase inside the warehouse.

The creature giggled from the birdcage, and Alek wondered what madness had gotten into it.

Zaven clicked his tongue sadly. "Ah, Lilit. You are your mother's daughter."

"He was talking to a reporter!"

Alek realized that Lilit was speaking German, deliberately letting him understand. He found it rather awkward, being threatened by a girl. Almost as embarrassing as mistaking her for a man.

"Nene will agree with me," Lilit said, fixing Alek with a cold glare. "Then we'll see who has the advantage."

He rolled his eyes at her. As if a mere girl could get the better of him. It had all been the creature's fault for distracting him. The birdcage seemed heavier than ever, climbing these endless stairs. How high up were they going?

"Mr. Malone was carrying a message for me," he explained. "From my friend aboard the *Leviathan*. I didn't tell him anything about your Committee!"

"Maybe not," Lilit said. "But I followed you an hour before you noticed me. Stupidity can be just as deadly as treachery."

Alek took a slow breath, wishing for the hundredth time that Volger were here.

But Zaven only laughed. "Fah! There's no shame in being trailed by my daughter, Alek. She's a master of the shadows." He thumped his chest. "Trained by the best there is!"

"It's true, I didn't notice you," Alek said, turning to Lilit. "But was anyone else following me?"

"No. I would have seen them."

"Well, then. I haven't given you away to the sultan's secret police, have I?"

Lilit *hmph*ed and climbed ahead. "We'll see what Nene says."

"In any case," Alek called up after her, "if the Germans find me, they won't bother trailing me. I'll simply disappear."

Lilit didn't turn to face him, but muttered, "That's useful to know."

The staircase continued up, dimly lit by a column of latticed windows letting in gray sunlight. As Zaven lead them above the swirling exhaust fumes on the street, the stairs grew brighter. Small touches of humanity appeared on the cold stone walls—family portraits and the three-barred crosses of the Byzantine Church.

"Zaven," Alek asked, "do you live here?"

"A masterpiece of deduction," Lilit said.

"We've always lived above the family business," Zaven said, stopping before a pair of wooden doors with ornate brass fittings. "Whether it was a hat shop or a mechaniks factory. And now that the family business is revolution, we live above the Committee!"

Alek frowned, wondering where this "committee" was. The warehouse felt as still as an empty church; the paint on the walls was cracked, the stairs in disrepair.

As Zaven unlocked the doors, he said, "No disguises at home."

Lilit gave him an annoyed look, but pulled the desert robes over her head. Beneath them she wore a brilliant red silk dress that almost reached the floor.

Alek noticed again how brown her eyes were, and how beautiful she was. What an idiot he'd been to mistake her for a man.

Zaven pushed through the doors into a riot of color. The apartments' divans and chairs were covered with vivid silks, the electrikal lamps decorated with rainbows of translucent tiles. A vast Persian rug was spread across the floor, its meticulous geometries woven in the hues of fallen autumn leaves. Sunlight spilled in from a large balcony, setting the whole mosaic aflame.

The furniture had seen better days, however, and the rug was worn through in places.

"Very cozy," Alek said, "for a revolution."

"We do our best," Zaven said, taking in the room with a tired sweep of his eyes. "A proper host would offer you tea first. But we're already late."

"Nene doesn't like to be kept waiting," Lilit said.

Alek straightened his tunic. Nene was obviously the leader of the group. It would be best to look smart in front of him.

They led him to another set of double doors. Lilit knocked softly, waited a moment, then pushed the doors open.

Unlike the outer apartments, this room was dark, the air heavy with incense and the smell of dusty carpets. The viscous light of an old-fashioned oil lamp turned everything the color of red wine. A dozen wireless receivers sat in the shadows, their tubes softly glowing, the chatter of Morse code filling the air.

Against the far wall stood a huge canopied bed covered with mosquito netting. It rested on four legs carved with drooping folds of skin, like those of a reptile. Within the netting lay a small, thin figure wrapped in white sheets. Two glittering eyes stared out from beneath an explosion of gray hair.

"So this is your German boy?" came a crackly voice. "The one you had to save from the Germans?"

"He's Austrian," Zaven said. "But yes, Mother, he's a Clanker."

"And a spy, Nene." Lilit bent to kiss the old woman on the forehead. "I saw him talking to a reporter before he came here!"

Alek slowly let out his breath. The fearsome Nene was simply Zaven's mother? Was this whole Committee nothing but an eccentric family hobby?

He set down the birdcage and bowed. "Good afternoon, madam."

"Well, you certainly have an Austrian accent," she said in excellent German—these Ottomans seemed to know half a dozen languages each. "But there are many Austrians working for the sultan."

Alek gestured at Zaven. "But your son saw the Germans chasing me."

"Chasing you straight to one of our walkers," Nene said. "A rather convenient introduction."

"I had no idea that machine would catch me when I fell," Alek argued. "I could have died!"

"You still could," Lilit muttered.

Alek ignored her, kneeling by the birdcage to untie the cover's straps. As he stood, he lifted the cage into Nene's view.

"Would an agent of the sultan have one of these?" he said, then whisked off the cover.

The creature looked out at them all, its huge eyes round. It turned from one face to the next, taking in Zaven's surprise, Lilit's suspicion, and finally Nene's cold, glittering eyes.

"What on earth is that?" she asked.

"A creature from the *Leviathan*, where I've served as engine crew the last two weeks."

"A Clanker, on the *Leviathan*?" Nene let out a chuckle. "What nonsense. You probably bought that beast from some backroom shop in the Grand Bazaar."

Alek drew himself straighter. "I certainly did not, madam. This creature was fabricated by Dr. Nora Darwin Barlow herself."

"A Darwin, making a cuddly trifle like that? Don't be absurd. And what use would it be aboard a *warship*?"

"It was meant to be a gift for the sultan," Alek said. "As a way to keep the Ottomans out of war. But then it hatched, um . . . ahead of schedule."

The old woman raised an eyebrow.

"You see, Nene? He's a liar!" Lilit said. "And a fool to think anyone would believe his nonsense!"

"Believe," the creature said, and the room fell silent.

Zaven took a step backward. "It *speaks*?"

"It's just a parrot," Alek said. "Like a message lizard, one that repeats words at random."

The old woman fixed it with a long, critical stare.

"Whatever it is, I've never seen one before. Let me take a closer look."

Alek opened the cage, and the beast climbed out and up onto his shoulder. He went closer to the bed, holding out a hand. The creature crawled slowly down his arm, returning Nene's cold stare with its own wide eyed gaze.

Alek saw the woman's expression soften, just as Klopp's and Bauer's did every time he put the creature in their care. Something about its huge eyes and wizened face seemed to generate affection. Even Lilit was struck silent.

Nene reached out and took Alek's hands. "You have never worked for a living, that's for sure. But there's a bit of engine grease under your fingernails." She rubbed his right thumb. "And you fence, don't you?"

Alek nodded, impressed.

"Tell me something about the *Leviathan* that a liar wouldn't know," she demanded.

Alek paused a moment, trying to recall all the wonders he'd seen aboard the airship. "There are fléchette bats, flying creatures made of jellyfish, and hawks who wear steel talons."

"Those beasts have been in the penny papers all week. Try again."

Alek frowned. He'd never read a newspaper in his life,

"NENE'S FAMILY."

and had no idea what was public knowledge about the *Leviathan*. He doubted the Darwinists had shown him any military secrets.

"Well, we fought the *Goeben* and the *Breslau* on our way here."

There was a long moment of silence. From the looks on their faces, it seemed that little fact hadn't been in the papers.

"The sultan's new toys?" Nene asked. "When exactly?"

"Eight days ago. We stumbled on them due south of the Dardanelles.

Nene nodded slowly, her eyes sliding to one of the chattering wireless receivers. "It's possible. Something was certainly afoot last Monday."

"It was quite a battle," Alek said. "The *Goeben*'s Tesla cannon almost put us all into the sea!"

The three exchanged glances, then Zaven said, "Tesla cannon?"

Alek smiled. At least he knew *something* that these revolutionaries might find useful. "That tower on her aft deck might look like a wireless transmitter, but it's an electrikal weapon. It makes lightning. I know that sounds absurd, but—"

Nene silenced him with a raised hand. "It does not. Come for a walk with me, boy."

"A walk?" Alek asked. He'd assumed the woman was an invalid.

"Onto the balcony," she ordered, and suddenly the

delicate sound of a clockwork mechanism filled the room. One of the bed's wrinkled legs took a slow, smooth step forward.

Alek jumped back, and Lilit laughed from across the room. The creature crawled back up to his shoulder, echoing her giggle.

"Haven't you ever seen a turtle move?" Nene asked, smiling.

Alek took another step back, getting out of the bed's way as it lumbered toward the double doors. "Yes, but I never thought of sleeping on one."

"You sleep on one every night, boy. The world itself rests on a turtle's back!"

Alek smiled at her. "My mother used to tease me with that old wives' tale."

"Old wives' tale?" Nene cried, her voice crackling. "The notion is perfectly scientific. The world rests upon a turtle, which itself stands on the back of an elephant!"

Alek tried not to laugh. "Then what does the elephant stand on, madam?"

"Don't try to be clever, young man." She narrowed her eyes. "It's elephants all the way down!"

The bed made its slow way from the bedroom toward the balcony doors. As he followed, carefully matching its turtle's pace, Alek wondered at the perfection of the mechanism. Clockwork machines ran on wound-up springs instead of noisy steam or gas engines, so the bed's movements were smooth and slow, ideal for an invalid.

But the woman lying in it had to be mad, with her talk of elephants. All three of them were a bit peculiar, in fact. They reminded Alek of his own poor relations, once-wealthy families who'd fallen on hard times but still had an inflated sense of their own importance.

The night before, Zaven had said they'd been part of the Young Turk uprising six years ago. But was this strange family a real threat to the sultan, or simply wallowing in past glories?

Of course, Zaven's walker had been nothing to sneeze at.

Out on the balcony Alek realized that the family's apartments were built atop the warehouse, the rooftop

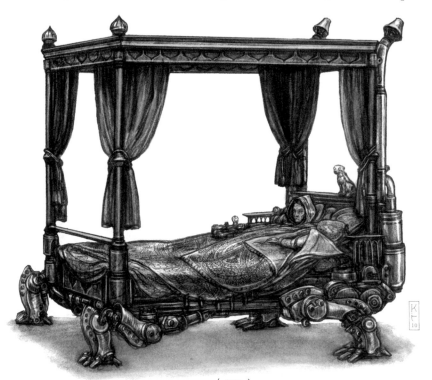

surrounding them like a small plot of land. An odd place
to live, but it had commanding views of the city. From this
height they could see both the Sea of Marmara and the
sparkling inlet of the Golden Horn.

There she was, just as Eddie Malone had said—the
Goeben, resting beside a long pier. Her huge kraken-fighting
arms were working above the surface, helping to load cargo.

Nene pointed a withered finger at the docks. "How do
you know about this Tesla cannon."

"It fired at us," Alek said. "It almost set the whole ship
aflame."

"But how do you know its *name*, boy? I doubt you
guessed it."

"Ah." Alek wondered how much to tell her. "One of
my men is a master of mechaniks. He'd seen experimental
models of the cannon."

"Your men have knowledge of German secret weapons, yet you served aboard the *Leviathan*?" Nene shook
her head in disbelief. "Tell me who you really are. At once!"

Alek took a deep breath, ignoring Lilit's cold smile. "I'm
an Austrian nobleman, madam. My father was against this war,
and the Germans had him killed for it. My men and I were
hiding in the Alps when the *Leviathan* crash-landed there."

"And they simply invited you aboard?"

"We helped the Darwinists escape. Our Stormwalker
was damaged, and their airship's engines were destroyed.

So we put the two together, so to speak, so that we could both escape the Germans. But once we were airborne, it became clear they considered us prisoners of war. We had to jump ship." He spread his hands. "So here we are, looking for allies to fight with."

"Allies," the creature repeated softly.

"I want revenge on the Germans," Alek said. "The same as you do."

There was a long silence, then Nene shook her head.

"I don't know what to make of you, boy. Clanker engines on a hydrogen breather? It's ridiculous. And yet . . . no spy of the sultan's would dare tell a story so unlikely."

"Wait," Lilit said, taking her grandmother's hand. "Remember when the *Leviathan* flew over the city yesterday? And we thought it funny how the engines were smoking, like Clanker airships' do?" She glanced at Alek. "Not that he's telling the truth."

Nene shook her head again. "No doubt this boy saw them as well, and that was what inspired this bizarre story."

"Madam, I don't enjoy being called a liar," Alek said firmly. "It makes me a stronger ally that I know both Darwinist and Clanker secrets! I have military training and gold. My men and I can pilot walkers and fix them as well. You must let us help you, unless you're only *playing* at revolution!"

Lilit sprang to her feet, her teeth bared. Zaven stood silent, but moved a hand to his knife.

Nene spoke very calmly. "Young man, you have no idea what this struggle has cost my family—our fortune, our station in society." She gently took Lilit's hand. "And this girl's poor mother as well. How *dare* you call us amateurs!"

Alek swallowed, realizing that he'd gone too far.

"I doubt you can help us," Nene continued. "I know an aristocrat when I see one. And spoiled brats like you never help anyone but themselves."

The words struck Alek like a kick in the stomach—this was how people always saw him, as a pampered fool, no matter how hard he tried. His knees bent, and he found himself sitting on the bed.

"I'm sorry for speaking like an idiot," he said. "And I'm sorry about your mother, Lilit. I lost my parents too. I just want to fight back somehow."

"You lost *both* your parents?" Nene said, and her voice grew softer. "Who *are* you, boy?"

Alek looked into the old woman's eyes, and realized that he had two choices—he could either trust her or go back to being alone. Without allies he and his men could do nothing but run into the wilds and hide.

But he was here in Istanbul for more than that, he knew.

"Who do you think I am?" he whispered.

"An Austrian nobleman, certainly. Perhaps an arch-duke's son?"

He nodded, holding her fierce gaze.

"Then surely you know your mother's full maiden name. And if you don't get every last syllable right, my granddaughter will drop you off this roof."

Alek took a breath, then recited, "Sophie Maria Josephine Albina, Countess Chotek of Chotkow and Wognin."

Belief dawned at last on the old woman's face.

"Our meeting is providence," he said. "I swear I can help you, Nene."

Inexplicably, Lilit burst into laughter. Zaven let out a low chuckle, and the creature joined in.

"What a charmer," Lilit said. "He's adopted you now, Nene!"

Alek realized his mistake. *"Nene"* wasn't a name at all, but simply a word for "grandmother," like *"Oma"* in German.

"I'm sorry my Armenian is deficient, madam."

The old woman smiled. "Not to worry. At my age one can never have too many grandchildren. Even if some of them are idiots."

Alek took a deep breath, managing to hold his tongue.

"Perhaps it's my old age, but I'm starting to believe you," Nene said. "Of course, if you are who you say, then surely you can pilot a walker."

"Show me one, and I'll prove it to you."

She nodded, then waved her hand. "Zaven? Perhaps it's time to introduce His Serene Highness to the Committee."

TWENTY-SEVEN

Lilit and Zaven led him to the far corner of the balcony, which overlooked a huge courtyard within the walls of several warehouses. The windows of the surrounding buildings were boarded up, and the whole courtyard covered with camouflage netting to hide it from the air.

In the shadows five walkers stood silently.

Alek knelt at the balcony railing, peering down. Over the last few days, he'd seen them in the streets, the motley array of combat walkers that guarded Istanbul's ghettos. These five were marked with the dents and scrapes of old battles, their armor decorated with a multitude of signs—crescents, crosses, a Star of David, and other symbols he'd never seen before.

"A committee of iron golems," he said.

Zaven raised a finger. "Iron golems is the Jewish name. The Vlachs call them werewolves, and our Greek brothers call them Minotaurs." He pointed at the walker from two nights before. "I believe you've met Şahmeran, my personal machine. She is a goddess of the Kurdish people."

"And they're all here together," Alek said.

"Another excellent observation," Lilit muttered.

"Hush, girl," Nene said, her bed making its slow way toward them. "For too long we were content to look after our own neighborhoods and let the sultan run the empire. But the Germans and their *mekanzimat* have done us a favor—they've united us at last."

Zaven knelt beside Alek. "The machines below are only a fraction of those pledged to us. We use these five to train, so that a Kurd knows how to pilot a werewolf, and an Arab an iron golem."

"So you can fight together properly," Alek said.

"Indeed. My own daughter has mastered all of them!"

"A girl piloting a walker? How utterly—" Alek saw Lilit's expression, and cleared his throat. "How exceptional."

"Fah! Not so strange as you think," Zaven said, raising a fist. "Once the revolution comes, women will be the equal of men in all things!"

Alek stifled a laugh. More of the family madness, it seemed, or perhaps the influence of the iron-willed Nene on her son.

"How does that Tesla cannon work?" Lilit asked.

"My man Klopp says it's a lightning generator." Alek

cast his mind back to Klopp's explanation a few days after the battle with the *Goeben*. "Mr. Tesla is an American, but the Germans fund his experiments. They've been working on this cannon for some time. How do you know about it?"

"Never mind that," Nene said. "Can it stop our walkers?"

"I doubt it. The Tesla cannon is designed to be used against hydrogen breathers. But the *Goeben* still has its big guns, and walkers like these are the perfect targets." Alek looked to the southeast, where smoke plumes rose from the sultan's palace—near the water. As long as the German warships waited there, the palace was safe from a walker attack. "That's the real reason those German ironclads are here, isn't it? To keep the sultan in power."

"And to starve the Russians." Nene shrugged. "A hammer can pound more than one nail. You've had a bit of military training, it seems."

"More than a bit, when it comes to walkers." Alek straightened his shoulders. "Give me the trickiest one you have, and I'll prove it."

Nene nodded, a slow smile spreading across her face. "You heard the boy, granddaughter. Take him to Şahmeran."

Alek flexed his fingers, looking over the controls.

The instruments were labeled with symbols rather than words, but the purposes of most were clear. Engine temperature, pressure gauges, fuel—nothing he hadn't seen in his Stormwalker.

But the saunters were a different matter entirely. They rose up from the pilot's cabin floor, like huge levers. The handgrips looked like the armored gloves of a medieval knight.

"How am I meant to walk with these?" he asked.

"You aren't. The saunters control the arms." Lilit pointed at the floor. "You use the pedals to walk, ninny."

"Ninny," the creature repeated, then chuckled.

"Your pet knows you quite well, doesn't it," Lilit said, stroking the creature's fur. "What's its name?"

"Name? Fabricated beasts don't have them. Except for the great airships, of course."

"Well, this one needs a name," Lilit said. "Is it a boy or a girl?"

Alek thought for a moment, then frowned. "The *Leviathan*'s crew always said 'it' when speaking of beasts. Perhaps they're neither."

"Then where do they come from?"

"Eggs."

"But what *lays* the eggs?"

Alek shrugged. "As far as I know, the boffins pull them out of their bowler hats."

Lilit looked more closely at the beast while Alek stared at the saunters. He'd never piloted a walker with arms before. This Şahmeran might be trickier than he'd thought.

But if a girl could pilot the monstrosity, it couldn't be too difficult.

"How do I know what the arms are doing? I can't even see them from in here."

"You just *know* where they are, as if they were part of your own body. But since this is your first time . . ." Lilit spun a crank, and the top half of the pilot's cabin began to move upward, huffing with pneumatics. "You can try it in parade mode."

"Parade mode?"

"For when Şahmeran marches in the Kurds' religious festivals."

"Ah, *that* sort of parade," Alek said. "This is a very odd country. All the walkers seem to be symbols as well as machines."

"Şahmeran is not a symbol. She's a goddess."

"A goddess. Of course," Alek muttered. "There certainly are a lot of females in this revolution."

Lilit rolled her eyes as she pulled the engine starter. The machine rumbled to life beneath them, and the creature imitated the engine noise, then climbed from Alek's shoulder to peek over the front edge of the control panel.

"Will your pet be all right?" Lilit asked.

"It has an excellent head for heights," Alek said. "When

we escaped the *Leviathan*, we climbed across a cable much higher than this."

"But why did you steal it?" she asked. "To prove that you'd been aboard the airship?"

"I didn't steal anything," Alek said, placing his boots carefully on the foot pedals. "It insisted on coming."

The creature turned to face them and seemed to smile at Lilit.

"Somehow, I almost believe you," she said softly. "Well, show us how clever you are, boy. Walking is the easy part."

"I doubt it shall be any trouble," Alek said, watching the instruments come to life. When the pressure gauges steadied, he pushed down on the foot pedals, slow and steady.

The machine responded, moving forward smoothly, the spiny legs along its belly moving in automatic sequence. He lifted his left foot from the pedal, guiding the walker into a slow turn.

"This is easier than my four-legged runabout," he exclaimed. "I could pilot that when I was twelve!"

Lilit gave him a strange look. "You had your own walker? When you were twelve?"

"It was the family's." Alek reached for the saunters. "And boys have a natural gift for mechaniks, after all."

"A natural gift for boastfulness, you mean."

"We'll see who's being boastful." Alek slipped his right hand into the metal glove and made a fist. A great pair of claws snapped shut on the machine's right side.

"Careful," Lilit said. "Şahmeran is stronger than any mere boy."

Alek pushed the saunter about, watching how the walker's arm followed his movements. The arm was long and sinuous, like a snake's body, its scales sliding against one another with a sound like a dozen swords drawn from their scabbards.

"The trick is to forget your own body," Lilit said. "Pretend that the walker's hands are yours."

The saunters were amazingly sensitive, the giant arms mimicking every movement of Alek's, but slowly. He paced himself to match the walker's scale, and soon he felt twenty meters tall, as if he were wearing a huge costume, instead of piloting.

"Now comes the tricky part." Lilit pointed. "Pick up that wagon over there."

In the far corner of the courtyard, an old wagon lay overturned. Its wooden side was scratched and gouged, like an ill-treated child's toy.

"Looks easy enough," Alek said, guiding the machine closer among the motionless forms of the other walkers.

He stretched out his right hand, and the machine obeyed him. From the control panel the creature imitated the sounds of hissing air and metal as they echoed from the courtyard walls.

Alek closed his fingers slowly, and the claws shut around the wagon.

"Good so far," Lilit said. "But stay gentle."

Alek nodded, remembering Volger's rule on how to hold a sword—like a pet bird, tight enough to keep it from flying away but gentle enough not to suffocate it.

The wagon shifted in the Şahmeran's grip, threatening to fall.

"Turn your wrist," Lilit said quickly. "But don't squeeze!"

Alek turned the claw upright, trying to settle the wagon in its metal palm. But the wagon had other ideas, tipping from its side onto its wheels. It began to roll.

"Careful!" Lilit said, and the creature repeated the word.

Alek twisted his hand in the saunter again, trying to flip the wagon back onto its side. But it wouldn't stay still, like a marble rolling back and forth in a bowl. The wagon reached the edge of his palm and teetered there, and Alek squeeze a little harder. . . .

The giant metal fingers shut with a sharp hiss of air, and he heard the crack of wood splitting. Splinters flew in all directions, and Alek ducked as something large sailed past his head. Tiny wooden needles stung his face.

He opened his eyes in time to see the wagon's pieces

"PRACTICE IN THE TRAINING YARD."

crashing to bits against the paving stones below. He stared at the empty claw, annoyed.

Lilit sat back up beside him—a few tiny splinters were caught in her black hair. The creature stared up at him from the pilot's cabin floor, making a sound like the creak of shattering wood.

"Having the power of a goddess is quite a responsibility," Lilit said quietly, flicking at her hair. "Don't you agree, boy?"

Alek nodded slowly, turning his wrist and watching the giant claw rotate on its gears. He still felt it, the connection between himself and the machine.

"I don't suppose you have another wagon," he said. "I think I've got it now."

TWENTY-EIGHT

Night was falling at last.

Deryn had spent a long, hot day among the crates on the cargo ship's deck, hiding from the crew and the merciless sun. It was the vessel she'd spotted from the beach at Kilye Niman, a German steamship carrying fat coils of copper wire, and turbine blades the size of windmill sails.

The ship had waited at the kraken nets till dawn, then had taken most of the day to steam to Istanbul. After spending seven weeks on an airship, Deryn was exasperated by the crawling pace of the surface craft. It didn't help that since her hasty supper the night before, Deryn had eaten only a stale biscuit she'd found among the crates. For drink she'd had only handfuls of dew scraped from a canvas lifeboat cover.

Of course, she was better off than her men, who were all either dead or held captive by the Ottomans. On the slow journey here, she'd replayed the scene on the beach a thousand times in her mind, wondering what she could have done. But against the scorpion walker and two dozen soldiers, she would only have been captured herself.

The cargo ship was not entirely without conveniences, though. The crew mostly stayed belowdecks, and a line of sailors' uniforms had been left drying in the sun. She'd found a set of slops that would fit well enough.

Once the sun set, she would swim for shore.

Istanbul was already lighting up before her. Clanker electricals were harsher than the soft bioluminescence of London and Paris, and what had seemed a ghostly glow from the airfield was dazzling this close. The city looked like a fairground coming to life, all glitter and brilliance.

Even the sultan's palace was alight on its hill, the minarets of the two great mosques lancing into the sky around it. Deryn had decided to head for that section of the city, the peninsula where both the oldest and newest buildings were clustered.

But as she stretched her swimming muscles, Deryn felt one last squick of doubt about her plan and considered the options. There were more than a hundred ships standing off Istanbul, some of them civilian vessels under British flags. If she swam across to one of those, it might carry her back out to the Mediterranean, where the Royal

Navy waited. Or north to the Russians in the Black Sea, who were Darwinists, at least.

But a thousand excuses crowded her head—the Ottomans would be searching British ships carefully. And why would any captain believe that she was a decorated officer in the Air Service and not some mad stowaway? What if without her middy's uniform and a ship full of beasties at her command, anyone could see straightaway that she was a mere girl?

And even if she did make it back to the *Leviathan*, what if Volger hadn't managed to escape? He could destroy her career with a word at any time.

But it wasn't any of those reasons that had set her on this course, Deryn knew. Alek was here in this city, and needed help. Perhaps it was daft to risk everything for some barking prince, a boy who didn't even know she was a girl. But it was no more daft than Alek walking across a glacier to assist a wounded enemy airship, was it?

When the water had turned into a black expanse, an upside-down sky shimmering with the city's radiance, Deryn left her hiding place. She stuffed the stolen uniform inside her diving suit and crept to the bow. After slipping over the gunwales, she descended the anchor chain hand over hand, then slid into the water without a splash.

She crawled ashore in the shadows beneath a long pier. Even at night, men and walkers worked the bustling docks, scurrying about beneath huge mechanical arms that chuffed smoke as they pulled cargo from half a dozen ships. Floodlights cast hard black shadows that jittered and swung.

Deryn stole into a maze of off-loaded crates and metal parts, and quickly found a dark spot where she could strip off the Spottiswoode suit. Pulling on her borrowed German sailor's slops, she felt a squick of vexation—demoted from an officer in the Air Service to a common seaman! And if the Ottomans caught her like this, out of uniform, they'd hang her as a spy for sure.

The diving suit had to disappear, so Deryn stuffed all but the boots and her rigging knife into a towering coil of copper wire. She reckoned most dock workers would hardly know what to make of the tangle of turtle shell and salamander skin, except to wonder if a mermaid had come ashore.

It was easy, staying hidden among the endless piles of crates—enough mechanical parts to rebuild Istanbul from scratch, she reckoned. They were all labeled in German.

Deryn crept inland, heading toward the city lights and the promise of food and water. At the edge of the warren, however, she found herself facing a chain-link fence. It was sixteen feet tall, with three coils of barbed wire glittering along its top side. The only gate in sight was wound shut with a massive chain.

"Just my luck," Deryn muttered. She'd come ashore at a top secret section of the waterfront.

It would've been simple enough to swim out and come in elsewhere, but Deryn was weak with hunger. The thought of plunging back into the cold, dark water made her shiver. What was so barking important about all this cargo, anyway? As she skulked along the fence, looking for an unlocked gate, she took a closer look.

It wasn't just mechanical parts, but electricals as well. There were giant rolls of rubber insulation, and a row of glass jar batteries, the same kind of voltaic cells that the *Leviathan*'s searchlights used. But these were the size of outhouses! Deryn remembered the turbine blades aboard the cargo ship. Were the Germans building a power station somewhere here in Istanbul?

She heard voices, and ducked lower into the shadows. It was a dozen men or so, one with a ring of keys jingling in his hand. Perfect—they were headed out.

Deryn crept behind them to a wide gate in the fence, with tracks leading through and out into the darkness. As their leader unlocked it, the men spread out across its length. They pulled it open, metal scraping over cobblestones.

Something huge and restless waited beyond the fence,

huffing and steaming in the cool night air. Then it began to move, a colossal machine rolling slowly into view. The engine at its front took the form of a dragon's head, and the cargo arms were folded on its back like black metal wings. White clouds of steam roiled from its grinning jaws.

"Barking spiders," Deryn said softly, realizing that she'd seen pictures of this contraption in the penny newspapers. . . .

It was the Orient-Express.

The great train eased forward, forcing Deryn farther back into the piles of cargo. But she was unable to take her eyes from it.

The Express seemed to be a strange crossbreed of Ottoman and German design. The engine suggested a dragon's face, with a great lolling tongue spilling from its jaws. But the mechanical arms that unfolded from its cargo cars were unadorned, and moved as smoothly as the wings of a soaring hawk.

The arms reached out into the piles of cargo, lifting metal parts, coils of wire, and glass insulators shaped like huge translucent bells. The train began to load itself, like some greedy monster ravaging a treasure trove.

Suddenly the dragon's single eye burst to life, a blinding headlight. As brilliance spilled across the darkness, Deryn stumbled blindly back, the shadows of her hiding place ripped away.

A cry sounded above the huffing engines of the Express—"*Wer ist das?*"—and Deryn understood enough Clanker to know what it meant.

Someone had spotted her.

She turned and ran, half blinded, stumbling on a bundle of plastic tubing. The tubes skittered underfoot, and Deryn hit the ground hard. She rose painfully to her feet and staggered into the darkness, where she curled up behind a large spool of wire.

Her knee was throbbing, her hands cut and bleeding from breaking her fall. Dizziness swept across her, twenty-four hours without proper food taking its toll. The pounding in her chest felt thin and weak, like a bird's heart instead of her own.

There was no way to outrun the men—she had to outsmart them.

Deryn ignored the pain, crawling back toward the Express on hands and knees, keeping low in the cargo stacks, squeezing through the narrowest gaps she could find. She hoped they hadn't got a good look at her, and wouldn't realize they were chasing a skinny wee slip of a girl.

Their voices surrounded her, echoing through the piles of crates and metal. Deryn kept crawling, pushing back toward the bright lights of the train. The shouting men flowed past her, thinking she was still running away. . . .

Then a shadow spilled across Deryn—a huge mechanical

"SKULKING IN THE SHADOWS."

claw reaching down for her. She dropped flat, and the claw's three rubber-tipped fingers closed around a coil of wire as big as a hippoesque.

The machine paused a moment, its grip settling around the coil, and Deryn saw her chance. She scampered up and climbed inside the cylinder of wire.

With a lurch the claw hauled it—and her—up into the air.

She looked down to see the ground sliding past, the electric torches of her pursuers spreading out across the maze of crates. But no one thought to look up at the cargo passing overhead.

The metal fingers squeezed tighter for a moment, and the wire pressed inward around Deryn. Had the arm's operator spotted her and decided to crush her?

But it was just the giant claw adjusting its grip. Soon she was being gently lowered, the coil of wire settling in among a dozen others.

She waited for the arm to swing away again, then climbed out into the belly of an open-topped freight car. The side walls were only a bit taller than Deryn was, and she scrambled up and peered out.

More men had arrived to join the search. Dogs, too—a pair of German shepherds was yanking their handler along, sniffing everything in sight. Luckily, traveling by mechanical arm didn't leave much of a scent trail. But she had to get out of this cargo car before the next incoming load crushed her flat.

Deryn made her way to the front end, peeking at the next car along. It had a closed top and a fancy-looking glass door at this end. She climbed over and dropped between the cars, then jimmied the door open with her rigging knife.

She slipped inside and closed it, holding the knife out in front of her.

"Hallo?" she called softly, hoping her Clanker accent was believable.

No one answered. As her eyes adjusted to the darkness, Deryn let out a low whistle.

It was a saloon car, as fancy as a box of peacocks. A row of small tables ran down one side. The brass handrails gleamed, and the gently arching ceiling was padded with dimpled leather. The armchairs looked absurdly heavy compared to the spindly furniture on the *Leviathan.* Each of these chairs had its own tiny footrest rising from the floor. A mechanical bartender wearing a fez stood motionless in the shadows.

She took a few steps forward, feeling out of place. Even empty and dark, the dining car had the smell of poshness, and Deryn half expected a man in a tuxedo to appear and smirk at her ill-fitting uniform.

She sat down at one of the tables, peeking out through

the curtains at the hunt outside. The electric torches of her pursuers bobbed in the darkness, but they were fanning out in the direction of the water, still thinking she'd run away from the Express. Barks and shouts echoed around the docks, but here inside the train it felt as if a fancy supper were about to be served. . . .

"Supper," Deryn whispered, and sprang to her feet.

She climbed behind the bar and hunted through the shelves, finding corkscrews and towels, and bottles of brandy and wine. This was just a saloon, separate from the dining car—there was no barking *food* here!

But then she discovered a drawer full of several fancy cakes wrapped up in thick cloth napkins. One of the crew must have set them aside and then forgotten them.

Deryn sat on the floor and began to gobble the cakes. Stale or not, they tasted better than anything she'd eaten since joining the Service. She washed them down with water from the bottom of a silver ice bucket, then had a few swigs from an open bottle of brandy.

"Not bad at all," she said, then burped.

Now that her head had stopped spinning with hunger, Deryn found herself wondering what exactly was going on here. Where were the Clankers taking all this cargo? According to the labels, it had all come from Germany. So why put it on the Express, which would be headed back to Munich?

"PETIT FOURS AND BRANDY BY LAMPLIGHT."

Deryn peeked out a window again—no sign of the search remained. Her pursuers were probably at the shore, having guessed that she'd snuck in from the water.

The mechanical arms were finishing up the last few pieces of cargo—huge glass jar batteries and insulators—and the train's engines were rumbling back to life.

What if it was headed to a place close by, somewhere it could return from before dawn? No one would notice it had slipped out of the city, or suspect the luxurious Orient-Express of carrying industrial cargo.

The train jolted into motion, and Deryn reminded herself that she wasn't here to spy on the Clankers. She was here to help Alek, not uncover the secrets of the Ottoman Empire.

The barbed wire fence was already sliding past on either side—she could jump off anytime now with no one the wiser.

Deryn went back to the bar and selected the fanciest bottle of brandy she could find. It was stealing, plain and simple, but she needed something to trade for money and a proper meal. This dusty old brandy was the best thing she could find.

The Express crept slowly through Istanbul, not calling much attention to itself. The tracks traveled near the water's edge, past darkened warehouses and closed factory gates. Deryn opened the door and stood between the cars, waiting for the right moment to jump.

As the train slowed for a turn, she stepped off as smoothly as some tourist arriving on holiday. She skidded down the embankment and crouched there until the steaming dragon had passed, then made her way into the unlit streets.

Even this late, the bright lights of the city still glowed on the horizon, but Deryn reckoned she needed rest more than food now. So she picked the darkest, shabbiest alley she could find and curled up for a few hours of fitful sleep.

TWENTY-NINE

She awoke before dawn to someone prodding her with a broom.

It was a young man in coveralls, who went about the task without particular enthusiasm. When Deryn scrambled to her feet, he turned back to sweeping the alley, never saying a word. Of course, the man would hardly expect her to speak Turkish. The port of Istanbul was probably full of foreign sailors lugging about bottles of brandy.

Drums were sounding in the distance, along with a vigorous chanting. It seemed a bit early for anyone to be making such a racket. The trio of cats she'd shared the alley with hardly seemed to notice, though, and went back to sleep after the sweeping man had passed on.

Deryn walked at random until she spied the forest of minarets near the sultan's palace. Surely there were restaurants for sightseers thereabouts. The fancy cakes in her stomach had been replaced by gnawing hunger, and she needed to be thinking clearly if she was to find Alek in this giant city.

Touring Istanbul on foot wasn't like looking down from an airship or the howdah of a giant elephant. The smells were sharper down here—unfamiliar spices and walker exhaust snarled in the air, and pushcarts full of strawberries passed, leaving a sweet haze in their wake, along with a few hungry-looking dogs. A dozen languages mixed in Deryn's ears; a jumble of alphabets decorated every news kiosk. Luckily, there were also simple hand gestures among all the babel. Making herself understood would be simple enough.

When men in seamen's slops called out to Deryn, she answered them in Clanker. She'd learned a handful of greetings from Bauer and Hoffman, and a few choice curses as well. It never hurt to practice.

She found a shop window filled with fancy liquor bottles, dusted off her brandy, and went inside. At first the proprietor looked askance at her disheveled slops, and almost tossed her out when he discovered that she was there to sell, not buy. But when he glimpsed the bottle's label, his attitude changed. He offered her a pile of coins, which grew by half when she gave him a hard look.

Most of the restaurants were closed, but Deryn soon found a hotel. A few minutes later she was sitting down to a breakfast of cheese, olives, cucumbers, black coffee, and a small bowl of a gloppy substance called yogurt, which was halfway between cheese and milk.

As she ate, Deryn wondered how she would find Alek. In his message to Volger he'd said that his hotel had a name like his mother's. That sounded simple enough, except that Alek had never told Deryn his mother's name. She knew his granduncle the emperor, of course—Franz Joseph—and remembered that his father's name was also Franz something-or-other. But wives were seldom as famous as their husbands.

She watched a group of sailors walk past, and wondered if any of them were Austrian. Surely they would know the murdered archduchess's name, if Deryn could only make her question understood.

But then she remembered the other half of Alek's message, that the Germans were looking for him. Questions about a fugitive prince from an English-speaking sailor in a Clanker uniform would only attract suspicion.

She had to find the answer herself. Luckily, Alek's family was famous. Wouldn't they be in history books?

All she needed was some sort of family tree. . . .

An hour later Deryn was standing on a broad marble stair, a brand-new sketchbook in her hand. Before her stood, according to her half dozen conversations in sign language and halting Clanker, the newest and largest library in Istanbul.

Its huge brass columns gleamed in the sun, and its steam-powered revolving doors gathered and disgorged people without pausing. As she passed through them, Deryn had the same jitters she'd felt in the saloon car of the Orient-Express. She didn't belong in any place so fancy, and the bustle of so many machines made her dizzy.

The ceiling was a tangle of glass tubes, full of small cylinders zooming through them, almost too fast to see. The clicking fingers of calculation engines covered the walls, fluttering like the cilia of the great airbeast when it was nervous. Clockwork walkers the size of hatboxes scrabbled along the marble floor, stacks of books weighing them down.

A small army of clerks waited behind a row of desks, but Deryn made her way through the vast lobby, headed toward the towering stacks of books. There looked to be *millions* of them, surely a few were in English.

But she found herself halted by a fancy iron fence that stretched all the way across the room. Every few feet there was a sign that repeated the same message in two dozen languages:

CLOSED STACKS—ASK AT INFORMATION DESK.

Deryn returned to the desks, screwed up her courage, and went to the one with the nicest-looking clerk behind it. He wore a long gray beard, a fez, and pince-nez glasses, and gave her a slightly puzzled smile as she approached. Deryn guessed that most sailors didn't spend their shore leave in the library.

She bowed to him, then tore two pages from her sketch

"THE LIBRARY CATALOG."

pad and set them down on the desk. On one she'd drawn the Hapsburg crest that had decorated the breastplate of Alek's Stormwalker. On the other she had sketched a branching tree, like the genealogies of the great airbeasts that Mr. Rigby was always making them memorize. No doubt the Clankers drew their family trees in a different manner, but surely a librarian would understand the concept.

The man adjusted his glasses, stared at the sketches for a moment, then gave Deryn a quizzical look.

"You are Austrian?" he asked in careful Clanker.

"No, sir. America." She spoke in German as well, but tried to mimic Eddie Malone's accent. "But I want . . ."—her brain raced—"to understand the war."

The man slowly nodded. "Very well, young man. A moment, please."

He turned to face what looked like a piano set into the desk, and clacked away at its keys. No music emerged, but as he typed a punch card emerged from a slot in the desk. He handed it to her and pointed.

"Good luck."

Deryn bowed and thanked him, then followed his gesture to a kiosk in the center of the room. She watched another patron use it first. The woman fed her punch card into what looked like a miniature loom. The card slid beneath a fine-tooth comb, whose tiny metal teeth jabbed up and down, as if scrutinizing the holes in the card.

After a moment's spinning and clattering, the card was spat back out. From the top of the kiosk, a clockwork machine climbed up and out, then went skittering away into the stacks of books.

Deryn felt queasy from following the Clanker logic of it all, but stepped forward to repeat the process with her own card. When the card popped back out, she discovered that it was stamped with a number. After a minute's wandering about the lobby, Deryn found a row of small tables labeled with numbers of their own. She sat down at the one that matched her card and pulled out her sketchbook.

As she drew, the whirr and clatter of the machines echoed around her, the sounds blending like the crash of distant waves. Deryn wondered how the Clankers managed it, translating questions into scatterings of holes in paper. Did every wee sliver of knowledge have its own number? The system was probably quicker than wandering through the ceiling-high shelves, but what other books might she have found, doing it herself?

She looked up at the calculating engines that covered the walls, and wondered what they were up to. Did they record every question that the librarians had been asked? And if so, who looked at the results? Deryn remembered the eyes peering at her through the slats of the throne room wall, and began to drum her fingers.

Surely in all this tumult of information, no one would

notice a few questions about the tragedy that had started this whole barking war.

Finally her clockwork machine scuttled back, like a dog with a fetched bone. It was weighted down with half a dozen books, all of them heavy and bound with cracked old leather.

She picked a few up and leafed through the gilt-edged pages. Some were in Clanker, others in a flowing script she'd seen on many of the signs outside, but one had hardly any words at all, only names, dates, and coats of arms. On its cover was the Hapsburg crest, and a Latin phrase she remembered from the first time Alek and Dr. Barlow had met.

Bella gerant alii, tu Felix Austria, nube.

"Let others wage war," the first part meant.

"Barking spiders," Deryn said softly to herself—there were a *lot* of Hapsburgs. The book was thick enough to stun a hippoesque, and the entries stretched back eight hundred years. But Alek was only fifteen; he'd have to be at the end.

She turned to the last pages and soon found him: "Aleksandar, Prinz von Hohenberg," along with his birth date and the names of his parents—Franz Ferdinand and Sophie Chotek.

"Sophie," Deryn murmured, leaning back and smiling to herself.

She left the stack of books on the table and headed back toward the revolving doors. After a quick trip down the marble stairs outside, she approached the first of a rank of six-legged taxis, all of them in the shape of giant beetles. Deryn reached into her pocket for the remaining coins.

"Sophie Hotel?" she asked. "Hotel" was the same in English or Clanker.

The pilot frowned, then asked, "Hotel Hagia Sophia?"

Deryn nodded happily. That sounded close enough—it *had* to be the one.

The taxi pilot inspected her handful of coins, then hooked a thumb toward the back seat. Deryn jumped aboard, for once enjoying the rumble of a Clanker engine beneath her. After tracking Alek down in a city of millions, she deserved to ride instead of walk.

THIRTY

The Hotel Hagia Sophia was pure dead fancy.

Deryn shook her head. She might have expected to find Alek in a place like this. The lobby alone was three stories high and lit by two gas chandeliers and a giant stained-glass skylight. Uniformed bellmen guided their clockwork luggage carriers through the bustling crowd. Marble staircases spiraled their way to the mezzanines and balconies, while steam elevators huffed into the air like sky rockets taking flight.

Even if Alek had chosen this hotel to match his mother's name, Deryn wondered if he might have found another clue to use—one that would have led somewhere a bit less . . . *princely*. The Germans were still looking for him, after all.

Of course, that meant that Alek wouldn't be listed under his own name. So how was she going to get a message to him?

Deryn stood there, hoping to catch a glance of Alek, Bauer, or Master Klopp in the lobby. But the crowd was full of unfamiliar faces, and soon Deryn felt the eyes of a white-gloved bellman on her. Her stolen uniform was rumpled and dirty from sleeping in the alley, and she stuck out like a clump of clart on a fancy china plate. She had only a few coins left, surely not enough to pay for a room, not here.

Perhaps she could buy coffee and some lunch. Judging by what she'd had for breakfast, there were worse places than Istanbul to crawl ashore half starved.

Deryn took a seat at a small table in the hotel dining room, making sure she had a view of the lobby doors. The waiter understood no English, but spoke Clanker no better than she did. He returned with a pot of strong coffee and a menu, and before long Deryn was feasting again, this time on lamb chopped into a hash with nuts and sultanas, covered with a plum jelly as dark as an old bruise.

She ate slowly, keeping her eyes on the hotel's main doors.

People came and went, most of them well-heeled old Clankers. The man at the table next to hers wore a monocle and a handlebar mustache, and was reading a German newspaper. When he left, Deryn reached over and snatched it up. She leafed through the pages to conceal that she was stalling with her food.

The last page was all photographs—the latest fashions, new clockwork house servants, and well-dressed ladies at a roller-skating parlor. Nothing earth-shattering, until Deryn's eyes fell upon three photos across the bottom of the page. One was the *Leviathan* flying over the city, another was the *Dauntless* kneeling in the street after its rampage, and the last showed two men under guard. . . .

It was Matthews and Spencer, the survivors of her disastrous first command.

She squinted at the caption, annoyed that Alek hadn't taught her any Clanker spelling. These three pictures together could hardly be good news. The *Leviathan* would be leaving Istanbul under a dark cloud today.

Unless the Ottomans had been angry enough to order the airship away early.

Deryn frowned. Count Volger had planned to escape last night, hadn't he? After her almost sleepless night, she'd forgotten all about him.

She lowered the newspaper, looking more closely at the stuffy old Clankers in the lobby. None had Volger's tall, lean frame and gray mustache. But the wildcount wouldn't have needed a trip to the library to learn Alek's mother's name. Maybe he and Hoffman were already upstairs, having a cup of tea with Alek and the others!

Just then Deryn noticed a young couple coming in through the lobby doors. They were dressed like locals, and the girl was perhaps eighteen and quite beautiful, with long dark hair in tight braids.

Deryn swallowed—the boy was *Alek*! She'd hardly recognized him in his tunic and tasseled fez. Not that he could wander about Istanbul in an Austrian piloting uniform, but somehow she hadn't expected him to look so . . . Ottoman.

Alek drew to a halt, his eyes searching the lobby, but Deryn snapped the newspaper up in front of her face.

Who was this strange girl? One of his new *allies*? Suddenly that word took on an entirely new meaning in Deryn's head.

A moment later Alek and the girl headed toward the elevators, and Deryn leapt to her feet. Whoever this girl was, Deryn couldn't afford to miss this chance. She slapped her remaining coins onto the table and headed after them.

An elevator opened up before the two, the attendant ushering them inside. Deryn waved her newspaper, and the attendant nodded, holding the door. Alek and the girl were talking intently in Clanker, and hardly noticed when she stepped in beside them.

As the door slid closed, Deryn opened the paper, pretending to read.

"Nice weather we're having," she said in English.

Alek turned toward her, a baffled expression on his face. He opened his mouth, but no sound came out.

"Dylan," she said politely. "In case you've forgotten."

"God's wounds! It *is* you! But what are you—"

"It's a long story," Deryn said, glancing at the girl. "And a bit secret, actually."

"Ah, of course—introductions are in order," he said, then glanced at the elevator man. "Or will be . . . quite soon."

They rode the rest of the way in silence.

Alek led them to a set of double doors that opened onto a vast room, all silk and tassels, with its own balcony and a shiny brass switchboard for calling servants. There was no bed in sight, just a pair of French doors half opened to reveal yet another room.

Deryn noticed the other girl's eyes widen, and she felt a squick of relief. Apparently this girl had never been here before either.

"Almost as fancy as your castle," Deryn said.

"And with rather better service. There's someone here you should meet, Dylan." Alek turned and called out, "*Guten tag*, Bovril!"

"*Guten tag!*" came a voice from nowhere, and then a wee beastie waddled from behind the curtains. It looked like a cross between a butler monkey and some kind of cuddly toy, all huge eyes and tiny, clever hands.

"Barking spiders," Deryn breathed. She'd forgotten all about Dr. Barlow's missing beastie. "Is that what I think it is?"

"*Mr.* Sharp," the beastie said sarcastically.

She blinked. "How in blazes does it *know* me?"

"An intriguing question," Alek said. "Bovril seems to have been listening while it was still in the egg. But it also heard your voice from that reporter's awful bullfrog."

"You mean that bum-rag was recording us?"

Alek nodded, and Deryn softly swore. What of Volger's threats had the bullfrog repeated?

The strange girl didn't seem surprised to see Bovril at all. She pulled a bag of peanuts from her pocket, and the beastie crawled over to her and began to eat them.

Deryn remembered her conversation with Dr. Barlow aboard the sultan's airyacht. The lady boffin had been quite vague about the creature's purpose. Deryn still didn't know what "perspicacious" meant, and there was all that business about nascent fixation, which had sounded a bit sinister, even if baby ducks did it too.

She'd have to keep an eye on this beastie.

"You named it Bovril?" she asked Alek.

"*I* named it, in fact," said the girl in slow, careful English. "This silly boy kept calling it 'the creature.'"

"But you're not supposed to name beasties! If you get too attached, you can't use them properly."

"*Use* them?" Lilit asked. "What a horrid way to think of animals."

Deryn rolled her eyes. Had Alek taken up with Monkey

Luddites now? "Aye, lassie, and you've never eaten meat?"

The girl frowned. "Well, of course I have. But that seems different, somehow."

"Only because you're used to it. And why in blazes did you name it *Bovril*, anyway? That's a sort of beef tea!"

The girl shrugged. "I thought it should have an English name. And Bovril is the only English thing I like."

"It's Scottish, actually," Deryn muttered.

"Speaking of names, I've been quite rude." Alek bowed a little. "Lilit, this is Midshipman Dylan Sharp."

"Midshipman?" she asked. "You must be from the *Leviathan*."

"Aye," Deryn said, giving Alek a hard look. "Though I *was* meaning to keep that a secret."

"Secret," Bovril repeated, then made a chuckling noise.

"Don't worry," Alek said. "Lilit and I have no secrets from each other."

Deryn stared at the boy, hoping that wasn't true. He couldn't have told this girl who his parents were, could he?

"But where's Volger?" Alek asked. "You must have escaped with him."

"I didn't *escape* at all, you ninny. I'm here for a . . ." She glanced at Lilit. "A secret mission. I've no idea where his countship is."

"But the bullfrog said you were going to help Volger escape!"

Deryn raised an eyebrow, wondering what else the bull-frog had repeated. Of course, Eddie Malone hadn't understood Volger's threats, and neither would Alek.

"*Mr.* Sharp," the creature said again, still chuckling.

She ignored it. "I was planning to help him and Hoffman escape, but then I was given a mission. Maybe they managed on their own." Deryn held up the newspaper. "But I reckon they didn't have time."

Alek took the paper from her and squinted at the captions. "'The *Leviathan* had been granted leave to stay in the capital for four extra days, but the night before last the brave Ottoman army discovered Darwinist saboteurs in the Dardanelles. All were killed or captured. In his outrage at this affront, His Excellency the sultan has demanded that the airship leave the capital immediately.'"

He let the paper drop.

"Aye, I thought so," Deryn said. "Volger was planning on escaping last night, but if the ship was sent away yesterday . . ."

"Then he's gone," Alek said softly.

Deryn nodded, realizing that the *Leviathan* was gone too.

"Where will they take him? London?"

"No. They'll head back down to the Mediterranean," Deryn said. "Patrol duty."

Of course, it would be much more than patrol. The airship would be awaiting the behemoth's arrival. There would be weeks of training missions, practice in guiding the huge beastie through narrow straits. Battle drills and midnight alerts. And here she was, stuck in this alien city, all alone except for Alek and his men, the perspicacious loris, and this unknown girl.

"But, Dylan," Alek said, "if you didn't escape, then why are you here?"

"Don't you see?" Lilit spoke up. "That's a German sailor's uniform—a disguise." She turned to Deryn. "You were one of the saboteurs, weren't you?"

Deryn frowned. The lassie was quick, wasn't she?

"Aye, I'm the only one they didn't catch. Those three poor blighters were my men."

Alek sat down in a tasseled chair, swearing softly in Clanker. "I'm sorry about your men, Dylan."

"Aye, me too. And I'm sorry about Volger," said Deryn, though she wasn't sure if she meant it. The wildcount was too much of a clever-boots for her liking. "He really did mean to join you."

Alek nodded slowly, staring at the floor. For a moment he looked younger than his fifteen years, like a wee boy. But he gathered himself and looked up at her.

"Well, I suppose you'll have to do, Dylan. You're a fine soldier, after all. I'm sure the Committee will be happy to have you."

"What are you talking about? What committee?"

"The Committee for Union and Progress. They seek to overthrow the sultan."

Deryn glanced at Lilit, then back at Alek, her eyes widening. Overthrow the sultan? What if Count Volger had been right, and Alek had joined some daft bunch of anarchists? And Monkey Luddite anarchists at that!

"Alek," said Lilit softly, "you can't go telling this boy our secrets. Not till he's met Nene, at least."

Alek waved her protests away. "You can trust Dylan. He's known for ages who my father was, and he never betrayed me to his officers."

Deryn's jaw dropped. Alek had already told this anarchist lassie about his parents? But he'd been in Istanbul only *three barking days*!

Suddenly she wondered if she should just walk out the door. She'd seen a dozen cargo ships flying British flags. Maybe one would take her out to the Mediterranean and back to sanity.

Why had she abandoned her sworn duty for some barking *prince*?

"Besides," Alek said, standing up and putting a hand on Deryn's shoulder, "fate has delivered Dylan here to Istanbul. Clearly he's *meant* to help us!"

Deryn and Lilit looked at each other, and they both rolled their eyes.

Alek ignored their skeptical looks. "Listen to me,

"DISCUSSIONS AT THE HOTEL."

Dylan. You Darwinists want to keep the Ottomans out of the war, right? It's the whole reason Dr. Barlow brought us all this way."

"Aye, but that's all gone pear-shaped. Everything we've done has only pushed the sultan into the Germans' hands."

"Perhaps," Alek said. "But what if the sultan were overthrown? Since the last revolution, the rebels here have despised the Germans. They'd never join the Clanker side."

"The British are just as bad," Lilit said. "All the great powers take advantage of us. But it's true enough, we don't want anything to do with your war. We just want the sultan gone."

Deryn stared at the girl, wondering whether to trust her. Alek apparently did, having blathered all his secrets. But what if he was wrong?

Well, in that case he needed someone he *could* trust.

"Great powers," muttered Bovril, then went back to eating peanuts.

Deryn let out a slow sigh. She'd come to Istanbul to help Alek, after all, and here he was, asking for help. But this was so much bigger than anything she'd expected.

If the sultan could be tossed out of his palace, then The Straits would stay open and the Russian army wouldn't starve. The Clankers' grand plan to extend their influence into Asia would be stopped in its tracks.

This was a chance not just to help Alek but to change the course of the whole barking war. Perhaps it was her duty to stay right here.

"All right, then," she said. "I'll do what I can."

THIRTY-ONE

"I do look rather Turkish, don't I?" Klopp said, regarding himself in the mirror.

Alek hesitated a moment, struggling for words. The man didn't look like a Turk at all—more like a zeppelin wrapped in blue silk with a tasseled nose cone.

"Perhaps without the fez, sir," Bauer suggested.

"You might be right, Hans," Alek said. "A turban would be better."

"Fez!" proclaimed Bovril, who was sitting on Dylan's shoulder eating plums.

"The fez is good," Dylan said. The boy's German was getting better, but he still missed words here and there.

"How does one put on a turban?" Klopp asked, but no one knew.

Bauer and Klopp had been stuck in the hotel for almost a week now, and it had been slowly driving them mad. A

cage was still a cage, however luxurious. But at last they were going out, headed to Zaven's warehouse to inspect the walkers of the Committee.

The problem was how to get them there without being spotted.

Alek and Dylan had tried their best to buy disguises at the Grand Bazaar, but the results hadn't been entirely successful. Bauer looked too fancy, like one of the hotel doormen, and Klopp's voluminous robes had turned him into a silken airship.

"We don't have to pass for Ottomans," Alek said. "We're just going through the lobby and into a taxi, then straight to the warehouse. Hardly anyone will see us."

"Then why aren't you dressed like a Hapsburg prince, young master?" Klopp pulled the fez from his head. "Seeing as how these anarchists already know your name."

"They're not anarchists," Alek said for the hundredth time. "Anarchists want to destroy all government. The Committee just wants to replace the sultan with an elected parliament."

"It's all the same nasty business," Klopp said, shaking his head. "Murdering one's masters. Have you forgotten those Serb boys throwing bombs at your parents?"

Alek bridled at Klopp's impertinence, but kept his anger in check. The old man had a dim view of revolutions in general, and Lilit's chatter about women's equality had hardly helped.

But meeting Zaven and the iron golems would put Klopp at ease. Nothing brought a smile to his face like the sight of a new walker.

"The Germans were behind that attack, Master Klopp. And allying with the Committee is our only way to strike back at them."

"I suppose you're right, young master."

"Indeed," Alek said simply. He looked at Bauer, who promptly nodded his head.

Dylan, however, was proving more difficult to convince. He'd taken an instant dislike to Lilit, and refused to tell Alek anything about his mission in Istanbul, saying only that it was too secret to share with "a bunch of daft anarchists."

Still, it was enough that Dylan was here in Istanbul, ready to help. Something about the boy's brisk confidence made Alek remember that providence was on his side.

"We have to bring the beastie," Dylan said in English, pulling on a silk jacket. His clothes fit perfectly—he'd spent an hour alone with the tailor getting them just right. "Dr. Barlow says it can be quite useful."

"But all it does is babble," Alek said, pulling his most important cargo—a small, heavy satchel—onto his shoulder. "Did she explain exactly *how* it's meant to help?"

Dylan opened the birdcage, and Bovril scampered over and jumped inside. "Only that we should listen to it. Because it's quite . . . perspicacious."

Alek frowned. "I'm afraid that word is beyond my English."

"Aye. It's beyond mine, too." Dylan reached into the birdcage and scratched the creature's chin. "But you're a cute wee beastie, aren't you?"

"Perspicacious," the creature said.

◉   ◉   ◉

When Klopp was finally ready, Alek used the switchboard to call for a steam elevator. A few minutes later the four of them were downstairs and headed across the lobby.

The hotel was bustling, and no one stared at their clothes or asked why they were carrying toolboxes. Alek dropped the key off at the desk, and the doorman saluted smartly as he led them all outside. One thing could be said for Istanbul, people minded their own business here.

Several of the city's scarab beetle taxis were waiting, and Alek chose the largest. It had two ranks of passenger seats, the rearmost big enough for Klopp's ample frame. Alek climbed into the front rank with Deryn, then handed the pilot some coins and told him the name of Zaven's neighborhood.

The man gave him a nod, and then they were off.

Above the noises of the street, Alek heard a rumbling from the birdcage. It was Bovril imitating the walker's engine. He leaned down to shush the beast, then slipped the small, heavy satchel under the seat.

"A lot of soldiers about," Bauer said. "Is it always this way?"

Alek looked up, frowning. The walker was striding down a wide avenue lined with tall trees. Ottoman soldiers stood on either side, forming themselves into double ranks. Most were in dress uniforms.

"I've never seen this many," he said. "Perhaps it's a parade."

The taxi was slowing now, the traffic growing heavier. Ahead of them a cargo walker in the shape of a water buffalo began to belch black smoke, and Klopp made a rude comment about poor maintenance. Hot steam clouds billowed from the surrounding engines, until the four of them were all tugging at their new clothes.

"Sir," Bauer said softly, "something's going on up there."

Alek peered through the water buffalo's exhaust. A hundred meters ahead a squad of soldiers was stopping every vehicle that passed.

"A checkpoint," Alek said.

"Foreigners are meant to carry passports in this country," Klopp said softly.

"Should we get out and walk?" Alek said.

Klopp shook his head. "That'll just make them curious. We're carrying these toolboxes . . . and a *birdcage*, for heaven's sake."

"Right," Alek sighed. "Well, then, we're tourists who've left our passports at our hotel. And if that doesn't work, we can bribe them."

"And if bribery doesn't work?" Klopp asked.

Alek frowned. They were carrying too much to run, and there were too many soldiers here to start a fight.

"Let me guess," Dylan said in English. "You're thinking about bribing them. They'll refuse. No soldier takes a bribe with so many captains about."

Alek swore softly. It was true—officers with tall plumed hats were everywhere.

"Can't you pilot this contraption?" Dylan asked.

Alek peered over the pilot's shoulder at the strange controls. "With six legs? Not me, but Klopp can handle anything."

Dylan gave him a grin. "Enough with your blether, then. When it comes time, I'll give the pilot a heave, and you and Bauer shove Master Klopp in front of the saunters!"

"I suppose that sounds simple enough," Alek said.

But of course it wasn't simple at all.

The next five minutes were quite excruciating. The line oozed along like heavy engine oil, while Klopp listed every conceivable disaster under his breath. But finally the belching water buffalo ahead of them passed the checkpoint, and the taxi strode into place.

A soldier stepped forward and gave them all a long, puzzled look. He held his hand out, saying something in Turkish.

"I'm sorry," Alek said, "but we don't speak your language."

The man offered a polite bow, and said in excellent German, "Passports, then, please."

"Ah." Alek made a show of checking his pockets. "I seem to have forgotten mine."

Klopp and Bauer followed suit, patting their silk robes and frowning.

The soldier raised an eyebrow, then turned to his squad and lifted a hand in the air.

"Oh, blisters!" Dylan cried, grabbing the startled pilot under his armpits and lifting him up. "Do it *now!*"

As Dylan dropped the man over the side of the taxi, Alek helped Bauer shove Klopp toward the front seat. He felt as heavy as a hogshead of wine, but a moment later he was sitting at the controls, his hands gripping the saunters.

The taxi reared up like a stallion on its four hind legs, scattering the guards around them. Then it bolted forward, sparks flying from its metal feet. Past the crowded checkpoint the avenue was clear, and soon Klopp had the machine at full gallop.

The soldiers cried out, unshouldering their rifles, and soon gunshots echoed around the taxi. Alek ducked, feeling as though his teeth were being shaken from his head. Dylan's arms were wrapped around Klopp's waist to keep them both from flying out of the taxi. Bauer had his hands on the toolboxes, and Alek reached down to secure the small satchel on the floor.

The only sound from the birdcage was Bovril's maniacal laughter.

"Hold on tight!" Klopp shouted, and leaned the taxi into a tight turn. Its six insectlike feet skidded along the cobblestones, making a sound like sabers dragged along a brick wall.

"RUSHING THROUGH THE CHECKPOINT."

Alek stuck his head up. This side street was narrower, and pedestrians were scattering as the taxi's beetle jaws hurtled toward them.

"Don't kill anyone, Klopp!" he shouted, just as the machine's right foreleg clipped a stack of barrels. One barrel split as the stack tumbled, and the sharp scent of vinegar sprayed into the air. At the next turn the taxi began to skid again, threatening to slide sideways through the large windows of a butcher shop, but Klopp wrestled it back under control.

"Where am I going?" he cried.

Alek pulled Zaven's hand-drawn map from his pocket, and made a rough calculation. "Head left when you can, and slow down. No one's behind us yet."

Klopp nodded, and brought the machine down into a six-legged canter. The next street was lined with mechanical parts shops and crowded with cargo walkers. No one looked twice at the taxi.

"I don't know how you can stand these daft contraptions," Dylan said, sitting up straight in his seat. "They're pure murder when they go fast!"

"Wasn't this *your* idea?" Alek asked.

"It worked, didn't it?"

"For the moment. They'll be after us soon enough."

The taxi made its way deeper into the industrial part of town, with Klopp following Alek's guesses. The markings of the Committee's mix of languages soon filled the walls. But streets signs were rare here, and nothing matched the few avenues labeled on Zaven's map.

"This is all quite familiar," Alek said to Klopp. "We're close."

"That might be a problem, sir," Bauer said. "Didn't you tell the cabbie where we were headed?"

"I told him what neighborhood."

"The Ottomans must have questioned him by now. They'll be here soon."

"You're right, Hans. We have to hurry." Alek turned to Klopp. "Zaven's warehouse has a view of the whole city. We should be able to see it from higher ground."

Klopp nodded, turning whenever a road led upward. Finally the taxi eased to a halt at the crest of a hill, and Alek saw the cluster of warehouses, with Zaven's apartments nestled on top.

"That's it! Maybe half a kilometer!"

"Do you hear that sound?" Dylan asked.

Alek listened. Even with the taxi idling, it was there— a buzzing at the edge of his awareness. He looked around, but there was nothing in sight except cargo walkers and a clockwork messenger cart.

"It's not down here," Dylan said quietly, staring at the sky.

Alek looked up and saw it. . . .

A gyrothopter hovering directly overhead.

THIRTY-TWO

"Find cover!" Alek cried.

Klopp urged the taxi forward again, rounding a corner into a narrow alley.

Stone walls loomed over them, the sky hardly wider than a sliver. The gyrothopter darted in and out of view. But however the alley twisted and turned, the machine's buzzing echoed in Alek's ears.

He noticed that the streets had cleared—the people knew that a military operation was on, and were anxious to get out of the way. Only a few dogs were left to scamper out of the taxi's path.

A light sparkled overhead, followed by a crackling sound.

"Fireworks!" Dylan cried. "The gyropilot's signaling that he's found us!"

Alek heard the shriek of whistles dead ahead.

"Klopp! Slow down!"

As it rounded the next corner, the taxi skidded to a halt, too late. A squad of soldiers waited, their rifles ready. Klopp pulled the saunters back as they fired, and the taxi reared up again. Alek heard the *ping* of bullets ricocheting from the machine's underside.

Klopp wheeled the taxi around with its forelegs still in the air, and bolted back the way they'd come. Another volley of shots followed, dust spitting from the stone walls on either side.

The taxi careened around a corner, but gears were grinding beneath the floorboards, and the smell of burning metal filled the air.

"Our engine's been hit!" Bauer cried.

"I know a trick for that," Klopp said calmly.

He turned them aside into a small plaza with an old stone fountain, and walked the machine straight into the water. Hissing clouds of steam rose up around them as the tortured metal cooled.

"She won't go much farther," Klopp said.

"We're almost there." As Alek stared at his map, he noticed a rumbling sound coming from the birdcage. What in blazes was the beast imitating now?

Then he heard it above the hiss of boiling water.

"A walker's coming." Dylan pointed ahead. "From that way, dead fast."

"It sounds big. We'll have to turn back and face the soldiers."

"Not if we take those," Dylan said, pointing at a stone staircase that led down from the plaza.

Alek shook his head. "Too steep."

"What's the point of legs if you can't take the barking stairs? Just get *moving*!"

In English or not, Klopp could tell what they were talking about—he was also staring down the steps. He looked at Alek, who nodded. The old man sighed, then grasped the saunters again.

"Hold on, everyone!" Alek shouted, planting one boot on the satchel at his feet.

The machine tipped slowly forward, then slid, its hooves rattling like a rock drill as they skidded down the steps. Stone dust flew as the taxi bounced back and forth, battering the ancient walls. Klopp somehow kept the machine from tipping over, and at last it reached the bottom, sliding onto level pavement.

Alek heard a *crack* and looked up. Soldiers were taking positions in the plaza above, their rifle muzzles flaring. A two-legged walker strode into view.

Alek blinked—it had Ottoman markings, but it was a German design, not like an animal in any way.

"Get down!" he cried. "And keep going, Klopp!"

The taxi ground back into motion, its gears whining

"OTTOMAN WALKER IN PURSUIT."

with every step. As it rounded the next corner, Alek dared to glance back up. Soldiers were streaming down the stairs, but the walker had come to a halt, its crew unwilling to dare the stairway on two legs.

Alek checked the map again. "We're almost there, Klopp. That way!"

The taxi was limping now, one of its middle legs flailing. But it managed to drag itself onto Zaven's street, staggering sideways like a drunken crab.

Lilit and her father had heard the commotion, of course— they were waiting with the warehouse door wide open.

"Go fast, Klopp!" Dylan shouted in crude German. "The gyrothopter!"

Alek looked up. He couldn't see the gyrothopter, but its buzzing sound was building in the air. They had to disappear *now*.

The taxi took another step toward the open warehouse door, then sputtered and died. Klopp whirled the starting crank, but the engine only hissed and spat like a fresh log tossed onto a fire.

"Barking stupid contraptions!" Dylan cried.

"Lilit, if you please?" Zaven said calmly, and she leapt to the controls of the mechanikal arm on the loading dock. It rumbled to life and reached out to slide the taxi through the warehouse door.

The door rolled closed behind them, and Zaven

stepped inside just as the last view of the street disappeared, plunging them all into darkness.

Alek reached down and checked the satchel at his feet—it was still there.

A moment later an electrikal light switched on.

"A most dramatic entrance," Zaven said, his smile gleaming.

"But won't someone tell them?" Alek panted, looking at the crack of sunlight beneath the door.

"Fah! Not to worry," Zaven said. "Our neighbors are all friends. They have ignored greater disturbances than this." He offered a deep bow. "Greetings, Masters Klopp, Bauer, and Sharp. I welcome you all to the Committee for Union and Progress!"

The Committee's walkers towered over them like five huge misshapen statues.

"What an odd collection," Bauer said. "Never seen any of these before."

"A few of those fought in the First Balkan War," Klopp said, pointing at the Minotaur. "They were a bit old-fashioned even then."

"War," said Bovril, staring up from Alek's shoulder.

Alek frowned. The first time he'd seen the walkers, he'd assumed the dents in their armor were from training battles. But with the noon sun flooding the vast courtyard, there was no denying it—these machines were ancient.

"You can fix them up, can't you?" he asked.

"Perhaps," Klopp said.

"Fah! We shall fix them together!" Zaven proclaimed. He was already treating Klopp like a long-lost brother. "You may have modern knowledge, sir, but our mechaniks have those skills that can only be passed from father to son—and to daughter, of course!"

"These machines are like family to us," Lilit said.

Klopp set down his toolbox. "Hmm . . . grandparents, I suppose."

No one laughed at this joke except Bovril, who climbed down and scampered across the courtyard to inspect the giant steel hooves of the Minotaur.

Dylan had been standing silently since they'd arrived, his arms folded. But now he spoke in halting German. "How many are there?"

"How many pledged to the revolution?" Zaven rubbed his hands together happily. "We have a half dozen in every ghetto in this city. Almost fifty in all; enough to sweep away the sultan's metal elephants. We could have done so six years ago, but we were not united then."

"And now, sir?" Bauer asked.

"Like a fist!" Zaven said, demonstrating with both hands. "Even the Young Turks have rejoined us, thanks to all the Germans marching about."

"And thanks to the Spider, too, of course," Lilit said.

Alek looked at her. "The Spider?"

"Shall we show them?" Lilit asked, but didn't wait for her father to answer. She ran to a large metal door in the courtyard wall, and jumped up to grab a chain hanging beside it. As she climbed it, her weight drew the chain down, and the door began to slide grudgingly upward.

A huge machine stood in the shadows.

Alek had no idea what it was for, but could see why Lilit had called it the Spider. A dark mass of machinery rested at its center, from which eight long jointed arms thrust out. A snarl of conveyor belts led into the core, like on a harvesting combine.

"Is that some sort of walking contraption?" Dylan asked in English.

"They called it 'the Spider,'" Alek translated, then shook his head. "But it doesn't look as though it can walk."

"This is no mere war machine," Zaven proclaimed. "But a far more powerful engine of progress. Lilit, show our guests!"

Lilit stepped through the doorway, almost disappearing in the shadows beneath the machine's bulk. A panel of dials and levers flickered to life, showing her in silhouette. She worked the controls, and a moment later the paving stones of the courtyard were rumbling beneath Alek's feet.

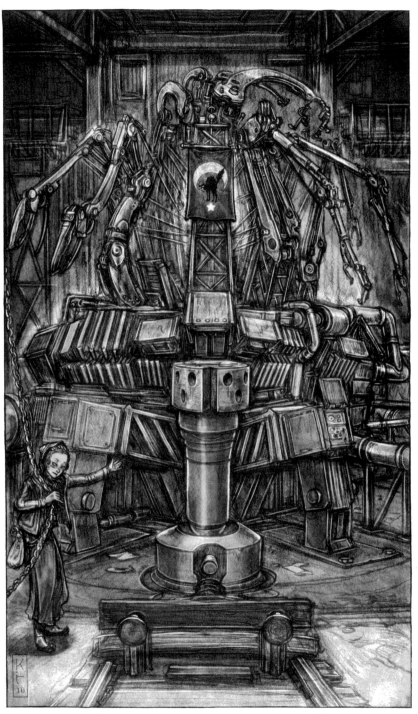

"UNVEILING A WALKER OF MESSAGES."

The eight arms began to move, stirring the air like the hands of an orchestra conductor, their manipulator claws making fine adjustments to the conveyor belts and other parts of the machine.

"It does look a bit like a spideresque," Dylan said. "One of the big ones that weaves parachutes."

Zaven nodded vigorously, answering her in his flawless English. "The Spider has woven the threads that hold our revolution together. Did you know, lad, that the word 'text' comes from the Latin word for weaving?"

"Text?" Alek said. "What does that have to do with . . . ?"

His voice faded as he saw a flicker of white within the gloom. A roll of paper was unspooling along one of the belts, disappearing into the machine's dark center. The arms began to whirl through the air, carrying about trays of metal pieces, pouring buckets of black liquid, then cutting and folding the paper with long, nimble fingers.

"Barking spiders," Dylan snorted. "It's a printing press."

"A Spider with a bark, indeed," Zaven said. "Far mightier than any sword!"

The machine whirred and spun for another minute, then slowed and darkened again. When Lilit emerged from the shadows, she was carrying a stack of neatly folded leaflets covered with inscrutable symbols.

Zaven lifted one up. "Ah, yes, my article on the subject of women being allowed to vote. Can you read Armenian?"

Alek raised an eyebrow. "Alas, no."

"How unfortunate. But the real message is just here." Zaven pointed at a row of symbols across the bottom of the page—stars, crescents, and crosses that looked like mere decoration.

"A secret code," Alek murmured, recalling the markings on the alley walls. With the profusion of newspapers sold on the streets of Istanbul, one more in a hodgepodge of languages wouldn't attract much notice. But for those who knew the code . . .

He felt Bovril tugging on his trouser leg. The beast was stepping from one foot to the other.

Alek closed his eyes, and felt the slightest tremor through his boots.

"What's that rumbling?"

"It feels like walkers, sir," Bauer said. "Big ones."

"Have they found us?" Alek asked.

"Fah. It's just the sultan's parade, for the end of Ramazan." Zaven swept one hand toward the stairs. "Perhaps you would all join my family on the roof. Our balcony has an excellent view."

THIRTY-THREE

The Ottoman war elephants paraded down the distant tree-lined avenue, leaving footprints of shattered cobblestones. Their crescent flags snapped in the wind, and their trunks—tipped with machine guns—swayed between long, barbed tusks. They turned in formation, as precise as marching soldiers, heading away toward the docks.

Deryn breathed a sigh of relief, handing the field glasses back to Alek.

"Mr. Zaven's right. They're not coming this way."

"This must be the parade they were getting ready for," Alek said, then handed the glasses to Klopp. *"Was denken Sie, Klopp? Hundert Tonnen je?"*

"Hundert und fünfzig," the master of mechaniks said.

Deryn nodded in agreement. If she understood him rightly, Klopp was guessing the metal elephants weighed a hundred and fifty tons each. Clanker tons were a bit larger than British ones, she recalled, but the point was clear enough.

Those elephants were barking big.

"Mit achtzig-Millimeter-Kanone auf dem Türmchen," Bauer added, which was beyond Deryn's Clanker. But she nodded again, pretending to understand.

"Kanone," repeated Bovril, who was sitting on Alek's shoulder.

"Aye, cannon," Deryn murmured, watching the shimmer from the steel turrets on the elephants' backs. The cannon were the important bit, after all.

Klopp and Alek went on talking in indecipherable Clanker, so Deryn strolled to the far corner of the balcony to stretch her legs. Her bum was still sore from the wild ride in the taxi, which had been worse than any galloping horse. She didn't understand how Clankers could ride about in machines all day—they way they moved was just dead *wrong*.

"Are you injured?" came Lilit's voice from just behind her, making Deryn jump a bit. The girl was always sneaking up on her.

"I'm fine," Deryn said, then pointed down at the war elephants. "I was just wondering, do they often parade about like that, smashing up the streets?"

The girl shook her head. "They usually stay out of the city. The sultan is showing his strength."

"That's for certain. Pardon me for saying so, miss, but you can't beat them. Those walkers carry cannon, and yours have only got claws and fists. It'd be like taking boxing gloves to a pistol duel!"

"The world is built on elephants, my grandmother always says." Lilit let out a sigh. "It is an old law—our walkers can't be armed, not like the sultan's. But at least we've scared him. His army wouldn't be tearing up the streets if he weren't nervous!"

"Aye, he might be nervous, but that also means he's ready for you."

"The last revolution was only six years ago," Lilit said. "He is always ready."

Deryn was about to say how cheery a thought that was, but an odd buzzing sound had filled the air. She turned to see a bizarre contraption headed across the balcony. It waddled along on pudgy legs, a cross between a reptile and a four-poster bed, buzzing like a windup toy.

"What in blazes is *that*?"

"That," Lilit said with a smile, "is my grandmother."

As they walked back toward the others, Deryn saw a mass of gray hair sprouting from the white sheets. It was an old woman, no doubt the fearsome Nene that Alek had talked about.

Bovril seemed pleased to see her. It scampered down from Alek's shoulder and across the balcony, then crawled up to the footboard of the bed. The beastie stood there with its fur ruffling in the breeze, as happy as an admiral at sea.

Alek bowed to the old woman, introducing Master Klopp and Corporal Bauer in a stream of polite Clanker.

Nene nodded, then turned her steely gaze on Deryn.

"And you must be the boy from the *Leviathan*," she said, her English accent as posh as Zaven's. "My granddaughter's told me about you."

Deryn clicked her heels. "Midshipman Dylan Sharp, at your service, ma'am."

"From your accent, you were raised in Glasgow."

"Aye, ma'am. You have a good ear."

"Two of them, in fact," Nene said. "And you have an odd voice. Your hands, please?"

Deryn hesitated, but when the old woman snapped her fingers, she found herself obeying.

"Lots of calluses," Nene said, feeling carefully. "You're a hardworking lad, unlike your friend the prince of Hohenberg. You draw a bit, and you do a lot of sewing, for a boy."

Deryn cleared her throat, remembering her aunties teaching her to quilt. "In the Air Service we middies darn our own uniforms."

"How industrious of you. My granddaughter tells me you don't trust us."

"Aye . . . well, it is a bit awkward, ma'am. I'm under orders to keep my mission here a secret."

"Under orders?" Nene looked Deryn up and down. "You don't appear to be in uniform."

"I may be undercover, ma'am," Deryn said, "but I'm still a soldier."

"Undercover," Bovril said, chuckling. "*Mr.* Sharp!"

Deryn glared at the beastie, wishing it would stop *saying* that.

"Well, boy, at least you're honest about your doubts," Nene said, dropping her hands and turning to Alek. "So, what do your men think of our walkers?"

Alek answered in Clanker, and soon Klopp and Bauer were peppering Nene and Zaven with questions.

Deryn couldn't follow half of it, but it hardly mattered what language you said it in—this revolution was well and truly stuffed without cannon. Zaven was barking mad to think otherwise.

Even Alek couldn't see the truth. He was always on about how it was his destiny to help the revolution, to get revenge on the Germans and end the war. That was a load of yackum, Deryn reckoned. Providence wouldn't stop the sultan's walkers from chewing up the Committee's antiques, as easy as a box of chocolates.

She pulled out her sketch pad and stared down at the parade again. The elephants were lining up beside a long pier, their guns elevating, readying to salute a warship. . . .

"The *Goeben*," Deryn murmured. The ironclad's new

Ottoman flags fluttered bright crimson, her Tesla cannon glittering like a steel spiderweb in the sun.

Lilit had been right—the sultan was flaunting his power today. Even if the Committee could beat those elephants somehow, they'd still have to face the big guns of the *Goeben* and the *Breslau.*

Or perhaps not. Less than a month from now the *Leviathan* would be headed up the Dardanelles, guiding a beastie hungry for German ironclads. Admiral Souchon might have fought kraken before, but nothing like the behemoth. The creature was supposedly powerful enough to sink the sultan's two new warships in half an hour.

Now, *that* would be a barking good night for a revolution to start.

The problem was, Deryn couldn't tell the Committee what was coming. If just one of them was a Clanker spy, letting the plan slip could spell doom for the *Leviathan.* She was duty bound to keep quiet.

A torrent of smoke poured from the war elephants' cannon, rippling into a vast dark cloud on the sea breeze. The sound arrived long seconds later, as tardy as distant thunder. Then the *Goeben*'s guns returned the salute, ten times louder and more fiery.

Deryn sighed as she began to sketch the scene—there were too many barking pieces to this puzzle. The behemoth might sink the German ironclads, but it couldn't slither onto land and fight the sultan's elephants as well.

Behind her the discussion had grown heated. Zaven was proclaiming in Clanker while Klopp shook his head, arms crossed.

"Nein, nein, nein," the old man kept repeating.

If only there were a simple way to handle a hundred and fifty tons of steel . . .

Then, all in a flash, it came to her.

"Hold on, Mr. Zaven," she broke in. "It doesn't matter that your walkers haven't got cannon. We can fix that!"

Alek shook his head tiredly. "There's nothing we can do. He says the army has strict control over cannon and ammunition."

"Aye, but you don't need anything so fancy," Deryn said. "When the *Dauntless* was hijacked, the attackers had nothing but a few bits of rope."

"Hijacked?" Nene asked. "I thought the *Dauntless*'s rampage was due to sloppy piloting."

Deryn snorted. "Don't believe everything you read in the papers, ma'am." She pointed down at the armored elephants. "See how there's a pilot for each leg? The hijackers lassoed our men and yanked them off, then climbed up to take their place. That's how you stop those metal beasties. Knock out a couple of pilots, and you stop them completely!"

"Perhaps on the *Dauntless*, where the pilots ride out in the open," Zaven said. "But the men down there are well shielded."

Deryn had thought of this already. "Shielded from ropes and bullets, maybe. But they must have vision slits, like Alek's Stormwalker did. What if something spicy got through them?"

"Something *spicy*?" Nene asked.

"Aye." Deryn grinned, turning to Alek. "I never told you about how I rescued the *Dauntless*, did I?"

Alek shook his head.

Deryn took a moment to compose her thoughts, knowing she had their full attention now. "It was my idea, in fact. The barking diplomats had no proper weapons aboard, so I snatched up a big bag of spice powder and hurled it at one of the hijackers. The smell of it knocked that bumrag right off his saddle! And armor will only make things worse—imagine being stuck inside a wee metal cabin with a snootful of spices!"

"Spices," Bovril repeated quietly.

"That hijacker could hardly breathe," Deryn said. "And my uniform was pure dead ruined!"

"The army doesn't control hot peppers," Nene murmured, and Alek began to translate for Klopp and Bauer.

Lilit turned to her father. "Do you think it could work?"

"Even a foot soldier can fight a walker that way," Zaven said. "The Committee can flood the streets with spice-wielding revolutionaries!"

"Aye, but think bigger than that," Deryn said. "Unlike the German walkers, yours have all got hands. I reckon that Minotaur beastie could throw a spice bomb half a mile!"

"Farther than that," Lilit said, then smiled. "If Alek can manage not to crush it first, that is."

Alek *hmph*ed a bit. "Klopp says he can rig something up—some sort of magazine to hold the spice bombs. We're standing above a mechanikal factory, after all."

"Parts aren't a problem," Zaven said. "But the hottest spices are sold by the pinch. We're talking about buying tons!"

"If I can provide the money, are you willing to try?" Alek asked.

Zaven and Lilit both looked at Nene. She raised an eyebrow, staring at Alek.

"We're talking about a lot of money, Your Serene Highness."

Alek didn't answer, but knelt to open his satchel—the small one he'd been lugging about all day. He slid out what looked like a brick wrapped in a handkerchief.

"*Junge Meister!*" Klopp said softly. "*Nicht das Gold!*"

Alek ignored him, unwrapping the handkerchief to reveal a metal bar. When sunlight struck it, a pale yellow fire burned across its surface.

Deryn swallowed. Barking spiders, but princes were *rich*!

"You really are him, aren't you?" Nene murmured. A thin few slices had been shaved from the bar's edges, but the Hapsburg crest was still plain.

"Of course, madam," Alek said. "I am a very poor liar."

The conversation started up again, shifting back to Clanker as Nene, Zaven, and Klopp began to plan.

Lilit turned to face Deryn, her eyes glittering.

"Spices! You're brilliant. Just perfectly brilliant." Lilit gathered her into a hug. "Thank you!"

"Aye, I'm dead clever . . . sometimes," Deryn said, pulling herself quickly away. "It's just lucky Alek brought that slab of gold along."

Alek nodded, but a pained look crossed his face. "That was my father's idea. He and Volger planned for anything."

"Aye, but it's barking lucky you brought it *today*," Deryn said. "Otherwise you'd have lost it."

"Pardon me?"

"Stop being a *Dummkopf*," Deryn said, shaking her head. "The taxi pilot knows what hotel we came from. And the way we're dressed, it's dead certain the management will remember us if the police come asking. So we'll have to stay here. We've lost the wireless set, but we've got Klopp's tools, Bovril, and your gold." Deryn shrugged. "That's everything important, right?"

Alek squeezed his eyes shut, his voice falling to a whisper. "Almost everything."

"Blisters! You didn't have *two* slabs of gold, did you?"

"No. But I left a letter behind."

"Does it say who you are?" Lilit asked softly.

"All too clearly." Alek turned to stare at Deryn, his gaze suddenly intense. "It's well hidden. If no one finds it, we can sneak back and fetch it!"

"Aye, I suppose so."

"In a week, once things have settled down. Please say you'll help me!"

"You know me, always happy to lend a hand," Deryn said, punching Alek on the shoulder. Though, frankly, it sounded a bit pointless to her. The Germans already knew that Alek was in Istanbul, so why risk getting caught?

It was only a barking letter, after all.

THIRTY-FOUR

"You *bum-rag*!" Deryn cried. "I was having a dead good dream!"

"It's time to go," Alek said.

Deryn groaned. She'd been helping Lilit with the Spider all day, carrying parts and trays of type, and every muscle in her body ached. It was no wonder that Clankers were grumpy all the time—metal was barking *heavy*.

In her dream she'd been flying. Not on an airship or a Huxley, but with wings of her own, as light as gossamer. It had been brilliant.

"Can we not leave it for another night? I'm knackered."

"It's a week since we left the hotel, Dylan. That's what we agreed."

Deryn sighed. She could see the desperate gleam in the boy's eye again. He got it every time he talked about his lost letter, though he wouldn't say why it was so bark-ing important.

Alek threw her blanket aside, and Deryn jumped to cover herself. But she'd slept in her mechanic's slops, as she always did now. She'd had to watch her step here. The pilots who came to train in Zaven's warehouse were all curious about the strange boy in the background, who knew none of the languages of the Ottoman Empire. So Deryn stuck with Lilit, working on the Spider, and helped Zaven with the cooking, learning the names of new spices, and slicing garlic and onions until her fingers stung.

"Leave off!" she cried. "I'm getting up."

"Hush. I don't want any questions from the others about where we're going."

"Aye, right. Just wait outside a minute."

He hesitated, but finally left her alone.

Deryn changed into her Turkish clothes, muttering about the various defects of Alek's character. She often talked to herself these days—living among Clankers was driving her mad. Instead of the murmurs of beasties and the steady hum of airflow, Deryn spent her days surrounded by the rattle of gears and pistons. Her skin smelled of engine grease.

Of all the machines she'd worked on this last week, the Spider was the only one she had a fondness for. Its dance of cutting blades and conveyor belts was as elegant as any ecosystem, a whirl of paper and ink converging into neat bundles of information, and its huge legs stretched out like the boughs of an ancient tree. But even that faint suggestion of a living thing only made Deryn miss her airship home the harder.

And all to help some barking *prince*.

She went out into the training courtyard, where the latest bunch of walkers stood, their spice-bomb throwers half finished. A djinn towered above the rest, its powerful arms crossed, its nozzles still wet from being tested. As fellow Muslims, the Arabs had a dispensation from the sultan to arm their walkers with steam cannon. The cannon didn't shoot projectiles, but in a pinch the djinn could disappear into a white-hot cloud.

The courtyard's outer door was wedged open a squick. Deryn slipped through to find Alek waiting out on the street.

Lilit was there too, dressed up in fancy European clothing.

"What's *she* doing here?"

Alek raised an eyebrow. "Didn't I tell you? We need someone the hotel staff won't recognize. Lilit rented a suite yesterday."

"And exactly how does that help us?"

"My room is on the highest floor, like Alek's was," Lilit said. "Two doors away. And they both have balconies."

Deryn frowned. She had to admit, climbing across balconies might be a wee bit easier than picking the lock. But why hadn't anyone told *her* the plan?

"I can sneak about just as well as you two can," the girl said. "Ask Alek how easily I trailed him."

"Aye, he's told me that story more than once," Deryn said. "It's just that . . ."

She tried to think of what to say. Lilit wasn't a bad sort, really. She was a dab hand with machines, as good at piloting as any of the men. In a way, she'd managed the same trick as Deryn had—acting like a man—without pretending, and that was a splendid sort of anarchy, one had to admit.

But the girl had a habit of turning up whenever Alek and Deryn were alone together, which was barking tiresome.

Why hadn't Alek mentioned that she was coming along? What other secrets was he keeping about her?

"Is it because I'm a girl?" Lilit asked stiffly.

"Of course not." Deryn shook her head. "I'm just sleepy, is all."

Lilit stood there, looking a little cross and waiting to hear more. But Deryn only turned and headed toward the fancy part of town.

The Hotel Hagia Sophia stood, dark and silent, a single gaslight burning above the doorway. Deryn and Alek watched from the shadows as Lilit made her way inside, the doorman saluting as she passed.

"It seems a bit daft, us *sneaking* in," Deryn whispered. "Do you really think they'd recognize us?"

"Don't forget," Alek said. "If they've found my letter, there'll be a dozen German agents in the lobby, day and night."

Deryn nodded. That was true enough—any trace of Austria's missing prince would stir up more ruckus than a stolen taxi.

"She's meeting us back here." Alek led Deryn around to a small lane, where rubbish was heaped outside the hotel kitchen door. He and Lilit had done a lot of planning together, it seemed.

Deryn shook the jealous thought from her head. She was a soldier on a mission, not some daft lassie mooning at a village dance.

She crept closer and peeked through a window. It was dark inside the kitchen, the motionless arms of a clockwork dishwasher casting eerie shadows. But after a few minutes a silent shape slipped through the darkness, and the door creaked opened.

"There's someone at the front desk," Lilit whispered. "And a man reading in the lobby, so keep quiet."

As they slipped inside, the scents of cooking filled Deryn's nose, as delicious as she remembered from her two days here. Bowls of dates and apricots and waxy yellow potatoes crowded a long and knotted wooden table, a row of aubergines shining purple in the darkness, waiting for the gleaming knives to gut them.

But the smell of paprika made her wince. Zaven had been mixing up spice bombs all day, and Deryn's eyeballs were still sore.

Lilit led them from the kitchen into a dark and empty dining room. The places were all set, the napkins neatly folded as if guests were about to arrive, and Deryn got the shivery feeling she always did in fancy places.

"There's a back stair for the servants," Lilit whispered, heading for a small doorway in the far wall.

The staircase was narrow and pitch-black, and complained at every step. Clanker wood always sounded so ancient and unhappy, like Deryn's aunties on a damp winter morning. That was what came of chopping down trees instead of fabricating your wood, she supposed.

The three climbed slowly to keep quiet, and it was long minutes later that Lilit led them out into a wide, familiar hallway.

Deryn felt a squick of chill as she passed Alek's room. What if his letter had been found, and half a dozen Clanker agents were waiting inside?

Lilit stopped two doors farther along, pulling out a key. A moment later they were all standing in a suite as fancy as Alek's had been. Deryn wondered again what was so barking important about this letter. Was it really worth spending money on this suite, money that could have gone to the Committee's walkers?

Lilit pointed. "The balcony."

Deryn crossed the room and stepped out into the cool of night. Here on the top floor the balconies were almost as wide as the suites themselves. Easy enough to get from one to the next—the sort of jump an airman made every day.

But she turned to Alek and whispered, "If you'd let me in on the barking plan, I could have brought a safety line."

He smiled. "Lost your air sense already?"

"Hardly." Deryn put one foot up on the railing, hands out for balance.

Alek turned to Lilit. "Stay here. There might be someone waiting for us."

"Do you think I can't fight?"

Deryn paused in her jump, wondering how Alek would answer. Was he more worried about Lilit's safety than his own? Or didn't he want a mere girl helping him?

Either would be dead annoying.

"It's not that you can't fight," he said. "But if you're captured, someone might recognize you as Zaven's daughter. That would lead the police straight back to the warehouse."

Deryn blinked—maybe Alek was just being *sensible*.

"What if you two get captured?" Lilit asked.

"Then you'll have to overthrow the sultan and set us free."

Lilit fumed a bit, but nodded. "Just be careful, both of you."

"Don't worry about us," Deryn said, and jumped.

She landed on the next balcony with a soft *clang*, then waited to give Alek a hand. He jumped with a grim look on his face, and his hand was shaking a bit when she grabbed it to steady him.

"Who's lost his air sense now?" she whispered.

"Well, it *is* rather high."

Deryn snorted. After skylarking at a thousand feet, half a dozen stories was nothing. She crossed the balcony, climbed onto the railing, and jumped again, hardly glancing at the ground.

She gestured for Alek to wait as she peeked inside.

The room was dark, but no one was in sight. Deryn slipped her rigging knife into the crack between the doors to lift the hasp, pushed them open, and listened—nothing.

She slipped inside and stole softly to the bedroom doors. The bed was empty, the covers and the pillows all straight. If anyone had searched this room, they'd cleaned up after themselves.

In fact, the whole suite looked exactly as Deryn

remembered it: the potted plants, the footstool that had been Bovril's favorite, the low divan she'd slept on while Alek had snored away in the splendor of the bedroom.

She heard a soft *thud* and turned around—Alek was stepping in from the balcony. He pulled a screwdriver from his pocket, heading straight for the shiny brass switchboard on the wall.

"Doesn't that contraption call the front desk?" she whispered. In her two days here Alek had used the switchboard to call delicious meals up to the room, as if by magic.

"Yes, of course. But I won't activate it." His fingers spun, and soon the front panel slipped off into his hands.

He set the panel carefully onto the floor and reached into the Clanker guts of the device. From among the tangle of wires and bells, he pulled out a long cylinder of leather.

Deryn took a step forward, squinting in the darkness.

"It's my letter," Alek said. "It's in a scroll case."

"A *scroll case*? Someone sent you a barking *scroll*?"

Alek didn't answer, slipping the screwdriver back into his pocket.

"Aye, I know—top secret," she muttered, crossing to the suite's front door. "We may as well take the hallway. No point testing your air sense again."

Deryn pressed her ear against the door—no sound at all. But when she looked back at him, Alek was still standing in the same spot, wearing a thoughtful expression.

"Forgot something else?" she whispered. "Another scroll? A bar of platinum?"

"Dylan," the boy said softly, "before we go back to Lilit, I should tell you something."

Deryn froze, her hand on the doorknob. "Something about her?"

"About Lilit? Why would I . . . ," Alek began, but then

his expression broke into a smile. "Ah, you've been wondering about her."

"Aye, a bit."

Alek chuckled quietly. "Well, she is quite beautiful."

"I suppose so."

"I was wondering when you'd notice. You've been quite a *Dummkopf* about it. And she's been trying awfully hard to get you to see."

"To get *me* to see? But why . . ." Deryn frowned. "What are we talking about, exactly?"

Alek rolled his eyes. "You're *still* being a ninny! Haven't you noticed how much she likes you?"

Deryn's mouth dropped open, but no sound came out.

"Don't look so surprised," Alek said. "She's liked you from the start. Did you think she had you working on the Spider for your mechanical skills?"

"But—but I thought that you and her . . ."

"Me? She thinks I'm a perfectly useless aristocrat." Alek shook his head. "You really are a *Dummkopf*, aren't you?"

"But she *can't* like me," Deryn said. "I'm a . . . barking airman!"

"Yes, she thinks that's quite romantic as well. You do have a certain swagger about you, I suppose. And you're not bad looking, to be sure."

"Oh, leave off!"

"In fact, when I first met you, I thought, 'Now, *there's*

the boy I want to be—or would, if I hadn't been born such a hopeless prince.'"

Deryn glared at Alek, who was clearly enjoying himself now, his eyes glistening with laughter held in check. It made her want to punch him, and yet . . .

"Do you really think I'm handsome?" she asked.

"Most beguiling, I'm sure. And now that you've masterminded the revolution, Lilit's affections are quite out of control."

Deryn groaned, shaking her head. She had to put a stop to this, before it got too blistering tricky.

"But we should discuss your romantic life another time." Alek held up the scroll case. "I need to tell you about this."

Deryn stared dumbly, trying to force her mind to stop spinning. She could deal with Lilit. It was just a matter of . . . well, not of telling her the truth, certainly, but of saying *something* sensible.

After all, it was true that women liked an airman's swagger—Mr. Rigby was always saying so. It was just part of being a soldier. Part of being a *boy*, really. She could make up a story of a girl back home . . .

"Right, then," Deryn finally managed. "What's so barking important about this scroll of yours?"

"Well, it's like this." Alek took a slow breath. "Along with our revolution here in Istanbul, I think this letter might end the war."

❋ THIRTY-FIVE ❋

The boy just looked at him, speechless again.

Standing there in the dark, Alek could hear his own heart pounding. Getting those first words out had taken all the willpower he possessed.

But now that Volger was gone, bearing the secret alone was too much. And Dylan had proven himself loyal a dozen times over.

"It's from the Holy Father," Alek said, holding up the scroll case.

It took Dylan a moment, but then he said, "You mean, the *pope?*"

Alek nodded. "It changes the terms of my parents' marriage, making me my father's heir. I suppose I've been lying to you—I'm not just a prince."

"Then you're . . . an archduke?"

"I'm the archduke of Austria-Este, royal prince of

Hungary and Bohemia. When my granduncle dies, it may be that I can stop this war."

Dylan's eyes slowly widened. "Because you'll be the barking emperor!"

Alek sighed, crossing to the large chair with tasseled arms that had been his favorite. He fell into it, suddenly exhausted.

He'd rather missed this hotel room, with all its Levantine splendor. In the week of hiding here he'd felt . . . *in command* for the first time in his life, with no tutors or mentors to appease. But now he'd joined a committee of revolutionaries, and had to argue over every detail.

"It's complicated. Franz Joseph has named another successor, but he chose my father first." Alek looked at the crossed keys on the leather case, a sign of papal authority that no faithful Austrian could ignore. "This document might throw the succession into doubt, if the war is going badly and the people *want* change. My father used to say, 'A country with two kings will always falter.'"

"Aye," Dylan said, coming closer. "And if there's been a revolution here, then Germany will be completely alone!"

Alek smiled. "Not such a *Dummkopf* after all, are you?"

Dylan perched on one arm of the chair, looking dizzy and astonished.

"Pardon me, your princeliness, but this is all a bit much. First you tell me about her . . ." The boy waved in the direction of Lilit's room. "And now *this!*"

"I'm sorry. I never wanted to lie to you, Dylan. But I learned about this letter the same night I met you. It's still quite strange for me."

"It's pure dead strange for me, too!" Dylan said, standing up again and pacing across the room. "Ending a whole barking war with a bit of paper, even if it *is* a fancy scroll. Who would believe it's *real?*"

Alek nodded. He'd felt the same way when Volger had shown him the letter. It seemed too small an object to change so much. But here in Istanbul, Alek had begun to understand what the scroll really meant. The *Leviathan* had been brought to that mountaintop, and then here. It was up to him, Aleksandar of Hohenberg, to end the war that his parents' death had started.

"Volger says the pope himself will vouch for me, as long as I keep this letter secret until my granduncle passes away. The emperor turned eighty-four last week. He could die any day."

"Blisters. No wonder the Germans want to catch you so badly!"

"True enough. It has made things dangerous." Alek looked at the scroll case. "But that's why we had to come back here. And why I'm willing to trade my father's gold to make the Committee's revolution work. What we do here can change *everything*."

Dylan stopped pacing in the middle of the room, his fists clenched, as if struggling with some secret of his own.

"Thank you for trusting me, Alek." The boy looked at the floor. "I haven't always trusted you. Not with everything."

Alek pulled himself up from the chair and walked closer, resting his hands on the boy's shoulders. "You know you can, Dylan."

"Aye, I suppose. And there's something I should tell you. But you have to swear not to tell anyone else—not Lilit, not the Committee. No one."

"I'll always keep your secrets, Dylan."

The boy nodded slowly. "This one's a bit trickier than most."

He fell silent again, the pause stretching out.

"It's about your mission here, isn't it?"

Dylan let out a slow sigh, a sound of relief and exhaustion. "Aye, I suppose it is. We were an advance party, sent to sabotage the kraken nets in the strait. It was all part of Dr. Barlow's plan from the beginning."

"But your men were captured."

Dylan shook his head. "My men may have been caught, but we did our job. Right now those nets are being eaten away by wee beasties. And it's happening so slowly that the Ottomans won't realize until it's too late."

"So you British aren't waiting for the sultan to join the war. You'll strike the first blow."

"Aye, in three weeks. Dr. Barlow says the nets will be in tatters by then. On the night of the next new moon, the *Leviathan* will guide a new beastie down the strait. It's the companion creature for the *Osman*, the ship that Lord Churchill stole from the Ottomans. It's called a behemoth, and it's barking huge, like the world has never seen before! Those German ironclads' days are numbered."

Alek clenched the scroll case tighter. The weakest link in the Committee's plans had always been the German ironclads. But with some kind of Royal Navy monster on its way, the odds had changed considerably.

"But this is exactly what we need, Dylan. We *have* to tell the Committee!"

"We can't," the boy said. "I trust Zaven and his family, but there are hundreds of others involved. What if one of them is a Clanker spy? If the Germans find out the *Leviathan* is coming, the *Goeben* could surprise it anywhere along the way with her Tesla cannon charged!"

"Of course." Alek shuddered a bit, remembering the lightning coursing through his body. "But what about Zaven's plan? He's leading walkers with spice bombs against the ironclads. Klopp says it's insane."

"Aye, completely daft," Dylan said. "But don't tell

Zaven that! If they strike on the night of the new moon, the *Goeben* will be sunk before they even get there!"

Alek nodded slowly, thinking it through. In an all-out battle for the city, the sultan would send his walkers into the streets, relying on the German warships to protect the palace. But if they lay at the bottom of the sea, the revolution could be over in a single night. Thousands of lives might be spared.

Of course, an attack in utter darkness would mean teaching the Committee's pilots how to drive their walkers at night. He'd already explained the principles to Lilit, and she'd picked them up quickly enough. If anything, it would give the revolutionaries yet another advantage.

"I'll order Klopp to say he's changed his mind, that he thinks spice bombing the *Goeben* will work. He might grumble a bit, but he'll do as he's told. But how do we get the Committee to pick that exact night?"

"Have Klopp say that it's best to attack the ironclads in darkness." Dylan shrugged. "Then we'll point out that September 19 is a new moon, and let them decide on their own."

Alek smiled. "And with your masculine charms, you can persuade Lilit to plead our case for us!"

Dylan rolled his eyes, turning beet red again. "Speaking of secrets, you won't tell Lilit about *that* discussion either, will you? It'll only complicate things."

Alek chuckled. He'd always heard that Darwinists were quite plainspoken about matters of biology, to the point of being vulgar. But Dylan looked positively shamefaced about the whole thing, more like a schoolboy than a soldier.

It was most amusing.

"As I said, all your secrets are safe with me."

"Aye, good, then." Dylan hesitated. "And . . . you're completely sure it's *me* she likes, not you?"

Alek laughed. "I should hope so. After all, if we did like each other, I'd have to run a mile."

"What do you mean?"

"For heaven's sake, Dylan. Lilit is a *commoner*, far more common than my mother." Alek held up the scroll case. "I grew up not knowing if this would ever happen. Not knowing who I really was, and always thinking how much easier it would be for everyone if I hadn't been born. I could never do that to my own children, not in a thousand years."

Dylan stared at the scroll case sadly. "Must be tough, being a prince."

"Not any longer, thanks to this." Alek clasped Dylan's shoulder again, happy that his only real friend knew his last secret. "Let's get out of here. We have a revolution to plan."

Lilit opened her door wearing a frown.

"Took you two long enough. I thought you'd got yourselves into trouble."

"We were having a bit of a discussion." Alek winked at Dylan, then held up the scroll case. "But we found this."

Lilit gave them both an odd look, and Dylan turned away in embarrassment, heading toward the servants' staircase.

Alek shrugged for Lilit's benefit, then followed.

As they descended the stairs, the hotel began to stir around them. The steam elevators rumbled and hissed, building up pressure for the morning traffic, and soon a clattering rose up from below.

Dylan came to a halt, raising his hand. "The cooks are in the kitchen already. We can't go back that way."

"Straight through the lobby doors, then," Lilit said. "If no one found your letter, there won't be any German agents about."

"Aye, but some of us are wanted taxi thieves!" Dylan said.

Alek shook his head. "It'll be fine. We'll be out the door before anyone gives us a second look."

"Just try not to act suspicious," Lilit said, nudging open the door to the dining room.

She led them through the empty tables, with a stride as confident as if she owned the hotel. A young boy in a fez looked up from polishing silverware and frowned, but didn't say a word.

They passed him and headed through the lobby, which

was empty except for one rather shabby-looking tourist waiting for a room. . . .

The man glanced up from his newspaper, smiled, and waved a hand.

"Ah, Prince Alek," he called. "I thought you might be somewhere hereabouts."

Alek froze in midstride. It was Eddie Malone.

THIRTY-SIX

"Of course, I never took you for a taxi thief," Malone said, stirring his coffee. "But then I heard the name of that hotel."

Alek didn't answer, just gazed at his cup in silence. The black surface of the liquid flickered, reflecting the dancing shapes of shadow puppets on the screen behind him.

The reporter had led them to a coffeehouse, well away from the curious glances of the hotel staff. Each table had its own tiny shadow play machine, and the place was dark and nearly empty, the few patrons all transfixed by their own puppets. But Alek felt as though the walls were listening.

Perhaps it was the beady eyes of the bullfrog staring at him from across the table.

"My mother's name," he said softly. "Of course."

Malone nodded. "I've been looking at hotel signs ever

since, and wondering. The Dora Hotel? The Santa Pera? The Angel?" He let out a low chuckle. "And then I heard about some Germans staying at the Hagia Sophia stealing a taxi. So the name Sophie started ringing in my ears."

"But how did you know to call me *prince*?" Alek said.

"I'm not the only Austrian with a mother named Sophie."

"That's what I figured, until I started looking into that Count Volger fellow. He and your father were old friends, weren't they?"

Alek nodded, his eyes closing. He was exhausted, and there was another long day of work ahead—a whole revolution to rethink.

"But we stole that taxi seven barking days ago!" Dylan said. "Have you been sitting in that lobby all that time?"

"Of course not," Malone said. "It took me three days of pondering, then another three to find out who Count Volger was. I practically just got there."

Alek winced a little. If only they'd gone to retrieve the letter a day earlier, they might have never laid eyes on the man.

"But once it all fell into place, I just *had* to find you again." Malone's face was beaming. "A missing prince, the boy whose family started the Great War! Biggest story I've ever covered."

"Should we kill him now?" Lilit asked.

Malone gave her a curious look; clearly he hadn't

understood her German. He pulled out his notepad. "And who might you be, miss?"

Lilit's eyes narrowed, and Alek hurriedly spoke up. "I'm afraid that's none of your business, Mr. Malone. We won't be answering any of your questions."

The man held up his notebook. "So I'll have to publish my story with so many questions left unanswered? And so soon? Say . . . tomorrow?"

"Are you blackmailing us, Mr. Malone?"

"Of course not. I just don't like loose ends."

Alek shook his head and sighed. "Write what you want. The Germans already know I'm here in Istanbul."

"Interesting," Malone said, his pen scribbling on the pad. "See? You're adding background already! But what's really interesting is young Dylan being with you. The Ottomans will be surprised to hear that one of the *Leviathan*'s saboteurs escaped!"

From the corner of his eye, Alek saw Dylan's fists clench.

But Malone had turned his gaze on Lilit. "And then there's the matter of your new revolutionary friends. That might raise a few eyebrows as well."

"My knife is ready," Lilit said softly in German. "Just say the word."

"Mr. Malone," Alek said, "perhaps we can convince you to delay publishing your story."

"A SHADOW PLAY AT THE SHISHA BAR."

"How long do you need?" the man said, his pen still poised to write.

Alek sighed. Giving Malone a date only revealed more about their plans. But they had to string the man along somehow. If the Ottomans learned that a Darwinist saboteur was working with revolutionaries here in Istanbul, they might begin to piece together Dr. Barlow's plan.

Alek looked to Dylan for help.

"Don't you see, Mr. Malone?" the boy said. "If you give us all away, then the story's over. But if you just wait a *wee bit*, it'll get heaps more interesting, we promise!"

Malone leaned back, drumming his fingers on the table. "Well, I suppose you've got a little while. I file my stories by messenger tern. That's four days to cross the Atlantic. And because I use birds, the Germans' can't listen in on their fancy new wireless tower."

"Four days is hardly—," Alek began, but Dylan grabbed his arm.

"Excuse me, Mr. Malone," the boy said. "What wireless tower are you talking about?"

"The big one they're just finishing." Malone gave a shrug. "It's meant to be a secret, but half the Germans in this city are working on it. Has its own power station, they say."

Dylan's eyes grew wider. "Is this tower somewhere along a railroad line?"

"I've heard it's somewhere on the cliffs, where the old tracks follow the water." Malone narrowed his eyes. "What's so interesting about that?"

"Barking spiders," Dylan said softly. "I should have realized the first night I was here."

Alek stared at the boy, remembering his story about the night he'd arrived. Dylan had secretly ridden a short way on the Orient-Express, which the Germans were using to smuggle parts out of the city . . . electrikal parts.

The pieces finally fell into place.

"With its own power station?" Alek asked.

Eddie Malone nodded, his eyes flicking between the two of them.

Alek felt a cold finger sliding down his spine. No mere wireless tower would need that much power. The *Leviathan* was flying straight into disaster.

"Can you give us a month?" he asked Malone.

"A whole month?" The reporter let out a snort. "My editors would have me brought home in a brown bag. You have to give me *something* to write about."

Dylan sat up straighter. "All right, then, I've got a story for you. And the sooner you publish it, the better. That wireless tower—"

"Wait!" Alek said. "I have something better. How about an interview with the missing prince of Hohenberg? I'll tell you about the night I left my home, how I escaped

Austria and made it to the Alps. Who I think killed my parents, and why. Will that keep you busy enough, Mr. Malone?"

The man's pen was scribbling, his head nodding furiously. Dylan was staring at Alek, wide eyed.

"But there's one condition: You can't mention either of my friends," Alek said. "Just say I'm hiding in the hills somewhere, alone."

The man paused a moment, then shrugged. "Whatever you want, as long as I can take some photographs too."

Alek shuddered—of *course* Malone's newspaper was the sort that published photographs. How perfectly vulgar.

But he could only nod.

"Mr. Malone," Dylan said, "there's still one other thing—"

"Not tonight," Alek said. "I'm afraid we're all quite tired, Mr. Malone. I'm sure you understand."

"You're not the only ones." The reporter stood up, stretching his arms. "I've been in that lobby all night. Meet me tomorrow in the usual café?"

Alek nodded, and Malone gathered his things and left, not even offering to pay for his coffee.

"This is all my fault," Lilit said when the man was gone. "I saw him when I followed you. I should have recognized him on my way up."

Alek shook his head. "No. I was the one foolish enough to involve a reporter in my affairs."

"No matter whose fault it is," Dylan said, "we should have told him about the . . ." He hesitated, looking at Lilit.

She waved a hand dismissively. "The Committee knows all about that tower. We'd been watching the Germans build it for months, wondering what it might be. Until Alek came along and explained everything."

"I did?" Alek asked, then remembered his first day at the warehouse. Nene hadn't believed a word he'd said . . . until he'd mentioned the Tesla cannon. Then suddenly she'd become quite interested, peppering him with questions—what it was called, how it worked, and whether it could be used against walkers. "But I thought we were talking about the *Goeben.* Why didn't you tell me the sultan had *another* Tesla cannon?"

"It hardly mattered—you said it couldn't affect our walkers." She frowned, looking at Dylan. "But it *can* shoot down airships, can't it?"

The boy cleared his throat, but only shrugged.

"And you both just turned green at the thought of that," Lilit said.

"Aye, well, you know," Dylan said. "Those contraptions are a professional hazard, when you're an airman."

Lilit crossed her arms. "And you were about to tell that reporter what this 'wireless tower' really was, to warn your

Darwinist friends!" She turned to Alek. "And you're willing
to spill your family secrets just to keep Dylan out of the
papers! There's something you two aren't telling me."

Alek sighed. Lilit could be annoyingly perceptive
sometimes.

"Shall I ask my grandmother to help me sort this all
out? She's very good at puzzles."

Alek turned to Dylan. "We should tell her everything."

The boy threw up his hand in surrender. "Aye, it hardly
matters anymore. We have to put a stop to the whole plan!
Just tell Malone about the Tesla cannon tomorrow. Once
that's in the papers, the Admiralty will know the plan is
too dangerous."

"We can't," Alek said. "The revolution will fail without
the *Leviathan*'s help!"

"But they'll never make it. If that cannon's got its own
power plant, it's got to be barking *huge*."

Alek opened his mouth, but couldn't find words to
argue with. There was no way to fly an airship over Istanbul
now, not with a giant Tesla cannon overlooking the city.

Lilit let out an exasperated sigh. "Well, since neither of
you boys can be bothered to explain, allow me."

She held up one hand, ticking off points on her fingers.

"One, the *Leviathan* is clearly on its way back to
Istanbul, or you wouldn't care about this Tesla cannon. Two,
whatever it's up to can help the revolution, as Alek just said.

And three, this all has to do with your secret mission." She hesitated a moment, staring at Dylan. "Your men were captured near the kraken nets, weren't they?"

Alek opened his mouth again, wanting to interrupt before she figured out the truth. But Lilit silenced him with a wave of her hand.

"Everyone thinks your mission failed, but they don't know that *you* weren't captured." Her eyes widened. "You plan to bring a kraken down the strait!"

Dylan looked miserable, but only nodded. "Not really a kraken, but close enough. And a fine plan it was too. But it's all ruined now! We have to tell Malone about the cannon, or get a warning to the Admiralty some other way."

"But this is perfect!" Lilit said.

"Perfect in what way, exactly?" Dylan cried. "That cannon is a death trap, and the *Leviathan* is headed right toward it! That's my ship we're talking about!"

"We're talking about the liberation of my people as well," Lilit said softly, her eyes locked on his. "The Committee will deal with this problem, I swear."

"But my mission was meant to be top secret." Dylan shook his head. "I can't let it go forward if a daft bunch of anarchists know about it!"

"Then we won't tell anyone else," Lilit said. "Only we three have to know."

Alek frowned. "The three of us can't destroy a Tesla cannon."

"No, we can't. But . . ." Lilit held one hand up, her eyes squeezing shut for a moment. "My father plans to lead the assault on the *Goeben* himself, with four walkers. But if the *Leviathan* and its sea monster can deal with the ironclads, we have those walkers to spare. So on the night of the revolution, we explain everything to my father, then head to the cliffs and tear this Tesla cannon to the ground!"

"Someone might find out," Dylan said.

"What if we only use pilots we trust?" Alek asked. "Lilit's walker, mine, Klopp's, and Zaven's. No one else has to know what's going on."

Lilit shrugged. "No one else is volunteering to fight the *Goeben*, after all."

Dylan stared at them both, a look of terror in his eyes.

"But what if we fail?" he said softly. "They'll all burn."

Lilit reached across the table and took his hands in her own.

"We won't fail," she said. "Our revolution depends on your ship."

Dylan stared at her hands for a moment, then looked helplessly at Alek.

"It's the only way they can win," Alek said simply. "And the only way to complete your mission. Your men sacrificed themselves for this, right?"

"Oh, you *had* to say that," Dylan said with a groan, pulling his hands from Lilit's grasp. "Aye, all right, then. But you barking anarchists had better not make a mess of this!"

"We won't," Lilit said, beaming at the boy. "You've saved the revolution again!"

Dylan rolled his eyes. "No need to get all moony, lassie."

Alek smiled. They really were the most amusing couple.

THIRTY-SEVEN

Deryn spread her arms out straight, and waited.

"R . . ."

She dipped her left arm forty-five degrees.

"S . . ."

She let her right arm drop, the screwdriver in her hand pointing straight down.

"G!" said Bovril, and ate another strawberry. Then it tossed the stem over the edge of the balcony, leaning its head through the rails to watch it fall.

"How do you like *that*?" Deryn cried. "It's learnt the whole barking alphabet!"

Lilit and Alek stared at the beastie, then at her.

"You taught it this?" Lilit asked.

"No! I was just practicing my signals. I was saying the letters out loud, I suppose, and after a couple times through . . ." Deryn pointed at Bovril. "The beastie joined in, as quick as a bosun's mate."

"And that's why you want to bring it along tonight?" Alek asked. "In case we need to send semaphore signals?"

Deryn rolled her eyes. "No, you daft bum-rag. It's because . . ."

She sighed, unsure exactly how to say it. The loris had a knack for noticing important details, just as Dr. Barlow had claimed. And tonight was the most important mission that Deryn had ever been a part of. She didn't dare leave the beastie behind.

"Perspicacious," the creature said.

"Aye, that's the word," Deryn cried. "Because it's barking perspicacious."

Two weeks before, Zaven had put his posh education to use and explained the loris's species name to Deryn. It turned out that "perspicacious" meant the same as "shrewd," or even "farsighted." And though that didn't sound like the sort of thing a beastie could be, it certainly fit.

Alek sighed, and turned toward the family's apartments, where Nene's tortoise bed was emerging, covered with maps fluttering in the breeze. The old woman called to Lilit and Alek.

As they walked away, Alek said over his shoulder, "All right, Dylan. But I have a walker to pilot. So you'll be looking after it."

"More than happy to," Deryn said softly, scratching the loris's wee head.

Only having the beastie about had made it bearable, working with Clankers and their lifeless machines, smelling of exhaust and engine grease. The bustling splendor of Istanbul was still so alien, its foreign tongues too many to learn in a lifetime, much less a month. Deryn spent her days printing newspapers she couldn't read, and wondering what the prayers gliding over the rooftops might mean. The intricate geometries of Zaven's carpets and tiled ceilings dazzled her eyes, and even the wondrous food often proved to be—like the rest of the capital—too sumptuous.

But hardest of all was being so close to Alek, while still hiding from him. He'd shared his last secret with her, and Deryn realized now that she could have told him that same night, in that dark hotel room with no one about to hear.

But every time she'd tried, Deryn had imagined the look of horror on his face. Not that she was a girl in boy's clothes, or that she'd lied to him for so long. All that yackum Alek would soon get past, she knew. And then he would love her, she *knew*.

But that was the problem, because there was one thing that would never change. . . . Deryn was a commoner. She was a thousand times more common than Alek's mother, who'd been born a countess, or even Lilit, an anarchist who spoke six languages and always knew which fork to use. Deryn

Sharp was as common as barking *dirt*, and the only reason that didn't matter to His Serene Highness, Aleksandar of Hohenberg, was that she was also, in his mind, a boy.

The moment she could be anything more than a friend, she *would* be, and then he'd have to run a mile.

The pope did not write letters to transform orphan daughters of balloonists, or girls in boy's britches, or unrepentant Darwinists, into royalty. She was dead certain of that.

Deryn watched Alek kneel by Nene's bed like a good grandson, the three of them going over the details of the attack one last time. This battle tonight was something they had helped make together, she and Alek, and this was the closest they would ever be.

"A, B, C . . . ?" Bovril asked, and Deryn nodded.

She prayed that her signal practice really would come in handy. If all went well tonight, the *Leviathan*'s crew would be taking a long hard look at the Tesla cannon after it had been destroyed. That could be her only chance to let them know that she was alive.

It might even be a chance to go home, and leave her prince behind at last.

The great outer gates of the courtyard swung slowly open, revealing a clear and moonless sky.

"Lucky it didn't rain tonight," Alek said, checking the controls.

"Right enough," Deryn answered. A midnight downpour would have turned the spice bombs into a useless, soupy mess, ruining the Committee's only weapons. That was the thing about battles, Mr. Rigby always said, one squick of bad luck could make all your plans go pearshaped.

Much like the rest of life, she supposed.

The courtyard filled with the rumble of engines from four walkers. Şahmeran, with Zaven at its controls, raised a giant hand and waved them forward as it slithered out the gates.

Lilit went next, piloting a Minotaur. The half bull, half man bowed low to get its horns through, giant hands out for balance. Spice bombs rattled in the magazine that Master Klopp had welded to its forearm.

Alek placed his feet on the djinn's pedals. Klopp had insisted that Alek pilot an Arab machine tonight; their steam cannon made them the safest of the Committee's walkers. Behind the djinn, Klopp and Bauer sat at the controls of an iron golem.

"Hold on tight, Bovril," Deryn said, and the beastie scampered up onto her shoulder. Its claws poked through her piloting jacket like wee needles.

Alek worked his feet, and the contraption took a huge step forward.

Deryn grasped the sides of her commander's chair,

queasy as always in the lumbering machine. At least the djinn was still in parade mode, the top of its head split open, so she could see the stars and breathe fresh air.

"Turn left here," she said. To keep this mission as secret as possible, the four walkers had no copilots. So Deryn was serving as Alek's navigator and, once the shooting started, as range finder for the throwing arm. Deryn had never been a gunner before, but altitude practice had made her a dab hand at estimating distances—as long as she remembered to think in meters instead of yards.

Deryn looked at her map again. It showed four separate routes to the Tesla cannon, with Alek's marked in red. These four walkers were headed out before the main attack began, so they couldn't afford to raise suspicions by traveling together. The trick would be arriving at their target all at the same time.

Also marked on the map were the positions of the other forty-odd walkers pledged to the Committee, poised to spring into action an hour later. Deryn wondered if there were any spies among those crews, ready to sell the Committee's plans to the sultan for a lump of gold.

At least she could be certain that this attack on the Tesla cannon had been kept secret. Zaven himself had heard about it only this afternoon. He'd fumed a bit about

"THE DJINN ADVANCES THROUGH THE STREETS."

being kept in the dark, until realizing that he wouldn't have to face the big guns of the *Goeben*.

Unless the Admiralty had changed the night of the behemoth's arrival, of course.

"Have you thought about how many things can go wrong?" Deryn said. "It's like the bard says, 'The best laid plans of mice and men.'"

"Fah!" said Bovril, imitating Zaven's tone.

"You see?" Alek said. "Your perspicacious friend is confident."

Deryn looked at the beastie. "I just hope it's right."

They made good time on the almost empty streets of Istanbul. The Committee's walkers had been practicing night walking for the last month, pretending to patrol for robbers, so no one gave the djinn a second glance.

The buildings thinned out at the city's edge, and soon the djinn was traveling down a dusty carriage road. The route was barely wide enough for the walker, and the skirt of steam cannon thrashed the tree branches on either side. When they passed a darkened inn at a crossroads, Deryn saw curious faces peering from the windows. Sooner or later someone would wonder what a walker from Istanbul's ghettos was doing in the country-side.

But they were too close to their target for that to

matter now. The landscape climbed, growing rockier as the cliffs rose. The city came into view out the walker's rear viewport, its glitter and brilliance garish in the moonless night.

A hundred masts and smokestacks were scattered across the water's black expanse, and Deryn wondered again what would happen if the *Leviathan* were shot down. Would the behemoth simply swim away, or go mad among all those unarmed ships?

She shook her head. They couldn't fail tonight.

They were only a few miles from the Tesla cannon when a spotlight lanced out of the dark.

Deryn squinted—her eyes caught a flash of steel, and the silhouette of a trunk and tail.

It was one of the sultan's war elephants, blocking their path.

"Range?" Alek asked calmly.

"About a thousand yards. That is, nine hundred meters."

Alek nodded, pulling a lever. A spice bomb rolled from the magazine into the djinn's hand. Deryn caught a whiff of it and winced. Even wrapped in oiled burlap, the bombs let off eye-burning dust every time they moved.

"Top down, please," Alek said.

"Aye, your princeliness." Deryn set to work on the

hand crank, and the djinn's forehead rolled slowly closed across the stars.

Alek stoked the engines, sending power to the steam boilers. The machine's right arm drew slowly back.

Someone in the war elephant shouted at them through a megaphone. Deryn didn't recognize any of the Turkish words, but it sounded more curious than angry. As far as the Ottomans knew, the djinn was unarmed.

"They're just wondering what in blazes we're doing here," Deryn muttered. "No reason to be nervous."

"Nervous," said the beastie.

Alek laughed. "Perspicacious or not, the creature knows you."

Deryn frowned at the loris. Of *course* she was a wee bit jittery. Only a fool wouldn't be, heading into battle. Especially on a finicky Clanker contraption.

"Loaded and ready to fire," Alek said.

"Hold on." Deryn watched the ranging gauge that Klopp had installed, its needle slowly climbing as steam pressure built in the djinn's shoulder joint.

The tricky bit was, Klopp hadn't been able to test every throwing arm in the Committee's army, so he'd marked the gauges using only math and guesswork. Until their first shot landed, there was no telling how far the bombs would actually travel.

The needle finally reached nine hundred meters. . . .

"Fire!" Deryn cried.

Alek pulled the release trigger, and the djinn's giant hand swung overhead. Clouds of steam gushed from its metal shoulder, turning the air in the cabin scalding.

The spice bomb struck fifty yards in front of the elephant, exploding into a cloud of dust that swirled as red as blood in the spotlight.

"Master Klopp knows his sums," Deryn said with a smile. "Next time we'll hit the bum-rags dead-on!"

"More steam," Alek ordered. "I'm loading another."

Deryn pulled the stokers, and the engines roared beneath them, but the ranging needle was slow to climb. The djinn had exhausted every squick of shoulder pressure with its first throw.

"Come on!" she urged it. "They'll be shooting back any second."

"If this were a proper walker, we'd be taking evasive action," Alek muttered. "What I wouldn't give for a decent gun sight."

"Or a decent gun!"

"These spice bombs were your idea, I seem to—"

The elephant's main turret roared to life, sending a shell screaming overhead. The explosion came seconds later, rocking the djinn on its feet.

"They overshot us!" Alek cried. "But they have our range now. Can I fire yet?"

"Hold on!" Deryn watched the needle climb. The loris dug its claws deep into her shoulder, imitating the whistle and boom of the near miss.

The needle passed nine hundred meters, but she needed another fifty at least. . . .

"Fire!" she finally cried.

The great arm swung again, rocking the cabin backward. The moment the bomb had flown, Alek grabbed the controls and took them charging ahead.

Through the rocking viewport Deryn watched the war elephant disappear into a roiling cloud of red dust.

"Bull's-eye!" she cried.

But the walker's crew still managed to fire—the main gun blazed again, setting the dust cloud around the elephant into a massive whirlwind. The air cracked once more as the shot zoomed past.

The djinn reeled from the blast—the shell had landed right where they'd been standing, Deryn reckoned. Alek struggled with the controls as the walker staggered forward.

The machine gun on the elephant's trunk opened up, setting the path ahead of them jittering with plumes of dirt. Then came a chorus of bullets striking metal, as loud as pistons misfiring.

"We need steam cover!" Alek cried.

"No chance!" Deryn stared at the motionless pressure

gauge. The engines were too busy keeping the walker moving to recharge its boilers.

But the elephant's main turret didn't fire again. Only its left front leg was moving, like a dog's pawing at the ground. The searchlight swung away aimlessly into the sky.

"They've got a snootful!" Deryn cried. Even hundreds of yards away, her eyes were starting to prickle from the spices. She pulled the goggles up from around her neck and snapped them on.

"Snootful," Bovril said, chuckling, then sneezed.

Alek twisted the saunters, putting the djinn's hands out for balance. But he kept the walker charging ahead.

"I'm going to knock them over. Brace yourself."

Deryn checked her straps. "Hold on, beastie!"

The elephant was stumbling in circles now, another of its legs trying to move. But the turret stayed motionless. Had the spice bomb struck it dead-on?

Then Deryn saw the airflow patterns made visible by red dust, and realized what had happened—the cannon's recoil had sucked the spices right into the main turret. The elephant's crew had done themselves in with their own shot.

"They must be positively gagging!"

"Not for long, though," Alek said. "Hold on!"

The war elephant had turned sideways, stumbling

into a barbed wire fence just behind it. As the djinn charged into the swirling red clouds, Deryn's throat began to burn, and she was glad for her goggles. But Alek didn't waver—he tipped the djinn's left shoulder down . . .

Metal crunched and tore around them, a shock wave thundering through the djinn's huge frame. The world spun in the viewport, sky and ground and darkness flashing past. Alek swore, twisting at the controls, and a lungful of spices set Deryn coughing.

Finally the djinn stopped spinning; it was listing at a crazy angle. Deryn sprayed a squick of steam to clear the air, unstrapped herself, and leaned out the viewport.

The white clouds around them parted, revealing the elephant lying motionless on its side.

"We got them!"

"Snootful!" Bovril shouted.

"But why are we leaning like this?" Alek cried. "And what in blazes is holding us up?"

Deryn leaned out farther, and saw glittering metal everywhere. The djinn had stumbled through the barbed wire fence, pulling up a quarter mile of it.

"We're tangled in that barking wire!"

Alek worked his foot pedals, and wires snapped and scraped. "There's more of them ahead. We need steam cover—now."

Deryn stoked the boilers, then looked through the viewport. Two miles in the distance the Tesla cannon rose up from the cliffs, half as tall as the Eiffel Tower.

Around its base three more war elephants stood waiting, their smokestacks belching to life.

THIRTY-EIGHT

"Are the others anywhere about?" Alek asked.

Deryn leaned out the viewport, looking backward. There was nothing on the horizon but the silhouettes of short salt-sheered trees along the cliff tops. Then she spotted them—a trio of smoke trails against the starlight, no more than two miles away.

"Aye, all of them! Three kilometers or so behind us." She glanced at the pressure gauge, which was only now beginning to climb again. "And a good thing too. It'll be a few minutes before we can throw again."

"We don't have that much time. Give us some cover while I shake this wire off."

As Deryn reached for the steam cannon lever, one of the war elephants fired. The shell landed short, but close, and Deryn was thrown backward from the controls. Gravel and dirt spat through the viewport, leaving a scratch on her goggles.

"If you please, Mr. Sharp?" Alek asked.

"*Mr.* Sharp," Bovril repeated with a chuckle.

Deryn scrambled up from the floor to pull the lever, and hissing filled her ears. The pilot's cabin was suddenly as hot and humid as a greenhouse.

Outside the viewport the world disappeared behind a veil of white.

Alek worked the pedals and saunters, blindly tearing at the tangle of barbed wire. More gunfire boomed beyond the steam cloud, but the answering explosions sounded in the distance.

"They're shooting at the others," Deryn said.

"Then now's the time to attack! Get me some pressure in my throwing arm."

"I'd be happy to, Your Highness." Deryn pulled the engine stokers again. "But we've emptied the boilers to make this steam, and now you're dancing about like a loon, which is taking even more power!"

"Fine, then," Alek said, bringing the djinn into a crouched halt. As the engines idled, the ranging gauge began to climb again.

Through the whiteness came the clatter of machine guns—the Ottomans were firing into the bank of steam clouds, listening to see where their bullets hit metal.

"They'll find us soon enough," Alek said. He pulled the release, and Deryn heard a third spice bomb rattle into place.

She wiped condensation from the ranging gauge. "Three hundred meters and climbing."

"That's enough—if we charge them!"

"Are you daft? There's *three* of them and one of us!"

"Yes, but we haven't much time. Listen to your beast."

Deryn stared at the loris. Its wee eyes were closed, as if it had decided to take a nap. But a soft noise came from its lips—a hum and crackle, like the static on Klopp's wireless. She'd heard the sound before . . .

"Barking spiders," she breathed.

"Indeed." Alek pushed at the pedals. As the djinn thundered forward, the hot clouds parted around them.

The Tesla cannon stood tall on the cliffs, its frame glimmering against the dark sky. Faint sparkles traveled along its lower struts, like fabricated fireflies flitting about on Guy Fawkes Day. Its shimmer spilled across the battlefield.

She leaned forward to squint up at the stars. No dark silhouette moved among them, but if the Ottomans were charging up their cannon, they must have spotted the *Leviathan* approaching.

The war elephants were still firing at the other walkers, their mortars elevated high. But as Alek charged ahead, one of the turrets began to spin about. . . .

Moments later its main gun billowed flame and smoke.

The shell struck close enough to send the djinn staggering. The needle on the ranging gauge trembled, then fell—pressure was leaking somewhere.

"We're hit!" Deryn cried.

"The trigger is yours, Mr. Sharp," Alek said calmly, his hands white-knuckled on the saunters. The djinn was limping now, the whole pilot's cabin lurching from side to side.

Deryn grasped the release trigger, her eyes flicking back and forth between the ranging gauge and the three steel elephants ahead. The needle had stopped at four hundred meters, trembling uncertainly, and the distance to the elephants was lessening with every step.

The nearest elephant swung its trunk toward the djinn, its machine gun blazing. Bullets struck armor with a sound like coins shaken in a tin. One bullet slipped in through the viewport, a sliver of hot metal striking sparks around their heads.

"Are you hit?" Alek asked.

"Not me!" Deryn said.

"Not me!" Bovril repeated, then filled the cabin with its maniacal laughter.

Another of the elephants' big guns was taking aim . . .

The ranging needle sputtered again, then climbed, and finally they were close enough. Deryn pulled the trigger, and the walker's throwing arm swung overhead as they ran,

"CLASH."

like a charging fast bowler unleashing a cricket ball at a batsman.

The spice bomb went straight into the closest elephant, exploding into a swirl of fiery red. The machine staggered, but the cloud moved hastily away, spreading through the shimmering lower struts of the Tesla cannon.

"Blisters!" Deryn cried. "The wind's too strong up here!"

Of course, the wind always blew hard against seaside cliffs. She'd been a *Dummkopf* not to realize it!

But Alek didn't falter, barreling straight at the elephant. The direct hit had done some damage, at least. The Ottoman machine was stumbling about like a newborn calf.

But just before they collided, the elephant's great head rolled on its neck, raising the two barbed tusks. . . .

Alek twisted at the saunters, but the walker was moving too fast to turn. With an awful metal shriek the djinn impaled itself upon one tusk, a white blast of steam shooting from the boilers in its chest.

The air in the pilot's cabin turned wet and scalding, every valve hissing like a teakettle. The elephant shook its head, tossing the djinn madly and throwing Deryn from her seat. She screamed as her hands splayed against the burning metal floor and the beastie's claws went deep into her shoulder.

"We're done for!" she shouted. "Abandon ship!"

"Not yet." Alek pulled a saunter back with one hand,

hitting the bomb release with another, and with the djinn's last squick of strength brought its throwing arm down.

Deryn stood, squinting through her goggles to watch the remaining spice bombs—almost a dozen of them—rattle down the magazine to burst against the elephant's back.

"Barking spiders," said the perspicacious loris.

"Open us up," Deryn said, unstrapping herself. "In another moment we won't be able to breathe!"

While Alek spun the hand crank furiously, she kicked open the locker in the back of the cabin, pulling a mass of rope from it.

"Aren't you glad we practiced belaying?" she shouted over the din of steam and gunfire.

"I'd rather not know what's coming," Alek said.

"Nonsense. This is easy compared with a sliding escape from a Huxley! I'll tell you about that some time."

As the djinn's head opened, Deryn tied the rope off and flung it over the back of the walker. Stepping up onto the cabin's edge, she peered down into the nebulous white cloud beneath them. The last steam from the djinn's boilers was still billowing from the tusk protruding from its back.

"I'll go first," she said. "So if you slide too fast, I'll break your fall."

"Won't that hurt a bit?"

"Aye. So don't slide too fast!"

Deryn clipped herself to the rope, taking one last look at the battle spread out around them. Another of the war elephants had been hit—it was stumbling in a circle, red dust splattered across its glittering steel armor. Lilit's Minotaur was charging forward while the iron golem stood back, its huge right arm launching spice bombs at

the remaining elephant. Even with the sea breeze at her back, the smells of spices and gunfire were choking.

Then she saw it—Şahmeran lying on her belly half a mile from the tower, pouring out black smoke and burning oil.

"Zaven's been hit!" she cried.

"And that's not all." Alek pointed toward the city, where a new column of smoke was rising in the distance.

"Blisters! Enemy reinforcements!"

"Don't worry. That walker's ten kilometers away, and the Ottomans don't have anything fast."

"Fast," Bovril said.

Deryn gave it a hard look. "What in blazes are you saying, beastie?"

"Fast," it said again.

A giant crash rolled across the battlefield—Lilit's Minotaur had charged straight into the last undamaged war elephant. Both machines went down, tumbling over each other like cats in a fight. A vast red cloud billowed out in all directions, driven by the steam from the two machines' broken boilers, turning the stars in the sky blood red.

The two walkers' tumbling came to a halt in the center of a swirling tower of dust and engine smoke, neither of them moving.

"Lilit . . . ," Deryn said hoarsely.

[428]

The Minotaur was down, but its head seemed to be undamaged. Maybe the girl was safe inside her metal shell.

"Look," Alek said. "She's opened the way for Klopp!"

Only one elephant remained standing, and it was covered with red dust, barely moving. The iron golem was lumbering steadily forward, with nothing between it and the Tesla cannon.

But Klopp didn't veer toward the wounded elephant or the cannon—he was headed straight toward them.

"What's he doing?" Deryn asked. "Why's he coming *here*?"

Alek swore. "Klopp and Bauer are following Volger's orders. They're coming to rescue me!"

"Blisters, this is what you get for being a barking *prince!*"

"An archduke, technically."

"Whatever you are, we have to show him you don't need rescuing. Come on!"

Deryn lifted the rope, and felt Bovril tighten its grip on her shoulder.

"Abandon ship," the beastie said.

She jumped, sliding down through hot clouds of vapor.

THIRTY-NINE

Before he followed Dylan, Alek looked down at the war elephant that had impaled the djinn.

Crewmen were abandoning the walker through its belly hatch, coughing and stumbling blindly. They wouldn't be much of a threat for the moment.

But seeing the ground so far below made Alek pull his piloting gloves tighter. Learning how to "belay," as Dylan called it, had taught him a healthy respect for rope burn. He swallowed, the tastes of paprika and cayenne heavy in his mouth, then jumped . . .

The rope whipped past him, wild and angry, like a stream of scalding water. He jerked himself to a painful halt every few meters, his boots banging against the hot metal of the djinn's armor. Steam clouds swirled around him, the engines inside the walker knocking and hissing as they cooled.

As his feet thumped down onto hard earth, Alek pulled off the gloves to stare at his burning palms.

"Took you long enough," Dylan complained, turning toward the iron golem. "Come *on*. That Tesla cannon's getting ready to fire. We need to show Klopp you're okay!"

Alek unclipped himself and followed the boy, who had broken into a dead run. The iron golem was still headed toward them, making its steady way across the battlefield.

Klopp clearly hadn't seen the Ottoman reinforcements coming from behind him.

As he ran, Alek squinted at the smoke trail in the distance. It seemed closer already, and he saw now how the column curved backward against the starlit sky.

Fast, the creature had said. But what walker was *that* fast?

Dylan let out a yelp from just ahead. He'd tripped and fallen face-first into the dirt. As the boy scrambled to his feet, Alek slowed, staring down at what Dylan had stumbled on—train tracks.

"Oh, no."

"What in blazes?" Dylan stared down at the rails. "Ah, this must be where the Orient-Express . . ."

"Express," the beast hissed softly.

Together they turned to stare at the approaching column of smoke. It was much closer now, charging along the cliffs ten times faster than any lumbering walker.

And it was headed straight for the iron golem.

"He can't see it," Alek said. "It's right behind him!"

"Klopp!" Dylan cried out, breaking back into a run, his arms waving in the air. "Get away from the tracks!"

Alek ran a few more steps, his heart thudding in his ears. But yelling was pointless. He searched his pockets for a way to send a signal—a flare, a gun.

The famous dragon-headed engine was visible in the distance now, it single eye glowing white hot, smoke spewing from its stacks. Dylan was still running toward Klopp, pointing back at the massive train.

The iron golem came to a lumbering halt, its head lowering for a better view of the tiny boy before it.

Alek watched as two huge cargo arms unfolded from the engine car of the Express. A dozen meters long, they stretched out in both directions, like a pair of sabers wielded by a charging horseman.

Klopp must have understood Dylan's cries, or heard the train behind him, because the walker began to slowly turn . . .

But in that moment the Express shot past, its left cargo arm slicing through the golem's legs. Metal shrieked and buckled, and a cloud of steam burst from the ruined knees.

The walker tipped backward, its huge arms flailing, and landed on the trailing end of the Express. Two freight cars buckled around the fallen machine, and the

"RAILROAD KNEECAPPING."

cars behind kept piling into it, hurling glass and metal parts into the air.

The shock wave from being pulled in half rippled up the train until it reached the engine, which skidded from the rails, plowing through the dirt. But the pilots had been ready for this—the Express's arms stretched out like wings to steady the engine car. A handful of coal and freight cars dragged behind the engine, sending clouds of dust into the air.

Alek saw Dylan running back toward him, Bovril a tiny silhouette on his shoulder, both of them about to be swallowed in the rolling mass of dust.

"Run!" he was shouting, pointing sideways from the tracks.

The front half of the train, skidding and derailed but still speeding along, was headed straight at Alek.

He turned and ran the way Dylan was pointing, directly away from the rails. Long seconds later the dust cloud overtook Alek, blinding him and filling his lungs.

Something flew out of the dark mass and knocked him off his feet, strong hands pushing his head down into the dirt.

A huge shadow swept overhead—the Express's cargo arm, Alek realized. A cascade of dirt and gravel flew over him, and a clamor like a thousand foundries rolled past, full of shrieks and clangs and explosions.

As the noise faded, the dust cleared a little, and Alek looked up.

"Well, that was close," he said. Not five meters from his head, the skidding claw of the cargo arm had carved a furrow as wide as a carriage lane.

"You're welcome, your archdukeness."

"Thank you, Dylan." Alek stood up, dusting off his clothes and looking dazedly about.

The front half of the Orient-Express had finally slid to a halt, almost skidding into the Tesla cannon itself. The iron golem lay hissing and steaming on the ground, the back half of the train in piles around it. Alek took a step closer, wondering if Master Klopp and Bauer were all right.

But Bovril was growling, echoing a low buzzing noise that drifted across the battlefield. A crackle was building in the air.

Dylan pointed toward the southern sky, where a long silhouette had finally appeared—the *Leviathan*, black and huge against the stars.

Alek turned back toward the Tesla cannon. As he watched, the awful shimmers began to travel up into its tip.

"We have to stop it," Dylan said. "There's no one else."

Alek nodded dumbly. Klopp and Bauer, Lilit and Zaven—they all needed his help. But the Tesla cannon was readying to fire, and the *Leviathan* had more than a hundred men aboard.

His fists clenched in frustration. If only he were in a walker now, with huge arms to tear the tower down.

"Express," Bovril hissed.

"The train," Alek said softly. "If we can take the engine car, we can use its cargo arms!"

Dylan gazed at him a moment, then nodded. They ran together, stumbling across the wreckage-strewn ground, dodging the piles of scattered cargo that had been thrown from the train.

The front half of the Orient-Express had come to rest only fifteen meters from the Tesla cannon. The cargo arms were motionless, but the smokestacks were still belching. A few soldiers stumbled out of the engine cars, wearing German uniforms, rifles strapped across their shoulders.

Alek dragged Dylan to a halt in the shadows. "They're armed, and we're not."

"Aye. Follow me."

The boy ran to the last car in the line, a freight carrier lying lopsided in the furrow dug by the train's passage. He climbed up and along its top, making his way toward the engine car. Alek followed, crouching low to keep out of sight.

The soldiers hardly looked alert. They were walking about in a dumbfounded state, gazing at the battle wreckage around them and coughing spices from their lungs. A few stared at the *Leviathan* in the sky.

Alek heard a familiar sound—the rumble of the airship's engines. He glanced up and saw that the *Leviathan* was halfway through a turn. The crew had spotted the glittering Tesla cannon and were trying to bring the ship about.

But they were too late. It would take long minutes to get out of range, and the Tesla cannon was buzzing like a beehive, almost ready to fire.

Dylan had reached the coal hopper behind the engine, and Alek jumped in after him. Coal skidded under his feet and turned his hands black as he caught himself from stumbling.

Dylan scrambled to the front and climbed out, reaching down to give Alek a hand.

"Quickly now," the boy whispered.

Alek pulled himself up between the two huge cargo arms. He could feel the air crackling; sparks from the giant tower were making the shadows quiver. But the engineer's cabin was just ahead.

"There's only one man inside," Dylan whispered, handing Bovril to Alek and pulling a knife from his jacket. "I can handle him."

Not waiting for an answer, the boy swung himself down and in through a window in a single motion. By the time Alek reached the door, Dylan had the lone engineer cowering in a corner.

Alek stepped inside and looked at the controls—a legion of unfamiliar dials and gauges, brake levers and engine stokers. But the saunters were metal gloves on poles, just like the ones that controlled Şahmeran's arms.

He placed Bovril on the floor, stuck his hands into the saunters, and made a fist.

A dozen meters to his right, the huge claw responded, snapping shut. A few of the German soldiers looked up at the noise, but most were transfixed by the glittering Tesla cannon and the airship overhead.

"Don't muck about!" Dylan hissed. "Tear it down!"

Alek extended his arm, reaching out for the tower. But the great claw clamped shut a few meters short of the nearest glowing strut.

"Get us closer!" Dylan said.

Alek stared at the engine levers, then realized that the train's wheels were useless without a track. But he remembered a legless beggar he'd seen in the town of Lienz, propelling himself along on a wheeled board with his hands.

He set both claws against the ground, one on either side, and scraped them backward. The engine car lifted a bit, sliding forward a meter or so, then settled back into the dirt.

"Closer," Bovril said approvingly.

"Well, we've got the Germans' attention now," Dylan muttered, looking out the window.

"I leave that matter to you," Alek answered, scraping the huge claws against the ground again. The engine car skidded forward with an ungodly screech, metal striking the bedrock of the cliffs.

Shouts came through the windows now, and a soldier leapt up to pound on the door. Dylan punched the engineer in the stomach, crumpling him to the floor, then turned to stand ready with his knife.

Alek outstretched the cargo arms again.

This time one great claw reached the Tesla cannon's lowest strut. As he snapped the claw shut, a crackle shot through the cabin. The metal gloves sizzled in Alek's hands, and an invisible force seemed to close around his chest. Every hair on Bovril's body was standing on end.

"Barking spiders!" Dylan cried. "The lightning's coming for us!"

Sparks danced along the controls and the walls of the cabin, and the soldier at the door yelped, jumping off the metal running board.

Alek set his teeth against the pain, pulling harder on the saunter. The engine car lifted into the air again, the strut letting out a metal groan as it slowly bent toward them. At the base of the tower, a ball of white fire was spiraling into being.

"It's about to fire!" Dylan cried.

Alek pulled as hard as he could, and a sudden shudder

passed through the car. The saunters went limp in his hand, and the lightning on the cabin walls flickered out.

"You snapped it, and the cannon's . . ." Dylan frowned. "It's tipping. The whole barking thing is tipping over!"

"From one broken strut?" Alek stepped to the window, looking up.

The tower was slowly leaning away, the lightning flowing down from its higher struts into a ball of white fire on its opposite side. A huge snakelike form clung to the struts there, halfway up, wrapped in a glowing cocoon of electricity.

"Is that . . . ?"

"Aye," Dylan breathed. "It's Şahmeran."

Zaven had somehow piloted his injured walker all the way to the tower. And now it was acting as a conductor, drawing the power of the cannon into itself.

Lightning spun in a whirlwind around the goddess walker, glowing brighter and brighter until Alek had to shut his eyes.

"He'll be done for in there," Dylan said, and Alek nodded.

A few seconds later the Tesla cannon began to fall.

"A GODDESS AND A MARTYR TOPPLE THE TOWER."

· FORTY ·

The tower toppled around Şahmeran in a maelstrom of white fire.

Tendrils of lightning leapt out in all directions, dancing on the frozen djinn and elephant, on the other fallen walkers, and along the wreckage of the Orient-Express. The metal walls of the engine car crackled with sparks and spiderwebs of flame.

As the lightning faded, the roar of the tower's collapse filled the air. A falling strut struck the engine car—the ceiling dented inward, and the windows shattered all at once. Bending metal howled around them, and smoke and dust billowed through the car.

Long moments later a heavy silence settled over the battlefield.

"Are you all right, Dylan?" Alek's words sounded muffled in his own ears.

"Aye. How about you, beastie?"

"Zaven," said Bovril softly.

Dylan took the creature into his arms. "Listen. The *Leviathan*'s still up there."

It was true—the soft rumble of the airship's engines had settled over the silent battlefield. At least all this madness hadn't been in vain.

"*Leviathan*," Bovril repeated slowly, rolling the word around in its mouth.

Alek stepped closer to the window. The Tesla cannon stretched out into the distance, jagged and broken, like the unearthed spine of some huge extinct creature. The djinn lay fallen beside the war elephant, both walkers battered by the cascade of debris.

A cold shiver went through Alek—most of the German soldiers had disappeared beneath the ruined tower.

"We need to see if Lilit's all right," he said. "And Klopp and Bauer."

"Aye." Dylan put Bovril on his shoulder. "But who first?"

Alek hesitated, realizing that his men might be dead, as Zaven certainly was. "Lilit first. Her father . . ."

"Of course."

They opened the door and stepped out into a hellish landscape. The smoke and spices and engine oil were choking, but the smells of burned flesh and hair were worse.

Alek turned his eyes from what the cannon's last discharge of electricity had done to the men outside.

"Come on," Dylan said hoarsely, dragging him away.

As they skirted the wreckage, Bovril raised its head and said, "Lilit."

Alek followed the creature's gaze, squinting through the darkness. There at the edge of the cliffs was a lonely figure, looking out over the water.

"Lilit!" Dylan called, and the figure turned to face them.

They ran to her, the cool sea breeze carrying away the smells of battle and destruction. Lilit's piloting gear was torn, her face pale in the darkness. A long canvas bag lay in the dirt beside her feet.

As they drew close, she stumbled into Dylan's arms.

"Your father," the boy said. "I'm so sorry."

Lilit pulled away. "I saw what he was doing, so I cleared a path for him. I *helped* him do it . . ." She shook her head, tears tracking the dust on her face, and turned to stare at the fallen tower. "Have we all gone mad, to want this?"

"He saved the *Leviathan*," Alek said.

Lilit just looked at him, dazed and uncertain, as if every language she knew had been knocked from her head. Her stare made him feel foolish for speaking.

"All gone mad," Bovril said.

Lilit reached out to stroke the creature's fur, her eyes still glassy.

"Are you all right?" Dylan asked.

"Just dizzy . . . and amazed. Look at that."

She pointed across the water toward the city of Istanbul. Its dark streets sparkled with gunfire, and half a dozen gyrothopters hovered over the palace. As Alek watched, a silent tendril of flame arced through the sky, then disappeared with a rumble among the ancient buildings.

"See? It's really happening," Lilit said. "Just as we planned."

"Aye, that's the barking strangest thing about battle—that it's real." Dylan looked out across the water. "The behemoth won't be long now."

Alek took a step closer to the cliff's edge and gazed down. The *Goeben* was steaming out, her kraken-fighting arms spread like the claws of a crab. Sparks glimmered across the tower on her aft decks.

"Another Tesla cannon," Lilit whispered. "I'd forgotten."

"Not to worry," Dylan said. "It's not as big, and doesn't have the range. The lady boffin has this timed to perfection."

As he spoke, a single spotlight lanced out from the airship's gondola, so bright that its beam sliced deep into the water. It slid toward the *Goeben*, a column of light rippling through blackness.

The gyrothopters above the palace moved toward the airship, and smaller spotlights from the *Leviathan* sprang to life, picking the gyrothopters out against the dark sky.

From this distance Alek couldn't see the hawks or bats, but one by one, the gyrothopters tumbled from the air.

"They've had a whole month for repairs and refits," Dylan said. "And to make more beasties."

Alek nodded, realizing that he'd never seen the *Leviathan* at full strength, only damaged and starved. Tonight it would be a different ship altogether.

"Beasties," said Bovril, its eyes glowing like a cat's.

The main spotlight reached the *Goeben*, and for a moment the warship's steel guns and armor glowed a blinding white. Then the spotlight flicked from one color to the next—purple, green, and finally blood red.

A pair of tentacles stretched from the water, spilling sheets of rain across the *Goeben*'s decks.

It was the behemoth.

The ironclad's kraken-fighting arms swung about, their snippers slashing at the sea monster's flesh. But the tentacles didn't seem to feel the cuts, coiling like slow pythons around the center of the warship. A huge head lifted up from the water, two eyes gleaming in the red of the spotlight. . . .

Alek took a step back. Unlike a kraken's, the behemoth's tentacles were only a small part of the beast. Its long body was all bony plates and segments, a spiny ridge traveling down its back. It repulsed him, like something dragged up from the deepest ocean, ancient and alien.

A desolate sound rolled across the water, the iron-clad's hull wailing as it bent in the behemoth's grasp. Her small guns were firing in all directions, the kraken-fighting arms flailing against the massive tentacles. Men and spent ammunition slid across the warship's decks as she rocked back and forth.

"Barking spiders," Dylan breathed. "Dr. Barlow said the beastie was huge, but I never thought . . ."

Something flared inside the *Goeben*'s broken hull, one of her boilers spilling flame. Hissing steam clouds shot from ruptures in the ship's armor plates.

The Tesla cannon tried to fire, but its half-charged lightning barely leapt into the sky, then tumbled back to coil around the behemoth's tentacles and dance on the metal decks. Explosions flickered up and down the warship's length as fuel tanks and magazines were ignited by white fire.

The searchlight turned a brilliant blue, and in one huge motion the behemoth hauled its body onto the superstructure, forcing the warship down. The *Goeben* resisted for a moment, but then her foredecks slipped beneath the waves. The aft end rose up, and the Tesla cannon climbed into the dark sky, still shimmering. With a metal shriek the warship split in two, both halves sliding neatly down into the water.

A lone kraken-fighting arm reached up from the

churning waves, its claw snapping at the air before it disappeared again. Then a burst of red light flared beneath the surface, sending columns of fresh steam into the air.

The water settled slowly, and then was still again.

"Poor bum-rags," Dylan said.

Alek stood silent. In the last month he'd somehow forgotten what the revolution would mean for the crew of the *Goeben*.

"I have to join my comrades," Lilit said, kneeling beside the long canvas bag. She pulled out a mass of metal poles and rippling silk, and set to work. The contraption expanded, driven by coils of springs inside. In moments it was five meters across, the wings as translucent as those of a mosquito.

"What in blazes?" Dylan cried.

"A body kite," Alek said. "But you'll never make it back to Istanbul in that."

"I don't need to. My uncle's fishing boat is waiting beneath the cliffs." Lilit turned to Dylan. "I'm sorry, but he can be trusted. And I had to tell someone else our plan, in case we needed a way back to the city."

"Now?" Dylan asked. "But we have to check on Klopp and Bauer!"

"Of course you do; they're your friends. But the revolution needs its leaders tonight." Lilit stared across the water, her voice falling. "And Nene will need me too."

As she stood there, fresh tears streaking the grime on her face, Alek thought of the night his own parents had died. Strangely, all he could recall now was repeating the story to Eddie Malone in payment for the man's silence. It was as if the telling had erased the real memory.

"I'm sorry about your father," he said, every word stiff and clumsy in his mouth.

Lilit gave him a curious look. "If the sultan wins tonight, you'll simply run off somewhere new, won't you?"

Alek frowned. "That's probably true."

"Good luck, then," she said. "Your gold was very useful."

"You're welcome, if that was meant as a thank you."

"It was." She turned to Dylan. "No matter what happens, I'll never forget what you've done for us. I think you're the most brilliant boy I've ever met."

"Aye, well, it was just—"

Lilit didn't let him finish, but threw her arms around him, kissing him hard on the lips. After a long moment she pulled away and smiled. "I'm sorry. I was just curious."

"Curious? Barking spiders!" Dylan cried, a hand at his mouth. "You hardly know me!"

Lilit laughed and lifted the body kite into the air. As its wings filled with the cool sea breeze, she stepped to the edge of the cliffs, her hands on the pilot strut.

"I know you better than you think, *Mr.* Sharp." She

smiled, turning to Alek. "You don't know what a friend you have in Dylan."

With that, she stepped off into the darkness . . . and fell from their sight.

Alek rushed to the edge of the cliff, looking down in horror. The body kite tumbled for a moment, but then steadied itself and angled out to sea. The wind lifted it up higher, almost level with the cliff tops, and for a moment they could hear Lilit's laughter once more.

The kite turned hard, banking toward the city lights. A moment later it had slipped away into the darkness.

"*Mr.* Sharp," Bovril said, and chuckled.

Alek shook his head, wondering at Lilit. Her father was dead and her city in flames—and there she was, soaring through the air, somehow laughing.

"That girl is quite mad."

"Aye." Dylan touched his mouth again. "But she's not a bad kisser."

Alek looked at the boy, then shook his head again.

"Come on. Let's go see about Master Klopp."

FORTY-ONE

The iron golem lay in a heap of train cars and scattered cargo, its legs twisted and torn. Only its upper half remained intact, the huge head leaning back against the wreckage of two freight cars, a sleeping giant with a crumpled metal pillow.

Deryn and Alek made their way closer, through electrical parts and shattered glass. The railroad tracks had been torn from the ground, and lay among the other debris like tangled ribbons of steel.

"Blisters," Deryn said as they passed an overturned dining car, its red velvet curtains spilling through broken windows. "Lucky there were no passengers aboard."

"We can get up to the golem's head that way," Alek said, pointing at the huge hand lying splayed in the dirt. They climbed onto it and up the walker's arm, and soon saw two motionless forms strapped into the pilots' chairs.

"WRECKAGE AND AFTERMATH."

"Master Klopp!" Alek cried out. "Hans!"

One of the men stirred.

Deryn saw that it was Bauer, his eyes glazed, his hands reaching feebly for the seat straps. She followed Alek up and helped him get the man out.

"*Was uns getroffen?*" he asked.

"*Der Orient-Express,*" Alek explained.

Bauer gave him a befuddled look, then saw the wreckage around them, belief dawning slowly in his face.

The three of them unstrapped Klopp and laid him on the golem's broad shoulder. The master of mechaniks still wasn't moving. Blood caked his face, and when Deryn put her hand to Klopp's neck, his pulse was weak.

"We have to get him to a doctor."

"Yes, but how?" Alek asked.

Deryn's eyes swept the battlefield. Not a single walker remained standing. But in the sky the *Leviathan*'s silhouette had swung into profile. It was just as she'd expected—now that it had dispatched the *Goeben*, the airship was coming about for a closer look at the wrecked Tesla cannon.

She opened her mouth to explain, but suddenly the beastie on her shoulder was imitating a soft thumping sound.

Alek heard it too. "Walkers."

Deryn turned toward the city. A dozen columns of smoke rose from the horizon.

"Could they be from the Committee?"

Alek shook his head. "They don't even know we're here."

"Aye, it was *meant* to be that way. But that anarchist lassie told her uncle, didn't she?"

Bauer rose unsteadily to his feet, lifting a pair of field glasses. One lens was shattered, so he held the other to his eye like a telescope.

"*Elefanten,*" he said a moment later.

Alek swore. "At least those things are slow."

"But we'll never carry Klopp out of here," Deryn said. "Not without help."

"And where do you suppose we'll get that?"

She pointed up at the dark shape over the water, still turning, its searchlights angling toward the cliffs now. "The *Leviathan* is on its way to take a closer look. We can signal them, and get Klopp to the ship's surgeon."

"A, B, C . . . ," Bovril said happily.

"They'll take us prisoner again!" Alek said.

"Aye, and what do you think the barking Ottomans will do, after all this?" Deryn swept her arm across the wreckage. "At least with us you'll be alive!"

"*Ich kann bleiben mit Meister Klopp, Herr,*" Bauer said.

Deryn's eyes narrowed. After a month working with Clankers, her German was much better. "What does he mean, he'll stay with Klopp?"

Alek turned to Deryn. "Your ship can pick Bauer and Klopp up, while you and I make a run for it."

Deryn's jaw dropped. "Have you gone barking mad?"

"The Ottomans will never spot us in all this mess." Alek clenched his fists. "And just think, if the Committee wins tonight, they'll throw the Germans out. And they owe both of us a debt, Dylan. We can stay here, among allies."

"Not me, you daft prince! I have to go home!"

"But I can't do this alone . . . not without you." His eyes softened. "Please come with me."

Deryn turned from him, for a moment wishing that Alek were asking this same question but in a different way. Not as some *Dummkopf* of a prince who expected everyone to serve his purposes, but as a man.

It wasn't his fault, of course. She'd never told Alek why she'd really come to Istanbul—not for the mission but for him. She hadn't told him anything, and it was too late now. They'd been together a whole month, working and fighting side by side, and still she hadn't convinced herself that a common girl could matter to him.

So what was the point of staying?

"There's more to do here, Dylan," he said. "You're the best soldier the revolution has."

"Aye, but that's my home up there. I can't live with . . . your machines."

Alek spread his hands. "It doesn't matter. Your crew will never see us."

"They have to." Deryn stared out across the battlefield, looking for something to signal with. But Alek was right; even if she had ten-foot semaphore flags, no one would ever see her among the wreckage of the train.

Then she saw them—the golem's arms stretched out in both directions. The right one was straight out, the left one at an angle, almost making the sign for the letter *S*.

"Can this contraption still move?"

"What, the walker?"

"A, B, C," Bovril said again.

"Aye. A giant sending signals would be barking hard to miss."

"The boilers are cold," Alek said. "But I suppose the pneumatics might still have some pressure in them."

"Then take a look!"

Alek gritted his teeth, but climbed back up to the head and knelt by the controls. He rapped at two of the gauges, then turned back, an uncertain look on his face.

"Can it work?" she called. "Don't lie to me!"

"I would never lie to you, Dylan. We can signal perhaps a dozen letters."

"Then do it! Follow my lead." Deryn held her right arm out straight, her left angled down.

Alek didn't move. "If I give myself up to your captain, he'll never let me escape again."

"But if you don't signal the *Leviathan* for help, Klopp is a dead man. We all are, once those walkers get here!"

Alek stared at her another moment, then sighed and turned to the controls, placing his hands in the saunters. The hiss of pneumatics filled the air, and then the great arms scraped slowly along the ground, exactly matching Deryn's stance.

"S . . . ," the perspicacious loris said.

Deryn swung her left arm across herself. This letter was harder for the iron golem, half lying in the dirt as it was, but Alek managed to bend its elbow just enough.

"H!" Bovril announced, and kept up as Deryn continued. "A . . . R . . . P . . ."

By the fifth letter the *Leviathan*'s huge kraken spotlight had found them, and together they repeated the sequence twice more before the giant arms' last squick of pressure hissed away into the night.

Alek turned from the saunters. *"Wie lange haben wir, Hans?"*

Bauer shielded his eyes from the spotlight's glare. *"Zehn minuten?"*

"We still have time to get away, Dylan."

"Not with only ten minutes, and there's no need to run." Deryn put a hand on Alek's shoulder. "After what we've done tonight, I can tell the captain how you introduced me to the Committee. And how if you hadn't, the ship would've been shot down!" She said it all fast. Breaking her silent promise to leave him behind was as easy as breathing.

"I expect they'll give me a medal," Alek said drily.

"Aye, you never know about that."

The spotlight began to flicker then, long and short flashes. Deryn was out of practice with Morse code, but as she watched, the familiar patterns came back into her mind.

"Message received," she said. "And the captain sends me greetings!"

"How very polite."

Deryn kept her eyes on the flickering spotlight. "They're getting ready to pick us up. We'll have Master Klopp to a surgeon in half a squick!"

"Then you don't need me and Hans anymore." Alek held out his hand. "I have to say good-bye."

"Don't," Deryn pleaded. "You'll never make it past all those walkers. And I swear I won't let the captain chain you up. If he does, I'll break the locks myself!"

Alek stared down at his offered hand, but then his dark green eyes caught hers. They gazed at each other for a long moment, the rumble of the airship's engines trembling on Deryn's skin.

"Come with me," she said, finally grasping his hand. "It's like you said the night before you ran away, how all the parts of the *Leviathan* fit. You belong there."

He looked up at the airship, his eyes glistening. He was still in love with it, Deryn could see.

"Perhaps I shouldn't run off without my men," he said.

"Mein Herr," Bauer said. *"Graf Volger befahl mir—"*

"Volger!" Alek spat. "If it weren't for his scheming, we'd all have kept together in the first place."

Deryn squeezed his hand harder. "It'll be all right. I swear."

As the airship drew closer, a whisper of wings came from overhead, steel talons glinting in the searchlights. Deryn let go of Alek's hand, and breathed deep the bitter almond of spilled hydrogen—the dangerous, beautiful smell of a hasty descent. Ropes tumbled from the gondola's cargo door, and seconds later men were sliding down them.

"Isn't that a barking brilliant sight?"

"Beautiful," Alek said. "If one isn't chained up inside."

"Nonsense." Deryn banged his shoulder. "That blether about chains, that was just an expression. They only locked Count Volger in his stateroom, and I had to bring him breakfast every day!"

"How luxurious."

She smiled, though the thought of Volger sent a squick of nerves through her—he knew her secret. The man could still betray her to the officers, or to Alek, anytime he wanted.

But she couldn't keep hiding from his countship forever. It wasn't soldierly. And besides, she could always toss him out a window if it came to that.

As the airship came to a rumbling halt, Bovril clung tighter to her shoulder. "Breakfast every day?" it asked.

"Aye, beastie," Deryn said, stroking its fur. "You're going home."

FORTY-TWO

"S-H-A-R-P!" said Newkirk from the mouth of the cargo bay. "Blisters, Dylan, it's really you!"

"Who else?" Deryn replied, grinning as she took the boy's offered hand. She pulled herself up in a single heave.

"And you found the missing beastie?"

"Aye." Deryn hooked a thumb over her shoulder at the wreckage-strewn battlefield. "One of my many accomplishments."

Newkirk looked down. "You *have* been busy, Mr. Sharp. But save your bragging. There are German walkers coming, and the bosun says you're wanted in the navigation room."

"Now?" Deryn glanced back at the rescue operation. Klopp was rising through the air, trussed to a stretcher, while Alek and Bauer waited on the iron golem's shoulder.

"The bosun says right away."

"All right, Mr. Newkirk. But make sure you get those Clankers up safely."

"Aye, don't worry. We'll not let the bum-rags slip away again!"

Deryn didn't argue with the boy. It didn't matter what Newkirk thought, as long as the officers knew that Alek had come back of his own free will.

Clanker or not, he belonged here.

On her way to the navigation room, the airship hummed and rumbled beneath Deryn's feet, the corridors full of scrambling men and beasts. Bovril took in everything with eyes the size of florins, awed into a rare silence. The beastie belonged here too, it seemed.

The lady boffin waited in the navigation room, staring out at the lights of Istanbul across the water. Deryn frowned—she'd expected to find the captain. Of course, with German walkers on the way, the officers would be up on the bridge. But why had she been ordered here instead of to a battle station?

Tazza leapt up from the floor beside Dr. Barlow, running over to snuffle at Deryn's boots. She knelt to cup his nose with her palm.

"Good to see you, Tazza."

"Tazza," Bovril repeated, then chuckled.

"A pleasure to see you too, Mr. Sharp," the lady boffin

said, turning from the view. "We've all been quite beside ourselves with worry."

"It's brilliant to be home, ma'am."

"Of course, it stands to reason that you'd make it back safe and sound, resourceful lad that you are." The lady boffin's fingers drummed the sill of the window. "Though I see you've caused a bit of trouble in the meantime."

"Aye, ma'am." Deryn allowed herself to smile. "It *was* a bit of trouble, knocking out that Tesla cannon. But we got it done."

"Yes, yes." The lady boffin waved her hand, as if she saw towers wrapped in lightning topple every day. "But I meant that creature on your shoulder, not this tiresome battle."

"Oh," Deryn said, looking at Bovril. "You mean you're glad to have it back, then?"

"No, Mr. Sharp, that is not what I mean." Dr. Barlow let out a slow sigh. "Have you forgotten already? I went to great pains to make sure that the loris hatched while *Alek* was in the machine room. So that its nascent fixation would be directed entirely at him."

"Aye, I remember that," Deryn said. "How it's like a baby duck, latching on to whoever it sees first."

"Exactly, which was Alek. And yet here it is on *your* shoulder, Mr. Sharp."

Deryn frowned, trying to remember exactly when

Bovril had started riding on her shoulder as often as Alek's. "Well, the beastie seems to like me just as much as it does him. And why wouldn't it? I mean, Alek is a barking *Clanker*, after all."

Dr. Barlow sat down at the map table, shaking her head. "It wasn't designed to bond with two people! Not unless they're . . ." She narrowed her eyes. "I suppose you and Alek have rather a close friendship, haven't you, Mr. Sharp?"

"*Mr.* Sharp," Bovril repeated, then giggled.

Deryn gave the beastie a hard look, then spread her hands. "Honestly, I don't know, ma'am. It's just that Alek was busy driving the walker tonight, so Bovril started off on *my* shoulder, and I suppose that—"

"Excuse me," Dr. Barlow interrupted. "But did you just say *Bovril*?"

"Oh, aye. That's its name, sort of."

The lady boffin raised an eyebrow. "As in the beef extract?"

"It wasn't me who named it," Deryn said. "They taught us all that in middy training, about not getting attached. But this anarchist lassie kept insisting on calling it *Bovril*, and the name sort of . . . stuck."

"Bovril," the beastie repeated.

Dr. Barlow stepped forward to peer more closely at the loris, then shook her head again. "I wonder if this excess of bonding is Mr. Newkirk's fault. He never quite kept the eggs at an even temperature."

"You mean, Bovril might be *defective?*"

"One never can tell with a new species. You say an 'anarchist lassie' started this *Bovril* nonsense?"

Deryn started to explain, but found herself wavering on her feet, and plonked down into a chair. It wasn't exactly good manners, sitting in a lady's presence, but suddenly all that had happened tonight was hitting Deryn hard—the battle, Zaven's death, the narrow escape of the *Leviathan* from a fiery end.

More than anything else, it was a relief to be home. To feel the ship beneath her feet, real and solid, and not burning horribly in the sky. And Alek aboard by now as well . . .

"You see, ma'am, when I found him, Alek had taken up with this Committee for Union and Progress, who were dead keen to overthrow the sultan. I didn't approve of them, of course, but then we found out there was a Tesla cannon being built. Knowing that it could destroy the *Leviathan*, I had to make sure it came down. Even if that meant joining up with anarchists—or revolutionaries, whatever you want to call them."

"Very resourceful, as always." The lady boffin sat across from her, reaching down to scratch Tazza's head. "Count Volger wasn't far wrong, was he?"

"Count Volger?" A squick of panic went through Deryn

at the name. "If you don't mind me asking, ma'am, what exactly wasn't he wrong about?"

"He said that Alek had fallen in with unsavory elements. And also that *you* would be able to find our missing prince."

Deryn nodded slowly. Volger had been sitting right there, of course, when she'd heard the clue about Alek's hotel. "He's a clever-boots, that one."

"Indeed." The lady boffin stood up again and turned to stare out. "Though he may be wrong about this Committee. However unsavory their politics, they have performed a valuable service for Britain today."

"Aye, ma'am. They helped us save the barking ship!"

"They seem to have toppled the sultan as well."

Deryn hauled herself up and joined Dr. Barlow at the window. The ship was under way again, heading back across the water. In the distance the streets of Istanbul were still alight with gunfire and explosions, and Deryn could make out swirling clouds of spice dust in the war elephants' searchlights.

"I'm not certain he's toppled yet, ma'am. It looks as if they're still fighting."

"This battle is quite pointless, I assure you," the lady boffin said. "A few minutes after the *Goeben* was destroyed, we spotted the Imperial Airyacht *Stamboul* lifting off from the palace grounds, flying a flag of truce."

"Truce? But the battle's hardly begun. Why would the sultan surrender?"

"He did not. According to the *Stamboul*'s signal flags, the Kizlar Agha was in command." Dr. Barlow smiled coolly. "He was taking the sultan to a place of safety, far from the troubles of Istanbul."

"Oh." Deryn frowned. "You mean he was . . . *kidnapping* his own sovereign?"

"As I said to you some time ago, sultans have been replaced before."

Deryn let out a low whistle, wondering how long this meaningless battle would go on. Out the window the dark water of the bay was still churning where the *Goeben* had gone down. She wondered if the behemoth was still down there, picking through the jumble of steel and oil for its supper.

The spotlight came on again, cutting into the water to bring the beastie to heel. The *Breslau* would be next on the menu.

"If the Committee's really winning," Deryn said, "then Germany will be the only Clanker power left!"

"My dear boy, there is still Austria-Hungary."

"Right, of course." Deryn cleared her throat, silently cursing herself. "Don't know how I forgot about them."

Dr. Barlow raised an eyebrow. "You forgot about Alek's own people? How odd, Mr. Sharp."

"Mr. Sharp," came a voice from above them.

Deryn looked straight up, and her jaw dropped.

Two small eyes were peering back at her from the ceiling. They belonged to another perspicacious loris, its tiny paws clinging to a message lizard tube. It looked almost like Bovril, except for missing the spots on its haunches.

"What in blazes?"

Then she remembered—there had been *three* remaining eggs. Bovril's, the one smashed by the sultan's automaton, and another that she'd forgotten all about. It would have hatched in the last month, of course.

Dr. Barlow raised a hand, and the other beastie swung

from one paw like a monkey, then dropped. It encircled the lady boffin's arm, sliding down to her shoulder.

"Mr. Sharp," the new beastie said again.

"*Mr.* Sharp," Bovril corrected, then they both began to giggle.

"Why does it keep laughing?" asked the lady boffin.

"I've no barking idea," Deryn said. "Sometimes I think it's cracked in the attic."

"Revolution," Bovril announced.

Deryn stared at it. She'd never heard the creature say something out of the blue before.

The new beastie repeated the word, rolling it around on its tongue happily, then said, "Balance of power."

Bovril chuckled at the phrase, then dutifully parroted it.

As Deryn watched with growing astonishment, the creatures began to jabber, each repeating what the other said. The single words became a torrent of phrases in English, Clanker, Armenian, Turkish, and half a dozen other languages.

Soon Bovril was reciting whole conversations that Deryn had shared with Alek or Lilit or Zaven, while the new beastie made declamations that sounded just like Dr. Barlow talking, even a few that had to be Count Volger!

"Excuse me, ma'am," Deryn whispered, "but what in blazes are they *doing*?"

The lady boffin smiled. "My boy, they are doing what comes naturally to them."

"But they're fabricated! What's *natural* to them?"

"Why, only becoming more perspicacious, of course."

· FORTY-THREE ·

The next morning Alek was allowed to visit Volger.

As his guard let him into the wildcount's stateroom, Alek noticed that the door wasn't locked. Alek himself had been treated politely the night before, more like a guest than a prisoner. Perhaps the tension between his men and their Darwinist captors had thawed a little in the last month.

Count Volger looked comfortable enough. He was at his desk eating a breakfast of soft-boiled eggs and toast, and didn't bother to stand when Alek arrived. He simply nodded and said, "Prince Aleksandar."

Alek bowed. "Count."

Volger went back to scraping butter onto a piece of toast.

Standing there waiting, Alek felt like a schoolboy called in for punishment. He had never been to school, of course, but somehow adults—whether tutors, parents, or grandmotherly revolutionaries like Nene—all wore their disappointment in the same way. Surely headmasters weren't so different.

Finally Alek sighed and said, "It might save time if I began."

"As you wish."

"You want to tell me that I'm a fool for having been captured again. That it was mad to involve myself in Ottoman politics. By now I could be safely hidden in the wilds."

Count Volger nodded. "Yes, there is that."

The man went back to scraping his piece of toast, seemingly intent on covering every square millimeter with butter.

"In not taking your advice, I risked my life and the life of my men," Alek continued. "Dr. Busk says that Klopp is recovering well enough, but I led him and Bauer into an all-out battle. Things could have turned out worse."

"Much worse," Volger said, then fell silent again.

"Let's see . . . Ah, I've also thrown away *everything* my father left me. The castle, all your plans, and finally his gold." Alek reached inside his piloting coat and felt for a hard lump sewed into a corner of the lining. He tore the fabric, pulled out what remained of the gold, and tossed it onto the table.

After a month of buying spices and mechanikal parts, the bar had been mostly shaved away. All that was left was the round Hapsburg crest stamped at its center, like a thick, roughly made coin.

Volger blinked, and Alek let himself smile. At least he'd finally provoked a reaction.

"Did you finance this revolution *entirely* on your own?"

"Only the finishing touches—a little spice on top." Alek shrugged. "Revolutions are expensive, it seems."

"I wouldn't know. I avoid them on principle."

"Of course," Alek said. "That's what you're really angry about, isn't it? That I overturned the natural order and deposed a fellow royal? That I forgot that revolutionaries want to overthrow *all* aristocrats, including me and you?"

Volger took a bite of toast and chewed thoughtfully, then poured himself more coffee. "There is that, too, I suppose. But there's one thing you've forgotten."

Alek wondered for a moment what his final failure might be, but then gave up. He took a cup from the windowsill, filled it with coffee, and sat down across the desk from Volger.

"Enlighten me."

"You also saved my life."

Alek frowned. "I did what?"

"If you had disappeared into the wilds as you were meant to, that Tesla cannon would have sent me and Hoffman to the bottom of the sea, along with the rest of this ship's crew."

The count stared into his coffee cup. "I owe you my life. Quite an annoying turn of events."

Alek hid his surprise by taking a sip of coffee. It was true—Count Volger had been saved along with the *Leviathan*. But was the man really *thanking* him for joining the Committee's revolution?

"This doesn't mean that you are any less of an idiot, of course," Volger added.

"Of course not," Alek said, a bit relieved.

"And there is also the matter of your newfound celebrity." Volger opened a drawer, pulled out a newspaper, and dropped it onto the desk.

Alek picked it up. It was in English—*New York World*, read the masthead. And there on the first page was a photograph of Alek, above a long article by "Istanbul Bureau Chief" Eddie Malone.

Alek let the newspaper fall back onto the table. He'd never seen a photograph of himself before, and the effect was distinctly disagreeable. Like looking into a frozen mirror.

"Are my ears really that large?"

"Almost. What on earth were you thinking?"

Alek lifted his cup, staring at the glimmering black reflection on the coffee's surface. He had steeled himself to face any amount of scorn from Volger, but not for this. As the newspaper's name declared, the whole world was gawking at him now. His family secrets were out there for anyone to read.

"That reporter, Malone, he knew too much about the Committee's plans. An interview was the only way to distract him." Alek dared another glance at the photo, and noticed the caption—THE MISSING HEIR. "So that's why the crew have been so polite to me. They know who I am now."

"Not just the crew, Alek. Britain has a consulate in New York, of course. Even their bumbling diplomats could hardly have missed this. Lord Churchill himself sent that newspaper to Captain Hobbes, carried by some sort of beastly eagle."

"But how in blazes did *you* get it?"

"Dr. Barlow and I have been sharing information for some time now." The wildcount leaned back in his chair. "She is proving to be a most interesting woman."

Alek stared at the man, a slight shudder passing through him.

"Don't worry, Alek, I haven't told her all my secrets. How is your friend Dylan, by the way?"

"Dylan? He's . . . quite astounding, at times." Alek sighed. "In a way it's because of him that I let myself be captured again."

Volger's coffee cup froze halfway to his lips. "What do you mean by that?"

"Dylan convinced me it was safer to give myself up

than to escape. There *were* a dozen Ottoman walkers headed toward us, I suppose. But it was more than that. He seems to think that I belong on this ship." Alek sighed. "Not that it matters. Once we're back in Britain, they'll put me in a cage."

"I wouldn't worry about that just yet." The wildcount glanced at the windows. "Haven't you noticed?"

Alek looked out the window. Last night when he'd grown too tired to stay awake, the airship had been headed back down the strait, guiding the behemoth back toward the Mediterranean Sea. But now there were mountains passing by, tipped with orange from the rising sun. Their long shadows stretched through the mist, trailing toward his left.

"Are we headed east?"

Volger clucked his tongue. "That took you some time. I'm sure your friend Dylan would have noticed right away."

"No doubt. But why are we headed for Asia? The war's back in Europe."

"When this war began, the German navy had ships in every ocean. The *Goeben* and the *Breslau* aren't the only ones that the British have been searching for."

"Do you know *where* in Asia we're going?"

"Alas, Dr. Barlow hasn't been forthcoming on the matter. But I suspect we will be in Tokyo sooner or later. Japan declared war against Germany four weeks ago."

"Of course." Alek stared out at the mountains passing by. The Japanese had been Darwinists since signing a cooperation pact with the British in 1902. But it was astounding to think that the war ignited by his parents' death had already outgrown Europe, and now encompassed the entire globe.

"This detour is inconvenient, but it keeps you out of that cage a little longer," Volger said. "Austria-Hungary is not faring well against the great fighting bears of Russia. The time for you to reveal yourself may be sooner than I thought." He prodded the newspaper as if it were a dead fish. "That is, to reveal what little you haven't already."

Alek pulled the scroll case from his pocket. "You mean this?"

"I was afraid to ask if you still had it."

"As if I would have lost it!" Alek said angrily, then realized that he had, in fact, lost it once already. But since the taxi incident, he'd kept the letter with him at all times.

The night before, the airman who'd searched him in the cargo bay had found the scroll case and opened it. But the letter's ornate Latin script had meant nothing to him, and he had politely returned it.

"I'm not a complete fool, Volger. In fact, this letter is why I ignored your advice and stayed in Istanbul."

"What do you mean, Your Highness?"

"A pointless feud among my family started this war, so

it's up to me to stop it." He held up the case. "This is the will of heaven, which tells me what I'm meant to do. Not skulk in hiding but take my rightful place and put an end to this war!"

Volger stared at him for a long moment, then steepled his fingers.

"That letter is no guarantee that you'll take the throne."

"I know all that. But the pope's word must count for something."

"Ah, I had forgotten." The wildcount turned away. "You've been in a land of heathens and heretics. You haven't heard the news from the Vatican."

"News?"

"The Holy Father is dead."

Alek stared at the man.

"They say the war was hard on him," Volger continued. "He wanted peace too much. Of course, what he wanted doesn't matter now."

"But . . . this letter represents the will of heaven. The Vatican will still confirm that it's real, won't they?"

"One would think so. Of course, someone there told the Germans about your father's visit." The man spread his hands. "We must hope that this someone doesn't have the new pope's ear."

Alek turned to stare out the window, trying to make sense of Volger's news.

After his parents' death, the whole world had gone mad, as if his family tragedy had broken history itself. But in Istanbul, somehow, things had started to fall back into place. The Committee's revolution, Dylan arriving with the behemoth in his wake, all of it revealed that it was up to Alek to stop the war, to put matters right. For the first time in his life, he had felt a certainty in all his actions, as if providence were guiding him.

But now the world was turning upside down again. Fate was taking him not back toward the center of the war but away from his homeland and his people, away from everything he had been born to do. And the letter in his hand, the only thing his father had left him that Alek hadn't thrown away, might now be worthless.

What mad providence was this?

AFTERWORD

Behemoth is a novel of alternate history, so most of its characters, creatures, and machines are my own inventions. But the historical locations and events are modeled closely on the realities of World War I. Here's a quick review of what's true and what's fictional.

The *Sultan Osman I* was a real warship, purchased by the Ottoman Empire and awaiting completion at a British shipyard in late 1914. As the war began, however, First Lord of the Admiralty Winston Churchill decided to seize the ship, worried that the Ottomans might join the Germans and use the warship against Britain. The Ottomans did ultimately enter the war, but partly because Churchill had stolen their ship. It is still debated whether they would have become involved without this provocation.

As in *Behemoth*, the Ottoman Empire was unstable in 1914. In the real world, in fact, the sultan and his grand vizier were no longer in charge. They had been overthrown during the revolution of 1908, and the Committee of Union and Progress (CUP) was already in power.

In the world of *Behemoth*, however, the 1908 revolution

was unsuccessful, leaving the sultan in power and the CUP split into many factions. I created a second rebellion in 1914 because I wanted my characters to be involved in a successful revolution, one that would perhaps nudge history toward a more positive outcome.

The German influence in Istanbul was very real; they owned a popular newspaper, while the British embassy had no one on its staff who could read Turkish. (Hard to believe, but true.)

Just as in this book, the German ironclads *Breslau* and *Goeben* found themselves trapped in the Mediterranean at the beginning of the war. They escaped to Istanbul and became part of the Ottoman navy, crews and all. In return for the two ships, the Ottomans put Admiral Wilhelm Souchon, commander of the *Goeben*, in charge of their entire fleet. On October 29, 1914, Admiral Souchon attacked the Russian navy without official permission, dragging the Ottomans into the war.

In the real world, the war resulted in the end of the Ottoman Empire, which was partitioned into a number of countries, including Turkey, Syria, and Lebanon. I wanted to create a history in which the empire remained intact and Istanbul retained its cosmopolitan nature as a model for the rest of the world.

And yes, you really should call it Istanbul, not Constantinople. Although the Ottoman aristocracy used the name *Kostantiniyye* for many centuries, and many westerners cling to the name in story and song, Istanbul was a more common name among its people. (Actually, most of them just called it "the City.") In any case, the Turkish post office stopped delivering mail marked "Constantinople" in 1923.

The Orient-Express was a real train, of course, running along various routes from Paris to Istanbul since 1883. In its heyday, the Express symbolized all that was elegant and adventurous about travel. On December 14, 2009, a few weeks after I finished this book, it ran for the last time.

There is no such thing as a "Tesla cannon," but Nikola Tesla was a real inventor, famous for discovering the basic principles of radio, radar, and the alternating current. He spent decades working on a so-called death ray, and in the 1930s he claimed it could "shoot down 10,000 planes at a rage of 250 miles." He offered the device to several governments, but no one took him up on it.

Maybe that's a good thing.